For Naraly

In frien

Aug 11, 2020

BY THE SAME AUTHOR

Son of the Dragon : Book One of Dracula Chronicles (Published December 2012)

Empire of the Crescent Moon

Book Two of Dracula Chronicles

By

Victor T. Foia

Dracula Chronicles

Book Two: Empire of the Crescent Moon

By: Victor T. Foia

First edition

Published by: Dracula Press, LLC

www.draculachronicles.com info@draculachronicles.com

Cover artwork by Justin T. Foia

Editors: Arlene W. Robinson and Terry Lee Robinson

ISBN-13: 978-1491296400

ISBN-10: 1491296402

Library of Congress Control Number: 2013914879
CreateSpace Independent Publishing Platform
North Charleston, South Carolina

For my sons, Justin and Timothy, artists,
entrepreneurs, and my best friends
And as always for Diane

TABLE OF CONTENTS

Maps of Dracula Chronicles xi

CHAPTER 1: Mein Gott, Nimm Mich!—My God, Take Me! . 1

CHAPTER 2: One Blunder at a Time 9

CHAPTER 3: A Forged Document. 21

CHAPTER 4: The Two Tower Gate 27

CHAPTER 5: Sultan's Wife 33

CHAPTER 6: In the Bedestan. 41

CHAPTER 7: Sultan's Musahib. 49

CHAPTER 8: Macedon Tower 57

CHAPTER 9: Dar al-Sulh—House of Treaty 67

CHAPTER 10: The Karaman Hostage 77

CHAPTER 11: The Mind behind the Plot 85

CHAPTER 12: A Fateful Step 95

CHAPTER 13: Disobedient Servant 103

CHAPTER 14: An Ancient Water Cistern 111

CHAPTER 15: The Auction Block 121

CHAPTER 16: An Impulsive Decision 129

CHAPTER 17: Pharmacopeia. 141

CHAPTER 18: Caring Hands 147
CHAPTER 19: Broken Loom 157
CHAPTER 20: Imperial Council. 167
CHAPTER 21: Help from an Enemy 173
CHAPTER 22: Underground Dungeon. 181
CHAPTER 23: The King's Challenge. 187
CHAPTER 24: Gruya's Catch 199
CHAPTER 25: A Woman's Plan 211
CHAPTER 26: Mehmed's Map Room 221
CHAPTER 27: A Trial of Arms 227
CHAPTER 28: At the Hamam 235
CHAPTER 29: Sultan's Gift. 245
CHAPTER 30: Storm on the Bosphorus 249
CHAPTER 31: Podestà Grimaldi 259
CHAPTER 32: A View toward Asia 265
CHAPTER 33: Arrow across the Water. 271
CHAPTER 34: An Unplanned Adventure 279
CHAPTER 35: Captain Throatcut 287
CHAPTER 36: Pantelimon Monastery. 297
CHAPTER 37: Bounty Hunters 301
CHAPTER 38: The Flight of the Hawk 309
CHAPTER 39: The Price of Sin 317
CHAPTER 40: Zaganos's Judgment 323

The Journey Continues 329

Glossary. 331

Who is Who and What is What 341

Story World of Dracula Chronicles 353

Houses of Dracula Chronicles. 365

Acknowledgments 375

About the Author 377

Maps Of

Dracula Chronicles

Maps Provided For Orientation Only

Borders Of Kingdoms And Empires Changed Continually And Cannot Be Represented Accurately

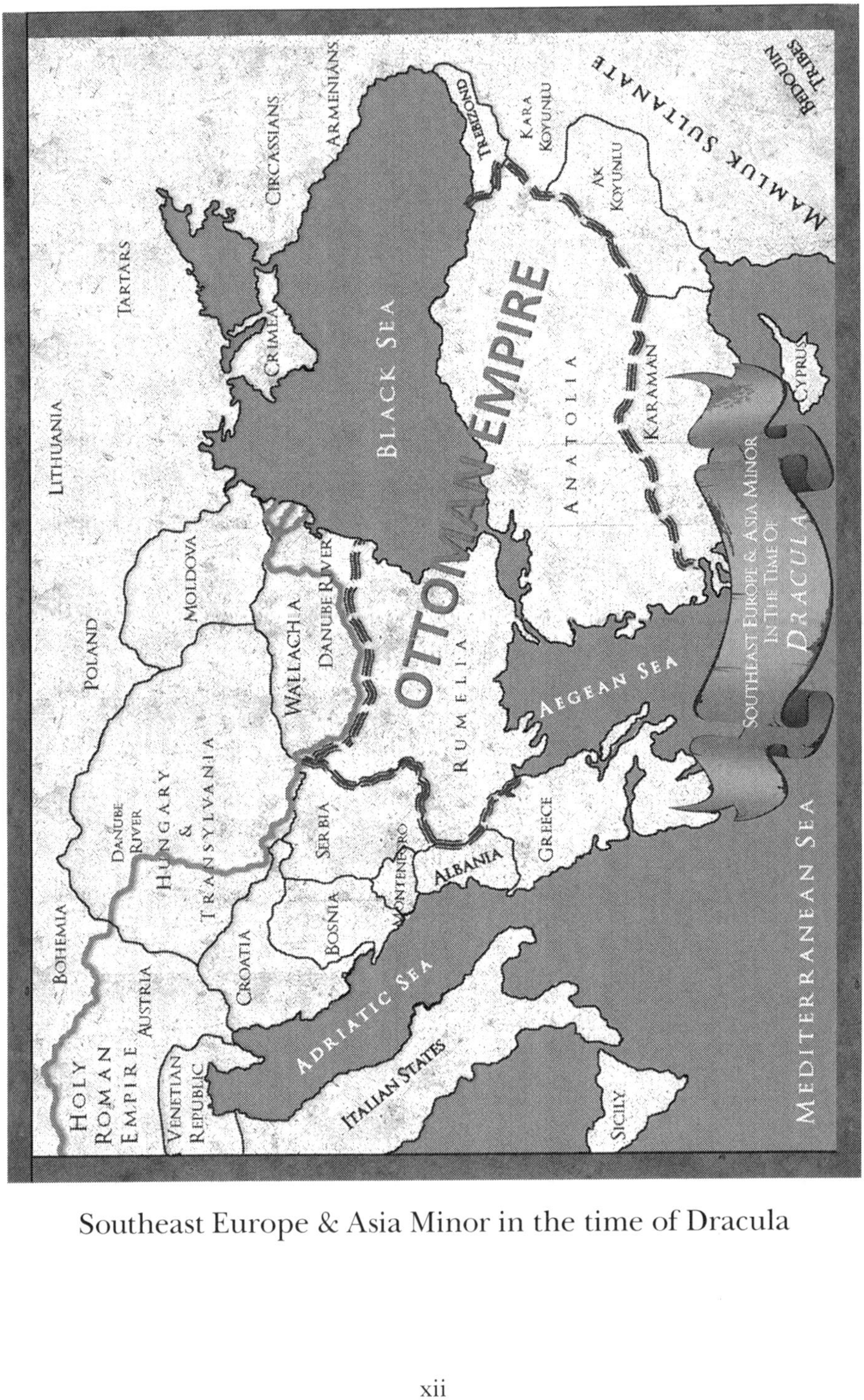

Southeast Europe & Asia Minor in the time of Dracula

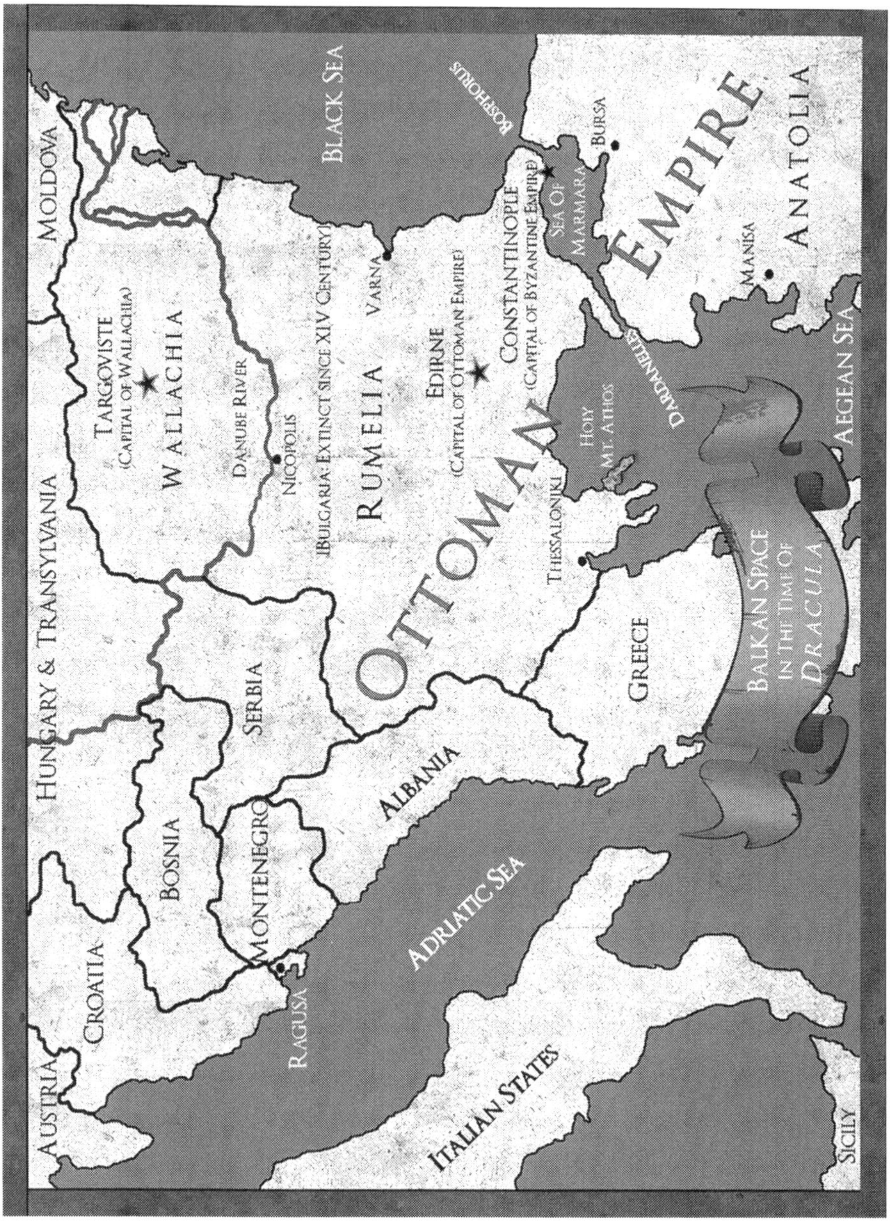

Balkan Space in the time of Dracula

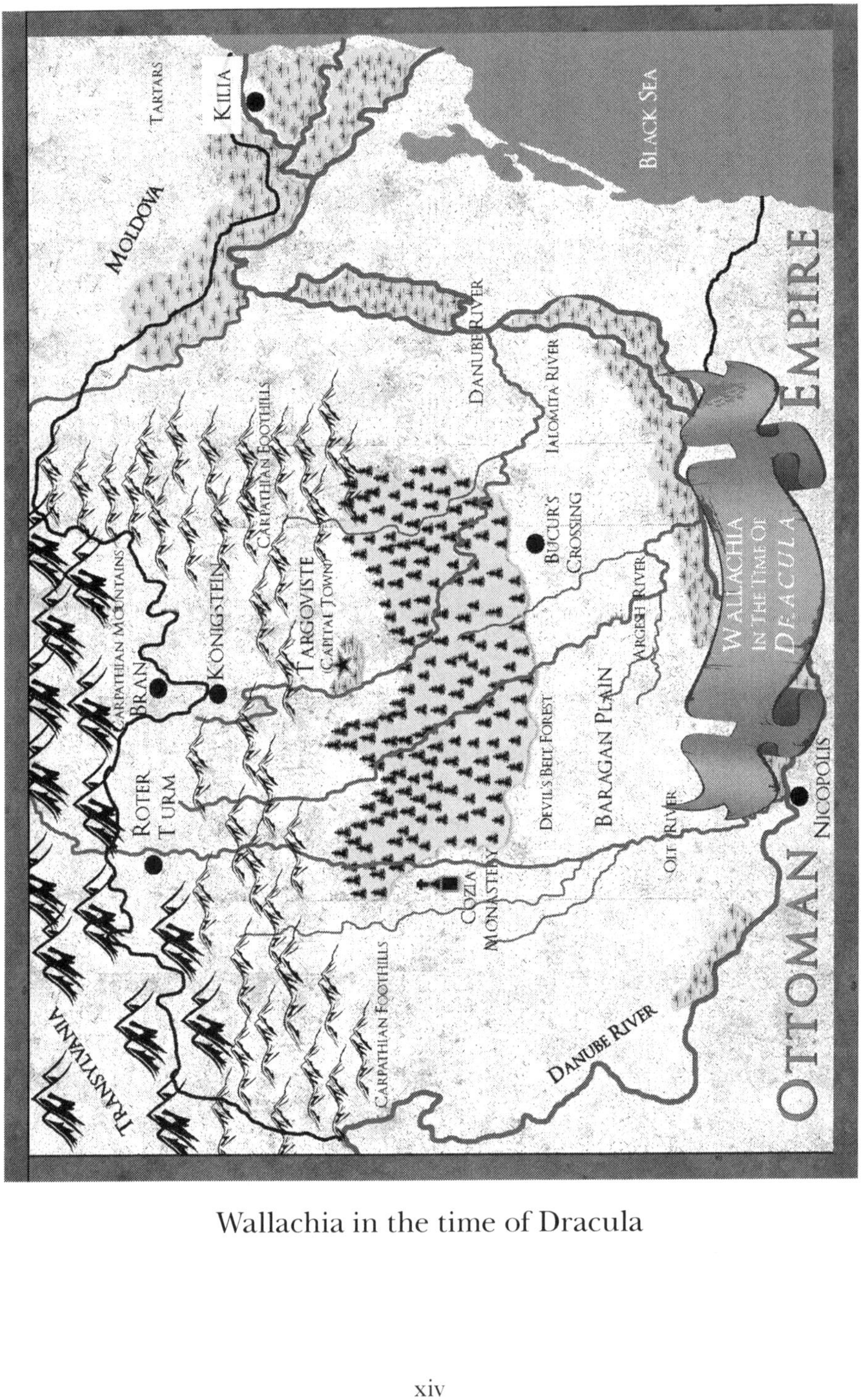

Wallachia in the time of Dracula

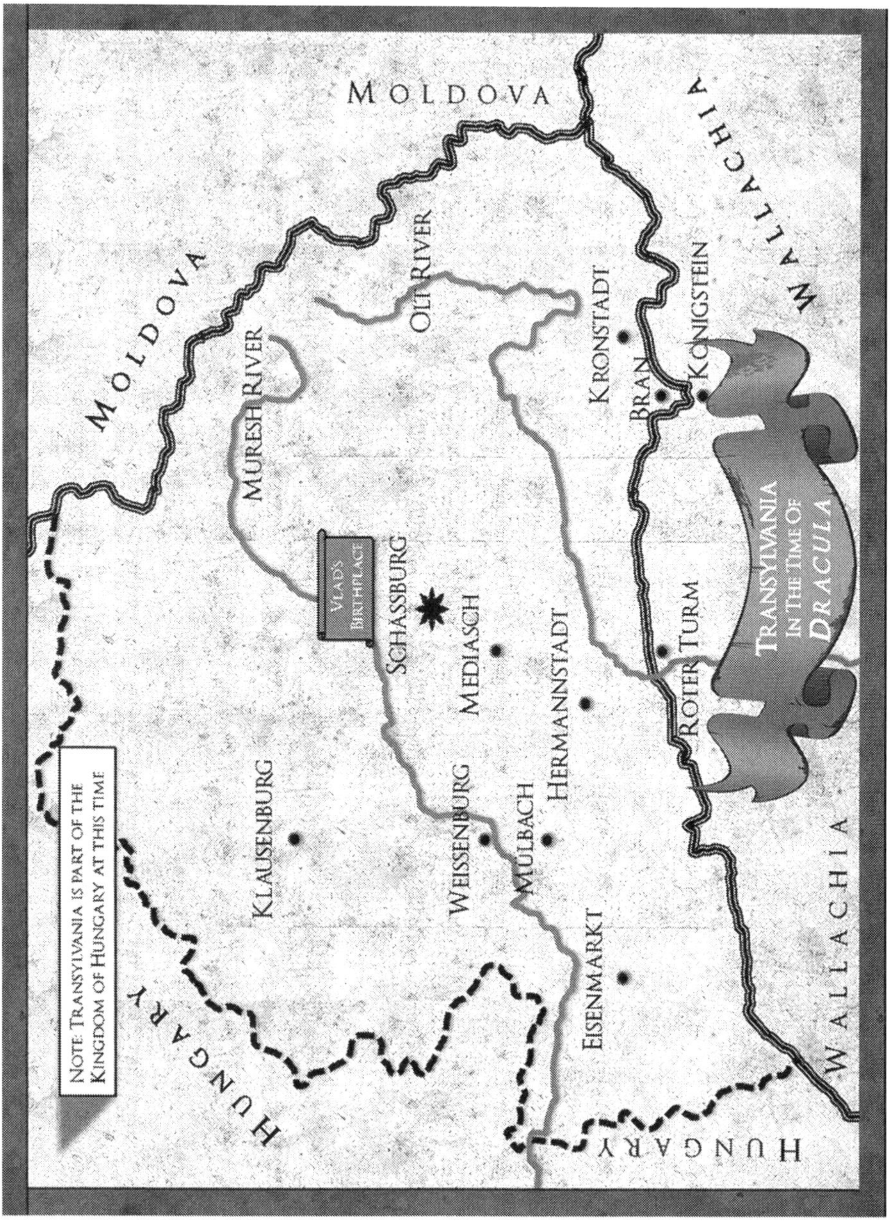

Transylvania in the time of Dracula

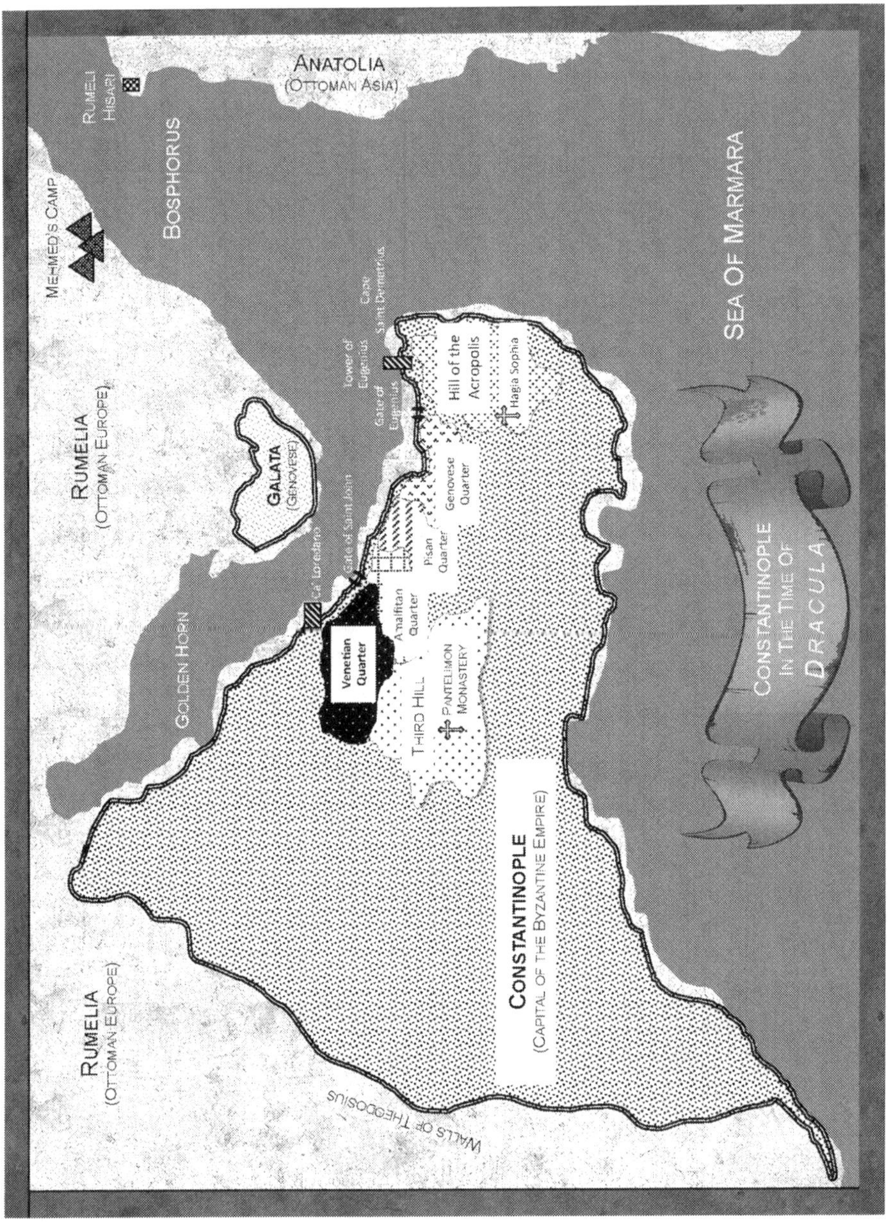

Constantinople in the time of Dracula

1

Mein Gott, Nimm Mich!— My God, Take Me!

June 1442, Rumelia, Ottoman Empire

"By the Pope's shriveled nuts, you've got to see this, Vlad," Gruya whispered. "That woman there is carrying a severed head by the hair."

Vlad and his squire were peeking by turns through a hole in the rear flap of the wagon's canopy. Their convoy had halted a couple of hours before, when the leading wagon's axle broke. Now they were being overtaken by a convoy of about thirty slaves, walking chained by the neck to each other. Six overseers on horseback were driving them.

The woman had caught Vlad's eye from far away because of her flying blonde hair, almost white in the strong sunlight. When she approached to within twenty paces he could tell her clothes, though torn and muddy, marked her of noble rank. Her proud bearing reinforced that impression. She stood out among the other prisoners, who marched with bent necks and drooping shoulders, by walking tall, face tilted to the sky. Now and then she'd stumble, and teeter on the verge of falling, yet was kept upright by the chain that tethered her to the prisoners in front and behind. But even when she flailed her arm to regain her balance, the woman's eyes never unfastened from whatever vision only she saw. She appeared to be talking to herself as well. When she reached the wagon, Vlad made out a phrase in German she kept repeating, "*Mein Gott, nimm mich!*, My God, take me!" *White skin, ruby lips, blue eyes.* A princess, he decided. Then he lied to himself it wasn't her beauty that kept his attention, but the man's head that dangled in her hand.

"It reminds me of an incense burner," Gruya said, "the way it swings back and forth by the tresses." He made a grimace of disgust. "But I bet it stinks like a witch's butt." He pushed Vlad aside, and spat through the hole in the canvas.

"I wonder what her story is," Vlad said. From the woman's looks, she was from the north. Bohemia? Poland? Lithuania? They all spoke German in those parts. How did she get far enough to the south to be captured by the Turks? So young, so beautiful, so far away from home. And now so doomed.

"That must be her husband's head she doesn't want to part with."

"Whosoever's head it is, she's not carrying it by choice," Vlad said, and resumed watching the convoy. "She's been ordered to do it. I see two other slaves doing the same back in the convoy."

"Why would the slavers need the heads? Can they sell them as trophies?"

Vlad knew the answer from Gunther's stories. "The overseers of these convoys are only intermediaries, hired to take the slaves to the market. They sign off for a number of heads, and must deliver that number at the destination, or pay for the missing ones."

"Ah, so the heads serve as receipts for those who die on the way," Gruya said. "Cruel trick on the poor survivors, but efficient for the owners."

The convoy moved past the wagon in a clinking of chains and a babble of wails. Two of the overseers kept prodding the prisoners with wooden rods to keep the pace. The other four brought up the rear, conversing casually in Turkish about the weather.

"I can't get that woman out my mind," Vlad said, when the sounds faded.

"And I can't get a massive portion of sausage and cabbage out of mine," Gruya said. "I've had enough prunes for a lifetime."

"I hope Father's drivers fix that broken axle soon, and we catch up with the slaves."

"Just thinking of prunes makes me want to go." Gruya held his belly in both hands and gave Vlad a pained look.

"We can't be too far from the inn," Vlad said. "We'll see the slaves there again."

"I hope we give ourselves up tonight, so I can sit in the privy for an hour, without fear of being discovered." Gruya moaned, and lay down in the fetal position.

"It's still too soon," Vlad said. "We aren't more than fifty miles from the Danube. At this distance, Father might turn around and boot us back across the river."

"Now, would it be really so bad to get back home?"

Until the arrival of the slaves, Vlad had secretly thought like Gruya. The ride was jarring, and the air inside their hiding place either stifling, or bone-chilling. For the past two and a half days, he and Gruya had subsisted on the dried fruit they discovered in the cargo of their wagon. The first night they were able to sneak out to drink water and use the inn's privy. But the second night, two of the muleteers set their sleeping blankets behind the wagon, and unwittingly trapped Vlad and Gruya inside. Hunger, thirst, and boredom pushed Vlad to despondency, and he fell to dwelling on the setbacks he'd suffered recently. There were Nestor's and László's duplicitous behaviors, Father's unfairness, and Vlad's own miscalculation regarding Omar. And then, more painful than all other setbacks, Gunther's death. These all contrived to make Vlad lose interest in this trip.

But the sight of that peculiar woman, the princess gazing at the sky, changed everything. Now he felt refreshed, energized, and purposeful. He had to see her again. And maybe do something....

"You'd better not be thinking about getting out now," Vlad said, alarmed at Gruya's look of panic as the squire groaned and clutched his belly again.

"It's like a knife ripping through my guts."

"For every prune I ate, you ate ten." Vlad looked through the peephole again. "It'll be dark in about three hours. Then you can run to the bushes."

Indistinct noises rose from the front of their convoy, followed by a whistle. Vlad heard steps approaching, and felt the wagon sway as their driver climbed up onto his seat. A few moments later, they were in motion again. The wagon began to lumber over the uneven terrain, lurching from side to side.

"Oh, no, I can't take this," Gruya hissed. "If you don't let me go now something bad's going to happen and you'll regret it."

Vlad sighed, and began to undo the thong that fastened the canopy flap at the rear of the wagon. "Had I known, I'd have brought diapers along. Next time, you're staying home."

Gruya sprang out of the wagon and dashed across an empty field toward a hedge, some twenty yards away. Before he could disappear behind the bushes an alert driver gave a shout, and Gruya froze. Then, concluding perhaps that secrecy had become moot, he strutted the rest of the way.

The convoy lumbered to a halt, and incredulous voices shouted, "That's Master Gruya," and, "There goes the sword bearer's son," and, "Will Lord Michael be surprised!" Guffaws followed when Gruya's proceedings behind the bushes became audible.

Vlad climbed down from the wagon and stepped over to the edge of the road, so all could see him too. The drivers, who stood on their seats to gawk and laugh at Gruya, now turned their eyes on Vlad. This time, out of respect for the king perhaps, or astonishment at Vlad's pluck, they fell to silence.

Vlad was prepared for his father's displeasure. He didn't care what form it would take, verbal, physical, or both, as long as it wasn't followed by a forcible return to Wallachia. Now he was determined to continue the trip, and find out the identity of that hapless princess.

It didn't take long for Dracul to emerge from his wagon, followed by a shaken Michael. The two men remained still for a while, heads leaned into each other, staring at Vlad with grave looks. They appeared to be conferring, but were too far away for Vlad to hear them. Finally, Dracul began to walk toward Vlad, leaning harder than usual on his walking stick, wincing with each step. Eight months had passed since Dracul shattered his right shinbone, because Vlad disobeyed his order to shoot an attacking wolf. The pain never left entirely, but whenever he was annoyed with Vlad, it seemed to flare up. And Dracul wore it as a silent reproach.

Being reminded once more of the part he'd played in his father's crippling tore at Vlad's insides. The recollection heightened his feeling of guilt for disobeying him this time too, and in such a brazen manner. Could Vlad blame Father if he chose to humiliate him in front of everyone? He both dreaded and welcomed his father's wrath. Perhaps the punishment would release Vlad from his guilt.

"You have no idea what you've done, Son," Dracul said when he reached Vlad. His voice was soft and controlled, not in concert with his hard face and cold eyes. Nor with the tension he betrayed as he held his walking stick with both hands, trying to flex it like the blade of a sword. "I've used every subterfuge I could for the past five years to avoid giving one of my sons as hostage to Murad. I temporized, I bribed, I cheated, I lied, as if I were a goddamn Hungarian. I would've perjured myself like one too, had that been needed."

As Dracul spoke, his voice gained a cutting edge, and the cypress stick in his hands began to bend despite its hardness. "I even chose to pay Murad a tribute larger than he requested, to keep you and your brothers out of his hands. You can't imagine what he does to hostages at the slightest provocation." The veins on Dracul's neck bulged and he bared his teeth in the way an enraged dog does before it snaps at its tormentor. Then he snarled, "*Can* you?"

The stick broke in his hands with a powerful report, but Dracul seemed unaware. His voice, freed of the shackles of self-restraint, exploded. "And now you walk into Murad's lair of your own free will?"

Dracul's initial calm unnerved Vlad. But when his father succumbed to sizzling anger, Vlad knew things were under control. He surmised that Father couldn't afford the delay of taking him back to the Danube, and felt relieved. "The sultan won't know about me. I'm already dressed as a stable hand, and I'll—"

"Things never turn out the way you want them with the Turks," Dracul shouted. "They've got a way to get the better of you every time." He stared at his boots, and bit his lower lip.

Vlad guessed his father had run out of bile. He never seemed capable of producing much of it. As if to confirm Vlad's suspicion,

Dracul assumed a calm demeanor and said, resigned, "I know something bad's going to come of this, and there isn't a damned thing I can do about it now."

"You said in Nicopolis you'll be home in a few weeks. What could go wrong in such a short time?"

Dracul gave Vlad a pained look. "Did I say that?" He turned his back on him and walked away, dragging his right leg. Vlad wondered how much of that limping was a show mounted for his benefit.

"That's the *caravanserai*," Vlad told Gruya, and pointed at a substantial brick structure in the distance. The convoy had stopped to let the mules rest on the summit of a slope they'd been climbing for more than two hours. Below them opened a valley already filling with a bluish evening haze. The inn was nestled among trees on the bank of a small river. In the last sunrays bouncing off the clouds, a slender tower rose from inside the inn's courtyard, gleaming white like a waterfall crashing down the steep face of a mountain. "There is a mosque inside the *caravanserai*, and what you see there is the minaret."

"All I can see is food." Gruya sounded drained. "A giant flitch of bacon, and a—"

"You'll have food, don't worry, but think only of boiled vegetables and rice. Get pork out of your mind for as long as we are inside the Dar al-Islam, House of Islam."

"It's a true mystery how anyone could build an empire without pork," Gruya said. "The Jews tried to, didn't they? And look, to this day they don't have one. If for no other reason than pork, the Ottoman Empire can't last much longer."

"Oh, you're so astute, Gruya. And to think of all the needless fuss the Pope is kicking up with his crusade. When all he's got to do is wait for the Turks to perish for want of swine flesh."

The inn, with an appearance of a small fortress, was a two-story edifice built around a rectangular courtyard. It was accessible through a single portal, just tall enough for camels and wide enough for wagons. Massive plank doors reinforced with iron bands protected this entrance. The windows, extant only on the upper floor, were tiny, shuttered openings. Along the perimeter of the building, a ditch four feet deep had been dug to serve as a dry moat. When Dracul's convoy reached the *caravanserai,* Vlad saw the slaves in this ditch.

"There's your woman," Gruya said.

But Vlad had already spotted *his* princess from far away. She was still alive; God hadn't answered her prayer yet.

The slaves, still chained to each other, were strung in single file along the bottom of the ditch. The chains of those at either end of the file were anchored to iron rods driven into the ground, so the prisoners couldn't bunch up together. With anxious looks, they followed the movements of an overseer who was pitching cabbage leaves and turnips at them from the rim of the ditch. He was quite adept at his job, but now and then a piece of food fell short of its target. On such occasions there was commotion in the ditch while men and women strained against their chains to reach the stray item.

The princess seemed oblivious to the hubbub around her, and didn't attempt to feed herself. Her male neighbors on either side took advantage of that to filch her portion. The sight gave Vlad a lump in his throat that stayed with him till late evening.

2

One Blunder at a Time

The inn's precinct was jammed with wagons, animals, and people. Vlad and Gruya were able to observe, in the open, the courtyard movements they only heard the two previous nights from their hiding place in the wagon.

Despite the lateness of the day, the agitation and noise inside the *caravanserai* rivaled that of any small-town market. A dozen stableboys ferried stacks of animal fodder on two-wheeled carts from the rear storehouses, and piled them up at various places throughout the yard. Muleteers and camel drivers watered and fed their animals, while their masters congregated to gossip and make business deals. Fruit, sherbet, and halva vendors moved from group to group, hawking their fares with loud cries.

Muslim travelers were doing their ablutions at a fountain in the center of the courtyard, in preparation for the Salah al-Maghrib, the sunset prayer. The mosque, whose minaret Vlad had noted from the hilltop, stood at the center of the yard. It was built on a platform above the fountain, and could be reached through an external staircase. The mosque wasn't large enough to accommodate more than a handful of worshipers at a time. When the muezzin sang the *adhān*, the worshippers lined up to take turns climbing the stairs.

"This is a perfect time for us to look around a bit," Vlad said to Gruya. "There will be nobody in the workshops for the next half an hour."

"That's not where the food is stored," Gruya said.

"There's no food until after Maghrib, so just follow me."

The long sides of the rectangle that formed the courtyard were built as open arcades. Travelers who didn't want to spend their coin on private rooms upstairs slept there free. The rectangle's short sides were reserved for kitchens, workshops, and storerooms. Vlad sniffed the air to locate the end with the kitchens, then headed in the opposite direction. Gruya followed, grumbling.

Several bays built against the back wall served as open workshops where wheels, saddles, and harnesses were repaired. There was also a smithy, for forging horseshoes and sharpening weapons. Vlad and Gruya found the shops lit but empty of workers.

"Look for a pair of carpenter's pincers," Vlad said, and pointed Gruya to the smithy. "If you find one hide it under your shirt, and get out of there fast."

"Don't the heathen cut off the hands of thieves?"

"This is only a loan."

Vlad stepped into the saddler's shop and in a few minutes located an ax handle, which he concealed in his sleeve. Gruya returned that moment, flashing a victorious grin. Vlad checked the pincers Gruya found and said, "Good. Now what we need is rope. I saw a coil under the driver's bench on Father's second wagon."

"You know, if I weren't hungry I'd be asking many questions."

"God has shown me kindness in many strange ways," Vlad said. "Your hunger must be just one of them." He peered down the colonnade, now lit by torches. "I see our drivers gathered by our sleeping area. It's a good time for you to get the rope. Stow it and the pincers in our wagon and wait for me there."

"You're sure we won't be missing dinner with all this running around?"

"I need something only Uncle Michael can give me. Then we're done, and can settle down to eat."

When Vlad reached the section in the arcade assigned to their crew for eating and sleeping, he heard Michael say, "There will be no talk either among yourselves, or with strangers, about what you saw today. And His Grace orders you to treat Prince Vlad as one of the crew."

"Does that mean to show him no respect?" one of the men asked, and the others chuckled.

Michael assumed a threatening tone that ill suited him. "Anyone betraying Vlad as being the son of His Grace will be sold into slavery to the Turks." Then he dismissed the crew and turned to Vlad.

"I'd like to have one of your spare shirts, Uncle Michael," Vlad whispered after the drivers moved out of earshot. "It doesn't have to be a good one."

"The only spare I have is the shirt my lady wife sewed and embroidered with her own hands for this trip. But I know you'll take good care of it."

Vlad hesitated, knowing how he intended to use the shirt. But this wasn't the time for fine sentiments. "It will be put to good use, Uncle."

Vlad took a lantern off a hook on the wall, and they walked to where the wagons were parked. Michael climbed inside his wagon and emerged with a blue shirt.

"Lady Mathilda even dyed it herself," Michael said, and patted the shirt with affection. "I think all that fuss over a simple shirt was her way of showing me she was worried about my safety while among the Turks." He chuckled drily and added, "If she knew about Zaganos's compromising letter awaiting us in Edirne, she would've tied me to the bedpost with this shirt, instead of packing it in my bags."

"I also need to borrow twenty aspers," Vlad said.

"That's a lot of silver, if all you're planning to buy is fruit or sweets."

"And please don't let Father know about any of this."

Michael threw Vlad a worried look. "There are those who say I go along too easily with your adventures." He sounded cross, and when he climbed off the wagon he refused Vlad's help. "That I never ask any questions, always trust your judgment ..."

"When the time comes I'll tell you everything, and you're certain to approve of what I've done."

Michael sighed. "People are right. All those troubles you keep getting yourself into are ultimately my doing."

The lecture over, Michael counted out the twenty aspers. Vlad pocketed the coins, and left to join Gruya by their wagon. "When you receive your food give me half of it," Vlad said, then stowed the shirt, the ax handle, and the money next to the pincers and the rope in the back of the wagon.

"I know what you're planning to do with the food," Gruya said, morose. "But you forget the inn's gate is closed, and won't open until the morning."

"They say hunger sharpens one's mind, but you're proving that's not the case," Vlad said. "I don't need the gate to be opened."

By the time Gruya and Vlad returned to their group, Michael had retired to join Dracul in a private room upstairs. The drivers were setting up sleeping pallets on a platform that extended along the wall from one end of the arcade to the other. This platform, the depth of an average man's height and elevated four feet off the ground, served as a communal bed for dozens of travelers. Men of all stations, merchants, footmen, wagon drivers, dervishes, and soldiers, sat cross-legged on their sleeping blankets and conversed while awaiting the dinner hour. Seeing that Muslims, Christian, and Jews could share such a cramped space without visible animosity fascinated Vlad. Greeks, Armenians, Turks, Kurds, Gypsies, Saxons, Hungarians, and Wallachians ignored ethnical enmities, and struggled to communicate in borrowed and broken languages. The hubbub of voices did not decrease even when kitchen boys appeared with the food.

"That's all?" Gruya said. "After waiting this long, all we get is boiled cabbage, carrots, collard greens, and rice? Not a shred of meat?"

"The food is free," Vlad said.

"In that case why don't I take an extra half, and give that to you instead of my own half?"

Vlad shook his head and gave Gruya a reproachful look. "That would be an abuse of courtesy. We're guests here, not beggars."

Under Gruya's doleful stare Vlad set aside two-thirds of his own vegetables. To that he added all but a pinch of his rice. He piled the saved food onto a spare trencher he borrowed from one of the drivers, and pushed it to the side. The rest, amounting to little more than what would fit in his cupped hands, he ate slowly, fighting the urge to wolf everything down.

Gruya divided his food into halves, counting fastidiously every leaf, every root, and every grain of rice. When he was done, he added one of the halves to Vlad's spare trencher. His own half he swallowed in two large gulps. "You didn't say I have to give you half of the fruit, did you?" Gruya said when the melon-seller approached their spot.

"You may keep to yourself all the fruit you can buy," Vlad said.

"You mean the fruit isn't free?" Gruya's face fell. "I've got no money, and you're toying with me. But I saw you stashed a good deal of silver in the wagon."

Vlad looked at the sky through the arch between two pillars. Both large and small stars were already visible. "Not long now before the nightfall prayer, Salah al-Isha. I'd say half an hour at the most."

"Does that have something to do with the food you confiscated from me?"

"Yes, indeed it does," Vlad said, and chuckled softly. "We've got to be in position by then, or we'll miss our chance."

Around them, the Christians and the Jews were settling in for the night. Dracul's drivers had covered themselves with sheepskins, and were asleep. Only the Muslim travelers remained alert. Soon, they left their places and headed for the fountain under the mosque for one more set of ablutions.

"Follow me with the food," Vlad said when the last of their immediate neighbors left. "And don't fall into the temptation to steal from it."

At the wagon, Vlad stuffed the food into the sleeves of Michael's shirt. If she knew what was happening, Aunt Matilda would never forgive the outrage done to her handiwork. The coins he piled on the shirt's tail, which he tied into a knot. At last he placed the shirt with its stuffed sleeves around Gruya's neck, as he would a pair of saddlebags on a horse. "This way you'll be close to the food until the last moment," he said.

"You want us to climb down through the window of one of the empty rooms upstairs, don't you?"

"Look at that," Vlad said, and clapped his hands in wonderment. "Hunger has sharpened your mind, after all."

"I knew when you mentioned the rope what you were planning. But I thought food might sharpen *your* mind. Those overseers outside are armed and won't be sleeping."

"An astute observation on your part. But only two of the six men are out there guarding the slaves. The other four came inside the inn before the gate closed."

"Two is all it takes to turn us into pincushions with their arrows."

"You aren't reckoning with Salah al-Isha, are you?"

They could hear the murmurs from the men washing up at the fountain.

"We've got to hurry," Vlad said. "The muezzin will begin his call soon."

He took the rope, the ax handle, and the pincers, and walked stealthily to the arcade on the opposite side of the courtyard. As on their own side, most of the people there were already asleep. He climbed the stairs to the second floor, and Gruya followed with the improvised food bags. There was no light on the landing, and only two torches at the very ends of the gallery above. A few of the rooms were empty, their doors open. They stepped into the first one they came to and shut the door behind them.

Vlad felt his way in the dark, and opened the shutter. He listened for sounds, but all he heard was the river flowing nearby. He placed the ax handle across the base of the window, tied the end of the rope to it, then tossed the coil out the window and climbed down into the dark. A few seconds later he found himself at the bottom of the ditch.

By the time he heard Gruya land behind him, Vlad had reached the end of the building below the workshops. Fifty yards farther along the ditch on that side of the inn, and he could peek around the next corner, at the space where the prisoners were confined. Darkness prevented him from seeing more than their shapes, huddled in solitary mounds. On the ditch's rim, only ten yards away, the silhouettes of the two overseers stood outlined by the light of a small fire. If the Turks discovered their presence and gave chase, Vlad and Gruya would never make it back to the room upstairs.

By necessity, the prisoners had defecated where they lay, so the air coming from their direction was near unbreathable. Vlad's lungs began to labor, and he covered his face to muffle his wheezing. That moment the muezzin's cry broke the silence, and though Vlad had anticipated the *adhān*, it startled him. The two overseers picked up their prayer rugs, and walked out of sight.

Vlad's plan was working.

"We've got only five, ten minutes at the most," he whispered over his shoulder to Gruya. "Quick."

He began to crawl on all fours, and immediately his hands landed on a clutch of nettles. A moment later he heard Gruya curse under his breath when his own hands touched the stinging weeds.

"Please assure me it's a smart thing we're doing," Gruya whispered, "because on my own I can't see it."

When Vlad thought he'd reached the place where the princess would be, he stopped and scanned the forms lying on the grass. The starlight was too faint for him to tell by sight whether they were men or women. He heard a man's snoring at his left, another's sleep-talking at his right, and silence in the middle. He knew then he was at the right spot, and groped ahead of him until he found a foot. A foot shod in a leather slipper with a hole in the sole. The princess.

His heart, already cantering, speeded up its pace.

"Wake up," he said in German, and shook the foot gently. The foot jerked with a rustling of fabric, and the princess let out a cry.

He pounced forward, guided by the sound of her voice, and clamped a hand over her mouth. She clawed at his face with both hands, but there wasn't much vigor in her fight. He placed his lips to her ear and said, "I'm here to help you escape."

The tension went out of her body.

"I'll let go of you, but you must be quiet."

She nodded. When Vlad removed his hand from her mouth she took in a big gulp of air before she whispered, "Did he send you?"

"If you mean God, then yes, I think He did."

"Not God," she said, angry. "He's abandoned me. I meant Saint Leonard of Noblac, patron saint of prisoners and slaves. I'm sure he sent you." She spoke with a determination and self-assurance that belied her miserable condition.

Vlad thought about the ease with which he and Gruya had found all they needed for their mission. "I suppose the saint had something to do with it." He reached behind him into Gruya's improvised food bag and fished out a boiled carrot. "Eat this," he said, and placed the carrot into her hand. "I'll give you more food, but save it for the road. Are you strong enough to walk?"

"I could run all the way home," she said between swallows.

"Where's home?"

"Poland. I was traveling down the Danube to my wedding in Belgrade. Akincis ambushed us, and most of the people in my wedding party drowned." She wiped her mouth with the back of her hand. "Why are you doing this?"

She might laugh to know how the trust of a naïve girl had marked Vlad. *Princes rescue people from danger,* Katharina Siegel, the *Schmetterling,* told him that winter, and her words seemed to give purpose to his life.

"Follow me and make no sound," he said. Though curious to learn her story, there wasn't time. The overseers might decide to inspect the prisoners after the prayer. He snipped her chain with the pincers.

They crawled back along the ditch, and Vlad was again stung by the nettles. He assumed the woman was too, but she gave no sign of it. When they turned the corner, he helped her stand.

"There is food here for a couple of days, if you eat sparingly," he said, and placed the bulky sleeves of Michael's shirt around her shoulders. "There is also some money. Buy food with it when you come to a Christian village. I saw a few on the way here from the Danube."

"Which way do I go?" she said.

He helped her out of the ditch, then climbed up after her. "What's your name?"

"Aśka of Rzeszów, Princess Lubomirska."

He took her by the shoulders and turned her around. "North is in that direction." Then he pointed to the sky. "Follow that star over there at all times. Travel on the road only at night, and hide in the daytime."

The princess turned her head, as if to say something, but uttered only a whimper. Vlad felt her body quiver, reminding him of a sparrow he once found caught in a snare. While he was untangling the bird, it remained still. But when it felt he was about to set it free, it started to tremble with anticipation. He still felt the sparrow's heart beat in his fist, and tasted the sensation of knowing the little creature owed him its life.

He gave the princess a gentle push. "You must get away before your guards return."

She took a few steps, and he lost sight of her in the darkness. Only then did he realize how every fiber in his body ached from the tension he'd endured for the past hour.

Back in the room, he gave Gruya the pincers, the ax handle, and the rope to restore to their places, then went to the fountain to wash up. Fiery blisters covered the back of his hands, but their heat felt like the glow of satisfaction that comes from knowing you've done the right thing. And done it the hard way.

Vlad slept through the call to the dawn prayer, and would've slept through breakfast had it not been for a general tumult that buffeted the *caravanserai.* Through his sheepskin cover, he heard steps running back and forth along the colonnade, accompanied by unintelligible shouts. When he made out the Greek words "woman" and "escaped," he sprang off the platform as if it had caught fire.

He shook Gruya awake, and said, "Get up. It seems somebody's run away."

"As long as it's not the cook, I don't care," Gruya said, and went back to sleep.

Vlad tied his *opinci* in a hurry, and ran out of the courtyard on the heels of other travelers who'd just awakened to news of the escape. A crowd had already gathered along the rim of the ditch, where four of the overseers were beating the slaves with rods.

"Who did this?" one of them screamed in Turkish, while all four showered blows upon both men and women alike.

Vlad searched the crowd, and spotted another overseer in heated discussion with a man who appeared to be a blacksmith. The sixth overseer wasn't in sight.

Vlad elbowed his way closer to the blacksmith in time to hear him say, "I swear by *Allāh* my cutting tools are all in my shop. Not one is missing."

"This is the work of Bulgarian infidels from the village down the road," an old Turk said. Other Turks around him nodded.

"Yes," the blacksmith agreed, "the Bulgarians are always causing trouble." He seemed poised to elaborate on his accusation when the sound of hooves came from up the road. The crowd fell silent, and all eyes turned in the direction of the rider. Vlad raised himself on his toes and caught sight of a man trotting at a leisurely pace toward the inn. He recognized the missing overseer, and noted with deep relief the man didn't have the princess in tow.

The crowd parted at the rider's approach, and he led his horse to the edge of the ditch. There, without uttering a word, he tossed a blue bundle to the feet of his colleagues. It hit the ground with a thud, then unraveled, letting a ball soaked in blood and trailing blonde hair roll into the weeds.

The crowd uttered a collective gasp. Vlad fell a step backward, and bumped into somebody. First revulsion, then remorse washed over him in slimy, foul-smelling waves. He felt hands on his shoulders, and heard Michael whisper, "Death is preferable to slavery for a woman of rank." As Vlad was thrashing to reach the surface of the mire that had just swallowed him, the kindness in Michael's voice was a lifeline thrown to him just in time.

"Who could have done something like that?" Vlad heard Gruya ask, two steps in the rear. "Imagine, cutting a woman loose, and sending her alone into the night." Vlad turned to look for him with a throbbing awareness of how right Gruya was.

"Oh, I can tell you who," Dracul said. He'd snuck up behind Vlad and put an arm around his shoulder. "A misguided soul who thinks he can make the world a better place, one blunder at time."

3

A Forged Document

When they resumed their journey, Vlad avoided contact with both his father and Michael. He walked behind the convoy, with Gruya trailing a few steps behind. The pain Vlad felt at Princess Lubomirska's death refused to dull with the passing of time. Why did it all go so wrong?

"You heard she prayed to God for death," Gruya said by way of consolation. "It's not your fault that Saint—I forgot his name—was too slow to respond, and God beat him to it."

"God could've chosen somebody else than me to do his work," Vlad said.

Two days later, in Filibe, his remorse finally began to lose its edge. Vlad saw three women from the north being auctioned in the slave market there. Same blonde hair his princess had. Their haunted looks left no doubt in him they too would prefer death to what awaited them after the auction. Perhaps God did choose Vlad to fulfill Princess Lubomirska's desperate prayer, "*Mein Gott, nimm mich!*"

That evening, he had the opportunity to make peace with his father. Well, perhaps not quite peace, since Father had too many reasons to maintain a state of war with his disobedient son. Their reconciliation was more of a truce.

Dracul asked Vlad and Gruya to join him and Michael in their chamber for dinner. They sat on the bare floor in a circle and ate in silence, Gruya alone showing signs of appetite. Dracul and Michael appeared preoccupied, lost in distant thoughts, and it troubled Vlad to see them in that state. He chewed his boiled vegetables without tasting them, and wondered when Father's recriminations would begin. Gruya finished his meal ahead of the others, then volunteered to remove the trenchers with the unfinished food and place them outside the door.

"Glad to see you're taking your role of a servant to heart, Grandson," Michael said with a sarcastic chuckle.

Gruya turned around at the door, sheepish, his mouth full. "You taught me to respect food, Grandfather," he said after he swallowed. "No waste."

Dracul took a scroll of paper from inside his shirt, and handed it to Vlad with a dark look. "I've got a serious problem with you and Gruya on my back."

Vlad felt relieved his father didn't bring up Princess Lubomirska's death. Dracul's anger at Vlad and Gruya's unauthorized presence in the convoy was something easier to face.

"This travel document Hassan Pasha gave me in Nicopolis states the number of people I'm supposed to have in my party," Dracula said. "The first official who asks for my papers will notice that my entourage has grown by two."

Vlad read the travel authorization signed by the Bey of Nicopolis. Indeed, it said the documented party was composed of two merchants, named Ulfer and Michael, plus six unnamed muleteers, all Wallachian subjects. The merchants had paid the required custom taxes, and were entitled to the protection of the sultan on their travel between Nicopolis and Edirne. Anyone causing these men harm, or injustice, would be brought in front of the nearest town's *kadı,* judge.

"Two unregistered men *will* cause trouble," Michael said. "They'll be assumed to be runaway slaves."

"Can't you send two of your men back home with some merchant traveling north, Father?" Vlad said. "I've heard caravans are always shorthanded."

"Caravans do their crew hiring in Edirne," Michael said. "Besides, a *kadı* would have to draw papers transferring our two men to another convoy. And the first thing he'd ask for would be your father's travel authorization, to adjust the number of muleteers downward."

"You and Gruya would be who I'd send back, if I could." Dracul scowled at Vlad. "But without proof that you're Wallachian subjects, I might as well hand you over to a *kadı* to be taken as runaway slaves."

Vlad didn't have to be told what such a treatment would entail. Severed toes, broken fingers, lopped-off ears. Lala Gunther had borne all those markings to chronicle his repeated failures to escape from servitude. Vlad inspected the paper again, and was hit by a thought. "What if I changed the document to say you had eight men crewing for you?"

Dracul shook his head. "Bad idea. If an Ottoman official thinks the document's been tampered with, I'll have bigger problems than just employing runaway slaves."

"His Grace is right," Michael said. "Even if we could clear the matter, in the end it will cost us a delay of a few days. As it is, we're behind the schedule."

"When I'm done, no one will notice I changed anything in the document," Vlad said. He didn't feel as confident as he sounded, but what alternatives were there? With another four, five days before reaching Edirne, there would be many occasions for a suspicious official to stop them. The prospect of solving a problem no one else could lifted his spirit. "I know from Father Gunther how the Turks make their ink. All I need is some gum arabic, lampblack, oak gall, and—"

"And where do you expect to find those things before we leave in the morning?" Dracul said in a mocking tone.

"I can substitute ordinary ingredients for the specialized ones," Vlad said, determined not to let his idea die. He turned to Gruya.

"Go to the workshop and bring me a handful of soot, two ounces of bone glue, and a thimble of sheep's tallow."

Gruya stared at Michael in disbelief, hoping perhaps his grandfather would countermand Vlad's order. But Michael just nodded, so Gruya headed for the door, resentful.

Dracul gave a scornful chortle. "Don't forget to bring a quill, too. Preferably from the left wing of a swan."

If Father wanted to disparage Vlad's initiative, so much the better. He'd have something to regret when Vlad proved he knew what he was doing.

"Show me the place where you'd change the text," Michael said.

Vlad flattened the paper scroll on the ground in front of Michael. Dracul leaned against the wall, and let his head fall onto his chest. Of course he'd want to remain aloof from this experiment he must consider childish. But at least he didn't squash the initiative. Vlad pointed to a set of squiggles, and said, "This is where it says there are six mulceteers."

"Show me how they write number eight." Michael handed Vlad a small knife, and pointed at the wall.

Vlad scratched the number eight on the ochre-colored plaster. "I know they look too different to simply turn a six into an eight. If the Turks used the Latin numbers, it would be easy. Because they don't, I must do something else."

Michael cocked his head, ready to ask for an explanation. But in his usual fashion, he held back to let Vlad volunteer it. That moment Gruya entered carrying a short board, like a tray, while concealing something behind his back. On the board Vlad saw a lump of charcoal, a mound of black grease, and a fist-size shard of something brown he guessed was congealed bone glue.

"Sorry," Gruya said, "no sheep's tallow. I hope this axle grease will do."

Dracul stood up with a groan of pain, and leaned over the board. "And no swan feather, I guess." He picked up a tiny pigeon feather that Gruya had planted like a standard into the mound of grease, and waved it under Vlad's nose. "Are we done with foolishness for tonight?"

Vlad rose as well. He weighed the hardened glue in his hand, thinking of a way he could liquefy it. He'd need a brazier to heat some water for that. Would he be able to get close to one without anyone asking questions? Then, he could grind the charcoal with a rock against the floorboards to get the black powder he needed. The axle grease would do just fine. But the pigeon feather was useless for anything resembling calligraphy. His heart sank.

He turned to Gruya, unable to hide his disappointment. "Is this the best you could do?" he said.

"With the things you asked me to find, yes," Gruya said. "But had you asked me to find plain ink, I could've let you have this." With a flourish, he produced a copper inkpot he'd been hiding behind his back. A hawk's feather stuck out of the pot.

Michael uttered a groan of surprise, but Dracul pretended to be unmoved. Vlad spread the paper in front of him on the floor, and weighed it down with the inkpot.

"I borrowed the ink from one of travelers when he left his place to go pray," Gruya said. "An itinerant scribe, I think. I saw him—"

"Never mind the stories, Grandson," Michael said. "Hold the candle so Vlad can see what he's doing."

"I need to return it quickly, before the loan becomes a theft," Gruya said. He sounded deflated that his success earned him no praise.

Following the place where the number of muleteers was recorded, Vlad added, "And two footmen, also from Wallachia."

"Remarkable," Michael said. "Your lettering is identical to that of Hassan Pasha's scribe."

When Vlad showed his father the inserted text, Dracul stared at it in silence, lower lip pushed forward in a reflective mien. Finally he said in a flat tone, "So Gunther taught you how to write like the Turks?"

Not quite the praise Vlad expected for having gotten them all out of an impasse. But then, it was Vlad who'd caused the problem to start with.

"You and Gruya can ride our mules from here on," Dracul said, "whenever Michael and I aren't riding them."

So, if not with praise, Dracul sealed the truce with a concession.

4

The Two Tower Gate

Edirne's Çiftkule Kapısı, the Two Tower Gate, bristled with archers looking down upon a long line of people and wagons awaiting admission to the city. Dracul's party waited for hours, like all others, while officers scrutinized the travelers' documents, and questioned them with the help of interpreters. When Dracul's turn finally came, no Romanian translator was at hand, so the officers had to send for one.

"I could translate, and save us time," Vlad said.

"It's best if they don't know you understand Turkish," Dracul said. "That way you can spy on them, as you did in Nicopolis."

Vlad didn't want to confess he was getting impatient. The Edirne air made him tingle with excitement. He'd forgotten all the dark feelings of the past few days. Now, the only thing he had in mind was to explore this town, and get a glimpse of its master. Here was the beating heart of the Ottoman Empire, the monster that kept much of Christian Europe sleepless. And here dwelled Sultan Murad, who with a single nod could set an army of a hundred thousand men in motion. Vlad heard the empire held ten million souls who lived, and died, at Murad's whim. To be within a few steps of the man who had dominion over such multitudes thrilled him. What did Murad look like? What was his disposition? His aura? Did he terrify the people around him with a mere glance?

Vlad pointed to the soldiers on top of the wall. "A wealthy man, Murad. He owns all of those men and thousands more like them. All his slaves."

"Ah, but his true wealth is not the men but the women he owns," Gruya said.

"So you're an expert on wealth now?" Vlad said.

Gruya snickered. "I heard Murad has three hundred concubines. That's what true wealth is all about." He became animated. "I conducted a study once to figure out—"

"A study? You?" Vlad was unable to hold back his laughter.

Gruya didn't seem to take umbrage. "I was curious to know how many yards of 'piping' you'd get if you put together the—*er*—the female parts of all those women, end to end."

"And to think that some people believe the science of engineering left Wallachia with the Romans, a thousand years ago." Vlad wished he hadn't mentioned Murad.

"I got help from a monk good with figures," Gruya said.

"Did he know what he was calculating on your behalf?"

"The answer is fifty yards." Gruya sounded dreamy. "Imagine, fifty yards of—you know what. I suppose most of those yards go untouched in Murad's house. They must be full of cobwebs."

"Next you'll tell me there'd be no cobwebs in the 'pipe' of your harem."

"Not if it were twice as long," Gruya said, and sucked air through his teeth with a grin.

Abdullah was the translator who came to help with Dracul's papers. He wore the iron ring of a slave around his neck, and spoke with the accent of Romanians from Transylvania's Kronstadt region. That reminded Vlad of Thomas Siegel, Katharina's father, and of his own rash promise to find him one day. Here was his chance to learn of Siegel's whereabouts, even if he had no money to ransom him. He tried to approach Abdullah, but when the man finished translating he scurried away, and disappeared behind the gate.

When their convoy finally set in motion, Dracul said, "You and Gruya look after our mules. Michael and I need to walk."

Passing through Çiftkule Kapısı was like entering a new world for Vlad. The thoroughfare leading to the center of the town, where their inn was located, was a slow-moving river of white turbans. Here and there, a colorful fez, the canopy of a wagon, or the bales of merchandise stacked up on a camel's back, broke the white monotony. A medley of languages filled the air, and Vlad experienced a charge every time he recognized one of them: Turkish, Persian, Arabic, Greek. Then there were languages he couldn't even guess. Armenian? Georgian? Circassian? Russian? Tartar? Hindi? Swahili? Aramaic? Gunther claimed he'd come across more than fifty languages and dialects in his forty years of being a slave.

Gruya also appeared fascinated by what he saw.

"If you let your mouth hang open like that," Vlad said, "people might take you a dolt, and fleece you at the first opportunity."

Gruya shrugged. "What I notice is there are no women in this crowd. Not even one to soothe a man's eyes. And where could all these folks be going, bunched together like sheep?"

"Friday's like our Sunday for the Muslims," Vlad said. "People come to town from nearby villages to pray at the Friday Mosque."

"There," Gruya exclaimed, "that's our translator." He pointed at a shop at their right.

When Vlad turned to look, Abdullah was just ducking in through the door.

"I've got to ask him something," Vlad said, and maneuvered his mule to the side of the street. A glance at his father and Michael, only steps ahead, assured Vlad they wouldn't be getting too far in the crawling traffic. He and Gruya tied their mules to a hitching post and went inside the shop.

"*Doamne ajută, bade,* May God help you, *bade,*" Vlad said upon entering the shop. The greeting startled Abdullah. He turned on his heels faster than his legs could handle, and toppled over a bale of cotton.

Vlad and Gruya laughed, and helped the old man regain his footing.

"*Luav-ar dracul*, the Devil take the two of you," Abdullah said with mock anger, his mouth stretched in a toothless grin. "I haven't been called *bade* in decades. I'm not used to such respect as a slave. Who are you?"

"You must be from around Kronstadt," Vlad said. "We don't have much time. I need to ask you—"

"Born and raised there," Abdullah said. "Also captured there by the Turks in 'twenty-two."

"You've been here for twenty years?" Gruya said, astounded. "Couldn't you escape?"

"Do you know a man from Kronstadt named Thomas Siegel?" Vlad said.

"Escape?" Abdullah kicked off his right slipper; all his toes were missing. "You think one can escape from the Turks?"

"But a man we knew," Gruya said, "Gunther of Bavaria, did escape a few years ago and—"

Vlad tapped Gruya's arm to silence him, and said to Abdullah, "Siegel was the alderman of the Weavers Guild. He was captured in Murad's raid in Transylvania."

"Oh, yes, that was in 'thirty-eight," Abdullah said. "I met Siegel when he arrived here, but he wouldn't have anything to do with me, on account of my being a Muslim."

"Why did you convert, *bade*?" Gruya said.

Abdullah kicked off his other slipper to show more mutilations. "Because I ran out of toes, I guess."

Gruya crossed himself.

"There is another Transylvanian in Edirne, named Gheorghe," Abdullah said. "A seminary student from Mühlbach, captured in the same raid with Siegel. The two of them are tight friends. Gheorghe will take you to Siegel."

Vlad felt a stab of excitement. "Where can I find this Gheorghe?"

"But are you a real Muslim, *bade*, or just pretending?" Gruya said.

"Let the man answer my question, Gruya," Vlad snapped. "We don't have all day."

"Gheorghe belongs to a shop owner in the *bedestan*, the covered market, next to the Friday Mosque. I don't recall the man's name."

Vlad left the shop aglow with the thought that he'd soon find Katharina's father. Upon returning home he'd figure a way to buy Siegel's freedom, if he had to sell a piece of his own lands. In his excitement he slapped his mule's rump.

"Hey, that's my mule you're beating on," Gruya said.

Only then did they both realize one of the mules was missing.

"If I'm a dolt, how come it's you who got fleeced?" Gruya said.

"*Kurva bitang*, you whore's bastard," Vlad cursed the unknown thief in Hungarian. His face turned hot. "You should've stayed out here," he shouted at Gruya, but knew he was being unfair. In the distance, Dracul's head bobbed up and down as he limped his way along the thoroughfare. No, Vlad couldn't face his father with one more blunder. "Don't just stand there, Gruya. Do something. Look around."

Vlad spotted a watchman in a booth ten yards away, and his hope revived. "I've been robbed of my mule," he said when he reached the booth. "I'd just stopped in a shop for a few minutes, and—"

"Don't feel bad," the watchman said with indifference, "it happens all the time."

Though enraged, Vlad felt a spark of pride at being so easily understood by the Turk. Still, he felt like breaking something. "But you're here to keep order," he said, barely able to control his tone. "Aren't you supposed catch the thieves?"

"Yes, but I rarely do," the man replied. He began to show signs of impatience with Vlad's questioning. "They're quite crafty, those mule thieves."

"What are they? Greeks? Albanians? Turks? What should I be looking for?"

"Most of them are Wallachians," the watchman said. "Where're you from? You've got a peculiar accent."

Vlad heard Gruya's whistle, and turned to see him atop a passing wagon. He was at Gruya's side in seconds. They ignored the driver, who shouted something in Bulgarian and threatened them with his whip.

"I see a brown fez and the head of an animal down there," Gruya said, and pointed back toward the city gate. "That man's the only one going the wrong way in the traffic. He must be our thief."

"Please keep an eye on this mule," Vlad called to the watchman. "I don't want it stolen too. I'll be right back."

"Bring me the thief, and I'll deal with him," the man replied, without sarcasm.

Vlad began to fight his way against the traffic, weaving left and right, ignoring the elbow jabs that greeted him. The thief hadn't made much progress, and Vlad closed the distance to him in less than two minutes. Gruya made a wide arc and appeared in front of the man, pretending to be just another walker in the crowd.

"I've got a message for you," Vlad said loudly in Romanian. The thief let go of the mule's reins and spun around. So he was a Wallachian, as the watchman had predicted. Being robbed by a compatriot made the crime even more disconcerting.

The thief was a sweaty ogre with bony knobs that thrust forward above bushy eyebrows. Broad in the shoulders like the door of an outhouse, he stood six inches taller than Vlad. When he saw that Vlad was alone, the thief broke into a lopsided grin.

"And I've got a message for you, Devil's snot," he said, and patted the hilt of a dagger stuck in his sash. "Why don't you show a bit of sense, and get lost before I gut you with this?"

At a glance, Vlad saw the dagger was a fine weapon of Persian design. Another thing the man had stolen, no doubt. "I can't do that without delivering my message first," Vlad said, and gave Gruya a sign by raising his eyebrows.

Gruya grappled the thief in a bear hug, and Vlad delivered a hard kick to his groin. The ogre drew a sharp breath and rolled his eyes so only the whites remained visible. Then he slumped onto Gruya, who stepped back and let him fall. The man's head hit the ground with a dull thud.

"I'll take your message now," Vlad said, and snatched the thief's dagger.

"What's going on here?" an elderly passerby asked, his tone severe. He wore a black turban, and was accompanied by a retinue of young men who looked upon him with respect. "There'll be no disturbances on Friday."

"My friend down there had a sunstroke," Vlad said, with a show of concern, "and I'm off to fetch a healer."

5

Sultan's Wife

Vlad and Gruya caught up with their party in front of the Friday Mosque, just as the muezzin began to sing the *adhān*. They could see their *caravanserai* in the near distance, next to the *bedestan*, but couldn't advance farther. They left their mules in the care of one of Dracul's drivers and worked their way into the crowd. People had lined up in two rows, twenty to thirty deep, to form a narrow passageway from one end of the plaza to the other, with archers posted every few feet. The crowd was hushed and an air of dignified expectation hovered over the place.

"The sultan and members of the Imperial Council are coming," a neighbor said when Vlad asked what the people were waiting for. That sent a sharp jolt through Vlad. Murad here? Only a few feet in front of him? If this were *all* he could see in Edirne, then be packed off to Wallachia, his trip would still have been worthwhile.

"Wait till Marcus finds out about this," he told Gruya, after explaining what was about to happen. "While he's chasing wenches by the Black Sea, I get to see the Sultan of the Ottoman Empire walk in front of my nose."

"Ah, if your brother were here," Gruya said, "all he'd think about would be how to assassinate Murad."

"Marcus is prick-hard and brain-soft," Vlad said. "Even assuming one could kill Murad, what would that accomplish? His namesake grandfather was stabbed to death by a Serb in Kosovo in 'eighty-nine. All that did was bring Beyazid to the throne: a war-loving sultan who went on to kick the Communion bread out of Christians for the next ten years."

Gruya squeezed Vlad's arm and hissed with an urgency unnatural to him, "Look! That's Omar."

Vlad followed Gruya's stare. There, in the front row across the passage, was the man whose face Vlad could never forget. A violent shiver coursed down his back, and his scalp tightened as if pulled down around his ears like a cap.

"It *is* Omar," he growled, and his hand clutched the dagger hidden under his shirt. His mouth went dry, and he found himself breathing faster. How much of that was fear, how much hatred? *I had you in my power once, and some madness made me set you free.*

A murmur started at the far right, and traveled through the plaza like a wave across a field of tall grasses. Vlad rose on his toes and peered above people's heads to see three men in oversized turbans and colorful silk robes approaching at a leisurely pace. Then he returned his eyes to Omar, but the Akinci had vanished. Involuntarily, Vlad glanced over his shoulder as if he expected his enemy to appear there.

In the passageway, the three men were talking among themselves, oblivious to the hundreds of onlookers around them. The man in the middle was the oldest of the three, and appeared the highest authority among them. Imposing in stature and self-confident, power radiated from him. He had white skin and features Lala Gunther had taught Vlad to recognize in Asiatic Turks: oval face, almond-shaped eyes, hooked nose, and a sparse chestnut beard. The other two men, short and swarthy, were decidedly from the Balkans: round eyes, straight noses, and black beards as dense as the bristles on a pig's back. Serbs? Bosnians? Albanians?

So this is Murad. Vlad's palms became moist, and Omar's presence vanished from his mind. He memorized every detail of Murad's appearance, intent on showing off to Marcus.

When Murad and his two companions passed in front of him, Vlad was surprised the viewers paid no attention to them. Instead, all heads turned to two men who'd just emerged into the passage. One was a young uniformed officer, the other a civilian a few years older. The latter had the appearance of a shopkeeper, dressed as he was in a coarse, brown robe and an ordinary white turban. Yet the officer seemed to defer to him.

"How's your hip, Lala Tabrizı?" the "shopkeeper" asked someone in the crowd. He listened for the answer with interest, then nodded, compassionate. A few steps farther, the man addressed someone else. "You keep promising to come hunting with me, Sheikh Nasiruddin, but never do." The distance prevented Vlad from hearing more than the laughter that rose around the sheikh. "Oh, yes, I know what you mean," the man in the brown robe said. "Well, pheasants and the ducks can wait, but new wives can't." More laughter from both sides of the passage, then the man resumed his walk.

The onlookers kept a respectful silence, and no one addressed the man unless prompted by his question or comment. Vlad concluded this man wasn't some low-level functionary, but the sultan himself, the all-powerful master of the empire. The realization caused Vlad's eyes to mist over. He felt as if he'd uncovered a magic lamp that illuminated everything around him. So this was what true power looked like? No fancy clothes, no jewelry, no prancing stallion. Just walking to the mosque in the middle of the afternoon, protected by a handful of archers, but otherwise looking like any ordinary person.

Once the sultan and his entourage disappeared inside the mosque courtyard, the crowd formed orderly lines in front of waterspouts jutting out of a stone wall nearby.

"That was Khalil Pasha, the Grand Vizier," a watermelon vendor said, when Vlad inquired about the tallest of the three men who preceded Murad.

"How do I get some of that?" Gruya whispered, and pointed at the seller's tray, piled high with melon slices. "I've got no money."

"And who were Khalil Pasha's companions?" Vlad said to the vendor.

"Next time we go on a trip like this," Gruya cried, "give me some notice so I can squirrel away a few coins."

"The Second and Third Viziers," the watermelon man said.

Gruya rolled his eyes in exasperation. "*You* might get a perverse pleasure out of going without food, or drink—"

"Which one was Zaganos Pasha?" Vlad said.

"—or sleep for days on end—"

"The one to the left of the Grand Vizier," the vendor said.

"—but *I* sure don't enjoy any of that." Gruya stepped between Vlad and the vendor.

Vlad shoved him aside, impatient. "What about the officer accompanying the sultan?"

"That one I don't know," the vendor said. "I'm from the countryside."

"As for the *other thing* I've got to go without," Gruya said, unable to stay his lamenting, "don't get me talking about it. It looks hopeless that I should find myself any female company, this side of the Danube."

The *caravanserai* was built on the same pattern as all the others Vlad had seen on the way down from Nicopolis: monumental stone gate, rectangular courtyard, central fountain, shops, kitchens, storerooms, and arcades on both floors. The major contrast this inn presented to those in the countryside was the absence of a mosque. With more than five dozen mosques sprinkled throughout Edirne, travelers had many options for places to worship Allah.

The innkeeper and his staff were still at the mosque when Dracul and his party arrived at the *caravanserai*. The only people around, other than the non-Muslim travelers, were two Janissaries guarding one of the rooms upstairs. When the innkeeper returned, he cast a businesslike glance around the courtyard, then ran to Dracul with open arms and an ingratiating smile.

"*Allāhu Akbar*," the man intoned, and touched his right hand to his heart, full of deference. "Praise and thanks be to Allah that Your Grace and Lord Michael are honoring my humble establishment with your presence again after so many years. It has been what? Three? Four years?" He spoke a fluent Greek that made Vlad suspect he'd converted to Islam as a grown man.

Dracul nodded in greeting, then winked and said, "No 'Your Grace' or 'Lord' this time, Hussein. Only 'Master Ulfer' and 'Master Michael.' We are here incognito. I'll explain it to you after we have a bite to eat."

Dracul's Greek was mangled, which both amused and embarrassed Vlad.

"Did I understand your father to say 'eat'?" Gruya whispered.

Hussein pointed to the upper arcade. "Well then, Master Ulfer, please follow me to your sleeping chamber. I'll have some food sent up to you, as well as some cold *ayran* you're sure to enjoy drinking after your long travel."

Gruya smacked his lips. "I heard the innkeeper mention drinking."

"It's a good thing I only taught you three words of Greek," Vlad said, not amused by Gruya's immature behavior. "You've used two of them already, and mercifully won't be needing to use the third one."

Gruya seemed ready with an answer, when a loud commotion took place by the gate. Vlad turned to see two beardless men with feminine faces stalking into the courtyard and driving everyone out of their way with shrill cries.

"Those are eunuchs, aren't they?" Gruya said, assuming an innocent air. "Men who can't get it up so they can't—wait, wait, I know how to say it in Greek—'*γαμώ*' ... gah-mo?" He snickered, proud of his cleverness. "I hope I pronounced the third and last word of my Greek vocabulary correctly."

From the foot of the stairs leading to the second floor, the eunuchs exchanged hand signals with the Janissaries standing guard above. Seemingly satisfied, the eunuchs bounded out of the courtyard. The passage they'd opened through the throng of travelers remained clear. A moment later they reappeared, followed by two women and a girl, all three Christians judging from their uncovered faces. Two more eunuchs, armed with bows and sabers, trailed them at close distance.

The women were of about the same age, perhaps in their mid-twenties. One wore a black hooded robe and a white wimple. The other was dressed in clothes sewn of expensive-looking fabrics. She and the girl held hands.

"The lady in black is one of the sultan's wives," Hussein whispered to Dracul, with a conspiratorial look. "They call her 'the empress,' because she's a king's offspring. All other of Murad's wives are slaves."

"Is she King Brankovich's daughter?" Dracul asked.

The innkeeper inflated his chest, clearly proud of his status of a person in the know. "Mara Brankovich herself."

"What's she doing here?"

"Visiting two secret guests, ones I was asked by the palace to put up at my inn."

"And who's the beauty walking with her?" Dracul said.

"Ah, Master Ulfer," Hussein said, and rubbed his hands unctuously, "your reputation as a man who can spot beauty a mile away is well deserved."

Dracul dismissed Hussein's flattery with a shrug. "What's her name?"

"You must have heard of Giovanni Grimaldi, the brother of the Galata's Chief Magistrate, Podestà Boruele Grimaldi."

Dracul scratched his beard, and furrowed his brow. "I recall a Grimaldi story I heard in 'twenty-nine when I was still living in Schassburg. Something about a marriage between a rich Venetian girl and the scion of a Genovese family from Galata. It was the first time that town became the subject of interest throughout Europe. Nobody understood why mighty Venice seemed so keen on courting a tiny Genovese colony in the shadow of Constantinople."

"Yes, that Grimaldi," Hussein said. "The marriage was supposed to forge an alliance between Venice and Genoa, which, of course, it didn't. You're looking at that same Venetian girl, Donatella Loredano, only now she is the widow Grimaldi. Giovanni died soon after the wedding."

"I remember now," Dracul said. "She's the daughter of Admiral Pietro Loredano, who got killed a few years back."

"Being a widow, she has the time to spend in Lady Mara's company. Donatella has been the empress's lady-in-waiting for the past two years. There are even rumors Donatella's position at the imperial palace owes something to her daughter Bianca's being promised to Murad as a ..."

Vlad stopped listening to Hussein's gossip and shifted his attention to the Venetian woman. For a reason he couldn't understand, the notion she was a widow, not someone's wife, pleased him.

The four eunuchs stationed themselves at the bottom of the stairs, ready to bar anyone's way. The women and the girl climbed to the second floor, where Lady Mara entered the room guarded by the Janissaries, while her companions remained waiting on the landing. Then a muffled wail came from inside the room, followed by loud sobs.

"The palace was quite secretive about the guests they wanted me to accommodate here," Hussein said. "But when I was told to expect a visit from the empress, it didn't take me long to figure out the guests were her brothers."

"What are they doing here?" Dracul said. "I heard they were locked up in the Amasya fortress, as high-value hostages."

At this, Vlad's attention returned to the innkeeper.

"And you heard right, Master Ulfer. The brothers, Gregory and Stefan, passed through here last year on their way to Anatolia," Hussein said. "It seems Lady Mara insisted the sultan bring them to Edirne so she could see them. They're to be taken back to their Amasya prison tomorrow. Imagine, such a long journey just for an hour-long visit with their sister."

"I heard Murad adores Mara, and grants her every wish," Dracul said. "But why such secrecy?"

Hussein leaned in a bit closer and lowered his voice. "Something's amiss with this entire affair. The brothers arrived yesterday by wagon, under military escort, and were led to their room, heads covered in blankets. They've been cooped up in there under guard ever since. I've even been told to let the Janissaries take the food in to them. I guess the palace doesn't want anyone to see their faces."

Ten minutes later Mara reappeared in the doorway, howling as if her own baby had been torn from her breast, and threw herself into the arms of the Venetian woman.

Vlad moved closer to the passageway the women would follow upon leaving the inn. When they finally descended the stairs, a look at Donatella told him why his father had been so taken with her. But what struck Vlad more than her singular beauty was the air of sadness that veiled her eyes. The same resigned sadness he remembered with a throbbing pain from his last and only encounter with his grandmother. And, as in Oma's case, he felt the urge to wipe away that sadness. But this time the impulse came from a part of his soul that stored feelings of longing and desire, not of pity and compassion.

6

In the Bedestan

The next morning, the officer who had accompanied Murad to the mosque appeared at the inn. He no longer wore his uniform, but a plain gray robe. Dracul and Michael, who were in the process of having their beards trimmed by the courtyard fountain, greeted the man in a friendly manner, and gave signs of knowing him. They sent the barber away, and huddled with the officer in secretive conversation.

Vlad crept to the other side of the fountain and listened while he pretended to wash his kerchief. Despite the fact the men talked in whispers, he caught a few words in Greek: "sultan … letter … Zaganos …" He even thought he heard the Pope being mentioned, but discounted that as improbable. What would Father have to do with the Pope? When Michael addressed the officer as "Tirendaz Agha," Vlad remembered the conversation he'd overheard at Hassan Bey's court in Nicopolis. Was this the Tirendaz that Hassan and his secretary were talking about? They said he'd been to Târgovişte, which explained Father and Michael's familiarity with him. And, more ominously, they hinted of a letter dangerous to Vlad's father that Tirendaz knew something about.

Trying to remain unobserved, Vlad moved closer to where the men stood. But Tirendaz noticed him and said to Dracul, "We'd better go somewhere else. There are too many ears around here."

When Tirendaz and Dracul were out of sight, Vlad edged over to Michael. "Did you find out what they want with Father?"

Michael betrayed concern despite a visible effort to control himself, and his anxiety infected Vlad. "Michael, who's Tirendaz?"

"The sultan's *musahib,* his confidant, as well as the Grand Vizier's nephew."

"Did he tell you about that secret letter we heard of in Nicopolis?" Vlad said.

Michael sat on the lid of the fountain with a pained expression. "I keep telling myself that the days of travel are over for me, yet here I am, three hundred miles away from my comfortable home."

Vlad interpreted Michael's reluctance to answer as meaning big trouble *was* on the horizon. "I heard Tirendaz mention Zaganos," Vlad said, and noticed Michael's upper lip twitch. "That's the Third Vizier. He's the one with the letter, isn't he?"

"Tirendaz has taken your father to the Grand Vizier's palace. From all I've heard so far, Khalil Pasha's on our side. The letter Zaganos claims to have—no one's seen it so far—is supposed to be from Hunyadi to Pope Eugene, and it portrays your father as conspiring against Murad. How it fell into Zaganos's hands, Tirendaz didn't say. We'll find out more when your father returns. In the meantime I'm to take our *peşkeş,*" their diplomatic gifts, "to the sultan's palace and have them recorded."

"I'm coming too," Vlad said. "Murad's palace is something I'd love to see."

"You father forbids you to set foot anywhere near that place."

"But—"

"He's in earnest about it, and so am I," Michael said, with harshness rare for him. "After the palace, I'll go to the market to sell the wagons, and all but two of the mules. We'll be needing all the money we can scrape together, if things go badly for your father." He crossed himself three times and mumbled an invocation.

Vlad did the same, and knocked on wood for an extra measure of prevention. He feared Michael knew more than he was willing to share. "What about the crew?" Vlad said.

"I'll have a *kadi* issue the men new papers, and send them home with a caravan traveling north."

As soon as Michael left, Vlad and Gruya did too, in the opposite direction. They strolled through the open bazaar, which covered a large area around the *bedestan*, and marveled at the array of goods from all over the world. The colors, smells, and sounds of the bazaar dazzled him. He thought back to the Târgovişte market, with its muddy animal pens and nearly barren stalls. When Father conceived his plan for drawing new commerce to Wallachia, he must've envisioned some version of the Edirne bazaar.

Gruya was in a state of childish excitement, darting from one vendor's counter to another. At one point he disappeared from view, and resurfaced half an hour later, his lips and mustache white with powdered sugar. "I discovered," he said, with the earnestness of an explorer, "that all I have to do is say please, and I get a free sample of anything that's edible. Fresh fruits, dried fruits, candied fruit, pastries, halva. Did you know there are five kinds of dates, and they all taste different?"

"I'm so proud of you for learning how to beg in Turkish," Vlad said. He wanted to upbraid Gruya for displaying his customary gluttony, but decided to leave him alone. Gruya had been away from home for near three weeks, and wouldn't return there for many more. No harm letting him be himself for a few hours.

"And just as I was beginning to suffer from thirst—"

"Of course," Vlad said, "we have to move on to drinking, your second most-favorite topic."

Gruya paid no attention to Vlad's sarcasm, and continued with unabated enthusiasm. "You'd think this was the last place on earth to find anything strong to drink. I've had it with *ayran* and—what's that vile thing made from fermented mare's milk?"

"*Koumiss*, and don't let the Turks hear you badmouth it."

"I met this old Bulgarian who took a shine to me," Gruya said. "He spoke a bit of Romanian. He traveled through Wallachia as a *rakija* merchant at the time your grandfather was king. Did you know *rakija* tastes much like the German burned water?"

They had reached the entrance to the *bedestan*. The market's rectangular hall was divided into three parallel sections. One section ran along the center axis, and served as a thoroughfare for shoppers. The other two ran on either side, and housed the shops inside bays with domed ceilings. Vlad glanced around, and wondered how he'd go about finding Gheorghe of Mühlbach here.

"If you're still walking straight, you couldn't've had much *rakija*," Vlad said. "So where's the story there?" He approached the first shopkeeper on the right aisle, and said in Turkish, "Do you know a slave named Gheorghe, who works here in the *bedestan*?"

The man regarded Vlad with suspicion, and shook his head.

"Oh, it's not the *rakija* that's the story," Gruya said. He crossed his hands behind his back, and inflated his chest like someone about to deliver important news.

Vlad left Gruya trailing him and walked from shop to shop, repeating his question. None of the dozen shopkeepers on the right aisle had heard of Gheorghe. When Vlad crossed over to the left aisle Gruya barred his way, begging with his eyes to be asked about the rest of his story.

"I am doing something important here," Vlad said, and pushed Gruya aside, exasperated. But after a few more people told him they hadn't heard of Gheorghe, Vlad relented. "Well, let me hear it. It must be something about sex, or you wouldn't be strutting about like a rooster with love in mind."

Gruya grinned conspiratorially. "I've got a plan that will make our stay in this heathen town a lot more tolerable." He waited for Vlad's reaction.

Vlad felt he'd conceded enough by letting Gruya speak, so he shrugged and continued his quest for Gheorghe. If there was no Gheorghe, there was no hope of finding Thomas Siegel. Why was even this small success being denied him? Only when he'd exhausted all the places he could inquire did he turn to Gruya. "Let me hear your plan."

"The Bulgarian told me there is a Gypsy quarter in town, where we can get all the—"

"You think Gypsy women will give you free samples of their—*er*—just because you say please?"

Gruya's face fell. "Yes, there is that pesky matter of the money. I was hoping you'd be able to talk my grandfather out of a few aspers for the purpose of buying love."

As Vlad was heading for the exit Gruya called after him, "What if your Gheorghe's known here by some other name? Maybe that's why nobody knows whom you're asking about." Then he climbed on a pile of empty crates, and shouted, "Gheorghe of Mühlbach."

The hall reverberated with Gruya's call, and all eyes turned on him. A nearby watchman stood up at his station, and scanned the hall with a threatening look. Mortified, Vlad was about to bolt out of the place when a short young man ran out of a shop, looked left and right, then cried in Romanian, "Here I am, here I am. Who's looking for me?" When he set eyes upon Gruya standing atop the crates, the man began to agitate his arms like someone chasing crows from a freshly seeded field. He was about twenty years old, with an unruly mop of black hair and unkempt beard. On his neck, Vlad spotted the slave's iron ring.

"Get back to work, Gorgon," someone shouted from inside the shop, in Greek.

"I thought someone finally came to ransom me," Gheorghe said a short while later, his face sagging with disappointment. He'd followed Vlad and Gruya out of the *bedestan,* and learned what they were looking for. "I prayed every day for the past four years to—"

"Don't stop praying, Brother Gheorghe," Gruya said. "Someone might be out there saving money for your ransom, as we speak."

"Now, instead of good news, I'll be getting a beating for just leaving the shop to talk with you," Gheorghe said. "My owner's a Greek renegade. He beats me every day, and won't let me use my real name. 'Gorgon,' he calls me."

"You need to run away," Gruya said.

"I tell you, converts to Islam make the worst kind of masters."

"So, where's Siegel now?" Vlad said.

"I'm writing down everything in a diary," Gheorghe whispered, and glanced over his shoulder. "On the sly, of course. Christian Europe has no idea of what's going on here. I plan to write a treatise on the Turks and Islam one day, if the Lord helps me escape."

Vlad struggled to conceal his impatience. "A Transylvanian renegade I met by the Çiftkule Kapısı claimed you and Siegel are friends. So you must know his whereabouts."

Gheorghe shook his head, as if to clear his mind of some bothersome thought, then said, "Friends, indeed. Thomas and I were brought to Edirne together. But you aren't going to find him. He was sold to a Christian merchant from Bursa two years ago."

Vlad felt downhearted. Michael was right when he said that once someone is swallowed by the Ottoman Empire, only a miracle would rescue him. *How reckless I was to promise Katharina I'd find her father.*

"Even Christians can buy slaves here?" Gruya said, incredulous.

"Certainly," Gheorghe replied. "All the sultan cares for is they pay him the sales tax." He spat in disgust. "Christians make the worst kind of masters." He'd forgotten his earlier indictment of converts to Islam.

In a state of dejection, Vlad left Gruya to chat with Gheorghe, and for the next several hours wandered aimlessly around the town. One day he'd have to tell Katharina that her father was lost without a trace.

When he finally returned to the *caravanserai*, exhausted and famished, he found Michael waiting by the gate. The old man's face was ashen, with new furrows etched on his forehead.

"Your father's been taken in for questioning by Zaganos," Michael said, "and won't be coming back tonight."

The fatigue of the day plunged Vlad into a heavy torpor, but worries over his father's plight kept sleep out of reach. To make things worse, his rest was frequently disrupted by Gruya's trips to the privy. The free samples at the bazaar had a price, after all. When Gruya left and didn't return for more than an hour, Vlad managed to finally fall asleep. Yet slumber didn't bring him solace. A dream in which Gorgon, the slave, turned into the three Gorgon sisters of the Greek myth, made his heart race painfully. The sisters had poisonous snakes for tresses, and the fruit they offered Vlad with false smiles turned to maggots in his hand. When Gruya shook him awake, Vlad was grateful to escape his nightmare.

"I've solved the mystery," Gruya said, agitated.

Vlad thought Gruya's excitement was out of proportion to anything he could've discovered in the outhouse. He was wrong.

"I'm sitting there minding my business," Gruya said. "You know there are six holes. Three on one side and three—"

"Do you think I need a description of the sitting arrangements in the privy?"

"Very well, then. I am sitting in the far corner—"

"Just the fucking mystery, please," Vlad groaned, "if you must tell me anything at all at this hour of the night—"

"—when, who should walk in but the two brothers from upstairs?"

Vlad sat up, his curiosity piqued. "Was the lamp in the privy lit? Did you see them?" The thought of the two hostages hadn't been far from his mind since he heard of them the first time.

"I hear the Janissaries' voices outside, but the two brothers come in by themselves. They've got hoods pulled down over their faces."

"So you didn't see them?"

"Now, I say to myself, 'You're in big trouble, Gruya.' If the sultan keeps his hostages under guard and covered up, he's got good reasons. So, I'm thinking, when the Janissaries discover I saw the hostages, they'll run me through with their swords, and throw me down the hole."

"Don't drag this on, Gruya," Vlad said, "my head's in pain."

"Just as I'm praying to Saint Ilie to blow out the lamp—he's the saint in charge of fire, candles, lamps, and such, isn't he?—the brothers pull back their hoods."

"They see you?" Vlad cried, now overtaken with excitement.

"They're sitting straight across from me, looking me in the eye. But, guess what? They can't see a thing."

"Oh, God," was all Vlad could muster, as the air rushed out of him at the realization of what that meant.

"Their eyes are as white as a pigeon's eggs," Gruya said, and his voice faltered.

From what he'd heard of how the Turks did such things, Vlad surmised Gregory and Stefan been blinded with boiling vinegar. He shook with a cold shudder, imagining the ordeal endured by King Brankovich's sons.

7

Sultan's Musahib

"It's dangerous to be in the possession of such state secrets," Michael said, when Vlad told him the gruesome news next morning. "Many an innocent man has been killed for seeing things he wasn't meant to see."

Michael had suspected that the Brankovich brothers were mutilated somehow, and that's why their sister, Mara, broke down at their sight. Perhaps their noses, ears, or lips had been cut off in response to something they'd done. But blinding? The value of any royal hostage was much diminished if he was rendered unsuitable to inherit his father's kingdom.

"Why is what happened to the brothers such a big secret?" Vlad said. "You'd think the sultan wanted to teach King Brankovich a lesson."

They were standing in the inn's courtyard, where the two hostages had just been helped into a wagon.

"I think the blinding was a rushed act on Murad's part, that perhaps he regrets," Michael said. "Now he's trying to conceal from Brankovich the condition of his sons, for as long as possible, in order to leverage them against the king's neutrality in the upcoming crusade."

"But won't Mara let her father know what happened?"

"Not if Murad extracted a solemn vow of secrecy from her in exchange for the visitation," Michael said. "She's a quite devoted Christian, and Murad counts on her keeping her vow."

Michael could tell Vlad was deeply shaken by what happened to the Brankovich brothers. And how could he not be? He had to remember Dracul's warning of a few days ago regarding Vlad's risk of becoming a hostage himself.

"Don't fret over the issue of hostages," Michael said. "You aren't in real danger, as long as we keep the lid on who you are. And if your father isn't freed up in a couple of days, I plan to send you home with Gruya, like the rest of the crew."

Vlad shuddered and his cheeks turned hot. "Oh, no, you can't expect me to desert Father."

"It won't come to that, I'm sure." Michael hoped his own uncertainty wouldn't show on his face. "I'll go see Tirendaz, and should return with your father."

"I came across an Orthodox church yesterday," Vlad said. "I'll go to mass there, and pray for him."

Michael found Tirendaz in a corner of the First Vizier's palace grounds. He was in uniform again, surrounded by two dozen archers wearing colors similar to his. The men were dressed in crimson tunics hanging to their knees, and tight white leggings tucked into yellow slipper boots. They wore elaborate headdresses, foot-high conical fezzes of cream-colored felt, topped with white feathers. Yet, despite the garishness of their attire, the archers appeared ready for a military mission, not a parade.

When he noticed Michael, Tirendaz broke away from his men and came to meet him.

"I'm leaving Edirne this afternoon and will be away for a few days."

He spoke in a lighthearted tone, but Michael thought the *musahib*'s insouciance was forced. Fear of impending bad news brought a tightening to his chest as Tirendaz continued.

"The sultan's going on a hunting trip, and wants me along as *solakbaşı*, commander of his bodyguard. These men are his *solaks*. You must've heard of the left-handed archers."

Michael had heard of the *solaks*, archers selected by contest from the leading bowmen of the empire. The sultan would never venture out of town without a dozen *solaks* at his right and a dozen at his left. On the battlefield he'd have ten times as many, on either side. In that war fifty years ago, when the Ottomans almost overran Wallachia, Michael got close enough to the *solaks* to receive a shot from one of their arrows. He said, "I was silly in my youth to think that if the sultan's bodyguard were left-handed, they'd be good at shooting arrows to the right, leaving the left flank poorly defended. So, I charged Beyazid's position recklessly from the left." He pulled up the sleeve of his shirt to show Tirendaz the brown scar of an entry wound, just below the elbow. "I have this to remind me not to take such names literally."

Tirendaz chuckled. "Perhaps we should call the Solak Corps 'Half Right-Handed and Half Left-Handed Archers,' if we want to be accurate." Then he became serious. "You must be concerned about your king's detention by Zaganos Pasha."

"Even more so, now that I've learned you'll be away from the city. How will I communicate with my king in your absence?"

"Let's go inside," Tirendaz said.

Tirendaz's office was surprisingly small, and had a Spartan bareness about it that impressed Michael. Whitewashed walls like those of a monk's cell, a divan covered with plain cotton pillows, a wooden chest, and a Qur'an stand. The only window in the room was placed near the ceiling, and covered with a wooden grate that allowed little natural light to enter the room. In front of the divan, where visitors were expected to sit, the plank floor was covered with a coarse, uninviting rug of a geometric design in gray and black. The simplicity of Tirendaz's office gave Michael a sense of the power wielded by the sultan's *musahib* that no display of luxury could. If the young man betrayed any tendency to self-indulgence, it was in the collection of about thirty bows that covered the walls, hanging from wooden pegs. Some were decorated in brilliant colors, and appeared lightweight, used perhaps for flight shooting. Others were plain but sturdy, clad in leather, and showing sign of long use on their grips. War weapons, which Michael knew had taken countless Christian lives.

"You've discovered my weakness, Lord Michael," Tirendaz said. "I simply can't pass the opportunity to acquire a bow that has once belonged to a notable archer." He walked to the wall facing the door and stared at the bows with a faraway look in his eyes. He finally lifted one off its peg. "Here's my greatest possession," he said, holding the unstrung bow reverently in both hands. To Michael the weapon looked like a gnarled root, dark and twisted in ways that made it difficult to imagine its shape when strung.

"It belonged to Iskender Bursalı, the best archer at Sultan Beyazid's court. He too was nicknamed Tirendaz, like me. But his accomplishments in flight shooting exceed mine."

"You're too modest, Tirendaz Agha," Michael said with a polite smile. "I've heard that no one at Sultan Murad's court can equal your prowess in either accuracy or distance."

"That might be so," Tirendaz said, without boastfulness, "yet it's nothing compared to what Bursali was able to do. He shot an arrow from the European shore of the Bosphorus to the Asian side, at the place where Anadolu Hisari, the Anatolian Fortress, now stands. Nine hundred and one yards. I haven't been able to match his record so far." Tirendaz replaced the bow on its peg, and said with veiled sadness, "With armies being more and more enamored of cannons and firearms, archery isn't an art with a future."

Michael surprised himself with an almost paternal feeling for this young man, and wanted to say something encouraging to him. By all measures, ethnicity, religion, and function, Michael should've considered Tirendaz a deadly enemy. Yet something in the man's nature prevented him from doing that. "Art born from skills, and applied with passion, is timeless."

"Well, you haven't come to hear me boast about my bow collection," Tirendaz said. "Please be seated."

"With your indulgence, Tirendaz Agha, I'd prefer to stand. At my age, once I sit on the floor I find it difficult to rise again. Besides, my visit will be quite short."

Tirendaz remained standing as well. "The matter has taken a turn for the worse. You won't be allowed to see King Dracul until the Third Vizier concludes his investigation." He looked directly at Michael for an instant, then averted his eyes. "Zaganos has finally produced the letter we all thought a boast on his part. It is addressed to Pope Eugene and bears Hunyadi's seal."

Michael felt the room sway, as when he'd arisen too quickly. "I'll sit down after all, even if only for a bit," he said, holding out both arms to steady himself. He couldn't see how a letter from Hunyadi to Pope Eugene could harm Dracul, but its mere existence in Zaganos's hands frightened him.

Tirendaz clapped his hands. The door opened instantly, showing Michael that someone had been listening on the other side. A man in his early twenties walked into the room. Tirendaz must've noticed Michael's concern because he said, "Ismail's been my secretary ever since I bought him ten years ago. I trust him without reservation." Then he turned to the slave. "Bring my guest a cup of ice water."

After the man disappeared, Tirendaz helped Michael sit on a cushion placed in front of the divan.

"What is Hunyadi accusing my king of?" Michael asked.

"Did King Dracul attend a war council in Eisenmarkt this spring?" Tirendaz watched Michael intently.

"Both he and I were in Eisenmarkt in March, for a royal betrothal."

"Was that at the time Regent Elizabeth died of tainted food?"

Michael saw no point in telling Tirendaz that Elizabeth was poisoned. "Did Hunyadi claim the occasion was a war council?"

"In the letter, Hunyadi praises King Dracul as a great strategist. He quotes him as recommending an alliance between the Christian forces and the Sultan of Karaman, prior to the launching of the crusade against us."

Now Michael was glad he sat down, or his reaction to this shocking news might've betrayed his knowledge of the reference to the Karaman alliance. Dracul had recounted to Michael his conversation with Cardinal Cesarini in the Eisenmarkt chapel, more as a laughing matter. Indeed, it sounded harmless at the time. Now, that throwaway comment about Karaman could cost Dracul his head.

"My king has declared publicly his disapproval of a crusade against the empire," Michael said, "and will not join when it's launched. He is committed to respecting the peace treaty he signed with Sultan Murad."

"Zaganos is bent on convincing the sultan that King Dracul is a conspirator and a perjurer." Tirendaz rubbed his beard, a troubled look in his eyes. "You understand, if he succeeds in doing that, Zaganos's next step is to call for King Dracul's deposition and Wallachia's annexation to the empire. That, of course, means war, which is Zaganos's ultimate goal."

The words "deposition" and "annexation" felt to Michael like a cudgel's blows to the back of his head. But he assumed an untroubled mien, and said, "If Hunyadi's letter is his proof of treason on my king's part, Zaganos Pasha is fishing on dry land."

Ismail arrived with the water. Although the shaved ice in it tasted of the sawdust pit from which it came, it cooled Michael's burning throat.

"The enmity between my king and Hunyadi is no secret to the sultan," he said. "How can His Highness give credence to Hunyadi's praises for King Dracul? It's an obvious ploy to compromise him in the sultan's eyes."

"That was the point raised by Khalil Pasha as well," Tirendaz said. "But Zaganos reminded His Majesty that Dracul and Hunyadi were close friends in their youth, and that further shook the sultan's trust in your king."

"All of this commotion, because of a letter written by a sworn enemy of both my king and the sultan," Michael said. "And how is it that such a damning letter conveniently found its way to Zaganos Pasha?"

Tirendaz hesitated, perhaps concerned with giving away too many of the Imperial Council's secrets. But his internal struggle resolved in Michael's favor, and he said, "Hunyadi's messenger was captured in Ragusa, and he was handed over to our consul there."

Michael lost his composure. "Ragusa?" he cried. "No one in his right mind would send correspondence from Buda to the Vatican through Ragusa. That place is hundreds of miles out of the way. Besides, Hunyadi knows Ragusa is an Ottoman protectorate, in all but name. Why, that's like practically handing the letter directly to the Imperial Council."

Tirendaz smiled at Michael's animation. "Indeed," he said. "That's the second point Khalil Pasha raised."

Hunyadi's design became clear now: backstabbing by praise. *Write a letter to the Pope in which you laud your enemy for masterminding an anti-Ottoman alliance. Then ensure the letter falls into Turkish hands. If the letter causes Dracul's downfall, he has no way of retaliating. If, on the other hand, he survives against impossible odds, he can't accuse you of calumny, since you only praised him.* That ignoble scoundrel Hunyadi had found a way to undermine Dracul with impunity, and look generous of spirit in the process.

"His Highness is listening to both sides," Tirendaz said, "but wants more proof of your king's faithfulness than mere logical arguments. He ordered Zaganos to get to the truth by—*er*—special means."

Michael held no self-deception about what that meant. A blend of hatred and helplessness swirled in his head. "How far will Zaganos carry torture to win his argument for war on Wallachia?"

"Khalil Pasha hasn't given up on trying to prevent the war. The longer King Dracul holds out against questioning, the better my uncle's chances of persuading the sultan not to believe Hunyadi's letter. The Grand Vizier's personal secretary will be the one recording the king's statements during the interrogation."

"At least Zaganos won't be able to manufacture a false confession," Michael said, and felt gratitude for Khalil's initiative not to leave things entirely up to Zaganos. "I'd like to provide the king with some nourishment during the interrogation."

"That's prohibited," Tirendaz said. Then he gave Michael a kind look and a hint of a smile. "But you know that in this town, money helps bend all rules. Zaganos keeps his prisoners in the Macedon Tower, by the Üç Şerefeli Mosque that is under construction."

8

Macedon Tower

The faster Michael tried to walk on his way back to the inn, the slower he advanced. The pain in his back made him stoop, and the one in his hips forced him to stagger like a drunk, making him self-conscious of his ungraceful stride. *Can't be fast and dignified at the same time.* He clenched his teeth and pushed on. When he stepped into a depression in the road, his left knee gave and he would've fallen, had a passerby not caught him in time.

Vlad and Gruya were waiting for him by the gate of the inn, and rushed to meet him when he turned the corner to their street. Breathless and overheated, he collapsed into their arms.

"Who's been chasing you, Grandfather?" Gruya said.

"Where's Father, Uncle Michael?"

Michael struggled to catch his breath, and tried to ignore a sharp stitch above his heart. *I'm feeling just fine. It's only stress. This isn't the time for illness.* "Take me to the innkeeper." Vlad's eyes brimmed with panic. "Your father's well, but I want us to bring him some food. You know he doesn't care for Turkish fare."

"Give me some money and I'll get him a pork sausage and some *rakija*," Gruya said, a bit too enthusiastic in Michael's opinion. "I have a Bulgarian friend in the bazaar who—"

"Why isn't Father coming here to eat?" Vlad said. "He's been gone for a day and a half already."

Michael gave Gruya four aspers. "Get the king onions, cucumbers, carrots, and fresh fruit too. And buy a wicker basket so we can carry all of that stuff to him tomorrow."

Gruya left, and Vlad met Michael's eyes. "What does the innkeeper have to do with Father?"

"You've been through town. Did you see a mosque under construction?"

"There is one, about half a mile from here. They're building a new minaret there now."

"The Turks are holding your father in a tower near that mosque."

At the word "holding" Vlad's head jerked, and his mouth opened halfway, but he remained silent. Michael could tell Vlad was fighting violent emotions, and decided to leave the rest of the explanations for later.

"There's our man," Michael said when he spotted Hussein in conversation with some newly arrived travelers. Then he leaned on Vlad's shoulder, and began to shuffle in Hussein's direction.

"Bribing prison guards is dangerous business, Master Michael," Hussein whispered, after Michael told him of Dracul's predicament. Then he rolled his eyes dramatically, and shook his hands in the air to emphasize his point. "How did His Grace, I mean Master Ulfer, end up in the Macedon Tower?"

"How much, Hussein?" Michael said, and shook his purse. "I doubt this will be the first time those guards receive *baksheesh* to let a relative visit one of the inmates." Slowly, he poured silver coins into the innkeeper's cupped hands, and watched his face. When Michael detected a flicker of surprise in the man's eyes, he stopped.

The sight and feel of the money seemed to reduce Hussein's conception of the risk involved. He became his old unctuous self. "I'll need a few days to make the right connection, my friend."

Michael noted the downgrade in title from "master" to "friend," which showed Hussein felt he'd gained advantage by being so needed. "I don't have that kind of time," Michael said. "I've got to see Ulfer in the morning. I'll double this amount if you do it by then."

"That's not possible for any amount of silver," Hussein said. "Interrogations take place from dawn until the afternoon prayer. Only then can—"

"Tomorrow afternoon then," Michael said, impatient.

Vlad helped Michael up the stairs to the room his father and his mentor shared, then left wordlessly. Michael kept the shutter closed and the lamp unlit, to avoid the sight of Dracul's empty bed. He lay heavily on his own bed, and waited for the pain in his joints to abate. As he did so, jumbled thoughts assailed him with pitiless determination.

How did the threat Dracul faced now come about? The king had been fastidious in his observance of the peace treaty terms, down to the minutest detail. This, despite the bitter cup he had to drink, knowing the people he now was forced to call allies were the same ones who'd raped his mother. But if he allowed hatred to rule over reason, he'd be condemning the land of his forefathers to annihilation at the hands of this insatiable race.

Sure, Dracul's comment about Karaman was damning, if viewed from the Turks' perspective. But how could such a tiny indiscretion become a lethal weapon in the hands of a Turk obsessed with destroying Wallachia? Unless a capricious God had so ordained, for His own inscrutable aims. The words of the prophecy Michael heard half a century before returned to him with sharp mordancy.

> *She brought forth a man-child who would become a dragon having a crown upon his head. And when the beast from the Euphrates saw that the dragon was cast unto the earth, he ... stood before the woman to devour her child and make him its own. But the angel of God sent the child into hiding....*

Once, the beast from the Euphrates had that man-child in its sight, but the angel of God snatched him away to safety. Now, the child become a king, the same beast held him in its claws. Would the angel save him once more? Or had the Lord's mercy run out?

"Are you asleep, Uncle Michael?" Vlad's whisper came from the doorway.

The shred of light that seeped through the shutter boards in the daytime had vanished. In the complete darkness of the room, Michael took several seconds to get his bearings. "Light the lamp, please," he said. He felt a surge of warmth at the thought of Vlad's companionship, even though he dreaded having to tell him details of Dracul's predicament.

Vlad sat on the side of his father's bed and listened, restless, to Michael's account of his conversation with Tirendaz. When Michael related the part about Zaganos's charter to interrogate his father, Vlad shut his eyes and bit his knuckles.

"Can the Turks torture a king?" Vlad said, after a few minutes passed in silence. "A king who's signed a peace treaty with them, and never broke it?"

"It won't do the Turks any good. Your father's a strong man and he'll never admit to what he said in Eisenmarkt about Karaman."

Vlad seemed to give thought to Michael's assessment, but his looks showed it didn't reassure him. "If he gives in to pain and confesses, Father condemns himself as a traitor. If he holds out until they tire of torturing him, he'll wish he were dead. One way or the other Father's doomed."

Vlad stood up, resolute, and said in a calm tone that surprised Michael, "There is only one way out of this." Then he headed for the door with the sure step of someone who'd already decided what needed to be done.

"You're thinking jailbreak," Michael called after him, "but that's impossible."

Vlad walked out of the room without a sign he heard Michael.

Vlad found the wait almost unbearable. The innkeeper finally returned late afternoon the next day from his search for a connection at the Macedon Tower. Hussein spotted Vlad, Michael and Gruya waiting by the fountain, nodded at them discreetly, then turned around and left the inn. They followed him at a distance of about twenty paces. When they reached the minaret's construction site, they encountered a large crowd of onlookers.

"What are they all marveling at?" Gruya said.

"This is Üç Şerefeli Mosque," Vlad said. "It means the 'three balconied mosque.' See the new minaret? They say it's the first one in the entire Islamic world to have three balconies."

"That must be where they're keeping the king," Michael said, pointing at a tower on the far side of the mosque grounds. The tower stood on a plot of land used as a dumping site for construction debris. On the side away from the mosque, the rubble piles appeared many years old, judging from the amount of shrubbery growing on them. On the side closer to the new minaret, the debris was fresh.

Hussein gave them a sign to wait, then walked across the rubble field and entered the tower, throwing a furtive glance over his shoulder.

While they waited for the innkeeper's return, Vlad took in the details of the place. The Macedon Tower was a circular structure about sixty feet high, with crumbling battlements on which weeds had sprouted. From the way brick layers alternated with fifteen-foot-high sections of sandstone wall, he guessed the interior was divided into four levels. Except for the lowest one, each of the other three levels had an opening that seemed to serve as window. He was pleased to note the windows weren't barred. *Large enough for a person to climb out through.* The lowest level opened to the outside through an arched passageway secured with an ironclad door.

The notion that his father was in a cell somewhere inside that tower gave Vlad a feeling he'd never experienced before. The king, descendant of a long line of kings, was now at the mercy of some illiterate jailer on whom he depended for food and water. And his father, for whose dignity and honor Vlad would kill without hesitation, had become the butt of a torturer's taunts and jibes.

Hatred and shame melded into one fiery lump that filled his chest to overflowing.

After a few minutes, Hussein reappeared in the tower's doorway, accompanied by a Janissary. The innkeeper pointed in Michael's direction, then took off across the rubble field and disappeared in the crowd. The Janissary made a beckoning gesture at Michael, then retreated into the passageway.

"I'm Aziz," the Janissary said in Greek when Vlad, Michael, and Gruya entered the tower. He was a dark, humorless man. "You tell somebody this I cut throat." His Greek might be shaky, but his message was clear.

The ground floor consisted of a windowless, circular hall with a high ceiling, from which hung a bronze chandelier of the type found in Orthodox churches. In the middle of the floor stood a brazier with a pot of boiling water on it. Two Janissaries sat cross-legged on the floor, playing *tavla* on a board that rested on their knees. A third Janissary crouched next to them, watching the game. The only furniture in the hall was a wooden panel bolted to the wall, on which the soldiers hung bows, quivers, and keys from iron hooks.

Aziz snapped the wicker basket from Gruya's hand, dumped its contents on the floor, and dispersed the mound of articles with the tip of his boot. Satisfied with the results of his inspection, he took a key from the panel and began climbing an iron staircase that led to the floor above through a trapdoor in the ceiling. Unable to control his impatience, Vlad followed closely on his heels, leaving Michael and Gruya to gather the food off the floor.

From the second floor, Vlad could look up into the hollow tower through iron grids that formed the floors of the next two landings. A square patch of sky was framed in the roof opening, and threw a bit of light into the tower's core. Aside from that, the only other light came from the windows Vlad had noticed from the outside. Now he saw with a sinking heart the windows were positioned too high on the wall to be reached without a ladder.

On the second floor, six bays with brick sidewalls were built against the circular wall. Five of them were enclosed with floor-to-ceiling iron grilles, and served as prisoners' cells. In the semidarkness of the place, Vlad saw the whites of many pairs of eyes observing him in silence from behind the bars. A heavy stink emanated from the cells.

The sixth bay stood open to the landing. From the hooks and pulleys that hung from the ceiling, and the jumble of strange devices that cluttered the floor, Vlad could tell it was a torture chamber. His nervousness about the visit increased at the thought of what Zaganos's "questioning" must've done to his father in two days.

Aziz proceeded to the next landing, and Vlad followed. This floor had the same configuration of cells, and its own torture room. Fewer prisoners appeared to be housed here, and the air was slightly less noxious.

"One more," Aziz said, and climbed to the fourth floor.

Even before he reached the top of the stairs, Vlad saw that on this level two of the cells were empty, and stood with their grille doors ajar. Two others contained an inmate each. At his arrival, the two prisoners stuck their heads through the bars, and watched him with curiosity. Between the two occupied cells there was another one that had to be his father's, but Vlad couldn't see him.

"Satan's balls on iron spits," Vlad heard his father shout. "Is that truly you, my faithful servant?" When he drew closer, Vlad saw Dracul seated on the floor in the rear of the bay, his back resting against the wall. The vigor in his father's voice gave Vlad hope that perhaps he hadn't fared too badly through the torture.

"Yes, Master Ulfer," Vlad said, and stifled the desire to shout for joy.

Aziz unlocked and opened a section of the grille that was hinged to form the door. "Half an hour," he said, then descended to the guardroom.

Vlad wanted to rush to his father's side, but to preserve the appearance of his humble station he waited for Michael and Gruya to arrive before entering the cell.

"My neighbors have been chosen with care," Dracul whispered in German, when all three visitors were inside. "The youth to the left is Kasim ibn Jihangir, grandson of the Karaman Sultan. I gathered from the little Greek he speaks he's been Murad's hostage for five years, since the age of twelve. This is the first time they moved him out of his regular prison."

Michael knelt next to Dracul. "Clever of Zaganos," he said, also in German. "When he sees he can't get a word out of you about Karaman, he'll make this Kasim confess to things you 'confided' in him."

"So, you know about Zaganos's accusation against me."

"Tirendaz has been helpful with that," Michael said.

"The other neighbor's a Greek who screams like the Devil's wife in heat when they torture him, but shows no trace of being hurt." In a voice lower yet, Dracul added, "He also speaks Romanian in his sleep."

"That might explain why we managed to find a way in here in such a short time," Vlad said. "Zaganos must've counted on our speaking Romanian openly in front of his man."

"You're learning the Turks' ways, Son," Dracul said.

"I've had enough learning, Father." The word "Father," even though whispered in German, gave Vlad a chill, for the risk it entailed if overheard and understood by the Greek spy. "We've got to get you out of here."

Dracul shot his arms up with an angry scowl, and appeared ready to yell at Vlad. But then he seemed to change his mind, and said in soft tone, "Even if there were a way to break out, do you see me scaling the walls with these feet?" He pulled away the rag covering his legs.

Michael and Gruya gasped. Vlad tried to say something, but the air wouldn't move up his windpipe. Dracul's feet were so swollen that the toes appeared as a single glob of purple flesh. The soles were blood-spattered and crisscrossed with open wounds.

"*Falaka* is what the Turks call it." Dracul spoke in the casual manner of someone describing a saddle. "It's *bastonata* to the Italians. They put your feet into stocks, hang you upside down, and beat the soles of your feet with rods."

Vlad regained his voice, and with it a new determination to act. "We can't let this continue. I've got a plan."

Dracul removed two rings from his fingers, and handed them to Vlad. "Take these home with you. Zaganos is starting on my fingers tomorrow, and I don't want this fine German workmanship damaged."

"How can you joke at a time like this, Father? I know they'll never break you, but what's the use of bravery if it gets you killed in the end?"

"If there were a chance for a breakout," Michael said, "I'd be for it."

"But there is more than a chance," Vlad said. "Look at this place. This isn't a real prison. There are only four guards, and they can't see what's happening up here while they're playing games downstairs. And, most important, there's a hole in the roof."

"I could easily climb this tower if I had a rope attached to the battlement," Gruya said.

"Yes, a rope, of course," Dracul said, sounding amused. "Why didn't I think of that? Then, once inside here, you could open the door to this cell, if you had a key. And I could dance the *saltarello* like a Venetian whore if my feet weren't a bloody pulp."

"Finding a rope is no problem," Vlad said, determined not to let his father kill the plan with ridicule. "They've got them at the bazaar. And I have an idea how to get the rope onto the battlement."

"The key's not a problem either," Gruya said. "They've got four identical ones downstairs, and that means all cells open with the same key. So, I borrowed one, just in case."

Dracul dropped his head to one side, and let out a feeble laugh. "Oh, the innocence of youth. Ropes, stolen keys, climbing on walls … what else? All like in a fun boys' game. I think this laughter will do me more good than all the food you've brought."

"They'll notice the missing key," Michael said, alarmed, "and they'll suspect something's afoot. We might not be able to return here if that happens."

"I'm planning to have a copy made tonight, and put the original back tomorrow," Gruya said. "I met this locksmith in the Gypsy Quarter last night—"

"Where?" Vlad said, incredulous. He remembered how cheerful Gruya had been the night before. There had to be a woman behind that, of course. "Did you spend the food money on … on *that*?"

"Oh, no," Gruya said, and winked. "Despite your skepticism, *that* was a free sample."

"Get any thought of escape out of your minds," Dracul said, and covered his legs with the rag, as if to put an end to the debate. "I won't have any of you risk your lives on such a foolish scheme."

"What about your life?" Vlad said. Frustration with his father's defeatist attitude began to wear him down.

"Travel papers for the three of you are awaiting at the Grand Vizier's palace, Michael," Dracul said. "I've made the arrangement with Khalil Pasha's secretary. They've got no interest in retaining you here. Go see him tomorrow afternoon, after he gets his work done here."

Michael rose with Gruya's help. "I'll send Vlad and Gruya home, but I'm not leaving you," he said in a rebellious tone unusual for him. "I took a sacred oath to—"

"Whether I'm here, lying on this filthy straw," Dracul shouted with a burst of anger that took Vlad by surprise, "or sitting at the head of the council table in Târgovişte, I'm still your king. I shan't be disobeyed."

Michael's body seemed to shrink under the weight of Dracul's outburst.

"Father's right, Uncle Michael," Vlad said. "Whether here or back home, he must be obeyed."

"If someone as stubborn as Vlad can accept the inevitable, so can you, old friend," Dracul said. "I'll wear Zaganos down, and he'll give up on his notion that he can prove me a traitor. In the meantime, I need you and Vlad home, to help Marcus hold on to the reins until I return. Now go, and let me be. We'll say our good-byes tomorrow."

When Aziz returned to lock up, Vlad noticed that the Karaman prisoner had retired to the back of his cell, and appeared to be asleep. The Greek, on the other hand, had his head still stuck out between the bars, and was watching them with keen interest. As they began to leave, Vlad took care not to let the man know he'd noticed his interest. *He'll make an inconvenient witness when …*

9

Dar al-Sulh—House of Treaty

Before Michael reached the Macedon Tower's ground floor, Vlad and Gruya had disappeared from sight. Vlad must've been embarrassed for caving in so easily to his father's order, after making such an impassioned plea for his escape. Of course, obeying the king wasn't just their duty; it was also the only sane thing to do. Michael was certain that attempting a prison breakout in the heart of Edirne was a suicidal idea. Yet he couldn't help being disappointed with Vlad, whom he would've expected to put up more of a fight against his father's refusal.

He didn't see Vlad and Gruya again until the next morning, when he found them whispering to each other by the fountain. At his approach, they took off in a hurry and disappeared outside the gate.

He rode his mule to the market where he bought travel provisions, which he dispatched to the inn with a porter. Next, he rode to the place where caravan masters gathered, and found a Turkish merchant leaving for Nicopolis the next morning.

Michael, Vlad, and Gruya would join the Turk's caravan, for safety. All the merchant demanded in exchange was fifteen aspers per person, and assurances that Michael would have a valid travel document. Michael gave him a Venetian ducat, worth five aspers more than the man had requested, as a way of ensuring additional good will.

"We leave after the morning prayer," the Turk said, and told Michael where his wagons were parked outside the town walls.

With every step Michael took in preparing for the inevitable departure, his mood became gloomier. Now he was glad neither Vlad nor Gruya were around, for he'd be unable to hide his growing heartsickness from them.

Dracul's assurance that he was going to "wear Zaganos down" and return home didn't convince Michael. Both he and Dracul knew this was the end of the road for the king. And if true to themselves, they'd also admit it was the end of Wallachia as a free country. Doubtless, the Hungarians under Captain General Hunyadi would hasten to occupy it when they learned of Dracul's plight. The only thing left to see was how soon that disaster would befall the country. Marcus, though heir to the throne, didn't have Dracul's clout to raise the great army of all free Wallachians. And the boyars wouldn't move a finger to help him. A fearless man, Marcus would fight till the end, with the Novak clan alongside. But ultimately, Marcus's two thousand men couldn't prevail upon the many thousands of mercenaries Hunyadi would bring. When it was all over, the boyars would make their accommodations with Hunyadi, asking only that he allow them to keep their estates and their Orthodox religion.

As for Vlad, Marcus, Baba, Gruya, and Michael ... if they didn't perish in battle, exile was their inevitable, bitter lot.

Michael went to Khalil Pasha's palace in the early afternoon, determined to catch the Grand Vizier's secretary the moment the man returned from the Macedon Tower. Michael was still crossing the second courtyard when, to his surprise, the secretary rushed at him, a scroll of paper in hand.

"This is your travel document," the secretary said, not looking Michael in the eye. "Signed by the Grand Vizier."

Michael read a bad sign in the fact the man had returned so early from his assignment at the tower. "Is the interrogation over already?"

"Your king is an exceedingly hardy man."

Michael's bowels churned. "But is he all right?"

"The hardiest I've seen under such circumstances. I've witnessed many interrogations, but have never seen anyone able to stifle even the tiniest moan of pain as King Dracul did." His face as enigmatic as his words, the secretary left Michael without further explanation.

Michael felt his strength drain away like wine from a leaky cask. He needed to sit, but the nearest ledge he could rest on looked impossibly far.

"Lean on me, Lord Michael," came a familiar voice behind him, and a powerful arm slipped under his. "The sun at this time of the day is at its hottest, and you don't have your hat on."

"Tirendaz Agha?" The unexpected sight of Murad's *musahib* amplified Michael's anxiety. "Back already?"

Tirendaz was dressed in travel clothes, his face grimy with the dust of a hurried ride. "I'd invite you to my office to rest for a while, but I think you'll want to return to your lodgings immediately, considering the latest developments."

Against his will Michael leaned heavier on Tirendaz's arm. "Developments?" Under normal circumstances his physical weakness would've embarrassed Michael. But now all he could think of was the new events that seemed to have occurred.

"The sultan was still in his camp by the river, just outside the walls, when the news caught up with us last night."

Michael looked Tirendaz in the eye with great foreboding. "Not good news, I suppose."

"A thousand mercenaries invaded Wallachia last Thursday, through Roter Turm Pass."

Michael didn't hear the rest. A metallic pounding began to ring in his ears, drowning out all other sounds, while his mind became stuck on one thought: *This is the end, the end, the end....*

"Do you know him?" Tirendaz shook Michael's arm gently, as one might do to awaken a sleepwalker. "Prince Nestor. He's said to be a pretender to Wallachia's throne."

What? That effeminate imp has turned into a warrior? "Hard to believe Nestor's behind this aggression. He doesn't have money to hire ten mercenaries, let alone a thousand. Hunyadi must be funding him. How reliable is your news?"

"We got information by messenger pigeons from two independent sources, one based in Hermannstadt, the other in Eisenmarkt." Tirendaz paused, troubled. "I'm committing a great political indiscretion, disclosing to you the placement of the sultan's informants. I hope I may count on your discretion."

"It would surprise me if His Majesty didn't have agents in all towns throughout Christendom, Tirendaz Agha. But rest assured, I won't betray you."

"The Eisenmarkt message said that Hunyadi has declared Nestor's claim to the Wallachian throne illegitimate. He sent out a call for eight thousand mercenaries, with whom he intends to chase Nestor out of Wallachia and hold it in safekeeping until King Dracul returns from Edirne."

Another villainous move masquerading as a *noble* act on Hunyadi's part. Michael's loathing for the Hungarian upstart gained in bitterness. "So Hunyadi found out about our visit here, despite all efforts at secrecy. It seems his sources in Edirne are as good as the sultan's in Eisenmarkt."

Tirendaz's face tightened, and Michael felt the notion was of concern to the Murad's *musahib.* This was an opportunity to sow additional discord between the Grand Vizier's and Zaganos's camps. "One could suspect Zaganos and Hunyadi, two mortal enemies, of cooperating with each other in their common goal of starting a war between the Christians and the Turks."

Tirendaz nodded, dark, pensive.

Michael continued. "With Wallachia as the prize for the winner. Hunyadi's turned Nestor's bid for the throne into his pretext for entering Wallachia with a sizable army. That, in turn, supports Zaganos's thesis that to keep Wallachia from falling into the Hungarians' hands the sultan must annex it."

Tirendaz raised his hands in a gesture of helplessness. "Sadly, your analysis is accurate, Lord Michael. Hunyadi's declaration of intent has made Zaganos's case for war unbeatable. The sultan's *tuğ*, the horsetail standard, has already been planted in front of the imperial palace, and the call to muster the army has gone out. Wallachia is in Dar al-Sulh, the House of Treaty, so the sultan can't allow the empire's enemies to take it for themselves. He has no choice but to annex Wallachia, making it part of Dar al-Islam."

Michael saw an opportunity to forestall disaster. "But His Excellency does have a choice, Tirendaz Agha. If my king is allowed to return home, he can put an end to Nestor's invasion. With that, Zaganos's and Hunyadi's pretexts evaporate, the status quo is preserved, and the empire is spared a costly war with Hungary over a tiny patch of land."

Tirendaz bit his lower lip and shook his head, rueful. "Khalil Pasha has argued this point as well, and the sultan agreed this solution would be preferable to war. But His Majesty's mistrust in King Dracul remains strong and prevents him from returning the king to Wallachia. Imagine the sultan's embarrassment if he were to free the king, only to see him join the upcoming crusade against the empire. In alliance with Karaman, no less."

"Even when three days of torture haven't yielded a confession substantiating Hunyadi's allegation against my king?"

"The sultan has taken that into account, and ordered Zaganos to cease questioning the king. He'll be removed from Zaganos's jurisdiction tomorrow, and transferred to the sultan's underground dungeons at the palace. Then, in a few days he'll be taken to Amasya and remain confined there until the resolution of the conflict."

Since for the Turks, "resolution" meant turning Wallachia into a *sanjak*, an Ottoman province, Dracul's confinement would be for life. Michael concluded he had no further means to influence the sultan's decision. He took his leave of Tirendaz and returned to the *caravanserai*, drowning in black despondency.

Back at the inn, Michael found Vlad and Gruya engaged in hushed discussion he thought was related to their imminent return to Wallachia.

"The worst of our fears have come true," Michael said, then related what he'd learned from Tirendaz.

"The Turks can't get their army in motion in less than eight weeks," Vlad said. He knew something about Ottoman war logistics from Gunther, who'd accompanied his masters in many campaigns. "They've got to rent thousands of draft animals. And they have to purchase fodder for all those beasts. If Father returned home now he'd have ample time to squash Nestor's invasion. Then would Murad still have a reason to wage war?"

"Of course not," Michael said, "but they won't let your father go, so war's inevitable."

Vlad dismissed Michael's assertion with an impatient gesture. "You said war would be avoided if Father returned home. That means neither the Hungarians nor the Turks will have Wallachia." He exchanged a look with Gruya. "And, as I told you, I have a plan for Father's escape." Then he returned to his discussion with Gruya as if nothing had happened.

Michael considered Vlad's attitude flippant, and a mild resentment against his pupil sprouted in him. He immediately regretted it. Vlad was still too young to grasp the seriousness of the situation, and Michael expected too much of him. A corrosive feeling of loneliness filled his chest. With Dracul about to leave for Asia as a prisoner, Michael was left alone to contemplate the impending disappearance of a way of life the Wallachians had defended with their blood for a thousand years.

He arranged the visit to the Macedon Tower the same way as the day before. This time Hussein asked for twice the amount Michael paid for the first visit.

"At his salary of three aspers per day," Michael said in protest, "your Janissary is already making a week's pay off me."

"Aziz says he wants more money because this will be your last visit to the tower," Hussein said. "And he won't accept copper *mangers*. Only silver."

"Yes, Aziz is right," Michael said. "It *is* his last chance to gouge me. We're returning to Wallachia in the morning."

"And Master Ulfer?" Hussein said, with an attempt at showing surprise. But Michael believed by now Dracul's case was no longer a secret for anyone associated with the palace.

When they arrived at the guardroom, Aziz appeared uninterested in checking their food basket for contraband. But Vlad tipped the contents on the floor, and grinned at the Janissary subserviently. Aziz muttered a curse under his breath and did a perfunctory inspection of the spilled items. This gave Gruya the chance to restore the borrowed key to its rightful place.

The first thing Michael said when he saw Dracul was, "I hope you feel strong enough for the news I bring."

"Yes, Master Ulfer," Vlad said, "it seems you're to remain the sultan's guest a while longer than you expected. So, we'll have to return to Wallachia without you."

Dracul looked at Michael inquiringly, then said, "You boys go up on the roof and get some air. Michael and I need to talk for a bit."

"How's that hand you're hiding?" Michael said as soon as the youths obeyed, and braced himself for what he was about to see.

Dracul took his left hand from inside his shirt. "I don't want Vlad to see this. What's good about progressive torture is that the new pain keeps your mind off the old one." The hand's four fingers had been smashed to a near flat shape, and the thumb was bent the wrong way.

Michael leaned over to inspect Dracul's feet. They appeared darker than the day before, but less swollen. "Can you stand now?"

"It'll be a while. We don't have much time, so tell me what you've learned."

When Michael relayed Tirendaz's news, he expected Dracul to fume against both Nestor and Hunyadi, but instead he just gave a dry chuckle. After a few moments of reflection Dracul said, "When Zaganos left earlier than his norm today, I thought he'd gotten bored with my lack of cooperation. Now I understand he no longer needed my confession." Then he rested his head against the wall, and fell silent.

"They're moving you out of here tomorrow," Michael said after an interval. "Then on to Amasya in a few days."

Dracul didn't seem to hear him. "I never thought I was born to set the world on fire," he said, eyes closed. "Only to keep the flame alive. And that I did, as long as the good Lord saw fit that I should."

"Alive, but for whom?" Michael said. He felt on the verge of tears. "Do you think Marcus can—?"

"I've been asking myself the same thing for some time." Dracul gave a tired sigh. "To whom was I supposed to pass the torch? It's taken me until today to see the flame wasn't meant for Marcus. You get to do a lot of thinking when your bones are being broken slowly, one by one."

"You think it was for Vlad?"

"Take Vlad to my cousin Bogdan in Moldova. He's got a boy too, Stephen I think, a couple of years younger than Vlad. Let him wait there until his time comes."

"And Marcus? Wallachia?"

"There is nothing Vlad can do about what's going on there now, but get himself killed." Dracul cradled his left hand into the right one, and winced with pain. "Marcus will fight Nestor until Hunyadi arrives. Then he'll fight Hunyadi until the Turks enter Wallachia. Finally, he'll join Hunyadi, and fight the Turks. He'll be happy doing any one of those things."

"And you think that one day Vlad will—?"

"Whether the Turks or the Hungarians take over Wallachia won't matter in the long run," Dracul said. "Vlad will take it back from either of them one day. Nothing will stop him once he catches his stride. He's bound to rule Wallachia with a 'rod of iron.' It's the prophecy, remember?"

These weren't words Michael expected to hear from Dracul. He looked closely at him, wondering if he was jesting. "For someone who's fought Vlad at every step when he tried to learn what his destiny was, you've certainly made a turnabout."

"Now say your goodbye before the boys return," Dracul said, and extended his right hand to Michael. "It doesn't do to let them see grown men weep like two jilted spinsters."

"Greeks believed peace was when sons buried their fathers, and war when fathers buried their sons." Michael wanted to continue, but his throat tightened painfully and his eyes welled with tears. Then he heard Aziz's steps mounting the stairs, and he summoned his strength to go on. "Though it's still peace, as I leave you behind I feel I'm burying my own son."

"You've been like a father to me indeed, Michael," Dracul said. "But I'm not dead. Just laying down a cross I'm no longer fit to carry."

Vlad and Gruya must've heard Aziz's footsteps as well, for they rushed down from the rooftop before the Janissary could see them there.

"We'll see each other sooner than you think, Father," Vlad said with conviction, and kissed Dracul's right hand. Then he headed for the stairs.

Michael was glad for that blindness youth often showed toward impossible odds. It made the parting from Dracul marginally more bearable. Michael and Gruya also kissed the king's hand, and followed Vlad.

"*Vergiß nicht deine Zukunft, Sohn des Drachen,*" Dracul shouted, when Michael, Vlad, and Gruya had reached the second landing. "Don't forget your destiny, Son of the Dragon."

The way his resonant voice poured down the hollow core of the Macedon Tower told Michael that Dracul had dragged himself with his one good hand to the iron bars of his cell.

Vlad stopped and looked up in surprise. Then he shouted back at his father with a happy grin, "*Zweifle nie an deinen Samen, König Drache,* Never doubt your seed, Dragon King."

10

The Karaman Hostage

Vlad decided to keep Michael in the dark about his and Gruya's plan until the last moment. That would be just before the *caravanserai*'s gate was shut for the night, when the two of them would be leaving on their daring errand.

They made a bet on how Michael would react. Gruya predicted his grandfather would be angry, and disapprove of their plan. Vlad thought the opposite would happen. "I see," is all Michael said when the two youths barged into his room and declared they were on their way to spring Dracul from the Macedon Tower.

To Vlad, Michael's expression had the studied indifference of someone caught in the situation of not being able to take a position. He couldn't wish his king left behind in his enemies' hands. But neither could he sanction an action his king had forbidden.

"Gruya and I need your help to get back up here after we do the job." Vlad took a rope he'd brought with him, and tied it to Michael's walking stick, to serve as an anchor against the window frame. Michael reached for the rope, and appeared to be absent-mindedly testing its strength. "When we give you the signal from down there in the street, all you have to do is throw this coil out the window. You mustn't do that ahead of time, because it might be spotted by the night watchman." Vlad didn't think there was any risk of that, since the rope would be impossible to see against the brick wall in the dark. But this was his ploy to show Gruya that Michael approved of their plan.

"You're angry, Grandfather, aren't you?" Gruya said, a transparent bid to goad Michael and win the bet. "You're saying to yourself, 'How are you going to get into the tower? And how is His Grace to walk, and climb, with his injured feet?'"

Michael looked at Gruya as if he were a stranger he saw for the first time, and frowned. Vlad noticed only now that Michael's shirt was dark with sweat stains, and his hands were shaking. He was clearly unwell. Was he even able to understand what they were saying?

Vlad took Michael's hands into his. "We attached a line for climbing to the battlements when we were on the tower's roof this afternoon. And don't worry about Father's feet. We'll be lowering him in a basket."

"I need to lie down now," Michael said listlessly. "I don't feel well."

"Do you know how expensive silk cord is, Grandfather?" Gruya said. "Vlad sold the king's rings, and spent all the money on it."

Michael turned on his side, facing the wall. Vlad took advantage of that to whisper to Gruya, "You're playing unfair. You can't *make* him angry. He has to get that way on his own." Then he threw a blanket over Michael, and puffed up his pillow.

"I met four monks from the Philotheou Monastery on Mount Athos at the church on Sunday," Vlad said. "They're on their way to Constantinople, to beg Patriarch Metrophanes for help with the repair of their church."

"Vlad promised the king will build them a new church if they helped him escape to Constantinople," Gruya said. "And I promised you'd have a new roof put over their dormitories. Do you think we went too far, Grandfather?"

Vlad jabbed Gruya with his elbow, and gave him a furious look. "One of the monks will remain hidden in the church here in Edirne. Father will take his place, and travel with the other three to Constantinople."

Michael began to snore.

"I won," Vlad said to Gruya. "Your grandfather clearly approved of our plan, but was too tired to show it."

"Oh, no, he didn't. But he was too tired to yell at us."

Vlad and Gruya argued about their bet all the way to the Macedon Tower. They crept on stealthily, and kept an eye out for the night watchmen who'd ask about their business, and perhaps arrest them. Their wicker basket with a hundred feet of silk rope would be hard to explain, especially after the curfew.

Although a three-quarter moon had already poked above the horizon, it was still dark on the far side of the tower. They couldn't see the monk who waited for them with Dracul's saddled donkey, and had to give a whistle signal to alert him.

"Have you got the frock for my father?" Vlad said.

The monk mumbled something, and Vlad had to repeat the question. The man was still a teenager and seemed petrified with fear.

"There is nothing to be afraid of, Father," Vlad said to calm him. If the monk panicked and ran away while Vlad and Gruya were up in the tower, the entire plan would collapse. "Once we get my father down, we'll walk you back to the church, for safety." Vlad would've loved to remind the monk that as a servant of God he ought to have a little more confidence in divine protection.

"I hope you get this done quickly, My Prince," the monk said, his voice aquiver.

"We can only climb up in about two hours from now," Vlad said, "after the prisoners and the guards will have settled down for the night." The monk let out a disappointed sigh. "Besides, we need a bit more light from the moon inside the place. There aren't any lamps up there."

"I'll pray for your safety to Saint John Chrysostom, our patron," the monk said. "His holy right hand is among our monastery's relics, and he's done many miracles for us over the years."

No need for a miracle here. The climb, the opening of the cell with Gruya's key, Father's descent in the basket ... all mere child's play. Vlad sat on his haunches, and looked up at the dark shape of the tower. This time, going against his father's direct order would draw Vlad thanks and praise. He began to hum to himself a bawdy tune he'd learned from Marcus.

The widow had a lively box
That many keys unlocked
Having lost my only key,
I had to use my—

The climb proved more difficult than Vlad expected. The rope, while strong enough, was too thin to give good purchase. They had to scale the wall as they would the vertical face of a mountain, by clawing at the gaps in the stonework. To Vlad's annoyance, Marcus's stupid tune kept running in his mind throughout the climb, "The widow had a lively box...."

Once they reached the rampart, they hauled up the basket with the rope meant for Dracul's descent. Vlad used the mule thief's dagger to cut a length of rope for a handle that would secure the basket to the main line. Then he looped the long rope around one of the merlons, and had Gruya sit in the basket to test the primitive tackle. Despite the friction against the stone, the smooth, braided rope glided easily under Gruya's weight.

Only now, with all preparations done, Vlad felt the full impact of what they were about to do. A light tremor took over his body, as if he'd just come in from a cold rain. "Are you scared?" he asked Gruya.

"I know a few other places I'd rather be right now," Gruya said in a strained voice.

Vlad handed him the dagger. "Take this and give me the key."

Vlad crept slowly down the metal steps into the darkness of the tower. Even with the moon now above the tree line, no light reached Dracul's landing. Vlad squeezed Gruya's arm three times, firmly. Gruya returned the signal, showing he understood that extra caution was needed.

When Vlad reached the bottom of the stairs he dropped to his knees, and crept on all fours past the Greek. The man was breathing regularly, as a light sleeper would. By prior agreement, Gruya stationed himself by his cell.

At Dracul's cell Vlad listened for a sound from his father, but couldn't hear any. From the next bay he heard the Karaman prisoner snoring softly. It made Vlad aware his own breathing sounded too loud in the enclosed space of the tower, and he tried to soften it. He counted the twelve iron bars he knew separated the hinged portion of the grille from the wall. Then he straightened up on his knees, and reached for the spot where the door lock would be. His hand touched air, and a painful stitch took hold of his chest. The cell door was wide open.

"Father," he whispered, and scurried on hands and knees toward Dracul's straw pallet. But even as he did this, his mind was screaming, *They've moved him already!* He bumped into his father's empty tin bucket, and it flew against the wall with a report that sounded to Vlad like a cannon shot.

A frantic rustle came from the Greek's cell, then the rattling of his grille door, and the cry, "Hey, who's there?"

The man's yell traveled down the tower's shaft, and back again. It struck Vlad in the pit of his stomach, and left him near paralyzed. He heard a brief scuffle where Gruya would be, then a thud, as something heavy hit the stone floor.

At the bottom of the pit a door opened with a grating sound, and a ray of light shot up into the tower.

"What's going on up there?" a voice shouted in Turkish.

Prisoners on the lower floors, awakened by the commotion, muttered curses and shifted about in the dark with scraping sounds. Vlad remained frozen. After a few moments, the door slammed shut with an angry bang and the tower returned to darkness. Vlad noted the Karaman prisoner had stopped snoring.

"How's the king?" Gruya whispered from the door of Dracul's cell. "We don't have to worry about the Greek anymore. I got him straight through the eye."

"Father's gone." Vlad's earlier fright turned to rage at the thought of what the failure of his plan implied. "They must've moved him after we left."

Gruya swallowed loudly with a smacking of lips, then remained silent for a while. Finally he said, "Let's get out of here."

"With the Greek dead, they'll know someone's broken into the tower," Vlad said. "If they suspect us we're done for. My father, and your grandfather too."

"We'll ditch the ropes, and deny everything."

"I've got an idea," Vlad said. "Go tell the monk what happened. Then give him the tackle to hide at the church, and send him off."

"What are you going to do?"

"On the way out, abandon the dagger on the roof in plain sight. I want the Turks to find it." When Gruya didn't move, Vlad pinched his arm viciously, and hissed, "Go."

Vlad stepped over to Kasim's cell. He couldn't see him, but smelled him nearby, and knew the Karaman had been standing there listening for some time.

"I was sent by Ibrahim Bey to spring you free," Vlad said in Persian, though the Karamans spoke a Turkic dialect.

"How did Grandfather know I'd be in this tower?" Kasim's tone wavered between hopeful and frightened.

Vlad was glad to note the man's Persian was stilted, as happened with a language learned in early childhood, then not used for a long time. Kasim might not be able to tell Vlad wasn't a native Persian.

"Did you come to kill me?"

"Here, hold on to my right hand as a gage while I open your lock."

Kasim fumbled in the dark, and when he found Vlad's hand he grabbed it tight in both of his. "Did my grandfather really send you?"

Vlad unlocked the cell and opened the door slowly to prevent it from squeaking. "I'm Emirzade al-Tabrizı," he lied. "I was hired by your grandfather for this job."

"I have kin in Tabriz," Kasim said. "If I ever come there, I'll look you up and show you my gratitude."

"Follow me to the rooftop and don't make noise."

On the rampart, Vlad grabbed the rope through the tail of his shirt, to prevent burning his palms, and launched himself into the void. Only when he was on the ground did he see, against the moonlit sky, Kasim's shape straddling the rampart. The man showed remarkable self-control not to precipitate himself on Vlad's heels, when his jailers might be close behind.

11

The Mind behind the Plot

June 1442, Wallachia

Women are like the Devil. Give them your little finger, and they'll take the rest of you. Imagine the gall. Alba, Lord Treasurer of the entire kingdom, being made to wait in his wife's antechamber like a sewing-needles hawker? Or like a—

"Would Your Lordship want me to refill your cup?" a tall and portly maid asked Alba.

He looked at her for the first time, though she'd been fussing around the room for a while. He was surprised she had a pretty face, for not being young anymore, and he wondered whether he'd taken her years ago. Well, he couldn't remember. There had been too many. But, probably not. He preferred his women short and skinny, so he could bend them whichever way, at his whim. The large ones required too much work. They also took note of his tiny manhood that couldn't hurt them, and were apt to smirk at him. Stupid cows. The little ones he could hurt, and that made him feel strong.

"What I'd like," he said, "is for Lady Helena to get done with whatever she's been doing for the past two hours, so I can speak with her."

"The lady's having herself made beautiful," the maid said, and turned her back to Alba.

He sighed. If Helena's beauty was involved, it would take forever. Alba thought about giving up the wait and returning to his quarters. But the plan he'd conceived was too exciting not to hold up to Helena as proof of his superior strategic thinking. The woman had a knack for always being a step ahead with plotting, and she loved to lord it over him.

Not this time, though. She'd have to bow to his cunning for a change.

"Her Ladyship will receive you now," the maid announced.

Alba thought the servant pronounced "receive" in a contemptuous tone. He, master of the domain, be *received* in his own house? He gave the maid a scornful look, and for an instant imagined her wriggling under him, begging to be spared. But she was nearly a head taller than he, and likely to put up a fight. His fantasy receded behind a screen of resentment.

"What could be so urgent that you should interrupt my rehearsal for the coronation, Lord Husband?" Helena spoke in a coquettish tone Alba hadn't heard since their honeymoon, two decades before.

He glanced around the dressing room, and saw clothes piled up on chairs, ready to be tried on. Then his attention was drawn to three pretty chambermaids who stood demurely behind Helena. *Oh, so fresh, so frail, so young, so—*

"Well? What do you say?" Helena cooed. She raised her hands and made a fluid motion, as if parting a veil to expose a rare treasure.

"A rehearsal ... yes ... I heard you ... I see the clothes," Alba stammered, his eyes unable to leave the sight of the girls. "But your maid lied to me, just now. She said you were being made beautiful."

Foolishly the girls giggled, and Alba realized his blunder, but it was too late.

Helena gave a roar, and pounced on the girls. She punched and scratched them at random, while they stood motionless, heads bowed. When she tired of abusing the maids, she rushed over to a dressing table laden with jars, brushes, and powder puffs. Alba recognized the articles as part of an enormously expensive shipment Helena had just received from Venice. Wasteful woman.

"Take this, you cruel man," she screamed at Alba, and began to throw jars at him.

When her fury was finally spent in a clatter of shattered glass, she dropped onto a couch and buried her face in a pillow.

"Get out of here," Alba ordered the girls. As they scurried out the door, he couldn't help sorting them in his mind by weight and height. He pulled a stool close to the couch and sat facing Helena. Her sobs reassured him. When she reached this stage she was beyond lashing out at him. Only in moments like this could he unwind in her presence.

"You are a monster," she said, through the pillow. "How could you be so unfeeling?"

"You know I've never been good at timing my jokes," he answered.

She stopped sobbing, but kept her face in the pillow. "Joke? What joke?"

"Well, you didn't really think I was blind to the hard work of your maids—" *Wait, wait.* Stressing their efforts implied Helena's beautification was a more onerous project than she'd be willing to admit. He decided to stick with plain flattery, so he said, with conviction, "Even without their work your beauty is—"

She sprang to a sitting position, and stared at him with girlish anticipation. "Yes? What about my beauty? Describe it."

Alba cast about desperately for persuasive terms to praise his wife's looks, while his eyes took in the debacle that was her face. Black paste had smeared around her eyes, and gave her the haunted look of someone who'd just witnessed an unspeakable tragedy. Her cheeks had been exceedingly white on his arrival, but now were dappled with yellowish spots where her skin showed through the gouged layers of cream that caked her face.

"Your beauty is glowing, radiant—*er,* statuesque."

Helena rewarded him with the sight of her receding gums, in a rare smile he was happy not having to describe. "It seems you learned something from that Italian poet, after all," she said, mollified.

"Oh, yes, Ser Piccolomini had an enviable way with words, when it came to the feminine charms."

"I wish he'd written a sonnet to preserve my beauty, as a painting would do." She sighed. "Alas, beauty doesn't last. Now that Esmeralda's about to become a wife, I fear my old age isn't far."

"You mean a queen, not just a wife." He stood up to lend gravity to the news he was about to deliver. "In forty-eight hours we're going to be a step closer to Esmeralda becoming the Queen of Wallachia."

Helena perked up, and hardened her look. Alba knew the mere hint of political intrigue had ended his grace period. A new skirmish would begin, on a battlefield Helena had long ago appropriated.

"I've just learned that our regent Marcus is on his way back to Târgovişte," he said, and paused to give his wife the chance to show her surprise. "Baba Novak asked him to wait at Nicopolis for Dracul's return, and leave the defense of the capital to Baba. But the regent ignored him, and is now heading this way to fight Nestor."

"Is Marcus bringing his two hundred cavalry with him?" Helena asked.

"He's coming with only a dozen men, and that's the reason I'm here talking with you." Alba was pleased to register Helena's rising interest. "My brother and I are planning an untoward event for Marcus, before he clears Devil's Belt Forest."

"How untoward?" Helena appeared as keen now as he hoped she'd be.

"Peter and I thought that a deadly accident for the regent would be the best."

"You thought that, because you employed logic." Helena's look reflected wonderment at his astuteness. Alba's breast swelled, and he almost believed the things he said about her beauty moments before coming from his heart. "You and Peter told yourselves that with the regent dead, and his father in some Ottoman dungeon, no one stood in our way to make Nestor king and Esmeralda queen."

"Precisely, that's what—"

Helena jumped to her feet and clutched at his shirtfront. "The logic of imbeciles," she screamed in his face, then pushed him onto the couch with great violence. "Did you and Peter think what would happen if you murdered Marcus, and then Nestor got himself killed in his next attempt at taking Târgovişte? Who'd make Esmeralda queen then?"

A jug of ice water dumped on his head would've felt hot compared to Helena's scorn. He wanted to look away, but knew that would only increase her choler.

Her lips flecked with white foam, she said, "I didn't persuade the regent to go against Baba's request, and come home, so you and your cretinous brother would foul it up for us."

The revelation sunk Alba's aspirations as strategist. "*You* did that?"

"I must share credit with our daughter. It was she who convinced Marcus to return."

Shock at learning Esmeralda was involved in this dangerous game made Alba inhale his spittle. "How could—*cough*—Esmeralda—*cough*—have such an influence on Marcus?"

"A man governed by his testicles is clay in a woman's hands." Helena made the gesture of closing her bony fist around a set of imaginary glands, and Alba winced. "You of all people should know that."

"But I don't ... see ... what she could have done to—?"

"All Esmeralda had to do was write Marcus a love note that said, 'I've eaten nothing since you left. The flowers you gave me are all I want to take to the grave with me. Adieu, my valiant king!'"

"King?" Alba shouted. "Do you understand the implication of that one word in the mouth of our daughter?" Though genuinely frightened, he was also gratified to have something he could throw back at Helena. "That letter is proof of our conspiracy."

Instead of backing down, she gave him a withering stare and jabbed a finger into his chest. "Play the role I reserved for you, and no one will be left to prove anything against us."

"What role?" Alba felt small and inconsequential, as if she had just asked him to clean up the mess of broken jars.

"Send Julius with twenty of his men-at-arms to meet Marcus and escort him to Târgovişte."

"Julius? Our nephew hates Marcus and will want to kill him when it is in his power."

"Tell Julius to be patient, and he'll have his way with Marcus soon enough. For now he's to deliver another letter from Esmeralda, telling Marcus she wants Julius to head the regent's bodyguard. Then leave it to Esmeralda and me to make Marcus do what we need done."

"But what can Marcus do for us?" Alba said.

Helena drilled her eyes into his, relentless. "He'll help us fix the mess Nestor made by disobeying my orders."

Alba resented Helena calling it *her* orders when she'd never spoken to Nestor. But he didn't feel safe to challenge her on that. "What orders were those, dear?"

She must've sensed her supremacy had been reaffirmed, for she softened her stance, and took a step back. "That future son-in-law of ours was supposed to take and *keep* Roter Turm Pass. Instead, he decided on his own to march all the way down here, then sit interminably outside Târgovişte, like a constipated old woman on the chamber pot. What did he think he'd accomplish?"

"Nestor found out somehow that Dracul was in Edirne, not by the Black Sea. So he thought it best to come here, eliminate Baba Novak, and take over Târgovişte. I completely approve of his initiative."

Helena's exasperation with Alba gave signs of resurgence. "Baba's ensconced with Dracul's army in the fortress, and can afford to wait in there until Nestor grows a tail." As she spoke her spit sprayed Alba's face, but he didn't dare wipe it. "Nestor's chances of getting to Baba are worse than a bull's for fucking a cow through the fence. And every day his mercenaries spend outside Târgovişte, whoring and drinking, costs *us* money."

"It's not Nestor's fault he has no siege equipment to storm the town, is it?" Alba said. "Nor that Baba Novak refuses to give him battle in the open field."

"If Nestor had stayed in the Roter Turm Pass, Baba would've been obligated to take the army there, and give Nestor his fight.

Baba couldn't have left the occupation of one of Wallachia's portals go unchallenged."

"But how would it have helped our cause to have Baba push Nestor back to Transylvania?"

"The moment Baba and the army left town, we could've taken over Târgovişte with fewer than fifty men. Then the Royal Council would've come over to our side, declared Baba an outlaw, and elected Nestor king. End of story."

The simplicity of Helena's plan left Alba with nothing to add. He'd have liked to point out it was her fault for not explaining it to him from the beginning. But that would be an admission that he accepted her as the rightful mastermind of the plot. So instead, he said, "I think Nestor's accomplished a great deal by coming here, battle or not. He's proven to the boyars he's got what it takes to be a king."

"The only thing Nestor accomplished was to give Baba Novak the chance to send five hundred men over the hills to occupy the pass behind Nestor's back, and cut off his retreat. And since he can't get rid of Baba, you and I will have to do it."

"How's Marcus going to help us do that?" Alba said.

"He's hot-headed and in love, a lethal combination of weaknesses. He'll do for us what Baba refuses to do: give Nestor battle on the open field."

"Marcus has no experience in battle. All the fighting he's seen so far has been only tavern brawls. Will Baba let him risk the army's safety in the field?"

"Marcus is the regent, and can do anything he wants to, if he has the backing of the Royal Council. It's your job to see he gets it."

"And Baba?"

"I'll have Marcus order him to hold Târgovişte with a nominal contingent of soldiers. When Marcus leaves for the battle, you and Peter murder that sheep-fucker Baba. Then give Julius the signal from the watchtower to kill Marcus. I hope you can figure the rest for yourself."

Alba had come to Helena's chambers to assert his mastery over strategy, but left further diminished in stature by her unremitting disdain. And to add depth to his humiliation, he was forced to acknowledge her deftness in mastering the intricacies of their plot.

Still, Helena was nothing but a backroom observer, fretting over her wrinkles and loose teeth. Anyone could come up with ideas, but only a true field commander could make them a reality. And Alba was one of those field commanders. The thought gave a bounce to his step, and soon the hurt inflicted by Helena vanished. *He* would be the true kingmaker.

Women's voices pulled him out of his reverie, and he discovered he'd wandered to the kitchen's door. A gaggle of maids was chopping meat and vegetables for supper inside, chattering lightheartedly. He stepped in and they fell silent.

He cast a look over the women, and the need rose in him for an outlet to release his repressed hostility. But they all were past their prime, ugly, sweaty, malodorous. Their looks told him they knew what he had in mind. Then, as if led by a common thought, their eyes flicked for an instant to a spot somewhere behind him.

Alba swiveled around in panic, stung by the thought he'd stumbled into an assassin's trap. But instead of imminent danger, he saw the beautiful face of a young woman seated on a crate, nursing an infant. As their eyes met the woman flinched, and her nipple popped out of the child's mouth. A howl of indignation rose from the nursling, which the mother quieted by shoving her nipple back into his mouth again. But in that brief interlude, the sight of the wet, pink patch of flesh channeled Alba's desire.

The women must have guessed his mind for they began wailing like one, "No, Your Lordship, don't do it."

Their cries only fanned the flames of Alba's desire, so he made no attempt to silence them as he continued to stare at the young mother.

"No, not her, Master," a voice said, sounding more distressed than the others. "She's my niece."

As if that had any bearing on Alba's intentions. He turned to the women and said, "Get out, and take the babe with you."

"She's only two days out of childbirth, Master," the young mother's aunt cried. "Take me if you must."

The sorrowful chorus intensified and began to hurt Alba's ears. "Out," he screamed.

"Take Ionuț, Auntie, Lord Alba won't hurt me."

The women retreated, beating their chests and pulling their hair. The aunt was the last to leave. She cradled the infant at her breast, and sobbed in loud, jarring waves. When they were gone, and the kitchen door closed, Alba turned to the young woman with a reassuring smile. "Let me sit on that crate, *nana,* and you kneel on the floor in front of me."

The woman complied, tears running down her cheeks. Alba saw confusion mingled with relief on her face, and realized she was ignorant of what he expected of her. That kind of innocence made his conquests so much the sweeter. At moments like this he felt imbued with a power raw, pervasive, inebriating. "If your husband hasn't taught you anything useful, I will."

He unfastened his codpiece and exposed himself to her. When she opened her mouth to scream, he thrust her head down onto his lap in a violent move. She gagged, and squirmed under his unrelenting grasp, but didn't bite his member. He knew her protests were for show only. *Deep inside, they all want it.* When, out of breath, the woman slackened her resistance, he chuckled and patted her shoulder, murmuring in a voice made husky by his arousal, "There, there, that isn't so bad, is it?" In the pleasant quiet that followed, his mind drifted to the upcoming events that would unleash his power and make his name something to fear and respect throughout the land.

Power over life and death.

He thought about the enemies he'd soon visit his vengeance upon, and a heady sensation flooded his being. The feeling stayed with him for minutes, until the woman began to squirm again, seeking release from his clutch.

Power to give pain.

He forced her head farther down on him, relentless against her unwillingness, until she began to choke. Then he eased the pressure, and waited for her to regain her breath. Next he reached a hand into her bosom and cupped her breast, firmly. She tensed with the anticipation of pain, and he squeezed her swollen breast savagely, to justify her fear. She gave a muffled groan.

Power to take pleasure.

He pinched her nipple and felt warm milk squirt into his hand. That instant his body began to convulse with pleasure, wave after wave.

When the short-lived ecstasy he wrested from the woman's suffering and humiliation evaporated, Alba was left basking in the warm glow that only power could radiate.

12

A Fateful Step

June 1442, Rumelia, Ottoman Empire

"Grandfather's waiting for us."

The moonlight played on Michael's white hair in the window frame. Vlad had hoped his mentor would be asleep and the rope for climbing up to the second floor not deployed, giving Vlad a reprieve before he'd have to confess his failure. When Gruya reached for the rope, Vlad let him climb up first, which he wouldn't have done if he were returning with good news. By the time Vlad made it to the room Michael had learned what happened, and gave Vlad a silent hug. Then the old man grabbed onto Gruya's arm for support, and sat on his bed, drained of color and strength.

Gruya untied the rope and tossed it out the window. "That's the last telltale sign." Then he took a long draft from a water pitcher, and passed it to Vlad.

"Some things aren't meant for us to change," Michael said, "no matter how much daring we put into trying."

The comment heightened Vlad's frustration. "We came so close, Uncle Michael. Everything worked exactly as I'd planned, except—"

"We must look to the future now, Vlad." Michael's voice had none of the conviction his words implied. Instead it sounded more like that of someone saying farewell from his deathbed. "Your father believes you are the one who must rule Wallachia when—"

"Me? Did he forget Marcus? Or the Turks and the Hungarians who're readying themselves, even as we speak, to take the country for their own?" Blood rushed to Vlad's face as he took in the measure of his father's ridiculous statement.

"He believes you are the one," Michael said, unaware of Vlad's reaction, "because of the prophecy that foretold your destiny."

"But he always thought the prophecy was nonsense." *Father is mocking me through Michael. But to what purpose?*

"It surprised me also to hear him say such things, but he spoke in earnest."

Michael knew Dracul better than anyone and could tell when he meant what he said. Vlad sat on the bed and tried to make sense of Michael's revelation. Why would Father, in the hour of his downfall, indulge in such frivolous banter at Vlad's expense?

Then it hit him, and he jumped to his feet. "When Father said I'm the one to *rule* Wallachia, he didn't mean it literally. He meant I should help him become free, so *he* could return home and continue to rule the kingdom." This did make sense.

"No, no," Michael said, "I can assure you that wasn't what he had in mind. He gave me specific instructions to—"

"Father's too proud to say he needs me, so he goes about it a roundabout way. He gives you a line about the prophecy, because he knows that will get my attention."

"You don't know your father like I do. He's resigned himself to the fact that his time's up, and that it's your turn. Not immediately, but sometime in years to come."

Vlad turned his back on Michael and went to the window. The sky had begun to get that pale bluish tint in the east that precedes the pink of dawn. Muezzins were this very moment climbing the stairs of their minarets throughout the town. They'd be trying to distinguish white from black on the threads wound around their fingers, to know when the time for prayer had arrived. Then their *adhāns* for Salah al-Fajr would awaken the city.

Father relied on me to set him free, and I let him down. Just "trying" counted for nothing when the fate of the country was in the balance.

"*Allāhu Akbar*"—Allah is the greatest.

"*Ash-hadu an-la ilaha illa llah*"—I testify there is no other deity but Allah.

The chant erupted, high-pitched and confident, from the nearby Friday Mosque. Hundreds of starlings in the trees lining the street below started to chirp in competition with the *adhān*. On singing the first verse, the muezzin held the "a" in the middle of "*Allāhu*" for several beats, then warbled the following words, sending them over the city like successive waves of an invigorating surf. When he finally paused for breath, the chant was reprised by dozens of other muezzins scattered across Edirne.

"*Hayya 'ala 'l-falah*"—Make haste toward reward.

Father's confidence in me is my reward. Haste was needed now to make good on his trust.

Voices came from the courtyard, and the scraping of wood on stone told Vlad the gate of the *caravanserai* was being thrown open, so the travelers could go to the mosque.

"What's preventing Murad from sending Father home is mistrust."

"We have Hunyadi and Zaganos to thank for that," Michael said.

"That mistrust would vanish if Murad had one of Father's sons as hostage."

Michael's head jerked back, and he clutched at the edge of the bed attempting to rise. "What are you saying?" he cried with sharp alarm.

Vlad placed his hands on Michael's shoulder and forced him back down. "That's precisely what Father had in mind when he spoke about my role. He didn't want me to risk everyone's life rescuing him from the tower. But he knew that if I became Murad's hostage I'd be safe, while he'd be free to return home and deal with Nestor."

"Your father had no such notion in mind," Michael shouted with unexpected energy. "You are completely wrong on this."

Michael's face displayed the kind of unquestionable authority Vlad remembered from the time when he was a child, and Michael his stern tutor. But Vlad wasn't about to relent. Now that he understood what he was supposed to do, the only question was why it had taken him so long to see the light. "As a hostage I incur no risk, as long as Father keeps the terms of his treaty with Murad, and maintains neutrality when the crusade starts."

"You can't be serious about this, Vlad," Gruya said, he too assuming a grave attitude like his grandfather. "You saw what they do to hostages."

"The Brankovich brothers brought that upon themselves, somehow," Vlad said. "I'm smarter than that."

"When the war breaks out, you, as a hostage, aren't safe at all," Michael said. "If Murad discovers that *any* Romanians are fighting in the crusade, he'll assume your father sent them. Then ..."

"I'm not planning to remain a hostage until the war comes," Vlad said. "I'll find a way to escape to Constantinople, and from there—"

"If you're staying here, so am I," Gruya said. "But this is insane. We'll both end up with our eyes boiled in our heads like Easter eggs."

"Don't be naïve, Vlad," Michael said. "One doesn't escape from the Turks so easily. Remember, it took Gunther four decades."

Gruya counted on his fingers, then said, "You'd be fifty-four and I fifty-six, if it took us forty years to get home."

"And if you make it to Constantinople, who do you know there?" Michael said. "It's not a place you can survive without money and friends."

"The Mount Athos monks told me there is a Wallachian monastery there, on the Third Hill."

"That would be the Pantelimon Monastery," Michael said, not mollified. "I know the abbot. He's one of Alba's men. Not someone I'd trust."

Michael's attempt at discouraging him didn't work on Vlad. "There is no time to waste. If Zaganos moved Father from the

Macedon Tower earlier than expected, he must be in a hurry to ship him off to Amasya."

Michael wrung his hands, looking more distraught than Vlad remembered ever seeing him. "Think of the price you'll pay if you get caught trying to escape, and give up this childish idea. Your father will never approve of it."

Vlad kissed Michael on both cheeks. "I'm on my own now, and Father's got nothing to say about this." Then he turned to Gruya and tried to embrace him.

But the squire waved him aside and headed for the door. "I'm not so easy to shake off."

"Suit yourself," Vlad said with a sigh. "But say your farewell to your grandfather first, as you won't be seeing him again until the winter." He turned to the door, and in passing broke off a wooden peg from the coat rack on the wall.

"Don't weep, Grandfather," Gruya said, and stood Michael up for a proper hug. "We know how to take care of ourselves."

Vlad stepped out of the room, shut the door, then jammed the wooden peg into the lock's eyebolts. Then he dashed to the stairs, while behind him Gruya pounded angrily on the door, screaming obscenities.

When Vlad reached the Friday Mosque, worshippers were already lining up at the ablution fountains. Only then did it dawn on him he had no idea how to accomplish what he'd set his mind to. Go to the sultan's palace? He'd never make it inside there. Besides, Murad was on a hunting trip. The Grand Vizier was against the idea of war, and favorable to Dracul's cause. He'd be the one most interested in bringing Vlad's offer to Murad. But, according to Michael, Khalil Pasha too was away with Murad's hunting party. Wait for them to return to the city? With the war preparations already in motion, the matter of Dracul's freedom couldn't be put off. Anguish invaded Vlad, and he slammed his fist repeatedly into his palm, searching for a solution. Then he remembered the Grand Vizier's nephew, Tirendaz, the sultan's *musahib*. Tirendaz had both Murad's and Khalil's ear, so he'd make a perfect go-between.

Vlad headed at a run for the Grand Vizier's palace, where Michael had met Tirendaz. The structure stood on the west side of a circular plaza, now empty of the customary vendors, petitioners, foreign visitors, and beggars who crowded the space at all daylight hours. The outer palace gate was closed, and five slaves armed with wooden staves stood guard in front of it, chatting.

Now and then a Judas door would open in the gate, and the guards would step aside to let a group of palace personnel pass through on their way to the mosque. Vlad stood by the side, scrutinizing their faces in the hope of seeing Tirendaz. When a long interval passed without anyone exiting the palace, Vlad approached the guards and said to no one in particular, "Is Tirendaz Agha inside?"

"Get away, Giaour," the slave who appeared to be the guards' leader shouted, without rancor. He seemed accustomed to rebuffing unwanted visitors.

Undeterred, Vlad stepped closer. "I've got information for Tirendaz Agha."

"You've heard me," the leader said, and this time menaced Vlad with his staff. Then he turned to his companions and resumed chatting.

"What I have is urgent. Take me to the sultan's *musahib* immediately."

The leader swiveled around nimbly and thrust his staff at Vlad's chest. Though it had a blunt tip, the weapon was handled with sufficient force to cause pain, and would've knocked an inexperienced person off his feet. Vlad sidestepped the blow and tugged hard at the staff. The man plunged forward involuntarily, and Vlad tripped him, then yanked the staff out of his hand. The leader crashed to the ground with a cry of disbelief.

The other four men gave a shout and charged Vlad as one.

Equally armed now, Vlad countercharged the closest of the four, and disarmed him with a harsh rap across the knuckles. The remaining attackers froze with sticks raised at the ready. "I'm not here to cause trouble," Vlad said. Then he maneuvered so as to have the gate at his back. "The *agha* will reward you for helping me bring him the news."

Before the guards could charge again, a voice came from a group of men gathered nearby. "What's the nature of this disturbance?"

Vlad recognized Tirendaz, and tossed his weapon at the feet of his assailants. "I'm Vlad of Basarab, King Dracul's middle son, and I wish to surrender as a hostage to Sultan Murad."

13

Disobedient Servant

"A*lea jacta est," the die has been cast. If I was meant to have my own Rubicon, this is it.*

With only nineteen words Vlad had unleashed events that would keep Wallachia from falling into the hands of either the Hungarians, or the Turks. Nineteen. *One* and *nine*, the numbers on his medallion, his numbers in the Book of Life. A euphoria overtook him. Why couldn't Michael, in all his wisdom, see this was the inevitable thing to do? At least Father did, even though he chose such an indirect way of asking for help.

Vlad recalled a snippet from Psalm 91, a psalm that he hadn't thought about since the night Oma died. "He will call upon me, and I will answer him; I will be with him in trouble, I will deliver him and honor him."

That February night at the Cozia Monastery, when Oma recited these words to him, Vlad couldn't grasp their meaning. But now it became clear that "he" meant Father, and "I" meant Vlad.

Tirendaz whispered something to a young clerk next to him, then entered the palace courtyard in the company of his entourage. The five gatekeepers gave Vlad hateful glances, then gathered their staffs and regrouped in front of the gate.

The clerk looked Vlad up and down with both curiosity and skepticism. "I'm Ismail, Tirendaz Agha's personal secretary." He spoke Greek without an accent, and Vlad guessed that was the man's native tongue. "Follow me."

They ducked through the Judas door and crossed the first court, still empty of outsiders at this time of the day. The court was a square enclosure with a covered platform along three of the walls, where authorized visitors could wait in comfort their turn to enter the palace. On the fourth wall, which separated this court from the next, there were hitching rings for riding animals. In the center of the court was a large circular fountain surrounded by flowerbeds.

Only a handful of palace slaves were present, engaged in various chores under the stern eye of an overseer. Some swept the ground; others weeded and watered the flowerbeds. A few stable hands tended to a string of saddled horses kept ready for riders in a hurry.

Ismail registered Vlad's inquiring gaze. "Horses for the Grand Vizier's messengers. This is the place whence they leave for all parts of the empire throughout the day."

The gate to the second court was guarded by soldiers with long pikes. A good thing pikers weren't stationed at the front gate, or things might've turned tragic for Vlad. He and Ismail passed through a vaulted corridor to reach the second court.

"This was the residence of the Venetian consul in Adrianople eighty years ago," Ismail said. "Before the town was conquered by the Turks and became Edirne."

"Was your family from this area?"

"My great-grandfather was the head of the Town Council." Vlad detected a note of pride in Ismail's voice. "When the Turks came, he fled to Athens with his family to escape slavery."

"How did you happen to be enslaved? The Ottomans haven't yet conquered Athens."

Ismail shot Vlad a reproachful look, perhaps due to that offensive "yet." Then he waved his hands as a warning that this wasn't a subject he wished to discuss. "This building also served as the main storehouse for the Venetian Quarter. That's why it looks more like a commercial structure than a palace."

The second court was a rectangular area about fifty yards long and thirty wide, lined with arcades on all sides. The center space was planted with rose bushes surrounding four artesian fountains. Animals weren't permitted in this court. Vlad knew there had to be a third court that housed the Grand Vizier's private quarters. No one, other than Khalil Pasha, his children, women, and eunuchs could enter that space.

Dozens of rooms opened onto the arcades, serving perhaps as government offices, kitchens, and storerooms. Ismail led Vlad to such a room containing only a divan, a washbasin, and a clay pitcher. "I'll have you wait here, and will be back in a while to write down your declaration."

With the *big step* now behind him, Vlad felt the weariness of the sleepless night settle on his shoulders like a coat of armor. He flopped onto the divan with the satisfying feeling of being right when all around him were wrong. He thought about his father dashing home to scatter Nestor and his mercenaries to the four winds. Well, perhaps Father wouldn't be able to dash anywhere with his injured feet. Khalil Pasha would do well to send him off in a carriage. But just the news that Father was on his way back would make Nestor soil his trousers.

When voices speaking Greek in front of his door awoke Vlad, he couldn't tell if he'd slept for minutes or hours. There was only a small window at the top of the wall, and the light that came in that way didn't help him guess the time of day. One of the voices was young, and he thought it might be Ismail. The other sounded old. Vlad tried to open the door: locked. No surprise there, since he had yet to be recognized for whom he claimed to be. But that shouldn't take long, if Tirendaz's secretary was smart enough to send for Michael.

Oh, that's who the other voice must be. Vlad pressed his ear to the door in time to hear Ismail say, "... thinks he should be treated as any impostor."

A key scraped inside the lock before Vlad could make sense of what he'd just heard. He stepped back, and the door opened to show Ismail and Michael regarding him with grave faces.

"Uncle Michael," Vlad cried in Romanian, and opened his arms wide. "I hope you'll forgive me for putting you through this. You'll see it's all for the better."

"You can stop pretending you're a prince." Ismail stepped between Michael and Vlad. "I've consulted both King Dracul and Lord Michael with identical results."

Vlad failed to grasp Ismail's meaning. If he were teasing, he chose a poor moment to do that. "What's there to consult?"

"It turns out the only truth you told was your given name, Vlad," Ismail said. "But you're no king's son. Only a liar."

Vlad leaned to one side to see Michael's face, and understood at a glance this was no teasing.

"You're a shameless and disobedient servant, Vlad," Michael said, in Greek for Ismail's benefit. "It's a disgraceful way to behave after being taken off the street into King Dracul's household."

This was a stunning development. Dracul had seemingly rejected Vlad's sacrifice, and ordered Michael to bear false testimony. Vlad turned to Ismail. "Don't you see my father's repudiating me out fear for my safety? It's on account of the terrible things that happened to other hostages." He would've liked to mention the Brankovich brothers, but remembered Michael's warning about the danger of knowing state secrets.

"I've seen the travel document Hassan Bey issued to King Dracul in Nicopolis," Ismail said. "It lists two merchants, six muleteers, and two footmen. There is no mention of a prince."

There was no mention of a king either, but Ismail seemed not to care about that detail.

Vlad was both stupefied and hurt. "Why's Father doing this? How could he throw away his chance to return home and save the country?" Outrage made Vlad's voice quiver, but he didn't care.

"Let me give this false prince a measure of royal justice, Ismail Efendi," Michael said, and shook his walking stick at Vlad.

Ismail stepped out of the way, and Michael shuffled closer to Vlad. "Your father wouldn't dream of buying his freedom in exchange for your *eyes*, your *hands*, your *feet*." Michael spoke Romanian this time, and at each mention of a body part, he laid the stick on Vlad's shoulder. The strikes were mere ineffectual brushes, but to Vlad they had the impact of a war hammer. His eyes stung, and his heart shriveled as if dipped in brine.

"What about Wallachia?" Vlad tried to sound persuasive, but his voice cracked and he came across as whining instead. "Has Father forgotten his kingly oath to defend it at all costs?"

Michael grasped Vlad's right hand and showed it to Ismail. "Look at these calluses," he said. "Is this the hand of a prince?"

Ismail probed Vlad's palm with his finger, and shook his head.

"Calluses mean nothing," Vlad shouted at Ismail, anger beginning to replace his dismay. "I like to shoe my horse, and forge my weapons. That doesn't make me a liar."

"The Turks believe you've lied to them and intend to punish you for it," Michael said, reverting again to Romanian. "It's a grave offense." He resumed Vlad's sham caning, but it was clear the need to do this upset the old man deeply. His face took on the purple hue of raw meat kept too long uncooked. "Don't worry, though. I'll sell my rings, the mules, everything we've got left, and ransom you by noon tomorrow." Michael appeared winded from his exertions. "But you've got to stop telling them—"

"The truth, Uncle Michael?" Vlad's bitterness burst into a loud and mirthless laughter that sounded, even to his own ears, like that of a person on the verge of insanity.

Michael staggered backward, as if appalled by Vlad's reaction.

"Come, Lord Michael," Ismail said. "Let stronger people apply due punishment to this brazen liar." He led Michael out of the room and locked the door.

Vlad sank his nails into the wood of the door, and stifled a scream. Then he kicked the thick planks, only to wrench his toe. This was so unthinkable on Father's part. And Michael should know better than to go along with him. Neither man comprehended that it was Vlad's destiny to take this course, and nobody could stop him. He collapsed on the divan and shut his eyes, trying to still the whirl of hateful thoughts that ravaged his mind.

Hours passed and the door remained locked. Vlad had to find a way to speak directly to the Grand Vizier. If Khalil Pasha was as keen on preventing war as Michael claimed, he'd jump at the opportunity Vlad presented. With a hostage in hand, Khalil could persuade Murad to trust Father, and send him home to deal with Nestor. Murad must be feeling quite the fool by now for letting himself be led to the brink of war by Hunyadi's letter.

But why wasn't anyone coming to talk to him? Neither Father's nor Michael's testimony was needed to establish Vlad's identity. A few minutes spent in conversation with Vlad would suffice to persuade Tirendaz and Khalil they were dealing with a prince. No simple servant could speak so many languages, or have such a vast knowledge of history and geography.

When he heard the *adhān*, he guessed it was time for the afternoon prayer. The day was passing fast, with no resolution for him. Would Father be sent off to Asia anyway, after he'd come so close to being saved?

Half an hour later the door opened, and Ismail came in with two blacksmiths carrying shackles, chains, an anvil, and a toolbox.

Vlad rose and confronted Ismail with a calm that masked his internal turmoil. "I want to speak to Khalil Pasha."

"The Grand Vizier's heard your false claim, and ordered you transferred to Zaganos Pasha's jurisdiction. Now lie on the floor and be still."

Vlad thought about resisting the chains, but concluded it would be pointless. "The same Zaganos who tortured my father over a deceitful letter from Hunyadi?" He lay down and the smiths placed iron shackles on his feet, with a two-foot length of chain between them.

"The Third Vizier is responsible for state prisoners," Ismail said, "even if they're no more than pretend princes."

When the smiths lifted Vlad's right foot onto the anvil, and hammered a rivet to fasten the shackle, his bowels churned. The time for convincing anyone of his truth was running out. "Ask yourself, Ismail, why would a man headed for prison refuse to be exchanged for a hostage?"

Vlad's left foot went onto the anvil next, and now his bowels felt as if they were being ripped to shreds. "Especially if the hostage was *not* his son," he shouted over the din of the hammer blows. "What would he have to lose?"

The blacksmiths were skilled at their work, and it took them only a minute to shackle Vlad's hands as well. The chain between the handcuffs was only two links long, to prevent him from attacking his keepers.

"The explanation isn't complicated at all," Ismail said with a patronizing smile. He handed one of the smiths a hinged iron ring with flanges at the open ends. The man closed the ring around Vlad's neck.

"Am I a slave?" Vlad was seized by a terror that strangled his voice to a whisper. Now he wished he'd resisted being bound. He could've killed all three of them and … then what? His life wouldn't be worth the lint in the Devil's bellybutton.

"King Dracul must've promised you a great reward to pose as his son," Ismail said. "Others have tried that trick. Your father hatched the scheme before he was tortured by Zaganos Pasha. Once he understood how the Third Vizier deals with liars, the king changed his mind, to save his neck. He just forgot to tell you to drop the impersonation."

The smiths pulled Vlad by the hair close to the anvil, and set the flanges of his neck-ring on it. When the rivet that locked the iron ring had been flattened, the smiths gathered their tools and left the room.

Two Janissaries came in and lifted Vlad by the armpits, then shoved him out the door.

"But what if I *am* King Dracul's son?" Vlad said over his shoulder. "Wouldn't the sultan miss an opportunity to spare the lives of thousands of his men?"

Ismail walked onto the arcade behind the Janissaries. "Prove to Khalil Pasha you are," he called after Vlad with a derisive laugh, "and he'll let your 'father' return to Wallachia immediately."

One of the Janissaries jabbed Vlad in the ribs with his thumb, and shouted into his ear, "Get moving, Giaour. We've got other business today besides you."

They were nearly at the gate when a thought shot through Vlad's mind, hopeful and sickening at the same time. "I can prove it, Ismail," he cried. He turned to see if the secretary had followed them, and received a vicious cuff in the ear.

"Let him speak," Ismail said and approached Vlad.

Vlad's ear was on fire, and his jaw felt out of joint. He'd never been hit in anger before, and now he found himself swamped with such a rage that his entire body quivered. He stood there, unable to speak, as Ismail's face turned from curious to scornful. When Ismail began to turn away, Vlad finally managed to whisper, "There is someone here in Edirne who can identify me."

The only sign the secretary heard him was a raised eyebrow.

"A Turk who returned recently from Wallachia saw me in Târgovişte and can prove who I am." Vlad felt his lungs beginning to fail him, and feared he'd be unable to finish what he wanted to say. "An Akinci named Omar. I spotted him by the Friday Mosque last week when we arrived here."

"Enough already," the Janissary who'd struck Vlad said. "We've got our orders, Ismail Efendi." He spun Vlad by the shoulders, and kicked him in the butt. Ismail made no attempt to interfere, and Vlad knew his last arrow had gone astray of the target. A heavy, sulfurous air descended upon him through which neither light not air could penetrate.

14

An Ancient Water Cistern

Vlad didn't know how he ended up in the alley where a group of men armed with thin rods barred his way. Awakened from his stupor, he recognized them as the five slaves he'd challenged that morning at Khalil Pasha's palace gate. He glanced over his shoulder, and when he saw his two Janissaries smirking he understood it was an ambush that concerned only him, not his escort.

"Only across the back, boys," one of the Janissaries said. He inserted a pole between Vlad's arms, then he and his companion hoisted the pole above their heads, on straightened arms. "And no broken bones." Vlad's feet dangled a couple of inches above the ground.

The five attackers scurried behind Vlad with gleeful yelps. The first blow took him by surprise, and tore a shrill cry out of him.

"The Giaour cries like a woman," a man said, and the others hooted.

Vlad clenched his teeth, and when the second blow landed, all he gave his tormentors was a hiss. On the third blow he denied them even that, and held his breath until the pain dropped to a bearable level. Then he stopped counting, and forced his mind away from the alley, away from these vicious dogs with their rods. Now he was galloping bareback on Timur, every blow to his back transformed into a bounce on the horse. Then Timur appeared to trip, and Vlad found himself thrown to the ground.

"Get up, Giaour," a voice came to Vlad through the haze of his pain. "You'll be late for supper if you don't get a move on."

Vlad rose to his knees first, and then to his feet. He was alone with the two Janissaries. His shirt seemed to have become tighter across his shoulders. When he tried to loosen it by shrugging, it felt glued to his back.

He walked slowly ahead, impeded by his leg irons, and the Janissaries followed in silence. Curiously, his back didn't hurt, only felt numb and heavy. A few blocks later they came to a gate that opened into a courtyard filled with ancient ruins. In the center of the yard there was a circular opening, about eight feet in diameter, with a scaffolding over it that supported a number of pulleys. A hemp rope attached to the pulleys hung down the center of the well and disappeared into the darkness below. Vlad guessed the installation served to move materials to and from underground storage.

"Over here," someone shouted from the back of the yard, and Vlad's guards led him to a tent in which about a dozen slaves stood bunched together. The men were shackled in the same manner as Vlad, and spoke in a language he didn't understand. From their appearance, Vlad thought they might be Russians or Poles.

A clerk who appeared in charge of the operations in the tent approached Vlad. "What happened to this one? Why's he all bloody?"

"Keep an eye on him," one of the Janissaries said. "He's a troublemaker."

"He got a thrashing for disobeying orders," the other Janissary added. Then the two soldiers left, grinning at Vlad.

The clerk grabbed one of the slaves by the arm and shoved him in the direction of a workbench, where a smith struck off his handcuffs. Next, another worker attached a metal tag to the slave's neck-ring, then led him back to where the clerk was waiting. The clerk peered at the tag then called out, "Twelve." A nearby scribe made an entry into a register resting on a portable desk strapped to his waist. Next the clerk measured the slave's height, and weighed him. "Five foot ten. One hundred and sixty pounds." An inspection of the slave's mouth followed. "Four teeth missing." Finally the clerk took a step back, appraised the man from top to bottom through narrowed eyes, and proclaimed, "Twenty years old."

An attendant appeared at the flap of the tent, and took Twelve away.

It went on like this until five more slaves were processed. Then the clerk looked at Vlad, and pointed at the workbench.

"Ninety-one," the clerk called out after inspecting Vlad's tag.

Nine and *one*? The occurrence of *his* ordained numbers shocked Vlad. Was this a joke on the part of the heavenly powers? He swatted the tag at his neck as if it were a poisonous spider.

"Five foot seven, one hundred and thirty pounds. Good teeth. Sixteen years old."

Only yesterday, Vlad would have been tickled to be taken for someone two years older than he was. Now the clerk's flattering error left him indifferent.

The attendant who came to take Vlad away had a mischievous smirk. "To the well," he said, and pointed at the center of the court, assuming Vlad didn't understand Turkish. When Vlad approached the circular opening he heard faint voices down below, but couldn't see anyone. "Catch the rope," the attendant said, and his smirk opened into a grin of blackened teeth. Before Vlad understood what he was supposed to do, the man shoved him into the well. Vlad tumbled head first, brushing his shoulder against the rope. At the last moment, before he was about to plummet into the void, his right hand seized the rope. It arrested his fall long enough so his left hand could also take hold of it. But the momentum carried him downward vertiginously, and the friction of the hemp fibers burned his palms.

"Hey, not so fast," a man's voice cried in accented Greek when Vlad hit the pavement at the bottom of the well. "You'll break your back if you don't slow down."

Stunned by the impact, hurting all over his body, Vlad sat where he'd fallen, waiting for his eyes to adjust to the dim light. The putrid odor of the place stung his nostrils.

"Come, get out of the way," the same voice said, with a note of caring, "if you don't want the next fellow to land on you." The man pulled Vlad up by his armpits. "Hey, what happened to your back?"

"Just a beating. And who are you?"

They had moved only a few steps away when another slave slid down slowly, breaking his descent with feet crossed over the rope.

"So you speak Greek?" Vlad's companion said, sounding pleased. "None of these other folks here do. They're new arrivals from somewhere north of the Black Sea." He picked up a small wooden bowl off the floor and wiped the food residue inside it with his elbow. "This is for both food and water. There might not be enough bowls if people keep coming like this, so don't let it out of your hand. Spencer's my name."

Vlad looked around. The darkness of the vast underground chamber was partly dispelled by a dirty light dripping through a number of grated openings in the ceiling. He saw men, perhaps a hundred, crouched with their backs against the walls and the supporting pillars. As he surveyed them, their cold stares of caged animals sharpened Vlad's feeling of doom. By contrast, his companion's unexpected solicitude kindled his hope. "Where are we?"

"This used to be a water cistern in the time of the Romans," Spencer said. "It's Zaganos Pasha's slave pen now. The way the man treats his slaves, you'd think he doesn't know his own interests. Big auction tomorrow, with dealers from Egypt and Syria. With a bit of luck you'll be out of here before he gets to starve you like he did me for the past two weeks."

In the past, the mention of Egypt or Syria would stir notions of heroic adventures in Vlad. Now the names of those lands, so distant from his own, chilled his heart. "From your red hair and freckled face I can see you aren't Greek. Norman or Dutch, perhaps. I've seen men from those parts who looked like you. How did Zaganos come to own you?"

"As an Englishman I should be offended to be taken for a continental. But slavery's beaten the ethnic pride out of me. Zaganos inherited me from my dead master, who owed him money."

A loud crash resounded behind them, followed by a scream of agony. A man lay in a rumpled bundle on the spot where Vlad had fallen. Even from the distance of about ten yards, Vlad could see the man's left shinbone had snapped, and was poking through the leg of his trousers.

"Let him be," Spencer said, trying to block Vlad from rushing to the fallen man's side. "He's as good as dead."

Vlad shook himself free of Spencer. "He's not dead yet."

The injured man had balled his fists and was groaning through clenched teeth. Vlad dragged him away from the landing spot by his tunic, and the movement wrested fresh screams from the man. "Is there any water we could give him?" Vlad said.

Spencer shook his head. "They'll be hoisting him up in the morning and putting him out of his misery."

"Does this kind of thing happen often?"

"A Christian's life is never worth much to the infidel. Besides, there is a glut of slaves in Edirne at the present, and prices have dropped to a record low for peacetime."

"So the guards can afford to have a little sport at the expense of the prisoners?" Vlad said.

"They almost can't give away some of the slaves," Spencer said. "The old, the weak, the sick. No one will buy them. So what if a few of them die? It saves the Turks the trouble of killing them."

Several more slaves descended the rope safely. Then another one fell and smashed his head against the stone floor. He expired silently on the spot, as the rest of the slaves watched with indifference. To Vlad's surprise, Spencer knelt next to the dead man and cradled his head in his arms, seemingly not mindful of getting blood on himself. After praying aloud in Latin and crossing himself a few times, Spencer stood up sprightly.

"What will happen to me?" Vlad said.

"That depends on the state of your health. You get sick, you die. Best to stay healthy and get sold. Let me take a look at your back before I read your fortune."

Spencer led Vlad to a far corner of the room, where he'd piled up the floor rushes to form a comfortable pallet. "This is my sleeping suite, and you're welcome to share it. But first, tie this tag to my neck-ring."

The metal strip Spencer handed Vlad was covered in blood. "You stole the dead man's tag?" So the prayer and the blessings were only for cover. Vlad rubbed the blood off with his thumb and read the number stamped on it. *Nine. God certainly jokes in mysterious ways.*

"My own tag identifies me as being too lightweight," Spencer said. "A hundred and twenty pounds, which is too little for my six-foot frame. So the Turks won't even try to sell me, knowing I'm too weak to interest a buyer. But with a new tag I've got a chance of being taken out of this hellhole, and, who knows, a decent peasant might buy me tomorrow."

"I don't want to be sold," Vlad said on impulse. "I've got to escape and—" Why tell a stranger his story? Spencer would laugh to hear that Vlad had been a free man until that morning, and that he'd given up his freedom trying to be a hero.

"Oh, I see," Spencer said with mock earnestness, "you aren't like the rest of us simpleminded folks who are just hoping to be passed from master to master until the end of our days."

"What I mean—"

"If the flesh on your back becomes corrupted, being sold won't be your biggest problem." Spencer took Vlad by the shoulders and turned his back toward the nearest skylight. "Strip your shirt."

Vlad began to pull the shirt over his head but it resisted, being stuck to his wounds. It took Spencer several minutes to pry the fabric lose without tearing the flesh.

"Your wounds are still too fresh to be infected. Though by tomorrow it might be a different matter."

"Will they try to sell me even with my mangled back?" Vlad said.

"You should hope they do," Spencer said. "The alternative is certain death." He spun Vlad around, and noticed his medallion. "This thing might just give you a fighting chance. The Turks love Christian amulets. Perhaps we can have one of them take it in exchange for bringing you a salve for your back."

"I can't part with it. It's something that—" Vlad realized he couldn't explain why that disk of black stone would be more important than having medicine that might save his life. "My back will be fine without any ointment." But the way his flesh was throbbing now, he knew that wasn't likely.

"If it's that valuable to you, hide it until you're with an owner who'll let you keep it." Spencer bent over and extracted something from his trouser hem. "Twelve years of slaving for three masters, and all I own is a needle and thread."

The words "slaving" and "masters" tore at Vlad's soul like the fangs of a bloodhound at a fallen stag. He took the needle and thread from Spencer and sewed the medallion into a fold of his drawers. With the light from above almost gone, he did the work mostly by feel. Then, exhausted and nauseated, he put the shirt back on, and was about to lie down when a commotion rippled through the pen.

"You don't want to miss this," Spencer said, and produced his own bowl from a hiding place in the wall. "Hurry, there is never enough food."

A wire cage holding two attendants and a large cauldron mounted on a four-wheel cart was being lowered on the rope. One of the men carried a lit torch, and used it to force back the slaves who mobbed the cage when it reached the ground. The other rolled the cart out of the cage and began to ladle a gray, watery broth into the prisoners' bowls. When Vlad received his portion, he took a few sips, then fed the rest of it to the slave with the broken leg. The man lay on the spot where Vlad had dragged him, still moaning in pain, looking much weakened by his ordeal. When the injured man felt the lukewarm liquid pour into his mouth, he clutched at Vlad's hand like a nursling at his mother's breast. In the torch's flickering light Vlad saw the face of an old, emaciated man. How did he ever fall into the net of the raiders and end up in a place where he couldn't make it even as a slave?

The attendants and their cauldron were raised to the yard level, and the pen was plunged into darkness. The slaves shuffled away to their sleeping places, grumbling.

"Stay here," Spencer whispered. "They're coming back with water in a few minutes."

Vlad shared his water with the old man. Then, holding on to Spencer who knew his way in the dark, he returned to their sleeping corner. On Spencer's advice, Vlad slept shirtless, lying facedown to allow the wounds on his back to dry up.

Far from offering respite from worries and pain, the night brought him only nightmares and blistering fever. At one point a hand tapped him on the head, and a disembodied voice said in Turkish, "Drink some water, Vlad of Basarab."

Vlad attempted to push himself up to a kneeling position, but toppled over to his side. His back felt as if a cat were sharpening its claws on it. He touched his open eyes and concluded with a shock he was completely blind. A fear of an unimaginable intensity invaded him. *I died and this is hell. But how did I get here?* He forced himself to recall the last scene of his life, leading to that moment when someone, or something, had put an end to it. Most likely a violent one. But his memory was unresponsive. Blind, in pain, and deprived of memory. Yes, he was in hell, and all alone. *And the Turkish voice?* "Do you know all the dead by name?" Vlad whispered, overwhelmed by timidity at the thought he was addressing the Devil himself.

"Oh, no," Spencer said, "only those who speak in their sleep." He chuckled, then pulled Vlad's head up by his hair and placed a bowl at his lips. "Here's water for you."

Vlad's memory came alive like paper tossed into a raging fire. "I'm not dead," he said, and immediately felt stupid. "I remember where I am."

"That's progress." Spencer tipped the bowl, and Vlad drank until there was no more. "A moment ago you were speaking to the sultan, shouting your name again and again, and telling him you wanted to be his hostage."

"Did you save your water for me?"

"Don't take me for a good Samaritan," Spencer said. "I've seen men in your condition. They're apt to be raving when the fever comes, and they keep everyone else awake. All I wanted was to buy myself some quiet time."

"You're a poor liar, Spencer. I'll reward your kindness one day."

By morning most of Vlad's strength had seeped away. He needed Spencer's help to rise from his pallet and put his shirt on. When he raised his arms the entire surface of his back moved with them like a heavy slab, sending waves of pain throughout his body.

"Your back looks much better," Spencer said, in an unconvincing tone that told Vlad his condition had worsened. "When the Turks come to select men for the auction, you've got to show them you're strong and healthy."

The feeding and watering ritual from the evening before was repeated. Then the attendants hauled up both the injured and the dead slaves. An hour later, the clerk and his scribe carrying the register descended into the pen in the company of three assistants armed with wooden staffs.

"They decide upstairs who among the slaves are likely to find buyers at the auction," Spencer said. "That's why they write down your height, weight, state of your teeth, and your age. Tall, strong, good teeth, and young is what they want, and that's what you can give them, Prince Vlad."

"You aren't old either, and have most of your teeth." Vlad saw that Spencer was terrified by the likelihood of being left behind. "What happens to those not selected?"

"They'll be sold as a lot for a few aspers to some mine owner from Anatolia. They'll all be dead inside a month."

The assistants herded the prisoners into a four-row formation. Then the clerk began to walk along the rows, reading the numbers imprinted on the prisoners' tags. The scribe would check the numbers against his register, and when they matched that of a selected slave, the clerk would grunt in satisfaction. Then one of the assistants would take the corresponding slave out of the formation.

Vlad noticed that Spencer let his shirt hang out of his trousers to hide his shrunken waistline. When the clerk read his tag, Spencer straightened up and pushed out his chest. His number turned out to be a lucky one, and the clerk, fooled perhaps by Spencer's posture, didn't bother to compare his notes with what was in front of him. Vlad emulated his new friend, trying to show the clerk the picture of good health and strength that would save him from being left behind. His number was lucky as well.

"When you become a slave, all you can think of, day and night, is escaping," Spencer told Vlad while the cage took them to the courtyard level. "Then, after you get caught a couple of times, all you want is to have a master who will feed you and not work you too hard."

"I'll never stop trying to escape," Vlad said.

"We'll talk after you collect a few souvenirs of your adventures," Spencer said, and laughed without joy. He pushed back the hair that hung over his left shoulder, and showed Vlad the scar left by his missing ear. At the same time, Vlad observed Spencer was also missing two fingers on his right hand.

Vlad counted thirty-two slaves who'd been selected for the auction. Except for Spencer they all were well built and healthy looking. The oldest could be no more than twenty-five. Vlad guessed Spencer was in his early thirties. They were told in sign language to form pairs, and to line up in a file by the gate. When they finally set in motion, the clerk led the way, and his assistants, now eight in number and armed with pikes, brought up the rear of the convoy. The clinking of the leg irons reminded Vlad of the scene he had so recently witnessed from the hiding place in his father's wagon train. He understood now how Aśka of Rzeszów, the Polish princess, felt being led in chains to a life of slavery.

15

The Auction Block

It took the company of slaves more than an hour to reach the neighborhood of the *bedestan,* where the auction hall was located. Despite his state of weakness, Vlad kept a stubborn lookout for Gruya and Michael, whom he expected to see awaiting to ransom him. But when the convoy entered the street ending at the market his hopes sank. Michael and Gruya would have no idea where he'd disappeared. By the time they discovered what became of him, he'd be lost forever in some distant land.

"This isn't the time to be falling apart," Spencer hissed. He grabbed Vlad by the waist and almost lifted him off the ground. "Dealers' agents are everywhere, trying to spot the best bargains among us. You don't want to be marked down as a weakling not worth the lowest price."

At their arrival, the narrow street was teeming with pedestrians on their way to and from the market. Now the shoppers flattened themselves against the walls, holding their sleeves to their noses. The luckier ones managed to step inside shops, and avoid contact with this human vermin. All traffic stopped, and voices could be heard arguing somewhere ahead.

"We must've run into other convoys, all competing for access into the hall," Spencer said.

Vlad feared he might not have enough strength left to make it to the auction block. He raised his eyes to the strip of blue sky visible between the upper floors of the cantilevered buildings that lined the street. *Don't let them take me back to the pen,* he prayed. There was no humility in his heart, only resentment against that God so bent lately on smashing him. While slavery was disheartening, it left some options open. The alternative, as Spencer had pointed out, was the end of the road.

"I've seen that man before," a girl cried in Greek from inside a shop at Vlad's left. He glanced in that direction, and saw the outline of a woman and a child in the recess of the darkened doorway.

"Hush, Bianca," the woman said. She sounded revolted. "You're just imagining you recognize anyone. Besides, these aren't the kind of people you should be noticing, even from a distance."

Shame made Vlad turn his face away, but he continued to listen. The woman and girl's voices felt soothing after the harsh treatment he'd been subjected to for the past twenty-four hours.

"You aren't even looking at the right person, Mother," the girl said, exasperated. "There, to the left. I remember him by his green eyes. He was at the *caravanserai* the day Lady Mara visited her brothers."

The words tore through Vlad's lassitude. The woman and girl were talking about him. His shame increased, and he turned his back to them. The mother switched to a language Vlad didn't understand. Her tone sounded reprimanding, and he imagined she was upbraiding her daughter for unladylike behavior.

The convoy began to move again. After a few steps, Vlad gave in to curiosity and glanced back over his shoulder. The woman had stepped out of the shop, and he recognized her as the person the innkeeper Hussein had called Donatella Loredano. Her face, framed in coppery tresses, had the paleness of a dove's breast. She looked Vlad in the eye with an expression he was at a loss to interpret. Pity? Horror? The sadness he had noticed in her eyes at the *caravanserai* seemed to radiate now with a greater intensity.

His interest in the woman didn't go unnoticed by one of the attendants. He came rushing at Vlad, and poked him in the ribs with the butt of his pike. "Move on, Giaour," he shouted. Donatella flinched, and bit her lip. To Vlad her reaction would've been worth ten such jabs from the attendant. But why was he given this image of beauty to take with him to that cesspool of indignities that was the slave market? God's capacity for inflicting pain was prodigious indeed.

The hall that housed the slave market was lit by gray daylight that filtered through dusty lunettes mounted high on the supporting walls. It was rectangular, and similar in construction to the *bedestan.* Like there, two rows of bays lined the external walls, each bay with its own domed ceiling. But in contrast to the *bedestan,* here the bays were used not as shops but as slaves' holding pens.

Vlad and his companions were herded into such a pen, and were told through signs to sit on the ground in silence. The attendants, pikes at the ready, took positions in front of the bay. At first Vlad was grateful for the opportunity to rest. But as hours went by in waiting, hunger and thirst threatened to sap his last drop of energy. Some of the slaves urinated on the walls, turning the already stale air more acrid.

Vlad glanced at Spencer for comfort, but his companion appeared in a worse state than he. Spencer's head was hanging onto his chest, and his face had acquired a sepulchral tint. Now Vlad felt guilty about drinking the man's water the night before. "Lean on me," he said. Spencer gave him a hazy look, dropped his head onto Vlad's shoulder, and within seconds was asleep.

Somewhere in the center of the hall, a chorus of loud voices indicated that the auction was in full swing. Now and then Vlad saw groups of slaves from adjacent stalls, men and women, being led in that direction.

Then the time came for Vlad's lot to be sold. Zaganos's clerk appeared with an official who counted the slaves, and made notes in a ledger.

"Two aspers per person for the use of the space," the official said, "and a hundred aspers per person in sales tax. That makes three thousand, two hundred, and sixty-four aspers."

"Here's the space-rental fee," the clerk said, and handed the official a handful of silver coins. "I'll settle the taxes after the auction. The way things are going out there, I might have to take back half of this lot."

Vlad and Spencer were in the second group of eight men taken to the auction block. They all crowded onto a platform of about nine square yards, where the auctioneer, a portly man in a dirty robe, began to tout their attributes.

"Each one strong as an ox, built for hard labor." The man waved a shepherd's crook above his head for emphasis as he spoke. "Whether you'll have them break stones in a quarry, row your galley, or dig in your mine, you're guaranteed years of service from these fine young men. Come, boys, take off your clothes, and show your muscles."

Except for Vlad and Spencer, who feigned ignorance, the slaves didn't understand what they were being told. When no one moved, the auctioneer pounced on one of the slaves, ripped open his shirt, tugged at his trousers, then screamed, "Off with your rags." This time the man understood the command and stripped naked. The other slaves followed his example.

When Spencer removed his shirt, a ripple of laughter traveled across the crowd of buyers.

"It's now that my troubles begin," Spencer said in a resigned tone. "I think I might as well say goodbye to you, Prince Vlad."

"How did that goat get among your oxen, Azarian?" someone shouted.

"Did you think we wouldn't notice his condition?" another voice said.

"I've always wanted to get me a living scarecrow," a third voice said, "but was afraid it would eat more seeds than the birds he kept away."

The mockery aimed at Spencer hurt Vlad as much as if it were meant for him.

Zaganos's clerk rushed onto the stage, flustered and apologetic. "It's a mistake, Azarian Efendi," he cried, and shoved Spencer out of the line. "Please forgive me." Spencer tumbled backward off the stage, and the clerk shouted after him, "I'll deal with you later, infidel dog."

"Now turn around," Azarian directed the slaves. When they didn't respond, he grabbed the first man in the row by the arm and swiveled him around violently. Then the other men, including Vlad, showed their backs to the buyers.

"As you can see," Azarian began to say, in his earlier confident tone, then stopped and walked over to Vlad.

"Is this another sleight of hand on your part, Azarian?" someone shouted. "Selling damaged goods, are you?" But this time no one laughed.

Azarian recovered quickly from his surprise at seeing Vlad's savaged flesh. "Here's someone who can take punishment," he said. "I count at least twenty lashes on this young man's back. Who among you would still be standing after such a beating? Yet look at him. Holds himself as if all he had was a few mosquito bites." He turned Vlad to face the crowd. "This boy is a fighter." Then Azarian inserted the crook of his stick into Vlad's mouth, and forced his jaw wide open. "And look, not a tooth missing."

A dwarf with a gray beard and beady eyes climbed with difficulty onto the stage. "No more tricks, Azarian," he said. "I want to see for myself."

Azarian pulled down on his stick, forcing Vlad to bend over. The dwarf inserted a long, yellow-nailed finger into Vlad mouth, and ran it along both his upper and lower teeth.

Vlad fought both the urge to vomit, and the rage that would have him crush the man's skull with a single blow.

"Three ducats," the dwarf said.

The offer drew a groan of protest from Azarian. "You're joking? You know this boy's owner will owe two ducats to the sultan in sales taxes, and me half a ducat as commission."

"Four ducats," someone shouted in Arabic.

A man dressed as a Christian, in dark clothes and a felt cap trimmed with fox, raised a finger, and Azarian shouted in Turkish, excited, "We've got five ducats. Who'll pay six?" He showed the next bid on his fingers for the benefit of the buyers who didn't understand Turkish.

Shout after shout rose from the buyers, adding a ducat to Vlad's price every time. With growing disappointment, he noticed the Christian remained aloof. The most active bidders were three men dressed in clothes distinct from those of the Turks from Edirne. They might be the dealers from Egypt and Syria whom Spencer had mentioned. Ending up as their property would make it impossible for Vlad to ever return to his home. He watched the Christian intently, willing him to make his bid.

"Twelve," Azarian shouted, and still the Christian didn't budge. "Thirteen ... fourteen ... fifteen." Then silence. Azarian glanced around the crowd, then raised both arms in the air, and said, "Fifteen—"

"Twenty," the Christian said in Greek, loud and confident.

Azarian waited a few moments, then shouted, "Sold, for twenty ducats."

Zaganos's clerk rushed to the Christian's side with a servile smile. "Come, Efendi, I'll have the *kadı* register the sale for you immediately."

Vlad put his clothes back on, then followed his new owner and the clerk to a booth where a judge was issuing ownership titles. When he understood he was out of Zaganos's clutches, the tension that had sustained him until then drained away. His legs began to tremble, and his vision dimmed. The ground below his feet seemed covered in fog. "Water," he said, aware his voice was too weak to be heard. "Water." The fog rose higher, and soon all sounds around him became muffled.

An arm came from nowhere and grabbed him by the back of his collar, just as he'd decided to sit on the ground. And a voice he recognized, but didn't know how, said, "I can help you take him home, Your Lordship. You can see he's in no condition to walk by himself." If the "lordship" replied, Vlad didn't hear him.

The familiar voice said, "Offer the clerk two ducats for taxes and your handsome hat as the price for me, my lord. He'll be happy to get rid of me, and you'll be making a great bargain."

Vlad let his knees buckle, and the arm holding him was unable to keep him standing any longer. The stone floor was cool to the touch, and Vlad set his forehead to it. All he wanted now was to sleep.

16

An Impulsive Decision

When Donatella awoke that morning, she had no reason to expect the day would be different from any other. Yet later on, when looking back at this day, she claimed to herself she had a premonition hers and Bianca's lives were about to change dramatically. Like every morning for the past two years, the first thing she did was to cross off another day on the calendar. The countdown had started with one thousand days, and now only three hundred and sixty remained before she'd lose Bianca forever. This ritual stirred up fresh pain in her heart every time. Yet she welcomed it as a reminder she needed to grasp and hold every moment of every remaining day. Then, when all the days had been crossed off, her own life wouldn't matter anymore.

She sat at her dressing table and looked at herself in the mirror. She didn't like what she saw, and wondered, though insincerely, why other people thought she was beautiful. Three hundred and sixty: *three, plus six, plus zero* ... The habit of reducing numbers to a single digit was something she'd acquired as a child. She was told then by a fortuneteller that nine was her lucky number. Now Donatella couldn't remember a single instance when nine had done anything good for her. She was nine years old when her father betrothed her to that Genovese brute, Giovanni Grimaldi. Father was assassinated on the ninth day of the ninth month of 1439. A year ending in nine. Lucky number indeed.

"I've got a surprise for you, Tella," a voice said from behind her. "Something amusing for you to try on." Donatella glanced in the mirror to see the head of her old nurse poking through the dressing room's door. "It will stop you from brooding for a few minutes."

"And why should I stop?" Donatella was becoming increasingly annoyed with Paola's recent determination to cheer her up at all cost. "Will the sand in the hourglass stop draining then?"

"If for no other reason, do it to save your face from aging prematurely." Paola entered the room and began to brush Donatella's hair, as she'd done daily since Donatella was an infant, twenty-six years ago. "Here, see those frown creases on your forehead? They come from dwelling on unhappy thoughts too long."

Donatella had a tiny start at Paola's observation. She leaned closer to the mirror and concluded with relief there was no trace of a crease on her forehead. "I care nothing for my appearance," she said, and averted her eyes from Paola's to hide the lie.

Paola braided Donatella's hair into a broad *coazzone,* and the plait hung to her waist. She then affixed to the back of her head a *trinzale,* and secured the gold cap in place with a *lenza,* rubyadorned string, that crossed her forehead. Donatella would've preferred a simpler hairdo, perhaps just coiling her braid inside a pearl-studded snood. But Paola was adamant that a Venetian lady like Donatella had to follow the smarter Milanese fashion, if she weren't to be laughed at. "Now, get naked," Paola said, "and I'll bring you the surprise."

Paola left the room and returned with a garment of white silk chiffon that Donatella couldn't identify. Bianca walked in just behind Paola.

Donatella regarded herself in the mirror, and thought she'd lost more weight in just the past few days. Her inner thighs were no longer touching, and her hips had become flat. Not something a woman would want to hear being said about her. She expected Paola to point out that all that brooding was robbing Donatella of her plumpness, reducing her feminine charms. Perhaps in this case, Paola would be right. Of course there was no one in Donatella's life to appreciate her charms, but just the same, she made a note to force herself to gain a few pounds. Not to preserve her beauty, she told herself, only to ward off Paola's reproaches.

"What are you doing, Mother?" Bianca shrieked when she saw Donatella getting into the two-legged garment Paola had brought. "You look like Grandfather."

When Donatella saw herself in the mirror she couldn't suppress a giggle. "Ladies' pantaloons? You went through the trouble of bringing me this ludicrous thing just to make me laugh?"

"It's the latest undergarment ladies at the de' Medici court in Florence have taken to wearing," Paola said. She knotted the white satin ribbon fastening the garment's waist. Then she crouched next to Donatella and tied the pantaloons' leggings below the knees with blue ribbons. "You've got loops everywhere so you can change the ribbons' colors every day."

"I want mine to have green and yellow ribbons, Mother," Bianca said.

"Ah, so now that you know the de' Medici ladies wear pantaloons," Donatella said, "this doesn't remind you of your grandfather anymore?" This trifle wouldn't distract Donatella from dwelling on Bianca's unhappy future for long. But if it took her daughter's mind off it for a while, it was worthy of attention. "I'll take you shopping for ribbons this morning, and ask Lady Mara to allow her seamstress to sew you your own pair."

"These pantaloons don't have a slit in the front like Grandfather's did," Bianca said.

"Of course they don't, silly," Paola said. "Your mother doesn't have anything that needs poking out through a slit."

"Then how's she going to—?" Bianca stopped, and covered her mouth with the back of her hand.

"That's right," Donatella said. "How am I supposed to…? With all my other clothes on, too? The *camicia*, the *gamurra*, the *giornea* …"

"And in the winter the *mantello*," Bianca said, and giggled. "By the time you lift up all those things, and unfasten your waist, it might be too late."

Paola scoffed. "If the de' Medici women have figured out how to piss with pantaloons on, you'll do it too, I'm sure. It will just take a bit of planning."

"Will you be wearing a pair too, Paola?" Donatella asked, feigning innocence. She knew well Paola's abhorrence to change when it came to *her* personal habits.

Paola assumed an offended mien, as if she'd forgotten it was she who introduced the article. "Not until someone proves to me the mother of our Savior herself wore such a frivolous thing," she said, and stalked out of the room.

"Come Bianca, get dressed quickly," Donatella said. "If we go shopping we've got to be back before noon. Mara's coming to have lunch with us."

Mara's visits to the lodgings Donatella and Bianca occupied in the Venctian ambassador's palace in Edirne were a source of amusement for them. Mara was a font of information about things happening at the sultan's palace. Especially in the harem, an area of particular interest to both Donatella and Bianca. With the ambassador away on a diplomatic mission to Crimea, the three women had the full use of his palace and staff. This was a more convenient place to meet than Mara's apartment in Murad's palace, where privacy was limited. Donatella had decided to make the most of this circumstance to help her daughter bond with this gracious lady, so when she finally had to leave Donatella, Bianca wouldn't suffer the full impact of the separation.

"When my time comes," Bianca said, "will I also be allowed to visit you outside the palace whenever I want to, like Lady Mara?"

"Go see if Fabrizio is free to chaperon us to the market," Donatella said. How much longer would she be able to avoid answering this question, which occurred to Bianca more and more frequently? Not only would Bianca be forbidden to leave the palace, but Donatella would never be permitted to visit her there.

"Will Uncle Boruele's spies tag along? I hate those two loathsome creatures."

Donatella had never been able to shake off her brother-in-law's footmen, whose job was to keep a perpetual watch on Bianca outside her residence. "We'll just ignore them as we always do."

Fabrizio Garzoni, the Venetian ambassador's majordomo, showed up to accompany Donatella and Bianca dressed as if he expected the onset of winter: black woolen overcoat and fox-trimmed cap. Those garments, coupled with a dignified gait, lent the elderly head steward the gravitas so dear to servants raised to high levels of responsibility.

In the ribbon shop Donatella looked absentmindedly at the merchandise, glad for the fact that Bianca appeared much engaged in choosing her colors. She was still a child, and could be easily diverted. But soon even such innocent outings would be denied her. To think Bianca would become practically a slave ... yes, kept in a gilded cage, but a slave nonetheless.

When Donatella's father took the unusual step of marrying his daughter to someone from a different nation, he didn't think of the possible consequences. Didn't he know a woman was safe only when protected by bonds of kinship? Away from that protection, the woman was nothing but the plaything of strangers who controlled her life. There was no one in Edirne or Constantinople from among Donatella's clan to protect her. In turn, she was unable to defend Bianca from the man who had sway over her future. What would Father say to learn that his granddaughter's Genovese guardian had bartered her off to a Muslim? Her father, the proud Venetian admiral who'd spent his life fighting Islam on land and sea? He'd cut off his own sword-hand to stop Bianca from becoming the concubine of an infidel.

"Come here, Mother," Bianca called from the shop's doorway, interrupting Donatella's dark musings. When Donatella joined her, Bianca pointed at someone in the street and cried, "I've seen that man before."

The space in front of the shop had become clogged with dozens of slaves being led to the market. None of the men in the convoy had anything remarkable about him to warrant such an outburst on her daughter's part. "Hush, Bianca. You're just imagining you recognize anyone. Besides, these aren't the kind of people you should be noticing, even from a distance."

Bianca stomped her foot. "You aren't even looking at the right person, Mother. There, to the left. I remember him by his green eyes. He was at the *caravanserai* the day Lady Mara visited her brothers."

After she studied the man for a few moments, Donatella switched to *Vèneto* and said, "You mustn't speak your mind in public, Bianca. Especially not in Greek, which some of these people might understand."

The slave Bianca indicated stood out among his companions by the black of his hair. All others were either blond or red-haired, like people from the north. Young, and about Donatella's height, the man appeared well built, though sickly and terribly unkempt. The back of his shirt was torn in places and stained with brown spots. But she saw him only in profile, and couldn't tell the color of his eyes.

From his beardless face, she guessed the man was about sixteen. Her motherly instinct, sensitized by thoughts of Bianca's slave-like future, made her insides reel. How painful it must be to find yourself torn away from your parents.

The slave column set in motion and, drawn by compassion, Donatella stepped outside the shop to observe its progress. The youth turned his head, and locked eyes with her: eyes of such a luminous green as she'd never seen. No wonder Bianca remembered him.

One of the guards shoved the butt of his pike into the slave's ribs, but the youth didn't flinch. For a few seconds his eyes flashed an emerald light into hers, then he turned and disappeared among the bobbing heads. She was seized by an inner frenzy, as if she were expected to do something important, with time running out too fast. But do what? She became agitated, wrung her hands, and bit her lip, while Bianca watched her quizzically.

"Are you unwell, Signora Donatella?" Fabrizio said. He'd kept himself out of sight all this time, and now joined Donatella and

Bianca outside the shop. "Would you like me to hire a litter to take you to the residence?"

The moment Donatella laid eyes on Fabrizio she knew what she had to do, and she pressed her coin purse into his hand. "Take this, Fabrizio. There is enough gold here to—" Her breathing became so fast she had to pause. Anticipation of what she was about to order Fabrizio to do made her mind race erratically. An incomprehensible feeling came over her, akin in intensity to that experienced when Bianca was born. It was as if a flower had just sprouted in the parched desert her life had become. "Follow this convoy to the market and purchase that young man for me."

"Mother," Bianca shrieked, and threw her arms around Donatella. "I was hoping you'd do it."

"Which man?" Fabrizio said, flummoxed.

"You'll recognize him by his black locks and green eyes," Donatella said.

"Forgive me, Signora Donatella, but I can't leave you and Bianca unattended in a place like this."

"You know Uncle Boruele's two spies are somewhere nearby, as always," Bianca said. "They won't let any harm come to us."

"There is a reward in it for you, Fabrizio," Donatella said, and pushed the majordomo into the lane. "Don't return without him."

"What are you going to do with that slave, Mother?" Bianca said when they left the congested area of the market. She could hardly keep pace with Donatella, who was almost jogging.

"We need to hurry so we don't make the empress wait for us," Donatella said, but she knew her quick pace had nothing to do with Mara's visit. Donatella and the sultan's wife had been close friends for over two years, and there was no formality to their relationship. She hurried because ... she didn't know why, but it felt exhilarating.

"I hope you're planning to keep him." Bianca grabbed Donatella's hand and forced her to walk slower. Grimaldi's two footmen, who'd fallen behind, caught up with them, giving signs of alarm at the women's unusual haste.

Keep him? A wave of hot air brushed Donatella's cheeks, as if she'd raked dormant embers. That wasn't why she asked Fabrizio to buy him. Or, was it? "I haven't thought about—it all happened so fast—I wanted to save him—" *I'm blabbering like a fool.* She took a few breaths, then said, "We'll take him to Constantinople, and put him on a ship to wherever he came from." As an afterthought she added, "He seems to be from a noble family."

At the ambassador's palace they found Mara's four eunuchs crouching by the gate. The empress was waiting for them on the second-floor loggia facing the street.

"Whatever happened to you, Tella? I can't tell if you're thrilled with something, or scared witless, but you aren't yourself today."

"Oh, it's nothing, Mara. I'm just flushed from hurrying home to receive you. Sorry I'm a bit late."

"Save your fibs for a more gullible audience." Mara smiled knowingly, and turned to Bianca. "You'll tell me what made your mother run, won't you?"

"Mother bought a new slave," Bianca said.

"But you have a palace full of them back home in Constantinople," Mara said. "What made you—?"

"A very handsome young man," Bianca said.

Of course Donatella was going to tell Mara what happened, but the way Bianca put it sounded wrong. "It has nothing to do with him being either young or handsome." Trying to correct the impression she was being too defensive, she added, "Young he is ... but handsome? I have no idea. I saw him only for a moment, and from a distance."

Mara giggled. "Oh, he can't be too plain if all it took was one look before you decided to buy him."

"Mother's going to send him back to his home," Bianca said.

Though her daughter only repeated what she'd been told, Donatella felt a tinge of distress at hearing her. Bianca's pronouncement seemed to turn the mere possibility of sending the slave away into an irreversible decision.

The ambassador's kitchen staff served them lunch on the loggia.

"Because it's too hot inside," Donatella explained when Mara inquired why they were braving the flies and wasps in the open air. The true reason was so Donatella could keep a lookout for Fabrizio. *Why is he taking so long to return with my—?* She found it difficult to think "slave," though the young man was that until she emancipated him. She'd taken the seat that gave her a view of the street below. Throughout the meal, she kept glancing discreetly over Mara's shoulder in that direction.

To Donatella's relief, Mara soon forgot about the slave story, and talked only about the upcoming war with the Hungarians over the invasion of Wallachia.

"Why are you so concerned, Mara?" Donatella said. "Your father's peace treaty with the sultan isn't in question. And Serbia isn't on the path of the armies going to Wallachia, is it?"

"True, but I'm fearful for the Christians who are already Murad's subjects," Mara said. "They suffer great hardships in times of war, even when the action takes place hundreds of miles away."

"But the sultan promised to protect them against abuse."

"Not even my husband can prevent hotheaded Akincis and Janissaries from terrorizing Christians on their way to the front." Then Mara related some horrific incidents of this nature that occurred in the previous war. "I'll ask Khalil Pasha to place military guards at churches and monasteries along the path taken by the army."

Donatella loved Mara's dedication to the welfare of the Christians fallen under the Ottoman domination. She never tired of learning how Mara used her influence with the sultan to rebuild a burned-down church, release a jailed priest, or intercede on behalf of a monastery whose vineyards had been vandalized by Muslims. But today Donatella had mind only for the mission she'd entrusted to Fabrizio. If he wasn't back yet, had he failed? Too much time had passed for things to have gone well. Awareness that she fretted exceedingly gave her a twinge of guilt. Perhaps her gesture wasn't as altruistic as she claimed it to be.

"Look, Mother," Bianca cried, "Fabrizio's coming."

Donatella jumped from her seat, mindless of displaying excessive interest. The majordomo had indeed appeared at the end of the street. But he was alone, and oddly, had lost his cap. She gripped the bannister to steady herself. Fabrizio did fail, and the young man was now on his way to a distant place from whence he'd never return.

Then another man appeared at the end of the street, unsteady under a heavy load. The rags he wore gave him the appearance of a beggar, but his leg irons showed him to be a slave.

"It's him, Mother, your new slave. Someone's carrying him on his back." Bianca clapped her hands and ran off the loggia.

Donatella followed her, skipping two stairs at a time despite her ample gowns. Mara came after them, without haste. Moments later the three women were crowding the doorway while the servants looked on, whispering to each other.

"The young man is affected with a great fever, Signora Donatella," Fabrizio said when he reached the entrance. "I'm afraid he might not make it if a doctor doesn't attend to him immediately."

"Please speak Greek, not *Vèneto,* in the presence of the empress, Fabrizio," Donatella said. She wasn't so much concerned with Mara's feelings as with buying time to steady her own heartbeat. "Is he unconscious?" She heard her voice tremble, and became aware of everyone's stares. To distract them she turned to the porter. "Who are you?"

"Spencer, your obedient slave. And please, someone give me a hand with my load. I'm about to collapse myself."

"I shall explain, Signora Donatella," Fabrizio said.

"Your new charge is in need of immediate care, Tella," Mara said, in the authoritative tone of someone accustomed to dealing with the sick. Then she addressed two footmen standing nearby. "Remove his leg irons and neck-ring. Then take him to the laundry room and clean him up."

Her friend's resolute attitude stirred deep gratitude in Donatella, but she said nothing for fear of betraying feelings best kept hidden.

"I'll send for my husband's *hekim,*" Mara said. "I don't trust those so-called doctors who treat fever by hanging a gecko around the patient's neck."

In the hour that passed before Hekim Solomon arrived, Donatella and Mara learned from Fabrizio what happened at the market. Spencer, whom Donatella ordered to bathe and put on clean clothes, told them who their patient was.

"A real prince?" Bianca said with a happy squeal. "Mother predicted he'd be of a noble family."

Mara said, her tone pensive, "King Dracul's at the heart of the upcoming war in Wallachia. I wonder how his son came to be sold off as a slave."

17

Pharmacopeia

Vlad. What an unusual name. Vlad of Basarab, Prince of Wallachia. Donatella had only a vague notion of where that country was located. As she listened to Mara's geographical explanation, Donatella conjured the lands north of the Danube River as dangerous, mysterious, beguiling ... lands of steep mountains and dark forests defended by men with fierce eyes and raven hair flying in the wind.

"The patient's condition is grave," Solomon said when he returned from examining Vlad, who'd been laid in a spare chamber on the second floor. "His lashing wounds have become infected. I've bled him, and applied an ointment of egg white, rose oil, and turpentine to his back. It's the strongest medicine I have, but I fear it might be too late for it."

Donatella gasped and clutched Mara's arm.

"What about *theriac,* Hekim Solomon?" Mara said. "I've heard it can do miracles."

The doctor made a disparaging grimace. "The sick man's humors are too severely unbalanced to treat with snake balms."

Solomon left, and Mara followed him soon, with the promise to return in the morning. Alone with Bianca, Donatella felt drained of energy, yet all she wanted was to see Vlad. She leaned on Bianca's shoulder as they mounted the stairs to the *piano nobile*. They found Spencer there, trying unsuccessfully to make Vlad drink water from a leather costrel. Vlad's eyes were open but he seemed unaware of the people around him.

"You're too clumsy." Donatella motioned Spencer out of her way, then handed him a handkerchief and said, "Pour some water on this." She sat on the bed next to Vlad, and let a few drops fall from her kerchief onto his parted lips. She noticed how regular and white his teeth were, how full his lips. At close range his eyes shone with an intensity that singed her, and she closed her eyes. But only for a moment.

"I want to give him water too," Bianca said.

Donatella lifted Vlad's head slightly, and his touch sent a delicious ripple through her body. His hair, wet from the wash, was heavy and smooth, like silk yarn.

Bianca dangled the wet kerchief above Vlad's mouth. When he swallowed she gave a shriek of delight. Donatella encouraged her with a nod to go on, wishing her own pleasure at holding Vlad never to end. Except for her father, she'd never touched a man's hair before. Her late husband wasn't the kind of man who'd tolerate a woman's hand on his head. Besides, she was close to him only once, on their wedding day, and it was he who did all the touching then. She never saw him again.

Was Vlad destined to also step into her life for only a moment, then die? She had no reason to care for him more than for any other sick person. Yet the thought that he might perish made her heart feel like a mouse trapped in an owl's claw.

"I heard the *hekim*, Signora Donatella," Spencer said in Italian, "and I think he's wrong. All that talk about humors might be fine. I'm not schooled in such matters to pass judgment. But I believe what Prince Vlad needs is some of that *theriac* Lady Mara mentioned."

Until then, Donatella had paid scant attention to this gaunt, red-haired man. She knew that without him Fabrizio would've had difficulty transporting Vlad to the residence. For that, she intended to give Spencer his freedom, and send him away with a few coins in his pocket. But his interest in Vlad's wellbeing made Spencer gain an unexpected value in her eyes.

"How is it you speak Italian so well?" she said.

"I was captured by Calabrian corsairs when only eight years old, and lived with them for a decade."

Vlad gave a moan of agony and rolled onto his stomach. The back of his new shirt was streaked with blood. Spencer lifted it gently and exposed Vlad's wounds, some of which had ruptured from over-swelling.

Donatella and Bianca gasped loudly, in unison.

"I've seen beatings like this, and they indeed can be deadly when the flesh becomes corrupted. But with a powerful salve, like the—"

"Where can I get *theriac*?" Donatella said, with urgency.

"I know a compatriot of yours who's licensed by the Venice Provveditori alla Sanita to make the drug. Many quacks will sell you fake *theriac* at a low price, but Ser Fioravanti is reputed to use only genuine ingredients." Spencer's confidence breathed new hope into Donatella, and she had all she could do not to hug him.

Shadows had become long and dusky on the street when Spencer led Donatella and Bianca to the Christian Quarter, where Fioravanti's establishment was located. Grimaldi's two spies kept close at their heels, muttering to each other, no doubt suspicious about the purpose of the women's outing. Inside the apothecary, Donatella discovered a collection of exotic objects that both repelled and enchanted her. Fioravanti, dressed in a brown cotton *jubbah*, reigned over a small army of servants occupied with grinding herbs and minerals piled on their workbenches. He was a man of about sixty, with thin lips, a powerful aquiline nose, and an air of unquestionable authority.

"Welcome to my emporium of miracles, Signora Loredano," he said, measuring Donatella up and down with covetous eyes. "I see you're wondering at my dress. I don't usually wear Levantine garb, but when I prepare my annual batch of *theriac* I feel more like an Arab alchemist than a Venetian pharmacist." He spoke much louder than necessary, and Donatella suspected he was hard of hearing.

"You're surprised I know who you are." This time his eyes came to rest on her breasts. "A young widow like you cannot to come to Edirne without a male protector, and hope not to become the subject of gossip."

"Signora Loredano is in a hurry, Ser Fioravanti," Spencer said, and once again Donatella sensed his value to her. "All she wants is to purchase some of your *theriac*."

"We have a friend who's ill," Bianca said. "If we don't hurry with the medicine he might die."

Fioravanti ignored both Spencer and Bianca. Instead he beckoned Donatella to follow him to the rear of the store. They passed shelves laden with ornamented caskets, sacks bulging with spices, and jars seething with live vipers. Not an inch of the walls had been spared from being decorated with rare animal skins and resplendent feathers. Wherever the space opened up between pieces of furniture, it was taken over by stuffed animals, realistically perched on dry branches.

When Fioravanti reached an ebony cabinet secured with a lock, he signaled to Spencer and Bianca to keep their distance. Then he leaned toward Donatella and whispered, loud, as deaf men do, "My eyes tell me that what you need foremost, Signora Loredano, is a remedy for passions of the heart."

Fioravanti's words whipped Donatella across the face, and for an instant she thought of running out of the shop. But she couldn't deny to herself that this overbearing man had diagnosed correctly her condition. Since that morning her heart had gone from its normal state of heavy and downcast, to throbbing with feelings she never experienced before.

With a smug grin, Fioravanti unlocked the cabinet, and handed her a small leather satchel. "This rare powder is called *mumia*. Some charlatans will make it from ground fake mummies that are nothing but dried-up bodies of executed criminals. There is a lot of profit to be made in my trade, if you are an unscrupulous pharmacist."

Donatella recoiled, disgusted, but held on to the satchel.

"I use only genuine mummies imported from Egypt," Fioravanti said, and relocked the cabinet. "I can't begin to tell you the cost of that ingredient. Why, this small amount you've just purchased costs four ducats. But the power—"

"Lady Donatella asked for *theriac*, not *mumia*, Ser Fioravanti," Spencer said, showing that he'd overheard the pharmacist. She threw Spencer a grateful look, and resolved to retain him in her service when she returned to Constantinople.

Fioravanti frowned at being interrupted, but went on. "The power of my *mumia* is legendary. It will cure paralysis, epilepsy, flatulence, incontinence, vertigo, fever madness, and—"

"What will *mumia* do for—?" Donatella checked herself. Saying, "passions of the heart," would be tantamount to admitting she was a fallen woman worthy of condemnation.

"Ah," Fioravanti exclaimed triumphantly. "One pinch of this powder will quench a woman's unwholesome desires for a week." He stared at her, perhaps hoping she'd confirm the presence of those desires in her. When she remained silent, he added, "A thimbleful will make her immune to passion for a year. Turn her heart practically to stone."

Before Fioravanti consented to dispense a jar of *theriac*, he insisted on giving a recitation of the sixty-four ingredients that made up the drug. Throughout the interminable ordeal, his eyes never left Donatella's bosom. The only ingredient she remembered afterward was the flesh of female vipers that had to be killed and dissected according to an ancient ritual. Fioravanti repeated that entry in his list three times, with ferocious relish.

Back at the ambassador's palace, Donatella fought her desire to look on Vlad, for fear she could no longer dissimulate her interest in him. "Administer the salve to Prince Vlad," she ordered Spencer, in a casual tone, "and report his condition to me in the morning." Then she put Bianca to bed, and summoned Paola to her own dressing room.

"I'm not sure *this* is better than brooding," Paola said after she stripped Donatella of her heavy garments.

Donatella avoided her eyes. "And what precisely do you mean by 'this'?"

Paola shook her head and pursed her lips. "When the woman is much older than the man, nothing good comes of it." Then she removed Donatella's chemise, but left her in her new pantaloons.

Only then did Donatella get a sense of how much things had changed since the morning. The day started with laughter and banter prompted by this ridiculous garment. Then Vlad, with his intriguing looks and fighting for his life, appeared, and made the morning levity seem to have occurred in another world.

In bed, she sifted through the day's images, peeling off and discarding the superfluous ones until she was left with only a handful that pulsated with life. There was the fleeting eye contact with Vlad on the street; the sight of him being brought to her, unconscious; his parched lips, burning eyes, glistening hair. Though she knew her intimacy with Vlad was the contrived intimacy between a patient and his caregiver, these images made her quiver with longing for him. Where did these feelings spring from, these "unwholesome desires," as Fioravanti called them?

She reached for the *mumia* on her night table. A single pinch of the drug would put a halt to this—what could she call it if not lunacy? He was too young, she was too old, and they belonged to different worlds with nothing in common. A thimbleful of *mumia* would … but the taste of passion she had never experienced before was too intoxicating, too pervasive for her to banish. At least not yet.

She sprang out of the bed and flung open the window to the interior garden below. A cool wave of lilac-scented air enveloped her. The bushes must have been in bloom for weeks, yet this was the first time she noticed their perfume. She inhaled deeply, then tossed the satchel of *mumia* into the garden and returned to bed, leaving the window open.

18

CARING HANDS

Tap ... tap ... tap.

A repeated, feather-light strike against his teeth plucked Vlad out of a dream in which he was lying on a bed, in a room with a gilded ceiling and curtained windows. The tapping stopped, but he kept his eyes closed, for fear of where he might find himself.

Then again, *tap ... tap ... tap.* He felt a cool spray on the tip of his nose, and concluded he was lying in the rain. He opened his eyes to dim candlelight coming from somewhere at his left, and saw a piece of cloth suspended a few inches above his face. A fresh drop had just formed at the tip of the cloth, and it fell into his mouth. He swallowed, and licked his lips.

"He's awake," a girl's voice shrieked. "Come see, Spencer, Vlad's awake."

The girl's outburst startled Vlad, and he tried to raise himself on one elbow. Pain engulfed his entire back, as if a hot object had lodged under his skin. He let himself fall back where he lay.

"I knew the Devil wasn't ready to receive you, Brother Vlad," Spencer shouted from a few feet away. Then Vlad heard the sound of curtains being pulled open, and the room filled with a bright light that shot needles through his eyes. He was lying on an immense bed, and above him stretched the gilded ceiling from his dream. A girl of about twelve years stood next to him, grinning.

"You aren't ready to get up, but you should be able to sit." Spencer lifted Vlad with great care by his nape. "Stuff those pillows behind him, Bianca, but mind his wounds."

"Where are we?" Vlad remembered the lashing, the slave pen, and the auction, but nothing that followed. He felt his shirtfront for his medallion, and his hand jerked when he didn't find it there.

"I wouldn't let something that precious get tossed away with your old clothes," Spencer said, and dangled the black disk by its leather thong in front of Vlad.

The girl snatched the medallion, and examined it closely. "Oh, look, number nine is carved all around it. My name has nine letters. Bianca Pia. May I keep it as my amulet?"

"Prince Vlad can't part with it," Spencer said, "it's got something to do with his destiny."

Vlad realized he must have spoken in his sleep, and wondered what else Spencer had learned about him. "Girls don't wear amulets with dragons and lions." Vlad pried the medallion out of her hand. "I'll find you a suitable one."

"No," she said, and stamped her foot. "I want this one, and if you won't let me have it Mother will make you do it. She owns you, so everything of yours is hers."

Vlad shot Spencer an inquiring look.

"Bianca's right," Spencer said. "Signora Donatella Loredano owns both you and me."

Loredano. That name brought Vlad back to the evening of his arrival in Edirne, and the beautiful widow with sad eyes. The same woman he spotted near the market on his way to the auction block. How was it possible for her to be his and Spencer's mistress?

"Mother bought you because you're handsome, and Fabrizio bought Spencer because you couldn't walk."

Spencer chuckled. "I've been saved a few times by my strong legs. It's ironic I should now owe my salvation to your weak ones."

"Mother wants to set you free so you can return to your family," Bianca said. "But I want her to keep you as my brother until I'm taken away."

Vlad had heard of people buying slaves only to set them free, in atonement for their own sins. If he were freed, he'd be able to return to the Grand Vizier's palace for one more try at convincing everyone he was the son of King Dracul. "Who's going to take you away?"

"Signora Donatella and Bianca live in Constantinople," Spencer said, "but they are Venetians."

"I've heard Lady Donatella's story recently," Vlad said.

"We're here for the summer to keep Empress Mara company," Bianca said. "Lady Mara teaches me how to be a good concubine."

The girl's shocking statement showed Vlad her imagination was too rich for him to trust a word she said. It meant he shouldn't believe her claim that Donatella planned to set him free either. Would he then have to escape from here, and make his way to the palace as a runaway slave?

"Do you even know what a concubine is?" Spencer said. He sounded as surprised as Vlad.

"My father was Genovese," Bianca said. "He died before I was born, and his will named Uncle Grimaldi my legal guardian. He's the *podestà* of Galata. Have you heard of that town? It's not too big, but Galata controls all the ship traffic through the Bosphorus."

"Your uncle must be very powerful," Spencer said.

"He's got a huge fortune. But Mother says no amount of money is enough for him. That's why he sold me as a concubine to Sultan Murad. So, when I turn thirteen next year, I—"

"Bianca Pia," an angry voice cried. "What possessed you to share family secrets with strangers?"

Vlad saw Donatella standing in the doorway, with knitted brows and fists pressed to her chest. Even in anger, her face was of a beauty that made it hard for him to look elsewhere. Her scolding carried with it the admission Bianca was speaking the truth. There, perhaps, was the root of the sadness that clung to Donatella so tenaciously.

"Has our patient returned from the dead?" said another woman who appeared behind Donatella.

"He still looks feverish, Mara," Donatella said.

The two women approached Vlad's bed.

Mara was dressed in the same black robe and white wimple Vlad remembered from his first sighting of her at the *caravanserai.*

Her face was serious like that of a physician's, but lacked the severity that comes with self-importance.

Mara felt his forehead, then slipped a cold hand through the opening of his shirt. "Your fever has broken, Prince Vlad," she said, then turned to Donatella. "Come see for yourself the miracle *theriac* has wrought in just one night."

In contrast to Mara, Donatella was bareheaded. Her reddish hair parted in the center and draped her ears, before descending to her waist in a thick braid. A black string circled her head and dangled a ruby on her forehead. She wore a blue velvet gown that matched the color of her eyes and framed her upper chest in a square, lace-fringed décolletage.

When Donatella bent over Vlad to test his fever, her breasts pressed invitingly forward and he caught himself staring at them. He narrowed his eyes to conceal his keen interest, and relished the chance to breathe her in at close range.

"He *is* much cooler than last night," Donatella said. Her hand was warm, and she kept it on his chest longer than needed to make that determination. "But you surely don't think he's ready to leave this place."

Vlad felt a thrill, imagining she wanted him longer in her house.

Bianca pushed her way between Vlad and Donatella, and said, "Let me check his fever too." Then she stuck a clumsy hand under Vlad's shirt. "I think he's too sick to travel. Besides, I want you to keep him forever."

"Don't be silly, Bianca," Mara said. "Your mother needs to take Vlad to Constantinople, and return him to his family as soon as possible."

So it was true. His new mistress intended to set him free, but also make him leave Edirne.

"I must remain in this town, Lady Mara," he blurted, and tried to get out of the bed. "My homeland is about to be taken over by enemies, and I'm the only one who can prevent it from happening."

Spencer rushed over and pinned Vlad down to his pillow. That made Vlad's back scream in pain, but he didn't care. He thrashed against Spencer's hold with all his strength, and only gave in when he saw Donatella join her hands, as in prayer, and whisper, "No, no, no."

Mara crossed herself, shaken. "Oh, dear. The infection has spread to his brain."

Donatella eyes opened wide, and she bit her lip. Her concern for his health felt like a tonic to Vlad.

"I'm not in delirium, Lady Mara," he said, much composed now. "The sultan wants to turn Wallachia into a *sanjak,* like Bulgaria, to prevent the Hungarians from taking it for themselves. All of this started because Zaganos Pasha convinced the sultan not to trust my father's faithfulness to the peace treaty."

"The apothecary had another medicine we might want to try," Donatella whispered. She seemed frightened by Vlad's condition. "It's made from ground-up Egyptian mummies, and Fioravanti said it cures fever madness."

"All it would take to restore the sultan's confidence in my father is to have me as his hostage."

At the word "hostage," Mara recoiled and covered her mouth with her hand. Donatella put her arms around her, but kept her eyes on Vlad.

"I tried to surrender to the sultan's *musahib.* That's how I got the lashing and ended up as a slave."

Mara looked doubtful. "I didn't know Tirendaz to be brutal with helpless people. His reputation is quite the opposite."

Although it exhausted him to speak, Vlad recounted the events of the past two days. He omitted only his attempt to spring his father from the Macedon Tower.

Donatella took Bianca into a protective embrace and held her silently for several minutes, eyes shut, oblivious to those around her. Finally she gave Vlad a moist look and said, "As a parent, I can see why your father would lie or even kill to prevent you from becoming a hostage."

Vlad turned his eyes on Mara. "But *you* understand why Father should want the opposite." Mara nodded, and Vlad felt encouraged to continue. "When you married Sultan Murad you became a hostage yourself. But that kept Serbia free from the Turks."

A transformation began in Mara, and she sat on the bed. "So, you believe your surrender would stop the war?"

"It would justify the sultan freeing my father." The prospect of winning Mara's support restored some of Vlad's strength. "And my father's return to Wallachia would render the war with Hungary unnecessary."

"We can't let Vlad fall into your husband's hands, Mara," Donatella said. "Not after what he's done to your brothers."

"Men like Vlad will do what they set their mind to, whether we let them or not," Mara said. She brushed Vlad's cheek with the back of her hand, a pained, faraway look in her eyes. "You say this Turk, Omar, can prove who you are?"

"But wouldn't that also be proof of bad faith against King Dracul?" Donatella said. "If he lied about his son, they'll think he's lying about everything else as well."

"In my husband's absence, it's the Grand Vizier who'll decide how to handle the matter," Mara said. "Khalil Pasha's a pragmatic man. If he can avoid war, he'll overlook a father's attempt to save his son by disowning him."

"Omar should be easy to identify," Vlad said, optimistic again. "He's got a broken nose and a bunch of missing teeth."

"If you're going to meet the Grand Vizier, you must get better first," Mara said. She stood, gave Donatella and Bianca hugs, then headed for the door. "You're fortunate to be in good hands, Prince Vlad."

"What will happen with Vlad if they do accept him as a hostage?" Bianca said. "Do we still get to keep him?"

"Please suggest they ask about Omar around the dervish lodges," Vlad called after Mara. "I heard him say he intended to join their brotherhood."

Vlad passed the rest of the day between intervals of restless sleep and hazy wakefulness. Despite Spencer's *theriac* regimen, the fever returned in wave after wave. Bianca applied cold compresses to his forehead under her mother's supervision, and fed him spoonsful of hot soup. In the late afternoon Mara's messenger arrived, with the news she had persuaded the Grand Vizier to search for Omar, and that a dozen çavuşes, palace sergeants, had begun to scour Edirne for him. The news made Vlad ebullient, but had the opposite effect on Donatella and Bianca.

"You'll go to the palace and won't come back," Bianca said. "Then soon you'll forget us."

"Forget? Never," Vlad said, looking Donatella in the eye. *One cannot forget such a face.*

"I'm afraid for what they'll do to you," Donatella said. She took the compress from Bianca and refreshed it in the washbasin. Then she sat next to Vlad and applied the wet cloth to his forehead. "The Turks keep their important hostages in the Amasya fortress. And, from what I've heard, in deplorable conditions."

"Once my father reaches Wallachia I'll escape, and return home," Vlad said.

Donatella shook her head, and gave him a look charged with pity. "Amasya is five hundred miles deep in Asia. Nobody escapes from there."

"Lady Mara said her brothers were only *suspected* of trying to escape," Bianca said, "and still were punished cruelly."

"And even if you succeeded, won't Murad ask your father to return you to him?" Donatella said.

"With the invasion in Wallachia repelled the sultan will forget about me."

Donatella said, "Murad never forgets what's his."

From her toneless voice and darkened expression, Vlad guessed this had to be an allusion to Bianca's fate.

As if to confirm his suspicions, Bianca said, "I sometimes pray God to take the sultan's mind, so he'd forget about *me*."

Unexpectedly Donatella's face crumpled, and she buried it in her hands.

"Don't cry, Mamma," Bianca said, and threw her arms around Donatella's neck.

Embarrassed, Vlad looked around for Spencer, hoping to share the awkwardness of the moment with him. But his friend was sleeping in a chair tipped against the wall. Donatella's crying didn't cease, and now Bianca began to cry as well. "Isn't there a way out of the deal Grimaldi made with the sultan?" he said, uncomfortable with prying into such private matters, but at a loss of what else to say.

It took a few minutes for Donatella to recover. She dabbed her tears with a lilac handkerchief, then hugged Bianca to her bosom. The girl quieted too.

"It's all my fault," Donatella said. "The Venetian ladies in Constantinople didn't want my friendship because I was married into a Genovese family. And the Genovese ladies hated me for being Venetian. I succumbed to melancholy and loneliness."

Vlad remembered the innkeeper Hussein's explanation of how Donatella was used as a pawn in an attempt to broker peace between Genoa and Venice.

"My brother-in-law is well connected at Murad's palace, so I asked him to introduce me to Mara. It turned out she was lonely too, being the only Christian among the hundreds of women in Murad's household. We became good friends, and I began to visit her in Edirne frequently."

"And it was on one of those visits that Murad noticed Bianca," Vlad said. He guessed the rest of the story. "When the sultan wants something, he gets it. Was that it?"

"It's as if I led my daughter to perdition with my own hand," Donatella said. Vlad thought she'd break down again, but she kept her composure. "Grimaldi signed a contract promising Bianca to Murad without asking my consent."

"Uncle Boruele wanted to place me into a monastery until the time came. Mother gave him a third of her dowry so he'd let me stay with her until the end."

"Couldn't you return to Venice?" Vlad said. "Neither Murad nor Grimaldi could reach you there."

"By law, Grimaldi was able to keep one-third of my dowry when my husband died. He extorted another third from me, just as Bianca said. The last third I've got is tied up in my Constantinople residence, and a few shops there. Without money, I'd be sentenced to beggary in Venice. And if Grimaldi found out I tried to liquidate my estate, he'd know what we're up to, and would take Bianca away from me on the spot."

"Grandfather left me a dowry in Venice," Bianca said. "But Uncle Boruele's people are watching my every step, so Mother can't send me away either. If he even just suspected she tried, he'd lock me up in the monastery."

"As a condition for letting Bianca stay with me, Grimaldi forced me to take four of his servants into my household," Donatella said. "Two maids take turns keeping an eye on Bianca inside the residence. And two footmen follow her every step when she leaves it."

"They travel with us wherever we go," Bianca said.

"But there's got to be a way to deceive them, and get away," Vlad said.

Donatella and Bianca exchanged a conspiratorial look.

"Mother had a plan, but it failed." The corners of Bianca's mouth sagged with remembered disappointment.

Donatella glanced at the door, then assumed a secretive tone. "A former sea captain of my father's is now in my employ. He agreed to take Bianca to Venice, if I found a way to get her onto his ship. Everything was arranged with an aunt of mine for Bianca's reception there."

"Last summer Mother had a secret rope ladder installed on the seawall below our palace," Bianca whispered. "And Captain Andrea sent a sailor up the ladder to take me to his galley, without Uncle Boruele's spies being the wiser."

"We were in the garden one evening," Donatella said. "I sent Grimaldi's maid into the house to fetch a blanket, so the sailor could spirit Bianca away in the meantime. But five rungs down the ladder Bianca panicked, and he had to bring her back up. Our plot was nearly discovered because of her shrieking."

A knock on the door saved Vlad from having to utter some platitude as comfort to the two women. One of Mara's eunuchs entered and handed Donatella a written message. She read it and turned pale.

"They found Omar," she said, barely loud enough for Vlad to hear her three feet away. "Khalil Pasha will question the two of you in the Imperial Council tomorrow, and you'll have the chance to tell your story."

The threat that loomed like an apocalyptic boulder over Wallachia was about to be rolled back, just because he'd refused to give up. This was reason to celebrate, but his joy was anemic. Success of his enterprise also meant Vlad would never see Donatella again. He read the same thought in her eyes, and his heart filled with something that had no name for him. Something that hurt, and gratified at the same time.

19

Broken Loom

"I don't want you touching my loom," Omar's mother said, when she saw him heading across their courtyard for the shed where she used to weave her *kilim* rugs. "Last time it broke down your father tried to fix it, and it hasn't worked since then. You're just as clumsy with such things as he was. I only trust Zekaï to work on it." She let go of her apron's tail, and shuffled over to bar his way. A handful of turnips fell out of the apron and rolled onto the ground.

In the past every mention of his father, who died a year ago, would have been accompanied by a bout of lamentations and tears on his mother's part. Now her mind was taken entirely with her youngest son. His name was the first word out of her mouth when Omar came home. "Zekaï?" she cried. "Where's my baby?" She didn't ask about Sezaï or Redjaï. Nor did she notice that Omar had all his front teeth knocked out and his nose broken.

Omar had intended to tell his mother the truth from the beginning. On the trip home from Wallachia, he rehearsed often the phrase he'd use on seeing her, so he wouldn't break down: *All three of my brothers have been martyred, and are now with Allah and the prophets*. But as his mother stood there on the threshold of her cottage, and looked eagerly past him for his youngest brother, Omar faltered. "Zekaï is still in Wallachia." The truth he uttered was gutted of meaning and hid a lie inside.

"Why did you leave him behind?" She stared at Omar incredulous and angry, giving no sign she saw the yellowish bruises under his eyes. "You promised me—"

"He's with Redjaï and Sezaï." This was another lying truth.

"Your father never parted from members of his band. I knew you weren't made to be an Akinci leader. When Zekaï matures a little more he will—"

His mother's cantankerous reception, so different from what he needed, unsettled Omar deeply. He'd been home for only a few minutes, after an absence of several months, yet he had decided to leave the cottage and spend the day at the Mevlevi Dervish convent. Although he didn't understand the deeper meaning of the whirling dervishes's *sema,* ceremony, their dancing, singing, and recitations brought him a peace he couldn't have hoped for.

When he'd returned home that night, his mother was asleep. But the next day she started all over again with, "Zekaï this," and "Zekaï that." That day, Omar had to remind himself that, "Heaven lies under the feet of mothers," not to snap with irritation.

He gathered the fallen turnips, put them back into his mother's apron, then pushed her gently aside. He pondered carefully every word he'd say, so he wouldn't actually lie. Lying raised a black cloud between Allah and the believer. The twisted truths Omar told his mother would likely raise a cloud too, but only a white one, he hoped. "You wanted to make Zekaï a new prayer rug, Mother." It was easier for him if he didn't look at her, so he went into the weaving shed and closed the door halfway. "Best you make that rug now, while Zekaï's still in Wallachia with his brothers. That way it will be a surprise when it's done." *True, a surprise, but only to you, Mother.*

Omar didn't know much about looms, but he could see the upper beam was broken. It seemed his father used a cheap piece of wood when he replaced the original beam, and it cracked under the tension of the warp. The lower beam, the shed stick, and the leash rod were intact. So if he could replace the broken piece, the loom should become functional again. "I'll get it working, Mother," he said, and waited anxiously to hear her reply. If she busied herself with weaving Zekaï's rug, she might stop asking questions about him for a while. Then Omar wouldn't have to think out new white clouds. "I'll replace the broken beam with one made of poplar wood, so it will last forever."

"And how are you going to pay for the poplar, since you came home without a *manger* from your raid?"

Of course, the moment he lost his cargo of slaves in Wallachia, Omar knew money would become an acute problem. That's why the first person he visited upon his return to Edirne was Hajji Mustafa, the wealthy merchant who'd lent him money for the raid. Mustafa was an old friend of Omar's father who could be trusted with the secret of an illicit raid into Dar al-Sulh. When he heard of the disaster that befell Omar and his brothers, Mustafa was apt to extend Omar's time for the repayment of the loan. And, hopefully, lend him a bit more money to tide him over until his next raid.

As Omar anticipated, Mustafa was full of praise for Zekaï, Sezaï, and Redjaï. "True mujahideen, your brothers," he'd said. "Just like the Gazis of the old days." Then he went on to quote the Hadith. "Allah is sponsor of him who goes forth on the road of Allah. If he isn't killed, he shall return home with rewards and booty."

"Well, that's the problem, Mustafa Efendi," Omar said. "I wasn't killed, and did return. But I lost my brothers, my booty, my wagon, my weapons, everything.... So, the money I owe you—"

"The Prophet, peace be upon him, tells us, 'Being killed in the road of Allah covers all sins, but the sin of debt'."

Omar felt humiliated having to grovel in front of this man, but had no choice. "The Qur'an also commands, 'If the debtor is in dire straits, then let there be postponement until he is in ease'."

"It's funny how the borrower always remembers the Qur'an when he can't repay his debt." Mustafa gave a dry cackle. "I heard you returned with three saddled horses. That will cover half of what you owe me. For the rest I'll wait a few months. Allah is merciful."

When Omar raised the question of a new loan, Mustafa shaped his lips into a beak, and shook his head with determination. So Omar had to sell the horses and pay down his debt. He consoled himself with the thought that he couldn't have fed the animals anyway.

"Don't pretend you can't hear me," Omar's mother shouted, then poked her head through the shed's door. "Not a *manger* to your name. Your father would be ashamed of you."

Oh, why must you invoke Father's memory to hurt me, Mother? She knew how much her son craved his father's respect, even now that he was gone, and often used that knowledge to lash at Omar. He felt like smashing the loom to get back at her. But she was right this time. Father would be ashamed of him. Not for failing to bring home booty, but for losing his three brothers to a couple of boys just out of childhood. Were his father alive, he'd disown Omar.

"Don't worry about money, Mother," he said. "We'll soon have more than we need. Just this morning I learned the sultan's *tuğ* has been hoisted in front of his palace, announcing *ghazwa*, a military expedition, against the unbelievers north of the Danube. I'll return from war with enough silver to put a new roof on the cottage, and even buy you a flock of sheep."

"Zekaï promised me a donkey, so I won't have to walk to the market with my bad knees...."

There you go again about Zekaï. "Please go away, Mother, and let me work." He shut the door all the way, and took a closer look at the loom's broken beam. Perhaps he could fashion a new one from some scrap of wood, as his father had done, until he'd have the money for a piece of hardwood. Now that war was imminent, he'd started to emerge from his depression. The Prophet promised that war on the path of Allah meant booty. But more important, this war also meant an unexpected chance for Omar to return to Wallachia. If Allah wanted him to avenge his brothers, Omar would find that green-eyed Shaytan, Dracula, rip out his bowels, and feed them to the stray dogs of Târgoviște.

Omar labored on the loom all afternoon. At first he removed a picket from the fence, and fashioned the pine wood with his knife into a member identical to the broken beam. Next, he strung up a fresh warp of cotton yarn, and made it just taut enough so his mother wouldn't complain. But not so taut that the beam would bow, and snap.

As he worked, his mind wandered back to the three days and nights he spent the week before at the Mevlevi convent. He'd returned there determined to begin his novitiate that would keep him sequestered in the convent for one thousand and one days. Enough time for Mother's pain to let up, when she learned what really happened to her other three sons. Omar's pride still smarted from being turned away by the Mevlevis, as not worthy of joining their order. But he knew they were right.

His sojourn at the convent had started well enough. Arif, the spiritual guide assigned to Omar, took him to the ceremonial hall and explained to him the elements of the *sema*.

"Music, recitation, and dance are the essential requirements for the attainment of the ultimate spiritual devotion and ecstasy," Arif said. He then revealed the meaning of the dervishes' clothes, incantations, and dance movements. "Now, when the ceremony begins, you'll see it as the manifestation of our mystic dedication to seeking the path to eternal existence. Absorb it as a recognition of Allah through the revealed knowledge of the Absolute. Even though beautiful in all its aspects, don't watch the *sema* like someone does a puppet show for amusement at a fair."

"Once I become a dervish, how soon will I reach a mystical union with Allah?" Omar said.

Arif regarded him sternly as if searching the meaning behind Omar's question. "Mevlâna has taught us, 'Only death is full union with Allah, and the day of our death is our wedding day'."

That evening Omar awaited the beginning of the *sema* with the anticipation of a boy taking his first meal outside the harem, with the men of the family. First, flutists, singers, and drummers arrived, and took seats on a dais in the musicians' gallery. They were followed by dervish dancers, who lined up on both sides of the hall. Omar was thrilled to decode the symbolism of their clothes, which before Arif's explanation he regarded simply as the order's uniform. The dancers' brown mantles represented their graves; the white shirts and flaring skirts signified their shrouds. Finally, their truncated, conical hats were the headstones of their tombs.

The *sema* began when Sheikh Bedreddın seated himself on the floor opposite the musicians' gallery, on a red pelt that stood for the Sufic throne. First, the chanters intoned a eulogistic litany of the prophets. They followed that with a laudatory oration to the founder of the order, "Oh blessed Mevlâna, beloved of the Almighty." Then the *ney*, the flute that served as symbol of perfection in existence, issued a long and deep-throated wail expressing longing for the attainment of the Ultimate. Arif glanced inquiringly at Omar, and he nodded to his spiritual guide in humble gratitude for his earlier lesson.

There followed the performers' communal procession around the hall, with the dancers paying homage to the sheikh. Two by two they bowed their heads to him, feet crossed as a form of veneration. Then the sheikh left his pelt throne, and moved to the center of the hall. This was the signal for the dancers to remove their robes, thus freeing themselves from their graves. One by one the dervishes approached the sheikh and kissed his hand, then began to whirl.

Omar still remembered how he felt his breast swell with hope. These men had once been like him, lost in a world of desire and ambition. Now, as each pivoted around his own axis, and whirled around the hall in flawless order, they became the ethereal beings of the esoteric world. He watched their upturned right palms that said, "We receive grace from Allah," and thought he saw Allah's grace pouring down upon the dancers. Then he watched their downturned left palms that signified, "We give Allah's grace to men." Omar *felt* that grace dripping down upon him as he knelt at the edge of the dancers' circle. "They possess nothing, and are nothing but empty vessels," Arif had said. "Their arms are a conduit for Allah's grace that comes upon the earth from the heavens. But their own existence is blotted out in Allah's munificence." How Omar longed to be like them. To have his pain, his rage, and his very existence annihilated through a mystic union with Allah.

The ceremony ended when the sheikh resumed his sitting position on the red pelt. Then the leader of the *sema* read Sūrat al-Fātiḥah, the first chapter of the Qur'an, and the dervishes returned to their cells.

When the hall had emptied, Arif presented Omar to Bedreddın as an applicant for the novitiate. Omar knelt in front of the sheikh and kissed his hand.

"Are you ready to renounce false pleasures?" Bedreddın said. "Greed, ambitions, instinctive desires, falsehood, and hypocrisy?"

"Yes," Omar said with deep sincerity.

"The way of the Prophet is the way of love. Love is the greatest guide on the mystical path, the only guide to spiritual enlightenment."

This was a troubling notion to Omar. Wasn't he supposed to hate the infidel without reservation? And the killer of his brothers above all? Bedreddın seemed to be waiting for an acknowledgment from him before continuing. Omar thought about his love for his mother, his brothers, and the memory of his father. Then he nodded with conviction.

"Mevlâna said, 'Be not without love that you be not without life.' Are you prepared to melt like sugar in the ocean of mystical devotion to Allah?"

Omar loved Allah unconditionally, so he nodded again.

"Rest your head on my knee," Bedreddın said. Then he took a *sikke*, dervish hat, blessed it, and placed it on Omar's head. "This is your first step on the road to becoming a dervish," the sheikh said. "It's a long and tortuous journey that only those with true love in their heart are able to complete." Then he dismissed Omar with a kind wave of his hand.

Arif took Omar to a niche by the kitchen door. There he was given a donkey pelt to sit, eat, and sleep on. "For the next three days you mustn't move from this spot, except to relieve yourself in the wee hours, before the others rise. From here you'll note everything that goes on in the kitchen, where you'll be spending the one thousand and one days of your penitential retreat. These three days, you'll eat and drink only what's put in front of you. And you'll observe absolute silence."

"What will happen after the third day?" Omar said.

"If you prove to be of pure intentions, your penitential retreat will begin in earnest. If not, you must leave the convent, and never return."

Doubts began to assail Omar from the first night. Not about his purpose, as his desire for enlightenment was genuine. Nor about the hardships of the novitiate, for his life of an Akinci had accustomed him to worse. But doubts over abandoning his mother for nearly three years. She'd lost already three sons. Did Allah really mean to deprive her of the last one? Soon pity for his mother led to a renewal of his hatred for the man who was the cause of all his misery: Dracula.

Omar tried to observe the workings of the kitchen as he'd been instructed, but hatred blurred his vision. At night it kept him awake and made his donkey pelt feel like a bed of sharp stones. When he awoke on the third morning and went to relieve himself, he found that his shoes had been turned to point outward. He understood he'd failed the test. His hatred must have poked its thorns through his cloak of deceit, and betrayed him as unworthy of becoming a Mevlevi dervish. He abandoned his *sikke* on the donkey pelt and slunk away with stinging eyes, before those who were supposed to become his brethren rose for the morning prayer.

A loud knock on the shed's door tore him from his brooding. Night had fallen and the room was steeped in darkness. He felt his way to the door, while the knocking continued.

"Come out Omar," someone shouted. "The sultan's çavuş is looking for you."

When he opened the door, the light of several torches blinded him for an instant.

"Are you Omar, the Akinci who has returned recently from Wallachia?"

Omar dropped the knife he still had in his hand, and took a step back. How could the sultan's men know such a thing? Except for his mother and Hajji Mustafa, no one knew where he and his brothers had gone. Now that his eyes had adjusted to the light, Omar recognized the uniforms of the men in front of him. Two of them were Janissaries, and one was a palace sergeant. To send a çavuş and two soldiers for a simple man like Omar was highly unusual. The palace must have found out about his raid in Wallachia, and intended to hold him to account.

"What does anybody care where I returned from?" he said. He tried to project self-confidence, even belligerence. "I'm a free man, not the sultan's slave, like you. I go and come as I please."

If the reason for him being investigated was just a rumor about his raid, all he had to do was deny it. They'd question him for a while, then let him be. But if the fuss was caused by an official complaint from the Wallachian court, the sultan was bound to make a show of conducting a full investigation. That could end disastrously for Omar. He'd heard of an Akinci being sawed in half as punishment for raiding a Serbian village belonging to King Brankovich. This concept of Dar al-Sulh, that gave protection to the infidel against the true believers, was certainly an invention of the Shaytan.

"You'll come with us to the palace now," the çavuş said, "then in the morning you'll learn why the Grand Vizier wants to know about your trip to Wallachia."

This was the end. If the Grand Vizier was involved, Omar's life wasn't worth the broken beam he'd just replaced. His mind thrashed and screamed with thoughts of escape, like a bird trapped in a drainpipe. He could shove these men to the side and dash away into the night. Hide somewhere until the town gates opened in the morning, then melt away in the countryside. But the thought of his mother finding herself completely alone and destitute made his legs feel like two millstones. *Maybe the Grand Vizier will take pity on Mother and spare my life.*

Meek, but seething with hatred, Omar let himself be led out of the yard.

20

Imperial Council

The man who came to fetch Vlad for his appearance in front of the Imperial Council was Ismail, Tirendaz's secretary. He had with him two porters with a stretcher.

"I would've expected you to bring a squad of Janissaries to prevent me from running away," Vlad said, "not a stretcher for me to lounge on." He'd been waiting by the gate of the Venetian ambassador's palace, in Fabrizio and Spencer's company.

"It was Lady Mara's contention that you couldn't walk," Ismail said. "To hear her say it, you were broken like a bundle of twigs stepped on by an ox. It didn't sound like there was enough left in you to run away."

Vlad stretched out his arms demonstratively. "As you can see, I'm as unbroken as you saw me three days ago."

"It seems that way." Ismail circled Vlad, and whistled in admiration. "Unbroken and dressed like an Italian patrician. Ruffled collar shirt, doublet, breeches, hose, soft leather boots. Why, you could pass for the Venetian ambassador himself." They both laughed, and took off for the sultan's palace, after Ismail dismissed the porters.

Vlad walked with the purposeful step of someone on an urgent errand. Until they reached the end of the street he kept his head high, his chest stuck out, and his back straight, despite the pain that posture caused him. He knew Donatella and Bianca were watching from the loggia. When they turned the corner Vlad relaxed his stance, and slowed his pace. He caught Ismail smiling furtively.

"For someone so determined to give the impression he's indestructible," Ismail said, "you're certainly going to great lengths to self-destruct."

"Wouldn't you do what I'm doing if you could reverse the occupation of your homeland by the Turks?"

Ismail cast a worried look over his shoulder. "That's a dangerous question. And don't believe you're doing your country any good. All you'll accomplish is to get yourself locked up for years in some forgotten place. Do you know what the prison guards do to someone like you?"

Vlad shrugged. "What shall it profit a man, if he shall save his ass, and lose his soul?"

"Misquoting Apostle Matthew in such a serious matter is just another act of bravado on your part," Ismail said. "You threw yourself into the fire, and, after your father and your tutor got you out, here you go again. Who's going to save you this time from falling into the abyss?"

"'Father' and 'tutor' you said? So now you do believe I am who I claimed to be?"

"Lady Mara is certain you're telling the truth, and I trust her judgment. But as long as your father denies you are his son, Khalil Pasha needs convincing proof to the contrary. He can't take the chance of canceling the war based on a woman's hunch."

"Has Omar been told why he's wanted?"

"That would influence his behavior," Ismail said. "Khalil Pasha wants to observe Omar's unpremeditated reaction when he sees you."

A chilling thought stabbed at Vlad. Might Omar deny knowing him? The Akinci had no reason to admit he'd been on an illegal raid in Wallachia. Indeed, to do so might cost him his life. "What if Omar lies? Will they torture the truth out of him?"

"Odds are in favor of your being tortured first," Ismail said. "Zaganos has accused *you* of lying, while no one has accused Omar of anything."

The optimism that had fueled Vlad since the night before, when Mara's message brought news of Omar, deserted him now. When he and Ismail reached the plaza in front of the sultan's palace, they found it thronged with hundreds of townsfolk.

"In case you wonder, they aren't here to welcome you, Prince Vlad," Ismail said, and gave a little chuckle. His attempt at humor fell flat, and Vlad remained dangling in the claws of apprehension. "It's to gawk at that." Ismail pointed to the top of a pole planted in front of the gate. A four-horsetail standard, Sultan Murad's personal *tuğ*, fluttered there.

"They'd better enjoy this sight now," Vlad said, and made a dismissive gesture at the standard. "As soon as I convince the Grand Vizier of who I am he'll take the *tuğ* down." Vlad hoped his bluster would mask his true state of mind.

"Don't expect to be thanked by these people for causing the war to be cancelled," Ismail said. "The sultan buys army supplies on the open market, and that means good business for many traders in town. He also rents three-quarters of the draft animals the army needs. Camels, oxen, mules. That's more good money to be made off the war."

They worked their way through the crowd, and entered the first court unchallenged by the gatekeepers. Ismail had to be a known figure at the palace. At the second gate, Vlad was frisked for weapons.

"The tradition goes back to the assassination of Murad I," Ismail said. "He was imprudent enough to let an armed Serb get close to him. Now all foreigners entering this palace are searched down to their drawers."

A page met them at the entrance to the audience hall where the Imperial Council was being held. "The trial of Mahmud Pasha is nearing its end, and you're on next," the page said. "Follow me."

Vlad and Ismail were led to an empty spot in the spectators' gallery at the back of the hall. A dozen men were seated there on a low upholstered platform.

"Who are those people?" Vlad whispered.

"Government officials who aren't members of the Imperial Council, but whom the Grand Vizier likes to call upon for advice. Most of them owe their appointments to him, so you might call them his clients."

Against the opposite wall, across from where Vlad sat, stood an empty, velvet-upholstered dais mounted by four steps. Being the highest platform in the hall, Vlad guessed the dais was Murad's throne. He was intrigued that aside from a few embroidered pillows scattered about, there was nothing ornamental in the hall.

At the left of Murad's throne, Vlad recognized the Grand Vizier seated on a floor cushion. Next to him sat an elderly man with a henna-dyed beard, who appeared to have fallen asleep, chin resting on his chest. Vlad nudged Ismail and indicated henna-beard with a motion of his head.

"Ah, that's Sadeddin Hoja, a very important member of the Imperial Council," Ismail said. "The *kadıasker,* the Chief Judge of the empire. A very cruel man, and a close friend of Zaganos. Luckily, your case is considered a political one, so you won't have to deal with him. The *kadıasker* only adjudicates cases involving Sharia."

Vlad recognized Zaganos seated at the Chief Judge's right. This was the man who'd tortured Vlad's father, and treated Vlad as his property to sell. Worst of all, the warmonger who'd set his sights on Wallachia. An impotent rage against Zaganos brought bile to Vlad's throat and tightened his jaw muscles.

Ismail must have noticed Vlad's reaction, and took it for fear. "You've got good reason to be scared of the Third Vizier. He'll do everything he can to keep the war fires burning. By trying to douse them, you've earned yourself a deadly enemy."

"Who's the child next to Zaganos?"

"That's Mehmed, the sultan's youngest son, and Zaganos's pupil. With a *lala* like him no wonder the boy's already preoccupied with nothing but war, though he's barely ten."

Mahmud's trial proceedings dragged on for another hour, conducted in tones barely audible to the people seated in the rear gallery. Occasionally Vlad caught a word like "taxes," "receipts," or "threats." Then, the Grand Vizier said something to his council colleagues, and a pitiful wail filled the air. It came from a man in a red satin robe who knelt in front of the Grand Vizier.

"That's Mahmud Pasha lamenting," Ismail said. "The men at his left are the Iznik delegation, bearing testimony against him. They've denounced Mahmud for having extorted unlawful taxes from the town during his tenure as Governor of Iznik."

No one seemed to pay attention to Mahmud's outburst. Pages carrying sheaves of documents scurried back and forth between the Grand Vizier and other members of the council. When all documents seemed to have been reviewed, Khalil Pasha dispatched a page to the spectators' gallery. The boy returned to the Grand Vizier's place accompanied by a portly man.

"The head of the treasury," Ismail said. "Not a good sign for Mahmud."

The treasurer knelt on the floor next to the Grand Vizier, and inspected a number of documents. When he was done he whispered something to Khalil. Then he turned to Mahmud, his palms open to the sky in a sign of regret. Mahmud burst into a louder wailing than before.

Khalil Pasha waved a black handkerchief, and two çavuşes who'd been waiting by a rear door rushed to Mahmud's side. One of them removed the man's turban, and placed it with visible respect on the carpet. The other slipped the loop of a silk cord around Mahmud's neck, and tugged at it vigorously for about four minutes. The hall fell into silence. When the çavuş stopped, Mahmud's body tumbled softly to the side in a rumpled pile of red fabric. The çavuşes returned to their posts by the door, and four servants carried the dead man's body out by the hands and feet.

A page scampered across the hall and asked Vlad to approach the council. Though he knew Ismail couldn't help him in any way, Vlad wished the secretary accompanied him. To stand *alone* on the spot where Mahmud Pasha had just been executed was intimidating.

"I was told you speak Turkish like one of us," the Grand Vizier said. His voice was resonant, laden with confidence and authority.

Vlad tried to keep his attention on the Grand Vizier but his eyes were drawn involuntarily to Zaganos. The Third Vizier's mouth was set in a severe grimace. Next to him, Mehmed regarded Vlad with curiosity. "I had a good teacher at my father's court, Khalil Pasha."

"Another thing I was told is you received a beating at the hands of some unknown attackers."

"Nothing I couldn't handle, Your Excellency," Vlad said.

"King Dracul has dozens of men trained to speak Turkish," Zaganos said. "He uses them to spy against His Majesty, the sultan. This young man is just one such spy."

This drew a murmur from the people in the rear gallery.

"If this man is a spy," the *kadıasker* said, "his case falls under my jurisdiction. It becomes a matter of Sharia when someone—"

"We aren't here to discuss our allies' intelligence-gathering methods, Sadeddin Hoja," Khalil said. Then he leaned forward, and looked darkly at Zaganos. "We're trying to determine if this man is the Prince of Wallachia, as he claims. If he is, he'll be held as surety for King Dracul's compliance with the peace treaty. If he isn't, the *kadıasker* may take over the case, and judge him as a spy according to Sharia. Now let's proceed with interrogating the witness."

One of the çavuşes ducked out the rear door, and returned a few minutes later shoving a hooded man in front of him. The witness wore a ragged tunic, yellow slippers, and a pair of dirty *shalwars*, patched in mismatched colors on the knees. Vlad recognized Omar's bearing, and when he drew closer, his odor as well. Hate for this murderer, mixed with fear Omar wouldn't acknowledge knowing him, quickened Vlad's heartbeat.

The çavuş turned Omar so he'd face Vlad, then looked at Khalil for an order. The Grand Vizier made a plucking gesture, and the çavuş yanked off Omar's hood. The Akinci recoiled as if he'd stepped on a jagged shard, and the men in gallery gasped collectively. Vlad, face-to-face with the man on whose reaction so much depended, held his breath.

21

Help from an Enemy

"So you know this man?" thundered Khalil.

Omar remained silent, while his eyes seemed to assess the situation, darting from Vlad to the Grand Vizier and back. "I've never seen him, Khalil Pasha," he finally said, and turned away from Vlad. Omar's missing teeth gave his speech an involuntary whistle, and caused spittle to dribble on his beard.

"There," Zaganos shouted, "another lie exposed. How much longer will we permit this Giaour to waste our time?"

Khalil raised a hand to silence Zaganos. "Why did you react so violently, Omar, if you don't know him?"

The confidence in the Grand Vizier's voice gave Vlad heart. The man wasn't easily duped.

"I got startled," Omar said. "I didn't expect to see an infidel right here in the sultan's palace." His tone showed he was regaining his composure.

"I would've had the same reaction as this poor man," the Chief Judge said, "if you'd sprung such a surprise on me."

A wave of snickers rolled along back of the hall. Seemingly encouraged, Omar gave a forced laugh and cast glances around him for support. "I'm more used to seeing infidels tumbling into the dust with my arrows in their backs."

Khalil's face showed indifference to the spectators' levity. "Do you deny having returned recently from Wallachia?" he said. "Lying to the Imperial Council carries a heavy penalty, I remind you."

Omar smoothed the tail of his tunic, straightened up, then wiped the sweat off the top of his shaved head. Vlad imagined the wheels of Omar's mind turning frantically while they milled the grist of his lies into something resembling truth.

"Not at all, Your Excellency," he finally said. "That isn't something that needs denying. I did in fact return a few days ago from that part of the world."

"And what business did you have there?" Khalil said. "You are an Akinci, not a merchant, if I'm well informed."

"Akincis too need to make a living somehow in times of peace, Your Excellency." Once again Omar looked about himself, and received encouraging nods from Zaganos and the Chief Judge. "I traveled to Wallachia and Transylvania, as a guard for the caravan of a Saxon merchant from Kronstadt. Many of us, Akincis, do this, while we're waiting for war to break out."

"So, you could've seen this man somewhere there," Khalil said. "Try to remember."

"No, I don't remember seeing him," Omar said without giving Vlad another look.

"It's what we all anticipated, isn't it?" Zaganos said. He flashed the Grand Vizier a mocking grin. "Come, admit it, Khalil Pasha. Even you didn't seriously expect a different outcome."

"I think Omar's been put through enough trouble," the Chief Judge said. He pointed a bony finger at the sergeant who brought Omar in and ordered, "Have my secretary give the man twenty aspers for his time, and send him home."

The Grand Vizier's face darkened, and he lowered his gaze. When the çavuş escorted Omar to the door, Khalil didn't interfere.

The precipitous collapse of his case paralyzed Vlad. Only when Omar was already by the door did Vlad regain his senses. "Liar," he shouted, and leaped after Omar with arms outstretched. Before he could take three steps, the second çavuş lunged at Vlad and put him in a headlock. The man's arm muscles were as hard as wood, and he seemed determined to throttle Vlad. In a trick Vlad knew from his wrestling with Gruya and Marcus, the çavuş pressed his own head against Vlad's temple. In less than a minute, that move would make Vlad black out.

"Restrain the accused," the Chief Judge commanded, unnecessarily.

"How can you forget someone who killed Zekaï, your baby brother?" Vlad managed to cry, with what he feared was his last lungful of air. Omar spun around and issued forth a bawl that shook the hall. Then he charged Vlad with fingers splayed, eyes bulging.

The çavuş let go of Vlad, and received Omar with a chop across the neck that dropped him to the floor. Then, in seconds, he and his colleague immobilized Omar, tying his hands and feet with the same cord they'd used to strangle Mahmud Pasha.

"What's the meaning of this," Khalil said to Vlad. "Do you confess to killing this man's brother?"

"He killed all three of my brothers, Your Excellency," Omar shouted as he struggled unsuccessfully to rise.

The gallery erupted in noisy vociferations. The Grand Vizier raised his hand requesting quiet, then jutted out his chin at the çavuşes. They stood Omar on his feet.

"Something seems to have refreshed your memory," Khalil said, and glanced with disdain at Zaganos and the Chief Judge.

"Yes, Your Excellency," Omar said, choking with venom, "now I recognize this son of Shaytan as the same one who ambushed the merchant I was working for. This murderer must've cast a spell on me that was broken only when he mentioned my brother's name."

"There was no merchant involved, Khalil Pasha," Vlad said, determined not to let Omar retake control of the situation. "Yes, my squire and I killed Omar's three brothers, but it wasn't murder. They all were armed, but we took them by surprise and we were better fighters. They entered Wallachia illegally, and captured more than two dozen boys."

Omar pointed a finger at Vlad, but kept his eyes on Khalil when he said, "This infidel is the head of a band of robbers, my vizier. All merchants who cross the big forest north of the Danube fear him and his cohorts. I've heard many Turkish travelers mention his name with dread: Dracula, which is 'Son of the Devil' in the Wallachian language."

Vlad felt a shock at hearing the nickname he'd almost forgotten, and realized that if there was a turning point in his standing with Khalil, this was it. "Dracula simply means 'Son of Dracul.' Any Wallachian can tell you that. Ask among your slaves, Your Excellency. If my father were a Turk named Dracul, I'd be nicknamed Draculoğul. It's the same concept."

Khalil seemed to grasp the implication of this revelation, and drove the point home. "Tell me, Omar, did you get the sense that this Dracula is an ignorant peasant turned bandit?" He paused and looked around the hall, to assure himself that all in attendance were paying attention to his line of questioning. "Or is he someone educated, whom others obey?"

Omar cocked his head, in an apparent effort to choose the most damning answer. "Not ignorant, my vizier." He sounded tentative and his eyes seemed to seek guidance from Zaganos and the Chief Judge. When Khalil encouraged him with a nod and a friendly smile, Omar said, with conviction, "Aside from Romanian, he speaks Hungarian, German, and Turkish. And when he gives orders, everyone in his band obeys him as if he were a king."

Khalil's face showed triumph, and Vlad's hope sprouted new shoots.

"Omar has proven to my satisfaction that this young man is the son of King Dracul," Khalil pronounced with finality.

The people in the gallery gave murmurs of approval, and Khalil acknowledged them with a nod.

"Even if that be the case, Khalil," the Chief Judge said, "we're left with a self-avowed killer of three Akincis. He might be the Prince of Wallachia back home, but here he's nothing but a Turk murderer."

"In fairness, *kadıasker*," Zaganos said, in a sugary voice that probably didn't fool many in attendance, "the circumstances of those killings remain in dispute. As of now we have the word of Prince Vlad against that of Omar."

The *kadıasker* turned to Zaganos with a fearsome scowl. "Do you expect me to take the word of an infidel over that of a true believer?"

"I will take both men under my care," Zaganos said, "and will extract the truth from them."

"You may have Omar, and do with him as you please," Khalil said. "But Prince Vlad is now a state hostage, and will remain confined in this palace until the sultan returns to town."

"I protest, Khalil Pasha," Zaganos said, and stood up with a show of indignation. "Hostages have always been under the jurisdiction of the Third Vizier."

"Must I remind you, Zaganos, that you've recently lost His Majesty's most important hostage? Kasim ibn Jihangir's escape from your custody turns the mere likelihood of a war with Karaman into a near-certainty." Khalil raised his right hand imperiously, palm outward, to show the discussion was over. Then he beckoned a scribe holding a portable writing desk, and began dictating. "In the name of Sultan Murad, from Khalil Pasha, Grand Vizier, to the Agha of the Household Cavalry—"

"I warn you, Khalil," the Chief Judge said, "I'll petition the sultan to allow me to exercise my prerogatives as *kadıasker.* I must judge and punish this murderer according to Sharia."

"I assure you, Sadeddin Hoja," Khalil said, "the sultan doesn't wish anyone to touch this hostage until King Dracul puts an end to the invasion of Wallachia. The day we receive notice of that, you may have your trial."

Vlad's mind became a jumble of thoughts, each vying for attention, like fledglings in a nest at feeding time. *Status as a hostage established ... be confined to the palace ... Zaganos no more a threat ... Donatella ... will I see her again ... Murad's tuğ will come down ... no war ... I won ... Donatella ... will she remember me in a few weeks?*

A mention of King Dracul in Khalil's dictation plucked Vlad out of his erratic rumination.

"The imperial escort is ordered to deliver King Dracul to Wallachia in the shortest time possible," Khalil said. "Under no circumstances are the sultan's troops to get involved in the Wallachian conflict, which must be resolved by King Dracul alone."

"Well, you've got your wish, Prince Vlad," Ismail whispered into Vlad's ear.

Vlad turned to see Tirendaz's secretary smiling, and felt a shot of warmth at the thought he might have a friend in this hostile and treacherous lair. "I want to say goodbye to my father, Lord Michael, and my squire. I left them precipitously."

"Haven't you been listening to Khalil Pasha?" Ismail said. "There wouldn't be enough time for that, even if they let you do it. Your father and his party are to leave Edirne under escort within the hour."

The çavuşes must've received a silent command from Khalil, for they grabbed Vlad roughly by the arms and forced him toward the door. Vlad struggled to turn his head to Ismail, despite the pain of his wounds. "Tell Lady—" *Tell Lady Donatella what? That I already miss being in her company?* Not something Vlad would ever share with another man. "Tell Lady Mara I'm grateful for her intervention."

The çavuşes led Vlad along a corridor lit by dusty skylights, then took him down several flights of stairs, deeper and deeper into the underground. Here, torches planted every twenty feet into wall sconces provided light at the cost of a heavy smoke that stung the eyes. When they reached a solid iron door that blocked the passage, someone on the other side slid open the cover of a grated wicket. A whiff of stale air came into the passage.

"Important state prisoner," one of the çavuşes said. "No one may visit him unless he shows an authorization stamped with the *ṭuğrā*, the grand imperial seal."

The man behind the wicket grunted, and unlocked the door. The çavuşes shoved Vlad across the threshold, then turned on their heels and left. Vlad found himself in a candlelit guardroom, its air heavy with smells of boiled cabbage and sweat. Two guards were playing *tavla* seated on the floor. The guard who let Vlad in locked the door, then pointed at a vaulted passage on far side of the room.

"I can speak Turkish," Vlad said, "so you can tell me what to do, and I'll understand."

The *tavla* players looked up but said nothing. The first man grunted again, as he'd done at the door, then motioned to Vlad to follow, and left the room through the passage.

Outside the guardroom, the air went from malodorous to pestilential. An ill-lit corridor stretched in front of Vlad as far as he could see. The jailor trudged along it in silence and, as Vlad trailed him, he observed cell doors set in the right wall every eight feet. They were iron-grille squares placed close to the floor and not bigger than two feet across. The thought flashed through Vlad's mind that his father's cell in the Macedon Tower, with its floor-to-ceiling grating and natural light, was luxurious in comparison to these cells.

The guard stopped at a cell whose door hung open, and Vlad crawled inside without waiting to be ordered to do so. The man padlocked the grille, then walked away.

22

Underground Dungeon

June, July, August, 1442, Rumelia, Ottoman Empire

"I need water," Vlad called after the guard.

The response was a growl.

The fever of the past two days had chapped Vlad's lips and parched his throat. He knelt by the grille and waited for the man to bring him water. The flame of a torch in the passage was his only source of light.

Vlad heard a cough in the cell at his left, and was glad for a neighbor. But when he thought about calling out to him, he realized he had nothing to say. Half an hour passed, and the guard didn't return. Vlad stood and felt his way around the cell.

His new home was about eight feet wide, and ten deep. He couldn't see how high the ceiling was. The only objects in the room were two chipped clay bowls, a wood bucket, and a pallet of rushes about three inches high. When he touched the rushes, he felt them covered in a velvety layer of mold. He fashioned his doublet into a pillow, then lay on the pallet. He kept his eyes on the light from the passage and tried to stay awake, not to miss the guard's return. But soon the stored fatigue of the past few days overtook him, and he fell asleep.

What awoke him was the faint sound of the *adhān.* The melody came through the walls amputated of its lower notes, the words barely distinguishable, sounding like a disjointed sequence of high-pitched shrieks. Yet Vlad was happy to hear it at all. Absent any indication of the passing of day into night, this sound was the only thing that would help him count the days.

He had no way of telling which of the five daily calls to prayer this was. But from the sharpness of his thirst and hunger he suspected he'd slept through the night, so it had to be the predawn *adhān.* Food and water would be brought as soon as the guards had finished their prayers. As he'd hoped, a short interval passed before sounds came from the direction of the guardroom. He grabbed his two bowls and stooped in front of the cell's opening, mouth dry and bowels rumbling.

He heard the wheels of a cart moving slowly along the corridor, accompanied by the shuffling of feet. The cart stopped at regular intervals; after some clanging of keys and clinking of bowls, it resumed its slow progress. Vlad noted the guard didn't exchange words with the prisoners.

"Was that the *adhān* for the Salah al-Fajr?" he asked the guard. He wasn't the one who'd locked Vlad up. But, like the other one, this guard didn't speak, only confirmed Vlad's guess with a nod. "When's the next feeding?"

"*No pot parlar,*" Vlad's coughing neighbor shouted in a horse voice.

He can't speak. Vlad guessed what his neighbor said from the similarity of his language to the Romanian. "What are you?" he said in Greek. "French, Italian?"

"*Jo sóc català,*" the neighbor replied. "*Jo no parlo grec.*"

Again Vlad understood enough to know his neighbor was Catalan, and that he had to try another language on him than Greek. "Do you speak Latin?"

"Not enough to pass for a priest," the Catalan said in a halting Latin, "but enough to ask a Genovese or Venetian sea captain for his gold." He gave a wheezy laugh, then coughed for several minutes.

"So you're a pirate?" Vlad said. He'd heard the Catalan corsairs had been the scourge of commerce in the Aegean Sea for centuries. "I'm Vlad. Wallachian. What's your name?"

"Don't bother with the guards. They all had their tongues cut off to prevent them from communicating with the prisoners. Add illiteracy to that, and you've got the most secretive detention possible." He chuckled softly. "But the knife cuts both ways. The guards can't report to the sultan what they hear us saying."

"Do you have things to hide?"

The Catalan began to eat his food noisily, with lip smacking and slurping, the way peasants did it back home in Wallachia. "Nothing but my identity," he said, mouth full. "Mother, who gave me birth on a pirate ship, named me Ferran. But to Sultan Murad I'm Don Enrique of Aragon and Pimentel, son of the Duke of Segorbe."

"I assume he's holding you for ransom."

"The real Enrique died in my arms on his way to the Holy Land, and left me his name," Ferran said, with feeling. "I did his family a favor writing them the false news of his survival. Old parents can be crushed by the loss of a son." He chuckled, and it made him cough again. "I was moved to tears when I wrote them again with my plea for ransom money. That moment I truly felt I *was* Don Enrique."

"How long have you been waiting for their reply?"

"What's the date?" Ferran asked, with apprehension in his voice.

"The twenty-fifth or twenty-sixth, I think," Vlad said. "June, that is."

Ferran sighed deeply. "Oh, my friend, it's the year I want to know. I've lost the ability to keep track of the time."

"Fourteen forty-two," Vlad said.

"*Oh, dolç Jesús,*" Ferran whispered, and fell into an interminable fit of coughing. Then Vlad heard the Catalan drag himself to the back of his cell, where he began to sob and mutter.

Vlad ate his bowl of over-boiled vegetables, and drank half of his water. Then he stowed the water bowl in a corner, not knowing when he'd get his next ration.

Ferran didn't communicate with Vlad for the next three weeks. The only way Vlad knew his neighbor still lived was his incessant cough, and the fact that the guard's cart continued to stop at Ferran's cell twice a day.

By counting five *adhāns* each day, Vlad kept a calendar that helped him visualize his father's progress on the way back to Wallachia. Even in his weakened condition, Father would be pushing himself to the limit to reach Târgoviște before it was too late. With horses changed at every stop, and without the encumbrance of the mule wagons, Father should be able to cover the three hundred miles in ten days. That meant he'd arrive home around July 6 or 7. If Baba Novak were able to hold Târgoviște until then, it would soon be over for Nestor. Maybe as quickly as in two, three days. News of Nestor's defeat should arrive in Edirne by carrier pigeon around July 10, and then Vlad would be taken out of the dungeon. True, he'd have to face the Chief Judge for the charge of murder, but that didn't worry him now. When he gave a full account of how he came upon Omar and his brothers, the judge would have to rule in Vlad's favor.

He paced his cell all day long, and did calisthenics regularly to keep up his strength. The wounds on his back had stopped hurting, and his spirits were high. Despite constant hunger and thirst, he slept well. But never before the last *adhān* of the day, so he wouldn't miss any of the calls to prayer and risk losing precise count of the days.

It was at night Vlad let his thoughts wander to Donatella. With eyes shut, he'd see her face, neck, breasts, hear the sound of her velvety voice. He'd trace on his palm the Cupid's bow of her upper lip, and imagine the feel of her kiss. From Gunther's old lessons, which made him laugh at the time, fragments of Persian love poems came to him, haunting and caressing.

On my lips the taste of your kiss
Blossoms like tulips reaching for the sun

"You won't understand the ethos of the Ottoman sultans until you know the poetry they read, and write," Gunther said. That might be so, but as Vlad recalled those poems now, he suspected Gunther was replaying his own love memories.

My bed of crushed flowers
Still bears the imprint of your body,
And my pillow that of your perfume,
Frankincense, musk, and amber

When July 10 arrived, Vlad was too excited to exercise. He knelt by the grille of his cell, and waited all day for a sound that would announce his release. The next day, he did the same. With crushing slowness, day after day passed without change in his routine. The Sultan should've received the good news from Wallachia by now. Unless Father failed to defeat Nestor. In that case Murad would hoist up his *tuğ* again and resume preparations for war. Everything would be lost for Vlad's homeland, and his sacrifice would turn out to be as meaningless as Ismail had predicted.

"Hey, Wallachian," Ferran called out one day, "are you still alive?"

What day was it, Vlad asked himself? The fifteenth? Sixteenth? His sleep pattern had been disturbed, and he'd stopped counting the *adhāns* as rigorously as at the beginning.

"It's been eleven years since I landed in this foul pit," Ferran said. "I was given as a gift to Murad on his ten-year coronation anniversary by the Mamluk Sultan. Is Murad still alive?"

Eleven years? Vlad couldn't imagine surviving that long in a place like this. Or wanting to. "And you're still hoping for a ransom to arrive?" His own voice sounded strange to him after three weeks of silence.

Ferran coughed, then remained quiet for such a long time that Vlad thought he'd retreated again into his solitude. "What else is there for me to do?"

That the Duke of Segorbe hadn't rushed to send a boatload of gold to Murad in exchange for "Enrique" didn't surprise Vlad. A letter written by an uneducated pirate couldn't fool a duke. Neither could the words of an impostor deceive a mother. But the fact that Murad lost track of his prisoner for eleven years made Vlad shiver with dread. Was this going to be his fate?

Soon Vlad became convinced his father had failed to quell Nestor's invasion. If no longer King of Wallachia, he'd be of no further interest to Murad. Neither would Vlad, whose value as a hostage would be annulled. Murad would forget Vlad in the donjon, as he did Ferran. Only Vlad wasn't someone who clung to an unworthy life at all cost.

While trying to become a hostage, Vlad hadn't once invoked God's help. After all, it was He who gave Vlad the idea. But now, when it was evident evil forces had claimed Vlad as their prize, his need for God's help glowed like charcoal under the bellows' breath. Yet a spiteful stubbornness prevented him from begging for mercy. He'd done the right thing, so why had God abandoned him? Yes, he needed help, but not to endure, only to escape through death. The image of Princess Lubomirska's face, upturned to a deaf sky, came to his mind, and he shouted, "*Mein Gott, nimm mich!*"

He decided to stop eating and drinking while he waited for God to take his life. With hunger and thirst gnawing at him, Vlad discovered that even thinking about Donatella no longer brought him solace. In the early days, her memory was a balm that assuaged his loneliness. But now he was unable to conjure more than a vague, colorless outline of her face. Then even that image faded, and he was left with only the darkness that surrounded him and sucked his energy drop by drop.

The fifth day of fasting crushed his will, and he crawled to the grille at the sound of the cart like a trained dog to his master. He slurped the water greedily, and devoured the boiled vegetables with a smacking of lips that outdid Ferran's. All along he loathed himself for cowardliness.

Next time his resolve lasted longer. When he finally drank and ate again, he wasn't sure anymore if it was really happening. Perhaps he was already on the other side. But if that were true, what a disappointment that his new world should look and feel just like the one he left behind. Only the pain in his guts reminded him that God hadn't yet done His work.

The last time Vlad crawled to the door he was too weak to return to his pallet. He curled on the floor under the grille, and told himself the end had finally arrived. From then on, he felt twice a day water pouring into his mouth, and had no will left to refrain from swallowing it.

23

THE KING'S CHALLENGE

July 1442, Wallachia

"What king rewards his enemies, and punishes his friends?" Baba Novak shouted, loud enough that soldiers outside Michael's tent could hear him. "His Grace gives Alba the command of the cavalry reserves, while he strips me of my sword bearer's function?"

"You aren't stripped, Baba, only suspended," Michael said.

Baba shook his fists and raised his eyes to an unseen sky. "And then he exiles me indefinitely to Kilia. If one looked for Wallachia's bunghole, that's where the search would end."

Baba's rages always amused Michael with their juvenile bluster. His son tried too hard to project anger and menace for Michael to take him seriously. When Baba was truly upset, he'd become calm and quiet, then strike at whoever crossed him with excessive force. Like the time when he split a horse thief in two, from skull to crotch, with one sword blow. Not for stealing Baba's charger, but for laming it in the process.

"Kilia's the king's most cherished spot in the country these days," Michael said. "He's exiling you there so you can supervise the construction work on the walls and wharf."

"And what do I know about such matters, Father?" Baba said, with a petulance that brought back to Michael memories of Baba's youth. "My job is to fight, not to—"

"You'll have Saxon master builders under you who'll transform Wallachia's bunghole into its gateway to the Silk Road."

"So instead of fighting battles I'm to wipe bricklayers' asses now?"

"The king said, 'indefinite exile,' so you'd drive the masons hard to complete the work quickly. When that's done, you may return and resume your office of sword bearer."

Baba scratched his groin and let out a big breath. "All of this, because I refused to let Marcus take the army into the field, where the boy would have lost it to that worthless usurper, Nestor."

"It's hot enough in this tent without your stomping about and blowing steam," Michael said. He filled a pewter mug with water from a barrel, took a swig, and passed it on to Baba. Then he replaced the barrel cover and sat on it. "You disobeyed the regent, who was your rightful liege while His Majesty was out of the country."

"But you know Marcus isn't experienced enough to command an army in battle," Baba said.

"The king knows it too, but has to show the rest of the country that a regent must be obeyed, just like the king."

"And Alba?" Baba's anger seemed to sprout new horns that made his face contort as if with pain. "How does that scrofulous villain get honored with a command post, when we all know he's got something to do with Nestor's invasion?"

"Sadly, we can't prove that," Michael said. "But giving him command of the cavalry reserves is the king's way of ensuring Alba is away from the battlefield, where he could spring a surprise on us."

"A command, even in the reserves, is still a more dignified thing than fighting like a plain soldier, the way the king wants me to do it," Baba grumbled.

"The king's feet are still sore from the bastinado, so he can't stand up in the stirrups to fight properly. And his left hand is so badly mangled, his shield had to be strapped to his arm. He'll be out there in the front, as he's always been, but he's relying on you to fight next to him."

This seemed to mollify Baba, but he was slow in dropping his show of anger. "If I had that depraved miscreant to myself for half an hour, I'd make him confess even the milk he suckled at his mother's breast."

"I don't think Alba bothers you more now than he did before Nestor showed up," Michael said. "Your true canker is that Gruya has run away."

Baba took the air of any frustrated father with unruly sons. "Oh, the beating that boy has coming to him when I get him back." He threw a fist at the tent's wall, and nearly toppled over when the canvas yielded without resistance. "He returns home after having gone where he had no business going, and doesn't sleep in his own bed one night before he runs away again."

"At least he had the sense to take Lash with him. The Gypsy's only two years older than Gruya, but ten years more mature. He can look out after your boy."

"I don't know who's looking after whom," Baba moaned. "They're both like two lost puppies, on account of being separated from Vlad."

"I can't blame them. They've been attached to him since the day he was born, and would die for him."

"I told Gruya there is nothing a sixteen-year-old can do to spring Vlad loose from the Turks, but he just scoffed at me and—"

"If we're going to talk about a disobedient son," Michael said, "I've got a few stories of my own."

Baba shot Michael an indignant look. "What do you mean? I've never—" He stopped short and snickered. "The good news is my men caught up with Lash and Gruya last night, and should have them back here soon."

"I'll take Gruya on as my squire while you're in Kilia," Michael said. "Though I can't promise he won't run away again."

"If I thought there was a chance of snatching Vlad from Murad's hands, I'd do it myself." Baba shook his head and made a sour face. "Gruya and Lash wouldn't accomplish anything but getting themselves killed—"

"Listen." Michael raised a finger to his lips. Dracul's voice haranguing his soldiers resounded in the mid-distance, and was immediately drowned by war cries. "Time we got ourselves suited for battle." Michael rose and tightened his sword belt.

Baba barred Michael's path, hands raised and brows knitted. "You're no longer fit, Father. Stay out of it."

"You know I couldn't turn down the chance of dying on horseback with a sword in hand. Death in bed isn't for me."

Heavy footsteps halted nearby, and a soldier poked his head in through the tent-fly.

"Got your son and Prince Vlad's Gypsy servant, my lord," he said, then lifted the flap to show Gruya and Lash standing sullen in the opening.

Baba straightened to his full height, and beckoned Gruya with his finger.

Lash rushed forward and threw himself at Baba's feet. "It was my idea, Lord Novak," he said, hands raised in supplication. "Punish me, my lord. Master Gruya didn't want to run away but I talked him into doing it."

"I thought Gypsies made good liars, Lash," Baba said, "but you seem bent on disproving that."

"Leave us, soldier," Michael ordered the man who accompanied the two youths. Then he tugged at Lash's arm to make him rise. "My grandson's old enough to pay for his own sins."

Gruya walked up to his father and stared him defiantly in the eyes. Michael was struck by how gaunt and haggard Gruya looked, especially now that his mustache and beard were more than fuzz. The blue of his eyes seemed to have darkened, and there wasn't even a hint of that mischievous smile that habitually curled his lips.

Baba glowered at Gruya, then slapped him across the face with his left hand. "This is for disobeying your father," he said. Gruya's cap flew and he staggered to the side, nearly falling. He steadied himself, threw out his chest, and stepped back in front of Baba, who took him into a bone-crushing hug. Just when Gruya seemed about to suffocate, Baba disengaged with a big grin and stepped back to examine his son from head to toe. "And this is for letting my men disarm you without getting a scratch on you," Baba said, then slapped Gruya again, now with his right hand.

No longer taken unawares, Gruya remained planted on his feet. "Next time I'll cut your men to pieces, Father, just to make you proud."

"There won't be a next time," Baba shouted.

"I'll never stop looking for Vlad, as long as he's in captivity."

Baba raised his hand for a third slap, but wasn't able to bring himself to hit Gruya again.

"If you're done with your display of fatherly affection, we should go," Michael said. "The king must be wondering what's keeping us here."

Baba put his arm around Gruya's shoulder, as casually as if they'd just finished a meal together and were parting ways. "Stay close to Father and see that he doesn't fall off the horse. He's got this stupid notion he'd like to die riding, like some goddamn Mongol." Then he turned to Lash. "And you don't let my son out of your sight from now on. If he runs away again, I'll turn your hide into a wineskin."

The field south of Târgovişte swarmed with riders and foot soldiers moving about in a disorderly manner. Michael saw Dracul ride back and forth among his troops, exhorting them and receiving their cheers.

"They aren't short on enthusiasm for the king," Michael said to Gruya. "Let's hope that's an adequate substitute for battle experience. They'll be facing hardened soldiers who kill for pleasure and profit."

"Why aren't our men in formation?" Gruya grumbled. "We must be looking like a herd of cattle to Nestor's mercenaries." He pointed to where Nestor's army had lined up along the crest of a small ridge, about three miles away. "You can tell from here those are trained soldiers."

Michael's eyesight was too weak to see much detail. But he could make out the dark blocks that represented the squadrons. Ten of them, probably at a strength of two hundred riders each.

"The king's letting the troops roam about freely on purpose, to make his army look larger than it is. He's got only twelve hundred qualified soldiers, two hundred of which came from our clan. The rest are simple folks whom the royal councilors have summoned from their nearby villages."

"Paltry help the boyars are giving His Majesty in such a time of crisis," Gruya said.

"They're invoking the right to keep their men-at-arms for the protection of their own estates. It's been like that from the beginning of time."

Gruya grimaced in disgust. "So they give the king peasants armed with pitchforks and scythes. What good are farm tools against armor and crossbows?"

"There might not be a battle, after all," Michael said. "It seems Nestor isn't so keen on fighting, now that the king is back in the country. Rumor is he's thinking of negotiating an end to the conflict."

"The coward." Gruya spat over his horse's head. "That would be too bad. I've set my heart on killing a few of his men."

"You might still get your chance, since the mercenaries aren't of the same mind with Nestor. He promised to let them sack Târgoviș̦te, as a supplement to their cash stipend. So now they're itching for battle."

Gruya drew his sword and tested the blade with his thumb. "Every other head I take will be for Vlad."

"It's your first battle, Grandson, so stay close to me and learn. Don't be in a hurry to get yourself killed." A pang shot through Michael's breast at the thought of losing his only grandson. Yet pride at seeing Gruya so unafraid swept away his concerns. "But don't count on killing mercenaries to be medicine for what truly ails you."

Gruya gave a derisive chuckle. "Do you have a better remedy? So far, all I heard from you and Father was that I should forget about rescuing Vlad. That's no medicine either."

Michael leaned down in the saddle and patted Gruya's hand. "We all want him back. But that's going to take a lot of money."

"What do I need money for? I can sleep under the stars and eat scraps. And I've got enough clothes to—"

"I wasn't thinking about your comfort. I meant money to organize a merchant caravan that would let us travel to wherever they're holding Vlad. Money to hire a crew, buy merchandise, pay custom taxes, obtain intelligence about Vlad's whereabouts, and most importantly, money to—"

"No disrespect, Grandfather, but this kind of adventure isn't for old men like you."

"—*most importantly*, money to bribe Vlad's jailers."

"Even if I thought it'd be a good idea to impersonate traders, where's that kind of money going to come from?"

"It will take some time, but it will come."

"A year? Two? Five?"

"The king's planning to mortgage one of his estates as soon as this mess with Nestor is settled," Michael said.

Gruya shook his head, lips puckered as if he'd bitten into a sour fruit. "I heard such deals take a long time to arrange. I don't want to grow old waiting, while my master languishes in a Turkish prison. Not Father, not you, not the king's army's going to stop me from running away and doing what's right for Vlad."

Gruya was being as stubborn as Michael knew he'd be; a new tack was needed. "You're right, I'm too old for adventures. And your father doesn't have the finesse needed to navigate among the Turks. He'd stand out like a cow in a wedding dress."

Gruya looked askance at Michael.

"It's clear *you* are Vlad's only hope, so go ahead, run to him. Only it's a shame to see that hope wasted because you're too impatient to wait for the money you need to succeed."

Gruya looked troubled and seemed to mull over Michael's observation. Then he reined his horse sharply, making it rear. "What's the king waiting for? We could've been done with Nestor and his mercenaries by now."

Michael wheeled his horse around to survey the field. "Nestor's got the advantage of holding the ridge. The king wants him to lose patience and charge us first. When that happens, we're all to feign a panicky retreat to the east."

"What about the swamp?"

Michael laughed. "Precisely. Knowledge of the passage through the swamp is worth three thousand additional footmen."

"And what happens if Nestor stays put, instead of falling into the king's trap?"

"Time's on our side. Every day Nestor doesn't deliver on his promise of booty to his mercenaries, the chance increases they'll revolt and strip him of everything he's got."

A horn signal came from the lookout atop the fortress tower behind them. Michael recognized it and said, "Your wish is about to be fulfilled, Grandson. They've spotted movement in Nestor's line."

Gruya stood up on his stirrups and scanned the horizon. "Oh, it's only a white-flag emissary," he said, crestfallen. "That milk-sop Nestor's decided to negotiate terms, after all. I hope the king won't listen to him."

Michael felt deep relief at the news. Regardless of the parley's outcome, Dracul would benefit from the additional time it would gain him. His feet would get a chance to heal further, and the peasants would get a modicum more of drilling before the battle. "Let's go see what this is all about."

"The concession Nestor is demanding in exchange for peace is that I cede a third of Wallachia to him," Dracul announced when the last member of the Royal Council had entered his tent.

The councilors stood in a semicircle around the king with various degrees of concern on their faces. "Which third, Your Grace?" several of them asked simultaneously.

Michael registered that not one of boyars showed outrage at Nestor's demand. They seemed interested only in knowing how their own estates might be affected.

"The only concession I'd make Nestor would be a quick death," Baba Novak thundered.

"That's what *I* had reserved for Nestor," Marcus said to Baba with hostility, "and you prevented me from delivering it to him."

"Nestor's asking for the lands west of the Olt River," Dracul said. "He wants to establish the Kingdom of Oltenia there. I told his emissary that Lord Michael will deliver my answer tonight."

Dracul had stripped off his armor, and was sitting now on a wooden chest in a relaxed posture. But Michael knew the pain in the king's feet had sapped his energy, and the casual demeanor was only for the benefit of the councilors.

"What's your counsel, my lords?" Dracul said. "You know the state of my army. Five hundred soldiers are away, holding Roter Turm Pass. Another five hundred are garrisoned in various towns and at border crossings. What's left here is near half what Nestor is fielding. Do we fight and risk defeat, making him king of all Wallachia? Or do we give him what he wants, and preserve the rest of the kingdom?"

Dracul's tone sounded mocking to Michael. He knew the king would never consider splitting the country with his once-removed cousin. But Dracul enjoyed baiting his councilors into taking a stand. Secretly the boyars welcomed a split, as a way to see the crown become even weaker. But to advise dividing the country would open them to the accusation of treason. On the other hand, if they counseled battle, they'd have to participate in it as the king's vassals, and thus risk their lives. Like the king, Michael relished the torment this choice inflicted upon the boyars.

"We should fight," Lord Ignatius said, without conviction. "As master of the horse, I'll be at Your Grace's side onto death, if need be."

Two or three other boyars mumbled something they probably wished to be taken as an endorsement of Ignatius's stand. But they stopped short of showing enthusiasm for fighting Nestor, just in case he ended up on top. The others stared at their boots and remained silent.

"And you, Lord Treasurer," Dracul said, turning to Alba, "will you also fight to the death to preserve me as your king?"

"Without the slightest hesitation, Your Highness." Alba made an effort to sound more convincing than the other boyars. "But wouldn't it be more prudent to give in to Nestor's demand for the time being, and avoid the risk of losing everything? Once things quieted down and Your Grace's army was restored to full strength, we could deal with the usurper from a position of strength. After all, Nestor won't have enough revenues to keep a standing mercenary army for too long."

Dracul nodded with a grave mien, and Alba looked around, triumphant.

Baba snorted and glared at the treasurer. "And your advice has nothing to do with the fact that most of your estates would fall under Nestor's jurisdiction?"

Alba made a show of being offended. "Are you insinuating that I'd welcome Nestor as my king?" He turned his back to Baba, and addressed Dracul. "If Nestor were to rule Oltenia, he'd naturally become my overlord with respect to my holdings there. But I have estates in the rest of the country as well, and you'll remain my true king there."

The one councilor Michael expected to oppose a land concession was Archbishop Varlaam, who stood to lose a third of his flock if the country were divided. Indeed, Varlaam wagged his finger at Alba, and said, "Both apostles Matthew and Luke tell us, 'No servant can serve two masters. For either he will hate one and love the other, or he will be devoted to one and despise the other'."

Alba rewarded the prelate with a withering stare. "I'll never consider Nestor my master more than in name."

"The loyalty Lord Alba has always shown the Crown," Dracul said, "compels me to decline his selfless advice. I won't split the country to save my own skin, and make him go against the admonition of not one, but two of Christ's disciples."

The boyars looked at each other with ill-concealed disappointment.

"So we fight, then?" Baba shouted, and clapped his hands with a jarring report.

Marcus raised his mace, and hollered, "I'm ready to turn Nestor's brains into mush."

Dracul scanned the faces around him with an impish smile. "No, we don't fight, and we don't split the country, either." He waited for someone to ask what he meant.

Michael guessed what Dracul had in mind, and wanted to stop him, but the king's warning glance checked him.

"I shall fight Nestor alone in hand-to-hand combat," Dracul finally said. "Let the winner rule an undivided country."

"Let *me* fight him, Lord Father," Marcus said.

"I claim that privilege for myself, as the sword bearer," Baba roared.

The others in attendance fell to a stunned silence, and their eyes turned to the treasurer for an indication of how they should react.

Alba's face went in seconds from surprise to delight. "Your Highness's courage will make this moment stand out in the history of Wallachia for—"

The rest of his sentence was drowned in the boyars' chorus of, "Long live the king!" Michael read joyful disbelief in their unguarded looks. What an unexpected gift the king had just made them. Nothing could be better than Dracul facing Nestor in single combat. Crippled and mangled as the king was, he'd surely fall to Nestor.

Dracul raised a hand to demand silence. "In these uncertain times, it's gratifying to receive the unanimous endorsement of my councilors for such a difficult decision."

"Not unanimous," shouted Baba. "Your Grace is in no condition to fight a man half your age."

"Now Your Highness can see who has faith in you and who doesn't," Alba said. "At half your strength, you're more of a man than Nestor will ever be."

"True, true," the other councilors said, nodding vigorously.

Dracul smiled as he returned nods to his councilors, one by one. "To say I'm touched by your confidence in my prowess would be an understatement." Then he paused, as if unable to hide his exhaustion any more. "Now, please retire to your quarters and allow me to prepare for this fateful confrontation."

The boyars, looking pleased and standing a bit taller than their custom, filed out of the tent, chattering gleefully.

"You two leave as well," Dracul said when neither Baba nor Marcus moved. "Michael and I can handle what remains to be done."

"I know you aren't afraid to lead your army against Nestor's in open battle," Michael said when he and Dracul were left alone. "So what, then, is this nonsense about a duel all about?"

"I can win against Nestor in a field battle, but the cost will be the loss of hundreds of my men. That means I won't have enough troops left to put down a boyars' uprising, should they decide to revolt against me."

"So, gambling your life is your solution?"

"Under different circumstances, Nestor wouldn't dream of accepting my challenge to a duel. But he knows of my health issues, and is certain to think this is his chance to kill me."

"And kill you he will, Ulfer," Michael shouted. "You can hardly walk and—"

"Enough," Dracul said in the tone he used when he'd tolerate no further discussion. "Go tell that worthless cousin of mine to meet me in the field tomorrow at noon. Then let me worry about who's going to kill whom."

24

Gruya's Catch

July 1442, Wallachia

Michael left with Gruya and Lash after dark to bring Nestor the king's message. They rode their horses at a slow walk, and took three hours to reach their destination, only ten miles away.

"No reason to hurry," Michael said when he called for a third rest stop. Nestor's camp, dotted with bonfires, was stretching over a wide front just ahead of them. "If I deliver the message after midnight, His Grace's 'tomorrow' naturally becomes 'after tomorrow'. I'll be buying His Grace an additional day."

"What difference will a day make, Grandfather? You've said yourself the king won't be steady on his feet for another two weeks."

"Lots of helpful things could happen in that extra day. A storm, for instance, which would postpone the duel and give the king more time for recovery. Or a mercenaries' revolt that would put Nestor on the run."

A light breeze coming from the camp brought a pungent odor.

"What's that abominable stench?" Gruya said, and covered his nose.

"I heard Nestor hired Gypsies from a nearby settlement to clear the camp latrines," Lash said.

As they drew closer, the odor became stronger. The sentries manning the gate wore kerchiefs tied over their noses. They waved Michael and his party through without asking their business.

"So much for security," Gruya said. "Perhaps Father should come over with a few men and finish off Nestor where he sleeps."

The camp thoroughfare was busy with soldiers, vendors, and prostitutes, milling about as if at a fair. They all pinched their noses when a wagon carrying a large wooden tub lumbered past them on the way out of the camp.

Lash chatted briefly with the two Gypsies on the wagon. "There are five such crews shuttling day and night between the camp and a creek a few miles away," he told Michael and Gruya. "They won't be done with their work for another two days."

"Bad timing for our mission," Gruya said.

They headed for the center of the camp, just as the sentries rang the midnight watch. Despite the late hour, drunken singing rose from all directions. Tents resounding with women's laughter drew crowds of soldiers, proving the vitiated air did nothing to dampen the men's libidos.

Michael easily recognized Nestor's pavilion, larger than all others, as befitted a commander. Unlike the rest of the tents that stood in the open field, his was raised in a grove of acacia trees still in bloom. Yet not even the fragrance of the acacia flowers could mask the fumes caused by the Gypsies' work. In the light of torches planted in the ground Michael saw a privy's overturned shape, only a few paces behind Nestor's tent. Two men equipped with buckets attached to long poles were transferring the contents of a hole in the ground to a tub set upon a wagon.

"Keep the horses saddled," Michael said to Gruya and Lash. "I'll deliver my message, then we'll get away from this stink as fast as we can." He looked around for a sentry to announce him, but Nestor's retainers had left their post for a bonfire some twenty yards away. A footman was feeding the flames with juniper branches, while four men-at-arms, probably Nestor's bodyguard, were fanning the aromatic smoke with their mantles.

Michael pulled aside the flap to Nestor's tent and stepped into a vestibule lit by a single oil lamp. "Chancellor Novak requesting permission to enter, Prince Nestor."

"Your master's exceeding cruel, Lord Novak, to send an old man on a diplomatic mission in the middle of the night. A mission made doubly unpleasant by our little housekeeping project."

Michael parted the curtain to see Nestor stripped to his shirt and drawers, face glistening with sweat, strands of hair plastered to his forehead. He was seated at a campaign desk reviewing the contents of a strongbox open in front of him. He'd piled up silver coins in columns three inches high, and at Michael's entrance he threw a swath of velvet cloth over them. With an experienced glance, Michael estimated there were about twenty thousand coins between the desk and the box, not even five hundred gold ducats worth of silver. If that was the extent of Nestor's war chest, he had good reason to worry about keeping his mercenaries under control. How careless of him to let an outsider see this.

Michael ignored Nestor's silent invitation to sit and said, "The king has no intention to split the country with you."

The corners of Nestor's mouth dropped, and anger contorted his face. "What are you saying, old fool? Doesn't Dracul understand I'm giving him a chance to save his dignity, as well as his crown?"

"What's going on, darling?" a voice said in Hungarian from behind a partition. Seconds later, a naked woman rushed into the room with an alarmed look.

"Get out of here, harlot," Nestor said.

"But you haven't paid me yet." The woman reached into the strongbox.

Nestor slammed the lid on her hand, and she screamed. That seemed to soften him a bit. "Come back in half an hour and I'll take care of you." Without rising from his chair, he picked a blanket off the floor and tossed it at the woman. "Now trot your sagging ass out of here before I split your head like a fucking log."

"You may have the entire country," Michael said, unperturbed, after the woman left. "But you must earn it by killing the king in single combat."

"What?" Nestor stood abruptly, overturning his chair. Michael noted the prince's drawers were dirty, his toenails yellow and overgrown.

"The king's giving you until noon tomorrow to set your affairs in order: make your will, write to your wife, see your confessor. Then he'll fight you one-on-one to the death. If you win, Wallachia's yours. If you die … the earth is rid of one more pile of ordure."

"Watch out, king's bootlicker," Nestor said, eyes flashing, "you're in my hands now." But when the meaning of Michael's message sank in, Nestor's face lit up. "For being the bearer of such good tidings, I'll let you lick *my* boots when I'm your king."

"His Grace will come alone. But you may bring two unarmed servants to take your corpse away. The rest of your men must remain in the camp."

"I'll gladly fight Dracul, but today, not tomorrow. I don't have time to sit around waiting for him to work up his courage."

"If you don't accept the king's terms in their entirety, I'm to withdraw his offer for the duel. So, one-on-one combat, or open battle … it's up to you."

"How do I know this isn't a trap?"

"The pleasure of killing a thousand men like you wouldn't induce my king to act dishonorably."

"You come with the king too, old man," Nestor shouted when Michael was already out of the tent. "I need a witness to tell the world what I did to that cripple, before I killed him."

Michael found their horses tied to a tree, but Gruya and Lash nowhere in sight. He decided Gruya must've gone prowling in search of a willing woman, and Lash kept him company in obedience to Baba's order. If wenching helped his grandson settle down, it wasn't the worst thing he might do.

Nestor's men were still hovering around the sweet-scented fire, joined by other soldiers who sought relief from the noxious air.

Michael sat on a boulder near the tent, to mull over the outcome of his mission. Having accomplished what Dracul asked of him, Michael felt responsible now for the king's probable demise. He blamed himself for not manipulating Nestor toward rejecting the duel. But Dracul was right: even a victorious battle would leave the royal army depleted, inviting the boyars to rise against him. They'd love to crown some weakling they could control from among the many bastards of royal blood scattered throughout Europe. On the other hand, a duel held the possibility of taking Nestor out, while keeping the army intact.

Michael's head weighed heavy, and he let it fall onto his chest. At first he struggled against slumber, then decided a wink wouldn't hurt while waiting for Gruya and Lash to return. He was just about to fall asleep when a woman's shriek came from inside Nestor's tent.

"The prince has run away." Nestor's prostitute emerged from the tent, still wrapped in her blanket, and repeated the news. Then she added, "And the prick took his money with him."

Nestor's four bodyguards rushed into the tent, tripping over each other, then reemerged with wild looks. "He's gone indeed," one of them shouted and held the empty strongbox above his head.

The news spread from tent to tent, and soon the camp was humming with the deep rumble of a swarming beehive. Soldiers, some brandishing lit torches, began to gather in front of Nestor's pavilion. Their number kept growing until it seemed the entire army of two thousand had congregated there.

Michael retreated behind his horse to avoid being crushed by the mob. He felt feverish with excitement, all earlier fatigue and despondency gone. If Nestor ran away, his army would scatter before the end of the day. It would become a child's play for Baba to mop up the countryside of the leaderless mercenaries.

"How could the prince have left without you seeing him go?" one man asked the bodyguards.

"It's a conspiracy to defraud us of our wages," another shouted.

"Treason too," a third person added. "Nestor's abandoned us to the mercy of the Wallachians."

Repeated by hundreds of voices, "conspiracy" and "treason" swept across the gathering like the breath of a forest fire. Swords were drawn, and before Nestor's men could react, they were cut down and trampled over. The massacre appeased the crowd for a brief while, but then it became clear matters wouldn't end there.

"We've got to find the prince and the money," someone said. "He couldn't have gone far."

"He cut a slit in the back of the tent, and slunk away through there," the prostitute said. "That's why no one saw him."

Hearing this reenergized the mob. "Check it out," someone shouted, and a handful of men charged the entrance to Nestor's tent. More followed, seeking to loot the place, and under their pressure the tent collapsed. The crowd watched with fascination the rumpled canvas heave like a sack stuffed with live piglets, before the men cut their way out with swords and daggers.

"Let's set up posses and go after him," someone shouted.

This idea had general appeal. With shouts and curses, the mercenaries dispersed, leaving the four corpses lying on the ground.

"What's going on here, Grandfather?" Gruya asked stepping into the light of the bonfire, followed by Lash. "Were you harmed by these rioters?"

"I'll tell you on the way," Michael said, giddy with the unexpected turn of events. "Let's leave before we end up like Nestor's bodyguard."

Lash procured a lantern from somewhere and rode ahead of Michael and Gruya to show the way. The plain around them sparkled with flickering lights, as the posses darted every which way in search of Nestor.

Michael waited for Gruya to ask again about the events that happened in front of Nestor's tent. But his grandson rode lost in thought, seemingly no longer interested. After a while Michael could repress his joy no longer, and had to share the good news. "Nestor agreed to the duel, but after I left him he vanished with his silver."

"*Hmm,*" was all Gruya said, with an indifference that left Michael perplexed.

An hour later their way was barred by a creek they hadn't encountered on the way to Nestor's camp. The only flowing water Michael knew of in this area was a small Ialomiţa tributary. But if this creek was it, they were off their return course.

"What's the idea of leading us this far south, Lash?" Michael said, restraining his annoyance with difficulty.

Gruya dismounted and took the lantern from Lash. "I asked him to, Grandfather, so I might show you something interesting." He pointed to a hulking shape rising a few yards away on the shore.

Michael dismounted too. As he approached the mysterious shape, a whiff of fetid air told him it was one of the Gypsy wagons he'd seen earlier. He was about to remonstrate with Gruya for what seemed an ill-timed prank, when his grandson gave a whistle. Two men emerged from behind the wagon, dark of clothes and skin, only the white of their eyes and teeth showing in the lantern's light.

"We've got your cargo, Master Gruya," one of them said.

"Let's see it," Gruya replied.

The two men hopped onto the wagon, extracted a bundle from the tub, and tossed it to the ground in front of Michael and Gruya. The bundle wriggled and moaned.

A gasp escaped from Michael's throat. "Is that—you've got—how did you—?" Michael hadn't been shocked into stuttering since … well, he couldn't remember when.

"Yes, Grandfather," Gruya said with a belly laugh, "I've got Nestor, and I'm planning to drown him like an unwanted kitten."

Michael took Gruya into his arms, and had to wait for a lump of pride in his throat to dissolve before he could speak. "No, no, you mustn't kill him, Gruya. The king will want to interrogate him about this invasion."

"If the mercenaries find Nestor in our possession they'll kill us."

That risk was real, but Michael wouldn't condone murder as a way around it. "We'll send one of these men to let your father know we've got Nestor, and he'll come for us with an escort. In the meantime, we'll hide. I remember a ruined watchtower somewhere along this creek." He turned to Lash. "You know it too, I'm sure. Can you find it in the dark?"

"It's about three minutes downstream from here," Lash said.

"Then take us there quickly."

Gruya sucked air noisily through his teeth. "Not before Nestor washes up, Grandfather. In his state of filth he'll stink up that tower." Indeed, Nestor was covered in slime and reeked appallingly. Gruya, knife in hand, bent over the prisoner, and said, "I'll remove your gag if you promise to be quiet."

Nestor nodded earnestly, then shook his tied hands at Gruya.

"Your feet yes, but not your hands." Gruya cut Nestor's foot bindings first, then the strip of cloth that served as his gag. "Give him a bath, men," he ordered the Gypsy drivers.

Nestor gulped air, then growled, "I'll kill you, you miserable—" A fit of vomiting followed, and before he could recover the Gypsies threw him into the water. Then they jumped in as well and began to dunk him repeatedly. When they finally hoisted him back onto the shore, he was clean enough for Michael to recognize the garments Nestor wore when they met earlier that night.

"My money," Nestor screamed at Gruya. "You took my money."

"Hush, Nestor," Gruya whispered. "It isn't smart to talk aloud about money in a place like this. The land is full of bandits who'd love to get their hands on your silver."

"I want my money back," Nestor wailed. "I saw you bundling it into my tunic. It's up there in that tub, isn't it?"

"Bad guess," Gruya said. "That tub is reserved exclusively for shit, as you've just learned. Your silver travels in luxury inside my saddlebag."

"So, you have his money, too?" Michael said, gaining more admiration yet for his grandson.

"It's what you said I needed to rescue Vlad."

"You're a thief," Nestor shouted, "and the product of a botched abortion."

Gruya struck Nestor across the face with the back of his hand, dropping him to the ground. "What happened to being quiet?"

The watchtower proved as close as Lash had estimated. Using the lantern's light to guide them, Michael, Gruya, and Lash climbed to the top on a decrepit spiral staircase. The Gypsies followed them in the dark, dragging Nestor along.

"Tie his feet, and sit him here," Gruya said, pointing to the center of the room.

The Gypsies did as ordered, then left, one on Michael's horse to fetch Baba, the other to hide Gruya's and Lash's horses in a wood across the creek.

The circular room at the top of the tower once gave shelter to archers, who shot at their attackers through slits placed every few feet around the wall. Over the years, the brick around the cross-shaped slits had collapsed, and the openings grew to the size of windows that permitted an easy survey of the surrounding area.

Lash peered through such an opening into the distance to the north, from whence they'd come, and said, "Posses. About two miles away. Two large ones, six small."

Michael followed the direction indicated by Lash and saw blurry torchlights scattered over a wide area. He couldn't tell if they were getting closer or moving away.

"I knew they'd be coming," Nestor said. "You'd better set me loose now, and run away before it's too late."

"It's touching to see how doggedly those mercenaries are looking for you," Gruya said. "They're like flies on a turd hunt."

"And they won't stop looking until they find me," Nestor hissed. "Then they'll flay all of you alive, and I'll shit in your skulls."

"We'll pray my father gets here before them, and I think you will too," Gruya said. He unwrapped a leather thong wound around his wrist, and gave it to Lash. "Get Nestor ready for prayer."

Nestor began to whine. "Don't let them kill me, Lord Michael! You said the king wanted to talk to me."

Lash tipped Nestor onto his back, then cut the string of his drawers.

"No, no," Nestor screamed, "you can't hurt me either. The king wants me unharmed, I'm sure." He began to squeal and thrash like a hog about to be castrated.

"The king wants your tongue, not your balls," Gruya said. "They belong to them who captured you." He stepped on Nestor's hair to pin him down.

"Lord Michael, help me. I'm the son of a king. Don't let them treat me like an ordinary villain."

Gruya and Lash glanced at Michael, and he gave them a nod. Whatever the boys had in mind, short of killing him, was less than Nestor deserved.

Lash fashioned a noose from the thong and tied it around Nestor's penis and testicles.

"Did you know," Gruya said, in a conversational tone, "black eunuchs have both their nuts *and* dicks cut off? They call that 'shaving'. White eunuchs are luckier: they get to keep their dicks."

Nestor's pleadings to Michael degenerated into a series of howls punctuated by unintelligible words.

"Keep him quiet," Michael said. "At night, screams like those carry for miles." He tried to muster pity for Nestor, but knowing him the reason for Vlad's dire predicament hardened his feelings.

Gruya cut a strip of cloth from Nestor's shirt and gagged him with it.

"I learned all of that about the eunuchs in Edirne," Gruya said. "You must be asking yourself, how do black eunuchs piss?"

When Lash finally stood, Nestor went into a frenzy, arching his back and wiggling his pelvis in an attempt to shake off the noose.

"They insert a metal tube into the stub of their dicks. I saw a black eunuch carry such a tube stuck in his turban, for that very purpose."

Gruya had brought along an empty feedbag, and now began to fill it with bricks he collected off the floor. When the bag was full he tied it with a rope, then lowered it out through an opening in the wall, as one would lower a bucket into a well. Lash knotted the rope's free end to Nestor's noose, then stood him up.

After Gruya paid out most of the rope, he placed the rest into Nestor's bound hands. "Hold on tight to this. Remember the eunuchs? If the bag slips out of your hands, the noose will shave *you*."

Nestor whimpered, but clutched at the rope with the purpose of the desperate. Then Gruya let go of it and the weight of the bricks yanked Nestor halfway out the opening. With great effort he managed to straighten up, but it was apparent he didn't have the strength to retrieve the feedbag.

"Regretfully Nestor, Lash and I have to leave before Father gets here," Gruya said. "He and I have a disagreement about my travel plans."

Nestor groaned repeatedly.

"I know you hate to see me go. Well, some friendships just aren't meant to last."

Nestor's groaning intensified and he craned his neck to see Michael.

"Yes, perhaps you can persuade Grandfather to spell you with that load. But I still think praying for Father to arrive soon is the better strategy."

Michael's earlier hope of dissuading Gruya from leaving began to crumble. Arguing with a willful sixteen-year-old who owned a saddlebag full of silver was hard. Michael's insides cringed at the daunting obstacles his grandson chose to ignore. He led Gruya to the top of the stairs, out of Nestor's easy hearing, and whispered, "You speak neither Turkish nor Greek. As a Christian you can't ride a horse or carry weapons in the empire, and it won't be easy to conceal the amount of silver you're carrying."

Gruya laughed and squeezed Michael in a rib-crushing hug. "You sure know how to be supportive, Grandfather," he said, pressing his lips to Michael's ears. "Why not also remind me I'll have Father's men on my tail from the moment he hears of my flight?"

Gruya's unbending determination reminded Michael of his own youth, and his resistance broke down. "I'll make your father believe you're on your way to the crusade in Hungary. That will give you time to cross over to the Turks. Now go find Vlad and bring him home."

Alone with the prisoner, Michael felt on the verge of weeping for his grandson, gone now on a dangerous, near hopeless journey. But seeing the man responsible for all this upheaval standing in front of him, bare-butt and fighting a load of bricks to save his manhood, all Michael could do was laugh.

25

A Woman's Plan

August 1442, Rumelia, Ottoman Empire

A moment came when Vlad found himself being carried by the hands and feet along an ill-lit passage. His head hung backward between his arms, and he saw the flagstones rush beneath him with dizzying speed. A vaguely familiar voice said in Turkish, "Don't shake him like you're dusting a carpet, men. You can see he's half-dead."

Who was half-dead? Vlad tried to raise his head, but it was too heavy. Ferran must be dying, poor man. Eleven years in this dismal hole. Vlad wouldn't let that to happen to him.

The movement stopped, and a torchlight appeared in front of him. Pain shot through his eyes, and he scrunched his eyelids tight.

"He's awake," the voice that had spoken before said.

Vlad felt the heat of the torch on his face.

"It's me, Vlad," the voice said, in Greek this time. "Ismail, Tirendaz's secretary."

Vlad kept his eyes closed against further pain. He wanted to say, "I remember you," but his lips were numb, his throat dry.

"I'm taking you to be washed, before you'll have something to eat," Ismail said. Then, in Turkish, "Mind you don't bang his head on the stairs."

The men holding Vlad changed their grips and Vlad felt himself being carried in an upward direction, jostled roughly whenever his porters fell out of step. When they reached a flat area, the movement became lulling, and next he was floating in a liquid that made his skin tingle. He awoke as something soft and fragrant tickled his nose, and found himself submerged in a tub of hot water, surrounded by mounds of soapsuds. Amber candlelight suffused the room.

"I see you've finally had enough rest," Ismail said, and rose from the stool he'd been sitting on at the foot of the tub.

What's this? Hot water, soap, soft light, a friendly voice? Vlad covered his face with his palms, and tried to collect his thoughts. The physical sensations were too palpable for this to be a dream. His hand went to his chest, and found his medallion in place; it wasn't a dream. A knot rose to his gorge, and his vision blurred.

"You're neither in heaven, nor in hell, Vlad," Ismail said, and laughed like a happy child. "Though you might find it hard to believe this isn't paradise, after what you've been through."

"My father?" Vlad said, but his voice didn't carry. He cleared his throat, and tried again, with more of an effort. "My father? Wallachia?"

"King Dracul chased the invaders away a month ago." Ismail approached with a mug in hand. "It's mid-August now, but I couldn't bring you the news earlier. The Grand Vizier was out of town until today, and he left strict orders against any visits to your cell in his absence."

So Nestor's attempt to usurp Father failed. As a consequence, neither the Hungarians, nor the Turks, had a chance to swallow Wallachia. Yet Vlad didn't experience the elation he anticipated in his cell, when he thought the good news would arrive any moment. All he felt now was a tide of shame rising in him. *While Father was fighting I was wallowing in self-pity, wishing to be dead.* "What happens now?"

Ismail pressed the mug to Vlad's lips. "Drink this."

"Will the sultan judge me soon?"

"Nothing but warm liquids for the next few hours. I described your condition to Hekim Solomon, and he sent this soup to get you started on your recovery. He remembers you from Lady Donatella's residence."

Vlad sipped the broth, and immediately shook with a wave of hiccups.

Ismail fidgeted for a while, looking somber, then said, "The sultan has listened to the evidence Zaganos gathered from Omar, and is inclined to find it credible."

Vlad wasn't surprised to learn the Turks took Omar's word over his own. But what evidence could he have produced? He stopped sipping.

"Omar provided the name of the Saxon merchant who hired him and his brothers," Ismail said. "Then, Zaganos uncovered tax receipts showing the Saxon's caravan left Edirne in late April. He was also was able to confirm with the Bey of Nicopolis that the same caravan crossed the Danube into Wallachia in early May."

"The timing is right," Vlad said. "But were Omar and his brothers identified by name on the merchant's travel document?"

"A copy of that document kept by the market inspector lists four unnamed Turks as guards."

Vlad understood his enemy's ruse. "Omar got the merchant's name from one of his friends."

"With no other testimony but Omar's, it's still only your word against his," Ismail said. "Khalil Pasha tried to convince the sultan that your value as a hostage should counterbalance Omar's unproven accusations, but—"

"Not something acceptable to the Chief Judge, I imagine."

Ismail nodded several times, and his face became darker. "Even the sultan cannot insult the Ulema, the class of Muslim scholars, by overruling its chief representative's opinion in a case governed by Sharia."

The *kadıasker's* influence on Murad, told Vlad what the Turks' plans were for him. The mug fell out of his hand and sank beneath the soapsuds. He let his head slump backward over the lid of the tub, and the weight of his wet locks tugged heavy at his scalp. A lassitude akin to drunkenness overtook him, and he slipped into a state of near-numbness.

"This isn't the time to sleep, Vlad," Ismail said, and fished underwater for the mug. "You must follow the diet ordered by the doctor, and exercise in all daylight hours. Hekim Solomon said you should regain half your strength within a week. You'll need it for what's coming up."

"Am I expected to get strong, just to be executed as a murderer?" The effort to speak made Vlad's body quiver. He saw Ismail's face lean over him as through a haze that seemed thicker by the moment.

"It's not going to be like that," Ismail said. "Mehmed persuaded his father to give you a chance to prove your innocence."

At first, Ismail's words floated above Vlad, disjointed and meaningless. When they settled upon him, Vlad turned them lazily in his mind, wondering why Ismail wouldn't just go away and let him rest. Then a bolt of hope shot through him, and he sprang forward in the tub, splashing water onto the floor. "Is there a way to prove my story without a witness to back me up?"

Startled, Ismail took a step back and threw his hands up. "Have you heard of a duel they call 'trial by combat'?"

Vlad watched him for a sign of levity and concluded the secretary was serious. "Combat in the German fashion, with real weapons?" This was too good not to be another Turkish trick.

"You've got one week to get ready," Ismail said. "Zaganos wanted the duel to take place tomorrow, but—"

"A combat to the death?" Vlad was still incredulous. "I didn't know the Turks followed German customs of settling disputes when there are no witnesses for either party."

"Now you see why there is no time to waste in restoring your strength." Ismail took the mug to a cupboard in the back of the room, and returned with it full. "Broth made from boiled lark bones and nettles to suit your particular humors, according to Hekim Solomon."

So, to prove he wasn't a murderer of innocent Turks, Vlad had to kill Omar in a duel. "I don't need bone soup to fight Omar. My hate for him is a strong-enough medicine."

"Well, there is a problem," Ismail said. "After he interrogated Omar, Zaganos sent him away, and no one has seen him since."

"But … what about the duel? How am I to—?"

"Zaganos will provide a substitute for Omar from among his slaves. I think they call such a person a 'champion' in Germany. It was another one of Mehmed's ideas."

A week to get in shape, so he could kill a man who'd done him no harm. The glow Vlad had felt at the prospect of confronting Omar in the arena faded. Its place was taken by the hollowness that comes from knowing you are under the thumb of forces you can't escape.

Ismail must have read Vlad's mind, for he said, "Whether it's Omar, or someone else, you've got to fight him to prove your innocence. Nothing else will satisfy Zaganos and the *kadıasker.*"

"It's not proof of innocence they are seeking," Vlad said. "All they hope is that I'll be killed. And if I'm not, they'll find other ways to do me in."

"Lady Mara has taken your side with Murad," Ismail said. "Though she wasn't successful in persuading him to forgo the trial by combat, it's she who got the duel postponed by a week."

Vlad rose from the tub, and looked around the room for his clothes.

"I had your old garments burned," Ismail said. "Lady Donatella sent you new ones."

When Vlad opened the parcel Ismail gave him, a cluster of fresh lilacs fell out of it.

"Oh, those are probably from Bianca," Ismail said. "When the girl heard you'd be released from the dungeon today, she couldn't contain her joy."

Vlad mumbled assent, but believing the flowers were from Donatella, he hid them under his shirt, where they seemed to sear his skin.

Vlad was assigned a vacant cell in the palace infirmary, off the first court, where he was allowed to walk freely. Despite Ismail's urging that he should begin exercising immediately, he remained in bed for the rest of the day. The fragrance of the lilacs he clutched to his breast transported him to the sickroom in the Venetian ambassador's palace. But although the recollection of the hours spent there restored Donatella's faded image, the effect only increased his despondency. Winning the duel meant he'd be sent to the Amasya fortress, to be kept as a beast in a cage for years, perhaps the rest of his life. Losing the fight would be preferable; it would put an end to everything.

Hekim Solomon came in the afternoon to check on Vlad, and scowled when he saw him. "Six weeks ago you were all muscle. How could they've starved you like this? The sultan must be told."

Vlad felt moved by this stranger's concern. "It was my own doing, Hekim Efendi."

Solomon observed Vlad in silence, and nodded with understanding. "It's that bad down there?" Then he checked Vlad's lashing scars, and grunted approvingly. "At least there is nothing to worry about regarding your back. Let's check your abdomen."

Vlad clenched his teeth to suppress a scream of pain when the doctor's aggressive fingers probed his stomach.

"How many weeks did you go without food?"

Vlad couldn't say. Three? Four? He shrugged.

"You're lucky to be alive," Solomon said. "And now, no more foolishness. You must eat only what I prescribe. A bit of yogurt and honey to start. Then tonight, a slice of watermelon. I'll send a pot of chrysanthemum tisane you must drink every two hours through the night."

The doctor headed for the door, mumbling something to himself about the recklessness of youth. "Just follow my instructions faithfully," he said from the threshold, "and you'll be in good shape for …"

"Entertaining people with a gladiator's fight?" Vlad said.

Solomon appeared embarrassed. "You can't blame people for being curious," he said. "Even the ladies in the harem have asked the sultan to let them watch the duel from behind the screen. There hasn't been one at the palace since 'twenty-three. That year, Zaganos accused Skanderbeg of being a false convert, and the sultan allowed them to fight it out in the arena. They're both Albanians. Hot blooded, you might say."

Vlad didn't know who Skanderbeg was, but the connection with Zaganos had him intrigued. "Since Zaganos is still alive, I assume Skanderbeg lost the duel."

"Oh, no," Solomon said. "Zaganos couldn't fight because of a broken arm, so he appointed a champion, who was killed in his place. Skanderbeg is one of the sultan's best generals today, with five thousand Sipahis under his command."

In the evening Ismail showed up, accompanied by Spencer.

"I won't hear a thing about your needing to rest," Spencer said. "Haven't you been doing just that for the past eight weeks?"

"Maybe he'll listen to you," Ismail said. "I can't seem to convince Vlad that unless he gets stronger—"

"I've got no intention to fight anyone, if it's only to amuse people," Vlad said.

"You've got no choice but to step into the arena a week from today," Ismail said. "The sultan's decisions aren't open for discussion."

"Oh, I'll step into the arena all right. But not to kill an innocent man, so I may earn the privilege of being locked up in some other stinky dungeon in Asia."

"You think anyone will care if you let yourself be killed on purpose?" Ismail said. "To them it will be a show just the same."

"Giving up on yourself isn't what I'd expect from a Wallachian prince," Spencer said, and lifted Vlad by the armpits. "I'll take you for a walk around the yard, and that should bring you to your senses."

Vlad tried to struggle free of Spencer's embrace, until he whispered into Vlad's ear, "I bring a message from Lady Donatella."

Vlad felt a palpitation in his chest, and lied to himself it was just from the exertion to stand.

"I want him back in one piece," Ismail said.

Only when Vlad stepped onto the uneven ground of the courtyard did he realize how weak he'd become by starving himself for so many days. He leaned on Spencer, and hissed, "The message."

The yard was empty, except for a few grooms on the far side tending to the messengers' horses. Nonetheless, Spencer dropped his voice to a low whisper. "Lady Donatella has an escape plan for you."

Vlad froze in his tracks, and the palpitations in his chest resumed.

"But you must win the duel first," Spencer said, "to prove you told the truth about Omar."

Why did Vlad have to purchase his freedom for such a dirty price? He thought about the melee in Eisenmarkt. True, there he'd been ready to fight strangers who hadn't harmed him. But those were Turkish soldiers captured on Christian lands, which meant they weren't innocent. Besides, they stood to gain their freedom if they prevailed. In this fight his opponent had nothing to gain. "Isn't there a way I can escape before the fight?" he said.

Spencer ignored the question. "After the duel, the sultan will order you shipped to Amasya. Lady Mara has persuaded him already to let you leave with Mehmed's convoy. The boy's being taken to Bursa by Zaganos Pasha to begin his Qur'an studies."

"How's Lady Donatella involved in all of this?"

"The key to Donatella's plan is for you to find your way into Constantinople," Spencer said.

Mara ... Donatella. Leave it to women to come up with a cockeyed scheme. "Oh, that should be easy," he said. "I'll just ask for a leave from Zaganos to view the relic of the True Cross in Hagia Sophia."

Sarcasm didn't seem to affect Spencer. "Lady Donatella said that if anyone can figure a way to slip his guards, and make it to Constantinople, it's you."

Vlad was far from confident about that. But Donatella's trust in his abilities brought a warm glow to his cheeks.

"Once in the city you're to go to her palace, Ca' Loredano," Spencer said. "It's in the Venetian Quarter, built against the seawall. But only after dark."

The request surprised Vlad. "Why such need for secrecy inside a Christian city?"

"Emperor John has a fugitive exchange agreement with Murad," Spencer said. "If Lady Donatella were discovered to have helped you, the consequences would be dire for her."

It hadn't occurred to Vlad that Donatella might be at risk by helping him. Now her generosity toward him took an even greater significance. "I know a place in Constantinople where I can hide until after the sunset."

"While on the streets in the city, you mustn't raise suspicions about yourself," Spencer said. "Murad pays large rewards for the return of even the most insignificant runaway. It's to discourage slaves from considering Constantinople a safe haven. And he pays for captured runaways dead, or alive. He's turned practically all residents into his bounty hunters."

Vlad and Spencer had reached the place where the grooms gathered, so they stopped talking for a while. "A captain of Donatella's father's will take you to Venice on his galley," Spencer said when they were alone again. "All you have to do is scale the seawall down to his ship waiting in the Golden Horn."

To elude Emperor John's men, Donatella would let Vlad use the secret ladder she'd installed for Bianca. This did have the makings of a serious plan, something more than just a lady's fancy. He felt tendrils of hope stirring his chest.

"I am to accompany Lady Donatella and Bianca to Constantinople right after the duel," Spencer said. "They're returning there to make the necessary arrangements. The rest is up to God's mercy and your abilities."

On the way back to the infirmary, Vlad felt his step become steadier. His mind, freed from hopelessness by Donatella's plan, began to race with new possibilities. But when he lay on his cot for the night, the thought of the duel returned to torment him. *I've got no choice: it's kill or be killed.* The rationalization gave him some relief. But the bad taste of this detestable choice wouldn't be repressed.

26

Mehmed's Map Room

Donatella was checking Vlad's fever by rubbing her forehead against his. Her touch was lighter than a butterfly's, but her perfume so intense it startled him awake. He found his face buried in a mass of pink roses. In great confusion he batted at the flowers with both hands, and sat up in bed with a violent jerk.

"Afraid of flowers, Prince of Wallachia?" a man of about twenty said in Turkish, then laughed foolishly.

Another man, who appeared a bit younger, joined in, his laughter mocking. "Perhaps Zaganos Pasha should arm Danakil with a flower stalk, instead of a sword."

So now Vlad knew the name of the man he had to fight in the duel. He'd be one of Zaganos's retainers, picked at random, a slave who had no say. Did this Danakil even know what was in store for him?

"It will make the duel a lot funnier," the first man said. "I can see Vlad running around the arena, chased by a man wielding a sunflower stalk."

"And bleating like a frightened sheep," the second man said.

"Quiet, you two," a boy of about ten shouted in a shrill voice. It was he who held the bouquet of roses. Vlad recognized him as

Mehmed, the sultan's son. The boy had pale skin, and a hooked nose that threw its shadow over a tiny pair of red lips. In profile, Mehmed's nose gave Vlad the impression of a bird's beak poised to pluck a cherry.

"I grew these flowers myself," Mehmed said with evident pride. "And since you probably know nothing about gardening—"

"Mehmed has learned gardening as his craft," the older of the two men said.

"Don't interrupt me, Hamza," Mehmed said in a cold tone, and swung the bouquet at the man's face. Thorns scratched Hamza's cheek and drew blood. Mehmed turned to Vlad and said, "These are Ispahan roses that normally bloom only in the spring."

"Mehmed is the first gardener able to delay their blooming until this late in the summer," Hamza said, undaunted by Mehmed's reprimand. "Me and Yunus watched him do it in the hothouse."

Mehmed tossed the bouquet to the floor, and watched with indifference as Hamza and Yunus scrambled to gather the flowers. Then he turned to Vlad. "I heard you know history. Who's your favorite general?"

"You have to be smart to be accepted into Mehmed's circle," Yunus said.

"He made an exception for the two of you," Vlad said.

Mehmed gave a squeal of delight. "Vlad's pegged you quickly."

Vlad stood and put on his breeches, before he said, "Lucius Cornelius Sulla."

"Never heard of him," Hamza said. Yunus just shrugged to show he too was ignorant of Sulla. They both gave Vlad hostile glances.

"Not a bad strategist, Sulla," Mehmed said with the casual tone of one commenting on fine weather. "But anyone who gives up absolute power voluntarily must be either insane, or a coward."

Vlad wondered whose words this ten-year-old was echoing. Zaganos was Mehmed's *lala*, so he'd be the natural suspect. But the Third Vizier didn't strike Vlad as a fancier of history. He looked closer at Mehmed, and concluded the words had to be his own.

"Mehmed's idol is Alexander the Great," Hamza said.

"What makes you like Sulla?" Mehmed said.

Vlad found a mound of yogurt and a slice of watermelon on a leather trencher by the door. He sat on the floor next to it, and began to eat the yogurt slowly, ignoring his guests. When he finished he poured himself a mug of Solomon's chrysanthemum tisane, then said, "I find Sulla's epitaph inspiring: '*Nullus melior amicus, nullus peior inimicus*'." Mehmed watched him with anticipation, and Vlad concluded Latin wasn't something Mehmed had mastered. "No better friend, no worse enemy."

Hamza and Yunus watched Mehmed, to determine from his reaction whether to laugh, or scowl.

Mehmed cocked his head and narrowed his eyes. "I like the sound of that. I'll have you read me Plutarch's account of Sulla's life, if you survive the duel."

"Hekim Solomon reported to the sultan you might be too weak to fight next week," Yunus said.

"True," Mehmed said, unhappy. "Father's considering another week's postponement."

"We're leaving for Bursa in eight days," Yunus said. "If the fight's delayed we'll miss it."

"I must see the duel," Mehmed said, petulant. "It was my idea, after all."

"You should tell the sultan," Hamza said, "that Vlad's in a perfect fettle, and is just pretending to be weak to get out of the fight."

Vlad felt a bit nauseous after eating the yogurt, but he pushed on, and began to eat the melon too. Since learning of Donatella's plan, he'd resolved to do all he could to restore his strength. "I could fight today," he lied. "I don't need a postponement."

Mehmed clapped his hands, and said, "Splendid. We all believe Danakil will win, but I'd love you to prove us wrong." He became jovial, and seemed eager to reward Vlad in some manner. "Do you want to see my maps?"

"You can't show him your secret maps, Mehmed," Yunus said. "He's an unbeliever, and a murderer of Muslims."

Hamza snickered. "What's the harm, Yunus? You forget he's going to be killed next week?"

Vlad's annoyance with Mehmed's two mouthy companions vanished at the prospect of seeing real Ottoman maps. But he thought it wise to play down his interest. "I'll look at your maps, but just for a minute. I've got more important things to do."

Mehmed flashed Vlad a happy smile. "Follow me."

They walked into the second court, and headed for the corner left of the entrance to the Imperial Council Hall. The center of the court was a beehive of activity, with porters carrying planks, carpenters sawing, and carters discharging sand from wheelbarrows. The makings of a square enclosure, about six feet high, was beginning to take shape.

"That's the place for your duel," Mehmed said.

Vlad felt a ripple of excitement, similar to the one he experienced in Eisenmarkt when Nestor promised to let him and Marcus fight in the melee. Blood rushed to his head, and his feet felt stuck to the pavement.

"Look at how scared Vlad is," Hamza said.

"How does it feel to gaze upon the very place you're going to die in?" Yunus said.

"If you're patient, I'll show you one day," Vlad said.

The map room was a sizable hall with a barrel-vaulted ceiling. Abundant light poured in through lattice-covered windows. Three of the walls were plastered with maps, floor to ceiling. Half a dozen scribes were drawing more maps at individual worktables. They didn't raise their heads when Mehmed and his companions entered the room.

"Father thinks I spend too much time in this room, and not enough in the garden."

"All men in the House of Osman have to learn a trade," Yunus said. "Mehmed chose gardening."

"His Majesty the sultan is a bookbinder," Hamza said.

Mehmed made an impatient gesture. "Some days I'm fed up with gardening. But I can never get enough of map-making."

Vlad scanned the maps on the wall, and immediately spotted that of Wallachia. Drawn in vivid colors, the map showed a number of rivers and lakes he was unaware of. His father's maps were quite sketchy by comparison with this one. Here the Transylvanian mountain passes were shown in great detail. They had markings that seemed to indicate width, distance, and elevation, something of interest to a military commander moving troops across the mountains. The Black Sea was sprinkled with ships flying the Ottoman flag, a red field pierced by a white crescent moon.

More such ships were drawn on the Danube, all the way to Nicopolis.

Vlad's father said the Black Sea belonged practically to the Genovese, and his plans for restoring Wallachia's economy rested on the hope of commerce with them. Yet this map showed the sea being under Ottoman control. The implication for Wallachia of a power swap between Christians and Muslims in the Black Sea chilled Vlad's blood. "Is your father planning to take the Black Sea from the Genovese? I didn't think he had a navy."

Mehmed chuckled and seemed pleased for the chance to boast. "What you see here is *my* navy, when I become the sultan."

Ah, so these maps weren't Murad's war maps, but only the toys of a precocious child, playing off his fantasies. Nothing to worry about then. With Mehmed having a seventeen-year-old brother, his chance of inheriting the throne was negligible.

"The map of Wallachia is the first I drew, and it's Lala Zaganos's favorite one. I copied it off a Hungarian map he brought me as a gift in 'thirty-eight, when Father and he raided Transylvania. The ships are my own embellishments, though." Mehmed took Vlad by the arm and said, "Come see my most treasured possession."

In a corner of the room stood a platform several square yards in surface. On it, reproduced in astounding detail, stood the miniaturized model of a city surrounded on three sides by water. Even from ten feet away Vlad recognized it as Constantinople, though he'd never seen the Byzantine capital. Driven by an irresistible impulse he rushed forward, and avidly took in the magnificent sight. There was the Golden Horn, the Bosphorus, and the Sea of Marmara, just as he'd seen them in Italian manuscripts back at the Târgoviste monastery. The blue waters seemed to be cradling a giant nest filled with golden eggs, the gilded cupolas of hundreds of churches. When he heard Mehmed giggle behind him, Vlad realized he'd betrayed too much interest in the city that held the key to his own freedom.

But instead of appearing suspicious of Vlad's intent, Mehmed just seemed flattered by his curiosity. "This was made half a century ago by the order of my great-grandfather."

"Sultan Beyazid," Hamza said.

"It's been maintained current over the years," Yunus said.

Vlad leaned over the mockup trying to locate the Venetian Quarter. "It seems every palace and every church is shown."

Vlad's genuine amazement made Mehmed beam. "Even the smallest inhabitable structure is there. Look at that grain of rice painted red. It's the house of a gatekeeper at the market."

"Mehmed can name every public building and every private palace," Yunus said. "As his secretary, I keep the list of buildings up to date."

"Whenever a building goes up, or is torn down," Hamza said, "this model is updated within a month. If not, it's my job to remove the head of whoever's responsible for the omission."

Vlad had to fight off the temptation to ask Mehmed where Ca' Loredano was situated. Instead he said, "Is it true there are entire quarters occupied by Italians?"

Mehmed took a rod from a stand and assumed an authoritative stance. "Here, here, here, and here," he said, pointing to areas along the seawall on the Golden Horn side. "Genovese, Pisans, Amalfitans, and Venetians."

Vlad scanned the Venetian Quarter and spotted, in a cluster of modest buildings, an imposing structure built adjacent to the seawall. It had to be Donatella's palace. Mehmed was watching with piercing eyes, and Vlad felt exposed under the boy's stare. Was Mehmed able to read his thoughts? "What's that building with the Ottoman flag on top?" he said, to distract Mehmed. He pointed to the church of Hagia Sophia, which he recognized from engravings in his manuscript collection. "Is that your father's embassy in Constantinople?"

Hamza and Yunus laughed rudely, but Mehmed remained serious. "That's Hagia Sophia, the largest church in Christendom. It was Beyazid's dream to turn it into the greatest mosque in the world."

"I suppose you left his flag in place for a good reason," Vlad said, only to bait Mehmed into disclosing more of his fantasies. "You're planning to make good on your ancestor's ambition one day, aren't you?"

Mehmed grinned and assumed a superior air. "Except for Lala Zaganos, all others have the same thought you do: nothing but a boy's dreams. It will feel that much better when those dreams come true."

27

A Trial of Arms

For the remaining days before the duel, Vlad walked daily inside the first court, did calisthenics in his infirmary room, and followed the diet prescribed by Solomon Hekim. The doctor returned for a second visit and declared himself pleased with Vlad's recovery. But although Vlad no longer felt lightheaded or nauseous, he knew his movements were too slow, his muscles too slack to count on an easy victory.

He waited anxiously for Ismail and Spencer to return with outside news, especially about Donatella. He even pined for Mehmed's company, wishing he could discuss history with him. But no one came, and Vlad had to bide his time in solitude.

At night he dwelled on his approaching escape, and gave homesickness free rein. He'd close his eyes, and walk down the shady path to his beloved cloisters, where a roomful of manuscripts awaited him. Or, he'd be in the armory, at swordplay with Marcus and Gruya. In the afternoons he'd take his horse to the fields outside Târgoviște, and ride it faster and faster until the wind whipped his hair, and his mantle sailed.

Danakil's necessary killing was a thought he banished from his mind. Almost completely.

The morning of the duel found Vlad resigned to the idea fate brought this fight to him as just another test. If he were to fulfill his destiny, he'd have to take many lives on the way, some guilty, some innocent.

His appetite returned in full, and he'd begun to look forward to his morning meals. Today, however, he left his food untouched, and only drank of Solomon's tisane. Then he sat cross-legged on the floor, closed his eyes, and let his mind take him into the arena in the second court. There, the man named Danakil stood a few feet in front of him, sword in one hand, shield in the other. A helmet concealed his face, and Vlad found that not seeing Danakil's expression lessened his qualms about having to kill him. The man was a couple inches taller than Vlad, and had Omar's wiry body. Vlad gripped tight the hilt of his sword, and made a few quick slashes in the air. The weapon's heft was adequate, and the blade sang with the voice of good steel. Danakil held his shield high, but Vlad knew a feigned thrust to the man's loin would force him to lower it. Then, with lightning speed, Vlad would plant his sword into the hollow space behind the man's left collarbone, and it would be over. He heard that well executed, this move caused an immediate loss of consciousness and a painless death. The thought eased his conscience.

"Ready?" a voice broke through his concentration. "I'm to take you there now."

Vlad saw Ismail in the doorway, hands clasped together, regarding Vlad with sorrowful eyes.

"You look as if you were staring at a corpse," Vlad said. "Do you think I'm doomed?"

"You'd be better prepared in a week or two," Ismail said. "The way things stand, this isn't a fair fight for you." He looked away. "Ladies Mara and Donatella have spent the night praying for you. They'll continue to do so from the women's gallery, above the Gate of Felicity."

Vlad no longer cared that the Turks turned his fight into a spectacle. But he would've preferred Donatella not to witness the degrading killing he was forced to commit.

More than fifty people had gathered in the second court, chatty groups sheltered in the shade of the arcade. At Vlad's approach, they all turned their heads and gave him curious looks. Vlad recognized some of the men he'd seen in the council hall. He glanced, without stopping, at the screened gallery above the Gate of Felicity and imagined a dozen pairs of women's eyes fixed on him, Donatella's blue ones among them.

"That man waiting for you there, by the arena's gate, is Skanderbeg," Ismail said. "Because of his experience with this kind of matter, the sultan's asked him to prepare you for the fight. I'll leave you with him and return home. I can't watch this."

Vlad didn't reply, his mind focused on the sight in front of him. Around the improvised enclosure, spectators' stands had been built, one section covered in red silk. *Murad and his dignitaries will stand there.* There was also a higher platform for someone of a short stature, covered in silk as well. *That's Mehmed's stand.*

"Your grandfather was my childhood hero, Prince Vlad," Skanderbeg said in lieu of a greeting. "Stories about King Justus's bravery at the Battle of Nicopolis are what I was weaned on."

Skanderbeg was tall, had broad shoulders, and radiated immense strength. His dense black beard grew from just below his eyes, adding fierceness to his overpowering presence. But what struck Vlad most was Skanderbeg's voice. With no apparent effort it reached an almost painfully loud volume as words tumbled out of his chest with the rumbling of a rockslide.

The mention of Vlad's grandfather had to be a provocation. "An Ottoman general confessing to admiration for someone who fought Islam all his life?"

"I was a Christian at the time. But you're right to be leery of me, since I'm a Muslim now." He winked as if there were more to the story. "Here, take this." He handed Vlad a short, single-edged sword whose blade had been recently sharpened. "It's my lucky weapon. It helped me win my first duel in this very spot, nineteen years ago."

It also helped Skanderbeg prove the sincerity of his Muslim faith, Vlad remembered. Though of good steel, the sword felt too light, and was barely two-thirds the length of Vlad's sword back home.

Next Skanderbeg gave Vlad a boiled-leather shield, only a foot across. "I heard you're still weak so I chose a lightweight one.

You'll be thankful not to be weighted down in this heat. Zaganos is making his man wear practically a barn door for a shield."

"A child's sword and a potlid for shield … have you got anything else that will ensure I lose the fight?"

A page opened the arena's gate and Vlad stepped through it, glad to be away from this duplicitous character. Skanderbeg called after him, "I'll tell you why people lose fights, and it isn't because of their weapons."

Was this the right moment for a philosophical chat? "I don't want lessons from a renegade."

But Skanderbeg appeared bent on sharing his views. "Ignorance of the enemy. Know more about him than he knows about you, and you'll win every time, no matter the balance of forces." He laughed deep and harsh, a bear's growl.

Impatient, the page slammed the gate in Vlad's face and secured it from the outside with a crossbar.

Vlad took stock of the space inside the enclosure, and concluded it was more a cage than an arena. He gauged it to be only four hundred square feet, offering little room to retreat when it became necessary. The ground was covered with loose sand that made the footing unstable. Under the midday sun, with no shade and not a breath of wind, the air in the arena was sizzling. Well, if these were hardships for Vlad, they'd also be for Danakil.

Vlad shaded his eyes and pretended to judge the direction of the sunrays, surreptitiously surveying the screen of the women's loggia. Four fingers, nails painted blue, poked through the latticework and seemed to be waving at him. That nail color was probably common, but still his heartbeat picked up at thinking Donatella had just connected with him.

That moment a *mehterân,* a military band, positioned somewhere in a side gallery, struck up a shrill martial tune. Kettledrums of all sizes, bells, cymbals, oboes, horns, and trumpets seemed to compete in creating a deafening medley of discordant sounds. The music had to be the signal for spectators to take their standing places on the platforms outside the arena. Within a few minutes, turbaned heads popped up everywhere above the enclosure, except in the area reserved for the sultan and his immediate circle.

The music stopped, and the spectators' eyes turned to the space left empty in the stand. Sultan Murad, Khalil Pasha, and Mehmed appeared there, chest-high above the wooden wall. Soon they were followed by Zaganos and Sadeddin Hoja, the Chief Judge.

Vlad hadn't seen Murad since the afternoon of the first day in Edirne. He appeared to be dressed in the same modest brown robe, and again wore a simple white turban. Just like that day on his way to the Friday Mosque, the sultan was jovial, and looked upon the people surrounding him as a benevolent father. His chestnut beard had become lighter in color and his face was deeply sun-tanned from the summer of hunting. At this close distance, Vlad noted striking similarities between Mehmed and his father: same amber-colored eyes ringed in dark brown, same hooked nose, same small mouth, same full lips.

"You may begin, Sadeddin Hoja," Murad said.

Hearing the sultan's melodious voice reminded Vlad this all-powerful ruler was known to love wine, music, and poetry more than the art of war. Yet he'd been defeating the Christians for over two decades. Was it because he knew his enemies better than they knew him?

The Chief Judge leaned over the wall, looked down upon Vlad with knitted brows, and said, "Vlad of House Basarab, you've been accused of the murder of three Ottoman subjects on Wallachian soil." He paused and looked around him. People nodded to show they understood his pronouncement. "And you, in turn, have accused the dead men and the only surviving witness of your attack, Omar Amasyalı, of committing an illegal raid in Wallachia. Under these circumstances, the truth of your accusation should normally be tested by torture. But His Majesty, the sultan, has shown you mercy on account of your having voluntarily surrendered as a hostage for your father." The *kadıasker* paused again for effect. "The sultan has granted you a trial by combat, after the fashion of the infidel. If you lose the duel but survive, your guilt will be proven, and you'll be executed by decapitation."

Sadeddin Hoja lifted his hand, and the *mehterân* burst into a fresh jumble of sounds that pained Vlad's ears. The noise covered all other sounds, and when it ceased, Vlad realized someone had entered the arena and was standing behind him. He could tell by the pungent odor of sweat redolent of unknown spices.

Danakil. Vlad's body tensed painfully, and blood rushed to his face. Then it occurred to him Danakil wasn't a true fighter, or he would've attacked without a warning. Vlad spun around and a wave of terror washed over him when his eyes landed on Danakil. The man was an African of a stature Vlad had never seen: seven feet tall, and twice as broad in the shoulders as he. The size of Danakil's sword made Vlad's look like a duck-roasting skewer, and his shield *was* a barn door. But Zaganos wasn't satisfied with giving his man oversized weapons; he also clad him in a mail coif and a long-sleeved, knee-length mail shirt that left few spots vulnerable to Vlad's attack.

Danakil kept his eyes riveted on Vlad's, seemingly not knowing how to start the fight. Sweat was already beading on the exposed part of the African's face, but he couldn't wipe it off with his chain mail gauntlets. He was baking inside his iron cocoon. *I have to get him moving until he can't take the heat anymore.*

Only five feet separated them. Vlad retreated slowly, step by step, while he stared his opponent in the eye. Danakil remained still, a predator fascinated by the futile movements of his tiny prey. When Vlad's back touched the wall, he rebounded and rushed at Danakil with all the speed he could muster. In the last second Vlad leaped into the air and slammed both feet into Danakil's shield. The man gave a cry, but didn't fall back under the impact, as expected. Instead, Vlad's feet took the shock of the encounter as if he'd landed on a brick wall. He tumbled to the ground and rolled over to his right. Danakil's sword descended in a big arc, but missed Vlad's shoulder and sank into the sand.

Vlad scrambled to his feet before Danakil could repeat his move, and dashed to the far wall. When he turned around Vlad saw Danakil five steps behind, shield and sword raised high. The African's mouth was bloody from the impact with his own shield, and his eyes, benign moments before, appeared murderous now.

Vlad waited until Danakil was within a blade's length of him before he stepped sideways. The giant, unable to check his movement, slashed the air with his sword, then crashed his shield into the wall with a loud bang. Vlad continued this game of cat and mouse for another ten minutes, observing Danakil's speed, and waiting to see him slacken enough for the move Vlad planned.

Only once did Danakil guess correctly the direction in which Vlad intended to dodge his assault. That time, Danakil's shield caught Vlad in the shoulder and pinned him against the wall. A shrill cry of "*Dio*, God," came from the women's gallery. The spectators, pleased to finally see Danakil gain the upper hand, exhaled collectively, and someone shouted "*Allāh*." Danakil stepped back to raise his sword, but by the time he was ready to strike again, Vlad was at the other end of the arena.

Vlad waited for Danakil to attack him again, but the lumbering giant's charge had become a slow shuffle. It was time to end it. When Danakil reached the center of the arena, Vlad shot up his sword arm, and assumed a running stance. Danakil stopped in anticipation. Vlad threw his shield at Danakil's face, and the African lifted his own shield to deflect the projectile. That moment Vlad sprung forward with a powerful yell. Two feet before he reached his opponent, Vlad dove headlong under Danakil's shield and past his left foot. While still airborne, Vlad spun his body to land on his back. At the same time he visualized his blade finding its way between Danakil's legs, and sinking unhindered by the armor into his bowels.

But, sword poised for the kill, Vlad discovered he lacked the store of hatred he needed to take this unfortunate man's life. Instead he swiped his blade across the back of Danakil's naked knees, then rolled away to safety.

With an agonized squeal Danakil dropped to his knees, then tumbled forward onto his face. In an instant Vlad straddled him, and shoved the tip of his sword under the mantle of Danakil's coif. He heard the excited talk of the spectators above him, and for the first time since the duel started, looked up at the stands. As he expected, Zaganos and Sadeddin Hoja cast him with venomous stares. But Murad and Mehmed were grinning, tapping the top of the fence in front of them in approval.

Khalil Pasha cupped his hands, and shouted over the din, "You've proven your innocence, Prince Vlad. You may kill Danakil. You've earned the right."

*Maybe the right, but not the obligatio*n. Vlad let his sword fall to the ground.

28

At the Hamam

The fight left Vlad drained of energy and dazed in the spirit. There was talk around him, but he could barely follow it. Someone picked up his sword and the blade flashed in the sun, showing a bloody edge. A moment of confusion, then the realization, *it's his blood.* He watched listlessly as palace hands carried Danakil out of the arena on a stretcher. The African's head, now stripped of his coif, was drenched in sweat. A look of panic, disproportionate with his injury, made his eyes appear as goose eggs marked with large drops of black ink. Danakil feared, perhaps, that incapacitated and masterless, his life was forfeit. Vlad felt sorry for his adversary, but had no way of helping him.

"He didn't fight fair," someone shouted from behind the half-open gate.

"I told you he's a coward," someone else said.

"You're both wrong." Mehmed's angry voice sounded from the same direction. The boy and his two inseparable companions barged into the arena. A water carrier with a string of brass cups dangling from his belt followed them. Striding in Vlad's direction, Mehmed called out, "I'd like to see either of you bring down a man of Danakil's stature with that puny sword Vlad was given."

Mehmed barked an order at the water carrier, and the man handed Vlad a cup filled from a leather costrel on his back. As he drank, Vlad felt the haze that clouded his mind slowly dissipate.

"I liked how you tricked Danakil," Mehmed said. "But why did you spare his life?"

Vlad shrugged. "He's not Omar."

"Come with me," Mehmed said, in the tone of one accustomed to being obeyed.

"Sorry, but I'm not up to looking at maps now. I need rest." Vlad stepped around Mehmed and headed for the gate. With the trial of arms behind him, he had mind for only one thing now: find a way to return home.

"Wait," Mehmed called after him. "You know I'm leaving for Bursa in the morning. You won't be my travel companion smelling as you do. Come have a bath." When Vlad didn't stop walking Mehmed added, "The Prophet, peace be upon him, said, 'Every man owes Allah at least one bath per week'."

"Vlad stinks as if he were months in arrears," Yunus said. "But today isn't the day for the infidels at the *hamam.*"

"You forget I can make an exception to any rule," Mehmed said.

Spurning Mehmed's company wasn't a smart thing to do, no matter how tired Vlad felt. Besides, this would be an opportunity to learn more about their upcoming trip. He waited for Mehmed, and the two walked together toward the gate of the second court. Hamza and Yunus followed, mumbling to each other, evidently not pleased with the attention Mehmed accorded Vlad.

"Are we going through Constantinople on the way to Bursa?" Vlad asked, aware that couldn't be the case.

Both Hamza and Yunus leaped at the opportunity to ridicule him.

"How can you ask such a stupid thing?" Hamza said. "Do you know what leverage Emperor John would gain over the sultan if he laid his hands on Mehmed?"

"No member of the House Osman has ever set foot in Constantinople," Yunus said. "They don't teach you anything where you come from."

"We'll be close enough to Constantinople to hear the chatter of the people on its wharves across the Golden Horn," Mehmed said. "But our crossing to Asia will take place from Galata on ships provided by the town's *podestà*. The Genovese are friends of my father."

By recalling Mehmed's model in the map room, Vlad could visualize Galata on the north shore of the Golden Horn. Constantinople was less than half a mile across the water of the inlet. As far as a springboard for his escape, Galata was an ideal spot. But even supposing he eluded his guards, he'd still need money for the ferry to cross the Horn. Swimming wasn't a viable option, as it would attract attention. This was a thing Donatella had obviously overlooked.

Woman's superficiality.

A bitter taste rose to his throat, and for an instant he resented Donatella for coming up with a plan that relied on an impossible step. Then he felt ignoble for giving in so easily to ingratitude.

"Before we cross to Asia we camp north of Galata, on the Bosphorus," Yunus said, "so Selim Agha can try to beat an old archery record."

Vlad shrugged, unable to hide his indifference to such meaningless details.

Hamza found in that a reason to put Vlad down again. "You have no idea how important Selim bin Sedad is. He's no other than the sultan's *musahib*."

"I was told a man named Tirendaz was that," Vlad said.

"One and the same," Mehmed said. "Selim Agha is nicknamed Tirendaz, master archer, because he's the foremost bowman in the empire. Father claims he assigned Tirendaz to my Asian entourage to teach me archery. But in reality, Father worries about Zaganos's influence on me, and wants to use Tirendaz as a counterbalance."

In his present frame of mind Vlad had interest in neither Tirendaz's archery prowess, nor his role in Mehmed's upbringing. What concerned him was how far this camp would be from Galata, and whether he would be able to get away from there before they boarded the ship for Asia. But those were questions he couldn't pose. "Why are we leaving the palace premises?" he asked when Mehmed led him out the front gate.

"Father prefers to bathe in town, where ordinary people do," Mehmed said. "So we don't have a *hamam* at the palace."

"When Mehmed becomes sultan," Hamza said, "he'll build a proper palace with its own *hamam*."

From the outside, the *hamam* was unimpressive. Its grandeur was revealed inside, through a multitude of domed rooms and arched passageways whose walls were clad in cream-colored marble that gave the interior a soothing appearance.

The patrons milling around the dressing hall gave no sign of recognizing Mehmed. But from their furtive glances, Vlad suspected Mehmed was known at the *hamam*.

"You wait for us here," Mehmed ordered Hamza and Yunus. "Vlad and I have had enough of your company for now."

The two youths looked at Mehmed, dejected, and seemed disposed to argue. But something in his stare persuaded them to obey, and they retreated slowly with the bent necks of dogs used to a cruel master's beatings. Their eyes turned to Vlad, reproachful and malevolent.

Vlad and Mehmed took to their dressing cabins and reemerged a few moments later, naked but for towels wrapped around their waists.

"Hey, is that an amulet?" Mehmed cried when he noticed Vlad's medallion. He reached out and touched the black disk with a tentative finger. "A dragon with a cross on its back. That's a combination I've never seen. I want it."

Yunus and Hamza rushed forward for a look.

"Don't touch it, Mehmed," Yunus said. "The dragon is the symbol of the Devil for the infidels."

"Vlad's a Shaytan worshiper," Hamza cried. "That explains Danakil's defeat."

"He carved a cross on the dragon's back to mask his own allegiance to the Devil," Yunus said.

"I don't care about any of that," Mehmed said, and stomped his foot. "I still want the talisman."

"A cross around the neck of a future sultan?" Vlad said, to dampen Mehmed's interest in the medallion. "I'm sure the Pope would celebrate that news with a special mass."

Mehmed winced, and his voice reflected hesitation when he said, "Some Muslims believe the cross is more potent against jinns than talismans with Qur'anic inscriptions."

"If I were a Muslim I'd call such a belief heresy," Vlad said. "I don't want to be accused of trying to convert you to Christianity with my amulet. So I won't let you have it."

Hamza stepped up to Vlad and assumed a threatening pose. "No one says 'no' to Mehmed," he growled. "Let alone a hostage from the backwaters of Dar al-Harb. If he asks you for something, you give it to him."

This was a fork in the road that forced Vlad to choose between submission and assertiveness. How easy that choice would be on horseback, with a sharp blade in hand. Not so easy when empty-handed and practically butt-naked. He noticed Mehmed was observing him with keen attention. *Give in to Hamza's bullying, and Mehmed would peg me as a coward, not worthy to take along as his companion. Deny Mehmed his request, and I might end up back in the dungeon.* Either choice seemed to place his escape plan in jeopardy. A heat wave coursed up his body and turned the tips of his ears hot.

He linked his hands behind his back in a gesture that said, "Take it if you must." Then he looked past Hamza, and bored into Mehmed's eyes with calm indifference. "You know an amulet taken by force brings a curse upon the taker."

Hamza and Yunus turned to Mehmed, seeking guidance on how to proceed. He hesitated a moment, then waved them away with an impatient flick of his hand. "Stop meddling in my affairs," he shouted in a tinny voice that betrayed his embarrassment at being forced to back down. "I can take care of myself without your help." Then he gave Vlad a smile, as if the unpleasant incident had been only a prank. "Time to go to the hot room."

Two masseurs approached and bowed deferentially, then led Vlad and Mehmed to an octagonal domed hall with niches for private bathing on seven of its sides. In the room's center stood a circular marble platform rising about two feet off the floor. Despite its name, the air in the "hot room" was cool. Vlad looked around, confused.

Mehmed anticipated Vlad's reaction. "You'll understand soon why they call it the hot room." He showed pride in initiating Vlad to the bathing ritual.

Vlad's masseur was a muscular Armenian named Alexan. He pointed to the marble platform and commanded Vlad gruffly, "Lay there until I tell you," then left the room.

The platform was crowded with sprawling bodies, heads at the center, legs fanning out like the spokes of a giant wagon wheel. Vlad took the place of a missing spoke and stretched out on his back. When Mehmed tried to get into the space between Vlad and his neighbor the man rose quickly and left the platform. One by one, all the other men departed in silence, leaving Mehmed and Vlad alone.

The marble surface turned out to be exceedingly hot. At first it scorched Vlad's skin, but after a while it gave him a pleasant sensation along the spine. Within minutes his eyes began to sting from the sweat pouring down his brow. Alexan returned with a towel dipped in ice water that Vlad pressed to his forehead. Slowly, the heat enveloped his body, and began to melt away the dull fatigue that had been clinging to him for so long. From above, a milky light seemed to drip down through a myriad of fist-sized holes that punctured the dome. More than an hour passed in a silence only occasionally broken by the splash of water when a bather would sluice himself in one of the alcoves. Vlad let his mind wander freely to peaceful scenes from back home, and an insidious vapor of contentment began to suffuse his body.

Mehmed raised himself on one elbow. "They say the ground gets much hotter than this in Mecca. Some pilgrims walk barefoot on it to blister their feet in homage to Allah." His shaved head glistened with perspiration. Naked and without his turban, Mehmed looked even younger than his ten years. Yet despite his youth, a disturbing air of earnestness emanated from him, as if he were a grown man trapped in a child's body. "I'll never see that for myself, though," he said, wistful.

"But you will, when you go on the hajj," Vlad said. "Isn't that mandatory for any Muslim who can afford the cost of the trip?"

"Jihad against the infidels is an acceptable alternative to the hajj for sultans and their sons. The hajj is too dangerous for people like us."

"So even your father, the most powerful man on earth, can never go to Mecca?"

"He'll use a surrogate pilgrim, an Emir-al-Hajj, to perform the hajj for him. And so will I."

"Unless you conquer Arabia from the Mamluks when you become sultan," Vlad said, to add a bit of levity to the discussion.

Mehmed didn't smile. "You know that Alexander told his friends at the age of ten he would conquer Babylon one day?"

The two masseurs reappeared pushing wheeled cauldrons filled with soapy water. Alexan beckoned Vlad with his index finger, showing him a missing upper tooth by the way of a smile.

"Be ready for some friendly torture," Mehmed said.

Vlad slithered to the edge of the platform, and turned onto his stomach, resting his forehead on a tin bowl Alexan provided.

"Say," Mehmed exclaimed, "where did you get those nasty scars? They look pretty recent."

"Ask Zaganos Pasha," Vlad said. "Though he's likely to deny having anything to do with them."

"He did that?" Mehmed said, incredulous.

"Why is he going with you to Asia? Isn't his place next to your father?"

"As my *lala,* he's expected to remain close to me at all times. But don't be afraid of him. If he knows you're my friend he won't touch you again, as long as you don't give him a valid reason."

That was far from reassuring to Vlad. "Not even you can prevent Zaganos from staging an accident," he said. "I cost him his war against Hungary and the conquest of Wallachia. He's not likely to forget that soon."

Mehmed too lay on his stomach on the edge of the platform, head-to-head with Vlad. "I can make Zaganos do anything I wish. He wants badly to replace Khalil Pasha as the Grand Vizier, but

Father won't hear of that. Zaganos knows I can make it happen when I'm on the throne."

Vlad was surprised Mehmed would speak aloud of such sensitive matters. He raised his head, and pointed with his chin at the two masseurs.

"Oh, don't worry about them," Mehmed said with a chuckle. "They've had their eardrums pierced out with hot irons so they can't hear a sound."

Alexan poured a bucket of soapy water over Vlad, and began to rub his back with a rough mitten that bit into his skin like a steel rasp. Mehmed received the same treatment from his own masseur.

"You seem to have no doubt about becoming the next sultan," Vlad said. "I wonder if your brother feels the same way regarding his chances."

"Only Allah can decide who succeeds Father onto the throne."

"Your great-grandfather Beyazid didn't wait for Allah's decision. He took matters into his own hands when his father died. Are you planning to do the same?"

Mehmed raised himself on his elbows with a jerk, and gave Vlad a reproachful look. "You're being provocative asking such a thing. True, Beyazid killed his brother to become sultan, but only because he had no other choice. His father had just been assassinated, and if Beyazid hadn't done it, the army would've been left leaderless on the battlefield."

This wasn't the reasoning of a ten-year-old. Zaganos must've worked hard on convincing Mehmed that killing a sibling to become ruler of the empire was Allah's will.

Alexan scraped Vlad's back with a demonic vigor, and Vlad had to bite his fist not to scream when his scars fell under the Armenian's perverted ministrations. Next came the turn of Vlad's legs, and soon his entire back side was aflame. Just as the feeling of being burned alive began to subside, a torrent of near-boiling water burst over him. Before he could recover from this surprise that cut off his breathing, Alexan flipped Vlad over and buried him under a mountain of suds. Then, without a moment's respite, Alexan relaunched his mitten on its merciless mission, this time on Vlad's front side.

"This was only the beginning," Mehmed said, when Alexan finished the scraping. "Brace yourself. It's going to get painful from here on."

Alexan began to knead Vlad's muscles with a mixture of cruelty and skill.

"If you wanted me to forget my worries—" A sharp pain Alexan inflicted to Vlad's inner thigh stopped him in mid-sentence, and took a few moments to recede. "—you've succeeded," Vlad groaned, with a mind to bash in Alexan's head.

Mehmed chuckled. "Save your breath for the next phase."

How much worse could it get? Just then Alexan twisted one of Vlad's arms, and bent it upward at an impossible angle. "*Kurva bitang*," Vlad cursed in Hungarian, between clenched teeth. Calling the Armenian a whore's bastard provided him a little relief.

"Oh, yes, forgot to tell you praying aloud is acceptable," Mehmed said, and tittered mischievously.

Vlad's grimaces and curses amused Mehmed but had no effect on Vlad's deaf masseur. Alexan just flashed his sardonic smile, and went on undaunted about his task. He was evidently bent on proving that human limbs were capable of bending, twisting, and swiveling in their sockets to a greater degree than they were given credit for. By the time there was nothing left to crush, pinch, or stretch in Vlad's body, he felt as if he'd tumbled down a long flight of stairs.

Yet when he rose from the marble slab he seemed to float, and moved about with a lightness never before experienced.

They walked next to the cooling room, where *hamam* attendants served bathers fruits and sweets.

"No bath is complete until you've quenched your thirst with pomegranate juice," Mehmed said, regarding Vlad with the pride of a host who'd just given a successful banquet.

If Lala Gunther cherished a memory of his years as a slave in Asia it was that of the pomegranate, which he called Allah's fruit. As Vlad let the fragrant, sweet-tart juice cool his overheated body, he agreed the fruit was divine indeed.

29

Sultan's Gift

Back at his cell in the palace infirmary Vlad was met with two surprises.

"You don't look, or smell like someone who fought for his life only hours ago," Ismail said from the doorway, his face crinkled in a happy grin. The secretary was concealing something behind his back. "Just don't get used to the pleasures of the *hamam*, Vlad. You won't be having one in the Amasya fortress."

"Thoughtful of you to remind me." Vlad pushed Ismail gently to the side, and entered his cell. "Ooh," he exclaimed, when he saw a new cot had been brought in, and someone was lying on it, covered head to toe with a sheet.

"That's your slave, Danakil," Ismail said. "Hekim Solomon has stitched his wounds, and given him milk of *kash-kash*, poppy seeds, so he could sleep."

"What am I to do with him?" Vlad wondered how deep his blade had cut into the backs of Danakil's knees. "Can he walk?"

"According to Solomon, the wound on Danakil's left knee isn't too serious. But you severed two ligaments on his right one. He won't be walking again without crutches."

Vlad dropped onto his cot, the earlier feeling of wellbeing lost. He'd reduced to a life of beggary the man who unwittingly helped him prove his innocence. Was this better than if he'd killed the unlucky bungler with a quick jab to the back of his skull? "Won't Zaganos take him back?"

"The vizier would have to buy him back from you. That's not likely to happen, damaged as this poor man is. Besides, Danakil's failure to kill you put him in bad odor with Zaganos."

"I'll emancipate him then, and he can try his luck working in someone else's harem."

"Please don't, Master," Danakil cried from under his sheet, in a plaintive and drowsy tone. He spoke Turkish with a heavy accent. "I want to go with you."

Vlad was taken aback by his outburst. "Don't you know I'm being taken to a prison?"

"I'll go wherever you go." Danakil threw off his cover, and tried unsuccessfully to sit up in bed. "You spared my life, so it belongs to you now."

Vlad felt vexed with this unexpected entanglement. "I don't want your life," he shouted, then immediately felt bad for the man and softened his tone. "I won't have much use of a servant in prison. Besides, I'm too poor to feed you."

With a mysterious grin, Ismail tossed the parcel he'd been hiding onto Vlad's knees. "You might not be as poor as you think. It seems you've impressed the sultan this morning, and this is his way of showing it."

"So, now I have a silk robe of no use to me," Vlad said, after untying the package, "and a servant who can't walk. What else could a hostage wish for?"

"It's not just a silk robe." Ismail lifted the garment and showed Vlad the gold-thread embroidery. "I've seen the sultan wear this robe in the Imperial Council Hall. You should feel honored by such a lavish gift."

Vlad thought about summer coming soon to an end. If he succeeded to escape, his journey home would take all autumn. And if he failed, he'd have to face winter in Asia. In either case, he'd need better garments than a fancy robe. "I'd feel more honored if Murad sent me clothes for the weather ahead."

"I've already taken care of that myself," Ismail said, and pointed to a burlap sack lying next to Vlad's bed. "You've got there the clothes you'll require for cold weather."

"Zaganos Pasha received a gift like this from His Majesty last year," Danakil said, eyeing the robe. "And he sold it to the treasury for two thousand aspers."

"Sell the gift?" Vlad said, incredulous, but his mind raced with the possibility of coming into some money. "Wouldn't that be an insult to him?"

"The sultan believes it's more delicate to show his favor with gifts than money," Ismail said. "But he expects people to sell his gifts. There is a clerk at the palace treasury responsible for just such transactions."

So Donatella's plan wasn't so flawed, after all. Here was the ferry money Vlad had worried about, and a lot more. Enough to disentangle from Danakil without guilt. "Then get me all the silver you can, Ismail."

Ismail left with the robe, and returned an hour later to hand Vlad a leather purse. "Quite a fortune," he said, visibly proud of his accomplishment. "There would've been three thousand aspers, but the head of the treasury gets three percent of all sales. He also retained a hundred aspers as tax on your assuming Danakil's ownership. Then there was the *baksheesh* to the clerk, the doorkeepers, the—"

"Never mind all of that." Vlad weighed the purse in his hand. "There is more left in here than I need."

"I've got to go now to supervise the packing for my master," Ismail said. "He requires special equipment for the conditioning of his flight bow when he attempts to beat an old archery record near Galata."

After Ismail left Vlad counted one hundred aspers from the purse, and tied them in the tail of his shirt.

"As my servant," he said to Danakil, "your first assignment is to look after this purse for me." He placed the heavy coin pouch on Danakil's chest.

"You trust me with so much money?" Danakil appeared stunned. "I'll hide it under my shirt when I travel, and—"

"You won't be able to travel for a few weeks," Vlad said. Danakil's face dropped, and he tried again to sit up. But the pain in his knees must've been intense, for he gave out a yelp and dropped back on his pillow.

"Your second assignment is to come find me in Amasya, and return the purse to me, as soon as you are back on your feet. Until then use money from it to pay for food, clothes, and lodging. No servant of mine should appear as a beggar."

Danakil's eyes filled with tears, and he pressed Vlad's hand to his heart. "I won't bring you shame, Master."

"Your third assignment is to see to it that no one disturbs my sleep tonight. I've got a long journey ahead of me, and I haven't rested well in weeks."

Vlad threw himself on his cot dressed as he was, and within minutes was asleep. When the predawn call to prayer sounded, he shot out of his bed, grabbed his burlap sack, and lunged at the door in the dark. There he stumbled upon Danakil, who was sleeping on the floor, his body sprawled across the threshold. The new servant had taken his third assignment literally. Vlad dragged him by his armpits just far enough so he could squeeze through the door, and left the cell.

The palace courtyard was seething with activity, strangely undertaken in near-silence. Horses were being saddled, camels loaded, and mules harnessed, without a single order being shouted, or disputed.

It was happening. The convoy that would unknowingly take Vlad toward freedom was about to set in motion. He wanted to laugh, remembering how certain Father and Michael were the Turks couldn't be outmaneuvered. And at how much they discounted his own ability to fend for himself. *Old men just lose their nerve and see everything in dark colors.* Well, he'd show them how wrong they were. A few weeks from now he'd walk into his father's castle in Târgoviște and sit at the dinner table, as if he'd just returned from exercising his horse in the countryside. When they all clamored to learn how he escaped, he'd shrug and say it wasn't something worth talking about. Father's and Michael's unsatisfied curiosity would be his secret revenge.

30

Storm on the Bosphorus

August 1442, Constantinople, Byzantine Empire

The last moments of Vlad's duel caused Donatella to hold her breath. When she realized he won, she exhaled noisily and stepped back from the screen, overcome by dizziness.

Mara embraced her with one arm and cradled her head with the other. "It's over, dear heart," she whispered into Donatella's ear. "The good Lord has answered our prayers."

Donatella felt her body shaken by a tremor. She hid her face in the crook of Mara's shoulder, and let the emotions held in check for days pour out in a stream of tears.

"Come to my apartment and rest for a while," Mara said. "You couldn't be more emotionally drained if Vlad were your own son."

Donatella knew the passion she'd developed for Vlad was no secret to Mara. Her friend's delicacy in pretending not to be aware of it filled Donatella with gratitude. "I must leave for Constantinople to provision Captain Andrea's galley for the voyage to Venice. That will take two days, perhaps more—"

"You'll have plenty of time," Mara said. "Even though Mehmed and his entourage are leaving tomorrow, they'll be traveling slower than you and Bianca because of their baggage train. And I learned this morning they're planning to spend an extra day outside Galata. It's for a silly purpose, something about an old archery record the Grand Vizier's nephew's trying to beat."

"I can't risk not having the galley ready for when Vlad makes his break."

"I'm glad to hear you're no longer saying, 'if he makes his break'." Mara wiped Donatella's tears, and kissed her on both cheeks. "I hate to lose you so soon. I was counting on having you here through the fall. But that was before you 'adopted' Vlad."

Donatella had never made the trip between Edirne and Constantinople in less than seven days. This time she drove her muleteers so hard they covered the hundred and fifty miles in only six days. Even Bianca, who usually begged her mother to maintain a slow pace, urged the men on relentlessly.

A novel and heady feeling of empowerment began to throb in Donatella's breast. Never in her life had she been able to stand up to the men who had power over her. Her father, with his misguided politics, bartered her off to the Grimaldi clan. "A woman's role is to submit," Father reminded her when she beseeched him not to do it. Submit she did, only to have her dignity trampled with impunity by that brute who called himself her husband. Later, her brother-in-law practically *sold* Bianca into concubinage, and nothing Donatella said could make him reverse his action. "The girl has to leave home sooner or later, so we might as well take advantage of this unique opportunity," he told Donatella. "If she's lucky to give the sultan a son, he'll marry her, and that will give us immense influence at the court."

But now Donatella's absolute submission to the will of men had come to an end. True, snatching Vlad away from Murad wouldn't make up for the loss of Bianca. But it would lift the veil of helplessness that had smothered Donatella all her life, and let in a whiff of fresh air.

"Do you realize, Mother, we'll never see Vlad again after he escapes?" Bianca said one evening while she and Donatella lay inside their wagon.

In denial, Donatella had repressed that thought with determination until now. Whenever it stirred, she'd squash it like a hated bug and focus instead on the escape plan. Or she'd bury it under a heap of mundane preoccupations: find a softer hair dye … try a more fetching tooth enamel … order a fresh supply of soap from Aleppo … shop for a chambermaid skilled in cosmetics. But now, when Bianca voiced what Donatella dreaded to contemplate, denial became pointless. "You're right, Bianca, we'll never see Vlad again," she said, and pain of a kind never experienced before pierced her heart. Then, thinking it would make Bianca feel better, she added, "We'll always remember him, though."

But will he remember us?

When they arrived at their Constantinople residence, Donatella was alarmed to learn Captain Andrea hadn't yet returned from Bursa. His last haul of the year was scheduled for mid-August, and it was almost the end of the month now.

"Go down to the harbor," she ordered her steward, "and find out if other ships have been delayed. Perhaps the weather's been bad in the Sea of Marmara." Ships returning from the Asian side were often held back by winds and currents, sometimes for more than a week.

The steward returned in the middle of the afternoon. "Several ships are making their way toward the city, my lady," he reported, "and Captain Andrea's galley is among them."

Donatella sighed, relieved. Then she noticed the steward was fidgeting. "Is there more to it?"

The man scratched the top of his head, before he said, "The winds are contrary, my lady, and they're preventing the ships from entering the Horn. The port master said he fears for the ships' safety, if they remain at large after dark."

Donatella looked out the window, and was reassured to see the sky was clear. Perhaps there was no reason to worry. Still she'd feel better to see for herself Andrea's progress up the Bosphorus.

"Take me to the lookout," she ordered the steward. When Bianca asked to go along, Donatella gladly acquiesced.

They walked across the Amalfitan, Pisan, and Genovese Quarters, down to the Gate of Eugenius, trailed as always by Grimaldi's two watchers. At the gate they all climbed to the top of the wall, where they were assailed by a sharp northerly wind. A large crowd had gathered there to watch the ships struggle against the current as they sought the shelter of the Golden Horn. Below them, the tip of the rocky promontory that marked the end of the Bosphorus and the beginning of the Sea of Marmara appeared submerged in boiling milk.

"Hold my hand, Bianca." The wind snatched the words out of Donatella's mouth. She looked up the Bosphorus, and was shocked to see a massive cloud advancing down the straights from the Black Sea. So much for clear skies.

"Look, Mamma," Bianca shouted, her hair turned into a golden streamer. "That's Captain Andrea's flag."

Donatella searched the churning waters where half a dozen galleys were fighting their way upstream. She located Andrea's galley by the gold and red colors of the Venetian flag, its six tails fluttering wildly. All other crafts were flying the Genovese colors. Donatella was disheartened to note how tiny and fragile Andrea's craft appeared. "Why is Andrea taking the ship straight up against the current?" she asked the steward. The man couldn't hear so she repeated the question, this time shouting into his ear.

"The galleys must first move up the Bosphorus, past the mouth of the Horn. Only then can it steer to the west, and glide into the inlet." The steward pointed at a ship that had advanced far enough north to be able to execute the maneuver. "There, watch that Genovese galley, my lady."

At first the ship appeared to stall against the current. But a few moments later its bow veered to the port side, and the craft began to describe a shallow arc until the bow pointed to the mouth of the Golden Horn. With the current at its stern now and the rowers pulling on their oars forcefully, the ship slipped into the calmer waters of the inlet.

Several other Genovese galleys followed the same maneuver, and they too gained the safety of the Horn. Then came Andrea's turn. Donatella leaned into the parapet to steady herself, as much against the wind as against a weakness that pervaded her lower body.

Andrea's ship had not advanced as far up the Bosphorus as the Genovese ones, when it began to turn to the port side. Perhaps the current had gotten stronger, Donatella thought, and the rowers were too exhausted to continue fighting it. Tensed, she watched the galley's movement, willing it to overcome the head wind, as the other ships had done. But to her dismay she realized that instead of turning, the ship stalled, and then began to move backward. Others in the crowd noticed this as well, and anguished shouts rose from all directions.

With unimaginable speed Andrea's ship floated down with the current, heading toward the rocky shore below the wall. With the distance to the galley closing fast, Donatella could see the slaves rowing madly, but ineffectually, the crew gesticulating and hollering at them. She searched for Andrea and spotted him standing erect on the stern deck, in front of the captain's tent.

Only a hundred yards remained before the ship would reach the rocks. Given the speed it acquired, that meant less than a minute. Why wasn't Andrea steering the galley clear of the promontory? That instant Donatella hated the man for wrecking his ship and ruining her plan for Vlad. Then it occurred to her she was looking at a man who might be dead in a few more seconds. But her disappointment was so vast, even knowing that, she couldn't forgive Andrea.

She tried to close her eyes, but the impending crash held a fascination she couldn't resist. Breathless, she watched the galley bob up and down on the waves, ever closer to the foaming rocks, then explode in a jumble of broken timber. No other sound reached the top of the wall from below except that of the sea, bellowing like a thousand wounded bulls.

Back at Ca' Loredano, Donatella shut herself in her sleeping chamber and flopped onto an armchair, not bothering to undress.

Rage and disappointment roiled inside her, their caustic burn threatening to pierce a hole in her chest. The disaster she'd just witnessed crushed her with its cruel and implacable finality.

If the shipwreck had affected only her, she'd have accepted the setback as her fate, the way she'd done on previous occasions. But this time her failure meant another's life would be ruined. Vlad was coming into the city on her promise to spirit him away, and she had no way to alert him the plan had collapsed. She could try to hide him for a while in her palace, but with spies everywhere, it would take the bounty hunters only a short time to ferret him out.

The loss of the galley and the crew had to be God's chastisement. His rebuke came at the moment when, for the first time ever, she tried to take control of events that would change someone's life. *Why did you have to thwart me like this?*

She reviewed her life of the past few months to see if, perchance, she'd committed any of the seven deadly sins. She knew gluttony, greed, sloth, and envy weren't her weaknesses. Wrath? The only wrath she felt was against Grimaldi and Murad, for what they were planning to do with Bianca. Surely God would understand a mother's ire, and not punish her for that. Pride? If primping and parading one's finery rose to the level of deadly sin, most of the ladies in Constantinople would be heading for hell ahead of her.

What about lust?

She couldn't lie to herself about what she felt for Vlad. All those nights when she lay in the dark thinking of him were steeped in a lust that made her body scream for his touch. She'd only been possessed by a man once, on her wedding day. Then, pain and humiliation taught her nothing but repugnance for the act. As a girl of fourteen, she learned to loathe that hidden place between her legs that men, in their detestable brutishness, desired more than gold. But the day she met Vlad, touched his skin, and looked into his eyes, something unexpected happened to her. That same despised place began to feel to her like a magic flower that opened its sap-engorged petals at night, ready to offer a thirsty traveler its cup of nectar. And in her nightly reveries, that traveler was always a dashing youth with black silken locks and luminous green eyes.

Donatella's spiritual adviser taught her that only chastity could redeem the sin of lust. So she remained chaste even from her own touch, despite the unsettling stirrings that now visited her body nightly. So if God were bent on punishing her it wasn't for her sins, but as a reminder women weren't supposed to meddle in men's affairs.

Morning found her slumped on the floor, her clothes rumpled and damp with perspiration. She felt worn out from a night of running aimlessly through rugged dreamscapes in a nightmare that seem to still roll in her head. Throughout the purposeless chase, unseen snags tore at her clothes again and again, stymying her progress. She sat up with difficulty, and examined her robe in the dim light through a crack in the shutters. To her confused wonderment, she found no tears in the fabric.

"Mother, Mother, wake up." Bianca's call came from the antechamber. Then the door flew open and the girl burst into the room, followed by Paola.

"What's wrong with you, Tella?" Paola said, in her customary reproaching tone. "Still in yesterday's clothes?"

Bianca didn't seem to register the state her mother was in. "Captain Andrea's alive," she cried, "and so is most of his crew. They were picked up early this morning in the Sea of Marmara, floating on debris from the galley."

Donatella refused to believe her daughter's presence in the room was real. The nightmare that tormented her sleep had many moments of false hope, when the path stretched clear in front of her, only to end in another trap. This had to be such a moment.

Bianca knelt, and took Donatella's face into her hands. "Don't you care, Mamma? If Captain Andrea and his men are alive, it means all you have to do is find him a new galley, and Vlad is saved."

Paola threw open the shutters, and a golden light filled the room. The unexpected glare melted the last vestiges of Donatella's dream, and allowed her daughter's words to sink in. The news of Andrea's survival ripped through Donatella's consciousness like a tightly wound steel coil suddenly freed of its restraints. Certainly, this was God extending His hand down to her, saying, "Don't give up."

"Yes, a new galley," she whispered, afraid to speak loud, as if that would invalidate the idea. "That's all we need."

"And just where are you going to get a new galley, Tella?" Paola said. "Galleys aren't mules, to be rented on short notice." She began to undress Donatella with rough moves that shouted criticism of her mistress's aberrant behavior. "Don't you think it's about time you get back to a normal life, and forget your hare-brained adventures?"

Normal life? That meant waiting passively for the time to come when Bianca would be taken away. No, Donatella didn't want "normal." She wanted to act, to be more than a simple observer, to feel what a man feels when he changes the course of events.

"Uncle Boruele has five galleys, Mother. He'd let you borrow one if you told him it was very important."

Donatella's first reaction at hearing her brother-in-law's name was to cringe. Ask a favor of the man who was the source of her greatest misery? But the rational part of her brain took over. If there was a chance to revive her plan for Vlad's escape, Grimaldi represented that chance. Besides, she wouldn't be asking for a favor. She had enough money to make Grimaldi a profitable business offer. And the lowly slug was all about profit.

"Have the girls draw me a bath immediately," she commanded Paola. "And air out my crimson velvet *gamurra*." The feeling of being in control she had before the shipwreck was coming back, and thrilled her.

"Mother, you hate that gown because it's cut too low," Bianca said.

"I'd say it's cut low, indeed," Paola said, "when your breasts pop out just as you're kneeling in front of the priest for the Holy Communion. You should've burned that dress the day it happened."

"Father Corelli said it was a forgivable accident," Bianca said.

Paola sneered. "Sure, he'd say that. All men are forgiving of such *accidents*."

"I'll wear a silk *colletto*, a partlet, to cover the décolletage," Donatella said.

"Tsk, tsk." Paola shook her head. "If you don't want to show your breasts to Grimaldi, why not wear the gold-cloth *gamurra* with the high neckline? You know a flimsy *colletto* isn't for concealing anything, but rather for drawing attention to your cleavage."

"Go tell the steward to fetch Andrea," Donatella said to Bianca, "and not to let him leave this place until I return from Galata."

"May I tell Captain Andrea you're getting him a new galley?" Bianca said.

Bianca's enthusiasm reinforced Donatella's feeling that she was doing the right thing. "Tell him that nothing in the plan I sent him last month has changed. He's to leave for Venice as soon as his special passenger arrives."

Donatella spent the next five hours at the hands of her slave girls, whom she ordered to make her as attractive as possible. After bathing her, the girls plucked and pumiced her hairline, adding an extra half an inch to her already high forehead. Then they bleached her hair with lye, and turned it into a rich gold with the latest dye from Venice's masters of *arte biondeggiante*, the art of blonding. Finally, they enameled her teeth in a peach color, and painted her nails a starling-egg blue.

Then came the whitening of her face. First, the girls rubbed *ceruse*, white lead cream, onto her skin. Next, they powdered her with ground alabaster laced with mercury, which turned Donatella's face to a pale ivory. When, as a finishing touch, the girls painted her lips with cinnabar vermilion, they stood out like two raspberries on a mound of powdered sugar.

Donatella took a last look at her image in the mirror, and was pleased with the results her girls had wrought. Then she had them put belladonna drops into her eyes to achieve that wide-eyed expression men found irresistible. Within minutes her pupils dilated till her irises appeared like thin blue rings encircling obsidian beads.

"Mother," Bianca exclaimed when the lengthy process was completed, "you are ravishing. No man could deny you any request."

If Donatella understood her brother-in-law's craving for power, she was ignorant of his interest in the weaker sex. But she knew, from years of observation, that powerful men always paid more attention to a pretty woman than a plain one. She'd see now if her own looks were enticing enough to make Grimaldi listen to her request for a galley. "I never thought I'd ask such a thing, Bianca, but pray to Virgin Mary your uncle is not blind to my charms."

31

Podestà Grimaldi

When Donatella left for Galata, she felt more beautiful than she remembered ever feeling before. She walked slowly the quarter mile to the Gate of Saint John, leaning on two slave girls. She needed their support to maintain her balance on the ten-inch-high *chopine* she decided to wear. The street was paved, so she didn't need platform shoes to keep her gown from trailing in the mud. But she hoped that standing taller than Podestà Grimaldi would make him take her more seriously.

In the twelve years since she left Venice to marry Giovanni Grimaldi, she set foot inside Galata only twice. Both were unhappy occasions. The first time was for the wedding banquet hosted by Podestà Grimaldi, Giovanni's older brother. One concession Donatella had obtained from the Grimaldi clan was that the married couple should reside in Constantinople, not Galata. Her father gifted her Ca' Loredano for that purpose, and the newlyweds were supposed to spend their wedding night there. But Giovanni was too eager to join his squadron for an expedition against the Mamluks to waste time on a romantic night with his bride. Instead, he simply raped her in the dining hall in front of the guests, then left Galata, never to return.

The second time she crossed the Golden Horn to Galata was when Boruele Grimaldi summoned her with the news he'd promised Bianca to Sultan Murad as a concubine. That was two years ago. Since then, Donatella avoided returning there at all costs. Instead, whenever family matters required her to deal with Grimaldi, she used lawyers as intermediaries. Not even his wife's funeral the year before softened her resolve to stay away from Galata.

But the problem she needed to solve today was too urgent to place in the hands of intermediaries. It was also of such an emotional import to Donatella that all her loathing for Grimaldi couldn't dissuade her from appealing to him in person. She summoned Vlad's image to boost her courage as she was ushered into the Palazzo Podestàle, Galata's government palace.

Grimaldi received Donatella in his study with a hostile growl that shook her fragile self-confidence. "You're wasting your time coming here to plead for your daughter, Donatella," he said in lieu of a greeting. "I told you, my decision is final. Even if I wanted to withdraw my offer to Murad, which I don't, it's too late. He wants the girl, and that's the end of it."

Grimaldi's tirade almost unhinged her. She sensed his anticipation at her debasement, his expectation she'd grovel for Bianca's freedom. The belladonna drops had rendered her vision blurry, and she was grateful she couldn't see his face with clarity. She'd shoot him such a hateful look that any further dialogue might become impossible. She used her near blindness as a shield behind which she gathered her strength for the counterattack.

"You know me little, Brother-in-law. Once I understood how promising the life of an imperial concubine is, I welcomed the arrangement you made for my daughter."

"What? You mean … I thought …"

She let him stammer while she crammed her hatred deep into her breast, hoping self-control would take its place. "Why, she'll be taught music, embroidery, calligraphy. And, as you said, if she gives the sultan a son—"

"But I thought you hated to have Bianca given to Murad."

"And if there was no child," Donatella continued with as much sincerity as she could sham, "Murad will marry her in time to one of his senior officials. She'll never want for anything." She feared she'd pushed her display of acquiescence too far, and Grimaldi would see through her pretense. Now she wished her vision were clear so she could read his expression.

"Well then, why are you here?" he said after a silence that tested her nerves.

She thought that stating her interest without further delay would be the best tactic. "I want to lease one of your galleys for two months."

"I heard about your shipwreck last night," Grimaldi said, without empathy. "Come back in a month, and I'll see what I can do."

"I need the galley today." She knew that exposing the urgency of her need weakened her bargaining position, yet she had no choice. If the galley weren't provisioned within the next twenty-four hours, it would be too late. "I'm prepared to pay a premium for giving you such a short notice."

"Women in commerce," Grimaldi said, and chuckled derisively. "I've heard of Venetian widows trying to take over the family business, as if they were men. A ridiculous conceit."

"A woman can do as well as a man if—"

"What would make you understand that women are but imperfect versions of men?" He stepped closer and said, in a tone half-mocking, half-angry, "You think you'll take *my* galley and build a fortune by trading with the Turks? You don't have what it takes between the legs to succeed in business: *coglione*. And what happens when you lose my ship, like you lost Andrea's?"

"I'll pay for the lease in advance, and I'll put up my brocade shop as collateral. You know it's worth two galleys."

"Come back next week. If you haven't regained your senses by then, I'll consider the transaction."

"I'll give you anything you want to let me have the galley today." Even before she finished the sentence, she knew saying that opened her to Grimaldi's greed. But was there anything she valued more now than Vlad's escape?

"Now *that* is intriguing," Grimaldi gloated, as if he'd uncovered a juicy secret. "Your request has nothing to do with commerce, does it? What could be so pressing that it can't wait a few days?"

"I swear this isn't related to Bianca in any way." Donatella felt as if she was sinking into quicksand, and every word she uttered sucked her deeper into the mire. "I'm not trying to—"

"Oh, I've got no worry about my sweet niece," Grimaldi said, and laughed heartily. "With my people in your house she can't take a piss without me knowing about it. And I've got spies at every one of Constantinople's gates. She couldn't leave the city if she were hidden inside a watermelon."

"I made some risky agreements the shipwreck prevents me from fulfilling," Donatella said, holding back tears of fear and frustration. "If I wait too long the fall storms will come, and I won't be able to make good on my obligations. That would ruin me." Unable to think of anything else she could say to soften Grimaldi's heart, she gave full rein to her despair. "You can have *anything* of mine you want, just give me the ship today. Money, shops … anything."

Grimaldi observed her in silence, and she feared what he'd say next. "I can't imagine what stupid venture you got yourself embroiled in, and don't really care. But it's madness to be impetuous." He began pacing back and forth, with the slow step of someone deep in thought. Then he stopped in front of her and said, "I don't want your money or your shops."

All is lost…. Oh, how I'd love to plant a knife into your gut right now.

Grimaldi cleared his throat. "There is something—" He took another ominous pause.

Here it comes.

"—something I do want."

"Anything," Donatella cried.

"You as my wife."

His words struck the pit of her stomach like a gauntleted fist. True, she had dolled herself up to get his attention, but didn't anticipate anything beyond that. Then *this*, coming from a man ten years older than her father would be now?

She stepped out of her *chopine* to steady herself, but shod only in her silk *pianelle* she felt small and insignificant. The effects of the belladonna drops had begun to wear out, and she could see Grimaldi's face more clearly now. An almost uncontrollable revulsion overtook her. She remembered his looks as being unappealing. But the face she saw now, perhaps in the light of his odious demand, was utterly repugnant. "I … *er* … meant anything material," she said in a voice so weak she knew it would only embolden him. "I have the means to make it worth your while to lease me the galley."

"My wife was barren, which you aren't," Grimaldi said. His nostrils flared out, making the hair that sprouted luxuriantly out of them appear like the business end of two paintbrushes. "And though you aren't quite young anymore, I'm sure your *figa* isn't yet dried up. You could still give me an heir."

Grimaldi's use of the vulgar term for female genitalia offended her. But it excited him, for when he spoke again, saliva oozed through his flabby lips. "Your *figa* must be dripping wet right now, just thinking about making another child."

Her mind flashed back to that miserable evening when this man's brother dragged her from the banquet table and threw her onto the floor. "I always knew I'd taste Venetian *figa* one day," he hollered, to the merriment of his drunken companions. "I just didn't think I'd have to marry to get my hands on one." With that he stuck his hand under Donatella's gown, and groped her vagina with rough fingers. Was she about to endure a similar treatment from this Grimaldi? Panic made her temples throb.

She glanced at the door to the antechamber where her slaves were waiting, but thought if she bolted Grimaldi might pounce on her. And even if she could get away, would she? Give up on the only chance she had to save Vlad?

"An heir, you said?" She willed the flutter of heart to quiet, and spoke with a calm she hoped would douse Grimaldi's fire. "A son, of course. An heir means a proper marriage contract, a last will and testament, witnesses, guarantors, a dowry."

Grimaldi's jaw slackened, and more saliva poured forth onto his chin. "Yes, yes … a son." His voice, harsh and commanding before, turned hoarse now.

"But are you sure you've got what is takes, Ser Grimaldi?" She felt the pendulum swinging in her direction, and became more confident. "At your age?"

Red blotches appeared on Grimaldi's narrow forehead, and his hands began to shake. "Oh, don't you worry about my manliness,

Donatella." He flashed her a wolfish grin. "I've been a wine merchant all my life, and you know the saying, '*Vino puro, cazzo duro*', pure wine, hard cock."

This time his vulgarity didn't touch her. She knew she'd gotten what she came for. Now it was only a matter of closing the deal from a position of strength. "Well, ask me again for a son when I return your galley in two months." She motioned him to stand aside. "I'll be the judge of how pure your wine has been."

Grimaldi's palsy became more violent, and the bristles of his nose brushes came to life under his labored breath. "A son, a son." An almost tender look came to his eyes, gone distant with a vision of what she could give him. "Two months, then?"

"Captain Andrea and his crew will be over within three hours to take possession of the galley." She headed for the door with a confident step. "He'll bring you the lease money."

Grimaldi sounded almost timid when he said, "And the collateral? The shop?"

She gave him a fierce look. "You're asking for a guaranty, when everything I have might be yours in two months?" Then she remembered her platform shoes. "Help me get onto my *chopine*, Ser Grimaldi." This was an order delivered in a severe tone she wouldn't have thought herself capable of before now.

She lifted the hem of her *gamurra* halfway up her leg, far higher than needed. Then she pointed her finger to the ground, and stared at Grimaldi with knitted brows. He picked up the *chopine* with a meek demeanor, and knelt in front of her. The sight of her hose made his eyes bulge, and he grabbed her calf with both hands. She slapped him playfully on the cheek and said, forcing a seductive smile, "There's plenty of time for that later, Podestà. I too believe it's madness to be impetuous."

32

A View toward Asia

September 1442, Rumelia, Ottoman Empire

"You left Zaganos Pasha behind?" Ismail said when he greeted Vlad and Mehmed in the camp north of Galata. Ismail had rushed ahead of the main convoy with the camp attendants, and reached the Bosphorus two days earlier.

"With a hundred riders at his disposal, Lala Zaganos couldn't pass the opportunity to conduct some war exercises," Mehmed said. "I expect he'll get here before midnight. He's got a keen interest in Tirendaz's flight shooting tomorrow."

The camp was situated on a plateau surrounded on three sides by slightly elevated ground. On the fourth side it was open to the Bosphorus, flowing about a hundred feet below. The plateau descended in a gentle slope for about three hundred feet before it met the flatland along the shore.

"How far is Galata from here?" Vlad affected a casual tone, but thought his voice sounded strained.

"Five, six miles," Ismail said. "I think you'd see it if you climbed on top of that hill." He pointed to a rise south of the camp.

Was that suspicion in Ismail's eyes? No more questions about Galata, Vlad decided. He turned to Mehmed and feigning ignorance said, "What's that land across the water?"

Mehmed made a sweeping gesture with his hand. "Asia. Imagine Alexander the Great crossing the water at this very place eighteen hundred years ago, to enter history."

"He actually crossed the Dardanelles," Vlad said, reflexively, not intending to correct Mehmed. His mind was on the fact that Asia swallowed Alexander, as it had many before and after him. Now it was trying to swallow Vlad.

But Mehmed was too much taken with the moment to register Vlad's observation. "One day I'll cross this water in the opposite direction to conquer Europe and enter history, like Alexander did. *Insha' Allāh.*" He looked at Vlad, as if expecting to be challenged. Vlad remained impassive.

"That fortress is Beyazid's Anadolu Hisari." Mehmed pointed to a structure with crenelated towers rising on the far shore, directly in front of them. The Ottoman red banner fluttered atop the tallest tower. "An angel told Beyazid the power capable of building two fortresses straddling the Bosphorus would rule Constantinople."

That moment a convoy of six merchant galleys flying the Genovese colors appeared from the direction of the Black Sea. The ships used both the current and their oars to glide with an astounding speed downstream. Mehmed, Vlad, and Ismail watched spellbound as the crafts passed in front of them, then disappeared minutes later in a bend of the narrows.

"The fortresses are useful only if they can control the ship traffic through the strait," Vlad said. Any power capable of that could threaten Constantinople's food supply. "But even with a second fortress on this side of the water, how could you intercept a ship convoy like the one that just passed?"

"You could blast them with bombards from the ramparts, couldn't you?" Ismail said.

Vlad had seen bombards in Eisenmarkt, and wasn't impressed. Though Governor Hunyadi claimed they were the best in Europe, the fist-sized iron balls they shot couldn't do much damage to a large galley. "That'd be like shooting peas at a running bull," he said.

"When the second fortress is built, there could be a chain strung across the water, like the Byzantines use for controlling the Golden Horn," Mehmed said. "The Bosphorus is narrow enough here for that. That's why the angel must've chosen this spot for the site of the two fortresses."

Vlad couldn't suppress his sarcasm. "The angel named *this very place* to Beyazid? If so, Muslim angels are more specific than Christian ones." He remembered how poor in geographical details Theodore's prophecy was.

Mehmed cast Vlad a reproachful look. "What the angel said was each fortress must be erected on a site marked by an arrow shot from the opposite shore. That made this place the only one to be considered, since the strait is at its narrowest here."

Vlad guessed the Bosphorus was half a mile wide where they stood, about the same width as the Danube at Nicopolis. How could anyone shoot an arrow over such a distance?

"Beyazid offered a prize of twenty Circassian virgins to whoever could meet the angel's condition," Mehmed said. "Ten for each of the two needed arrows. The best archers in the empire tried to win the prize, but only Iskender Bursalı succeeded."

"He shot an arrow from here to where Anadolu Hisari stands," Ismail said, "and received his portion of the prize."

"What happened to the second fortress?" Vlad said.

"No one has yet managed to shoot an arrow from Asia to Europe," Ismail said. "It's something to do with the wind."

"So, ten of those virgins are still waiting to be awarded to the strongest archer," Vlad said.

Ismail laughed, but Mehmed just furrowed his brow. "It's not the strength of the archer that counts, but his art."

"True," Ismail said. "Tirendaz is fond of quoting Bursali's creed, '*Menzil zor ile atılmaz, sanat ile atılır*', a flight record comes from art, not strength."

"And Tirendaz has more art in flight shooting today than anyone alive," Mehmed said. "If he beats Bursali's record, I'll have him shoot an arrow from Asia to Europe one day. Then I'll build Rumeli Hisari, sister to Beyazid's fortress, and Constantinople will fall into my hands."

Vlad glanced at Ismail to see if he was surprised at Mehmed's claim. But the secretary must have been used to the boy's boastings, for he showed no reaction.

"My master has already shot arrows to distances of nearly nine hundred yards," Ismail said, "so I think he has a good chance of matching Bursali's performance."

"The channel width is only seven hundred and twenty yards here," Mehmed said. "But you must add the distance from the archer's footstone to the water's edge. And on the far shore, the distance from water to the pillar marking Bursali's record. That makes the distance to beat nine hundred and one yards."

"Where's Bursali's footstone?" Vlad asked.

Ismail indicated the shore with a sweeping motion. "It's somewhere down there, obscured by fifty years' worth of vegetation growth."

"Tirendaz asked me to lead a search party for it," Mehmed said. "It will be the three of us, plus Hamza and Yunus. I'm also going to use ten of my pages to help." He glanced at the sun just then dipping behind the hills, and said, "Too late now to start the search, so we'll do it in the morning. But we have to start early. Tirendaz wants to shoot his arrow before the sun gets hot and causes strong air currents over the water."

Vlad figured the best time for him to sneak away would during the search for the footstone. When it was found, there would be great excitement, and everyone's attention would turn on Tirendaz. Then, whether he succeeded or failed in beating Bursali's record, confusion in the camp would delay discovery of Vlad's disappearance. By the time someone sounded the alarm, he'd be in Galata.

"You look preoccupied, as if you're planning something," Ismail said when he and Vlad retired for the night in the tent they shared.

He lit a lamp, and lifted it to Vlad's face with a penetrating look. "You've been agitated since you arrived. It surprised me, because I've learned to think of you as self-controlled, no matter what comes your way."

He's onto me. How stupid to let my guard down. Vlad rubbed his eyes as if he were tired, trying to conceal the redness burning his cheeks. Though Ismail had given him proof of sympathy, the man was in the service of the Turks. He probably was told to gain Vlad's trust, then report any suspicious behavior.

"You've got a keen eye, Ismail," Vlad said, and was glad to see the secretary break into a satisfied smile. "Perhaps I've been preoccupied."

Ismail put his arm around Vlad's shoulders, in a brotherly gesture. "Is it the thought of crossing over to Asia?"

Watch out. He's testing you. Discussion of the crossing was a subject Vlad had to avoid, or risk giving himself away. "Nah, Asia's something I brought upon myself, so I've come to accept it. If I'm troubled, it's by something too petty to discuss."

Ismail chuckled. "I've been troubled myself by trifles many a time, only because I had no one to talk with. Remember the proverb, 'A burden shared is a burden shed'."

"Not much to share," Vlad said. "It's just that I used to think of myself as a good archer. I can shoot any bird that flies within the range of my arrow. But that range isn't even a hundred yards. And now, here comes Tirendaz, ready to shoot an arrow over nine hundred yards."

"Don't envy him, Vlad. People like him are never happy, because chasing records is a journey without end. Even if Tirendaz shoots his arrow nine hundred and two yards tomorrow, he'll be agonizing over his next record attempt."

Vlad lay back on his blanket, and Ismail launched into a dissertation about the art of flight shooting. Vlad's mind wandered off to his own concerns, but occasionally he'd make a sound that indicated interest. That seemed to stimulate Ismail to carry on.

The first thing Vlad would have to do in the morning was figure out the guards' emplacement. Likely, the best-guarded stretch of the camp perimeter would be on the landside. The waterside didn't present much risk to Mehmed's party, so it should be lightly manned. Vlad hoped no one from the camp would be paying attention to the search party down by the shore, so he could take off undetected.

"The flight bow is quite different from the war and target bows," Ismail said. "It's lighter and longer. Those other bows don't require special conditioning, but the flight bow is quite temperamental."

Vlad would wait for the search to begin, before he'd make his move. Mehmed, overly anxious to be the one who found Bursali's footstone, would drive himself madly. And his two companions, Hamza and Yunus, would step all over themselves helping him. That meant all three would have their noses stuck in the weeds, and wouldn't notice Vlad's absence.

"The flight bow is clad in beech bark, which absorbs moisture," Ismail said. "It needs to be heated in a special box before each record attempt. This makes the bow lighter, and increases its drawing weight."

Once the search was in full swing, Vlad would drift slowly along the shore, until out of sight, then follow the Bosphorus to Galata.

"That's why I had to get here two days ahead of my master," Ismail said. "I brought with me a drying box, in which I heated Tirendaz's bow over a low fire for forty-eight hours."

Ismail droned on a while longer, but with no further reactions from Vlad he extinguished the lamp and went to sleep.

33

Arrow across the Water

Knowing what he was about to do the next day made it hard for Vlad to sleep that night. He lay face up the dark, kneading his hands, cracking his knuckles, and tugging at his locks until it hurt. He tried obsessively, but with limited success, to visualize every step he'd be taking from the moment he left the camp until he set foot on the Venetian galley.

When he tired of this futile exercise, he began to think about his arrival in Venice. He'd locate his father's agent there, and have him send word to Enea Piccolomini at Emperor Frederick's court. The influential Poet Laureate would rush over with a troop of men-at-arms to escort Vlad to Vienna in person. There, he would introduce Vlad to his imperial patron as the man who saved Piccolomini's life in the Devil's Belt Forest. Frederick and his court would want to hear all about Vlad's experiences inside the Ottoman Empire. And every one would be enthralled by his daring escape. Imagine, King Dracul's son giving Sultan Murad the slip. Vlad would become the talk of Europe. Then, he'd return home, almost a hero.

Quite a glorious outcome to a seemingly doomed adventure, Vlad told himself. Yet, he was aware his feelings about repatriation were halfhearted. Going from the prospect of a life behind bars, to being celebrated as the man who stopped Murad's war, should've overjoyed him. Why then wasn't his heart racing with anticipation?

It certainly wasn't fear of the risks awaiting him. After weeks of suspense and torment, the escape promised to be laughably simple. All he had to do was get away from here unobserved, and slip into Constantinople. There, the friends destiny brought onto his path would do the rest. The monks at the Pantelimon Monastery would shelter him until dark, then Donatella would help him get onto a galley bound for Venice.

The moment his thoughts touched upon Donatella, he knew he'd found the source of his malaise. Yes, she was one of those unexpected friends, but also more than that ... much more. What was she to him? He asked himself this again and again. But that space stretching beyond the boundary of friendship was *terra incognita* for him. All he understood was that she'd become someone he longed to be near all the time. Mere friends didn't make you feel that way.

By tomorrow night she'd be out of his life forever, and soon forget who he was. A troubled young man from some backward principality, she'd say to herself. Somebody she helped as an act of Christian charity.

At that thought, a diffuse heaviness settled on his chest, and the deeper he breathed to shake it off, the more oppressive it became. He wished Gruya or Marcus were here, or even Lash. He wouldn't share his intimate feelings with them, but their presence would fill part of the void he felt inside.

At dawn, when Ismail and the others left to do their prayer on a nearby rise, Vlad strolled through the camp and took stock of the guards. Several of them were posted on the landside, but, as he'd hoped, only one man guarded the waterside.

"Everyone will be responsible for searching inside a square," Mehmed announced when the search party assembled in his pavilion for breakfast. All fifteen men were seated on the floor in a circle, bowls of gruel and slices of melon in front of them.

Mehmed unfurled a scroll of paper, and held it up for all to see. On it he'd sketched the strip of flatland between the shore and the bottom of the slope leading down from the plateau. He'd divided the area with the precision of a land surveyor into fifteen equal-size squares, stretching in a straight line parallel to the shore.

"You each get nine hundred square yards to search," he said. "Because dirt washed over the area for the past fifty years, you'll have to poke the ground with a spear to find the stone."

He took a piece of lead and wrote his name inside a square. "You can choose your own," he said, and passed the scroll on to Hamza.

By the time Vlad's turn came, half the squares had been taken. Mehmed had chosen the square located at the center of the search area; Hamza and Yunus had picked those adjacent to his. Vlad wrote his name in the southernmost square. So far, all signs pointed to an easy getaway.

"The prize for finding Bursali's footstone is five gold ducats," Mehmed said, and all the men gasped. "You'll find the squares delineated with strings, so you should have no trouble staying inside yours."

Even before he reached his square, Vlad realized the hill south of the camp extended all the way to the water, blocking access to the shore. He'd have to climb that hill and take an inland route to Galata. This would expose him a little longer to a chance observer, but he had no other outlet.

He began to poke the ground with his spear, and watched the other men do the same. When he was satisfied no one was looking in his direction, he began to walk slowly toward the hill. He figured his calm movement wouldn't raise alarm if he were noticed. But if it did, he'd claim he was looking for a place to relieve himself.

When he reached the bottom of the hill, about forty yards from his square, he threw a last glance to the search area. The men were scattered over a distance a quarter-mile long, still agitating their spears up and down. He'd remained calm until this moment, but now his heart began to pump like that of a horse in full gallop. He dropped his spear and started to scramble up the hill, bent from the middle to minimize his profile. Fortunately the slope was neither steep, nor long, and he reached the summit in less than a minute. There, instead of the open field he anticipated, his eyes fell upon cluster of tents erected only a few hundred yards away. Zaganos and his riders had arrived in the night indeed, and set their camp across Vlad's only escape route.

Like a hare faced with the sudden appearance of a hunter in front of him, Vlad didn't waste time reflecting upon what happened. Instead he turned around and tumbled down the hill. He dreaded hearing someone from below shout his name, but no other sound than his own panting broke the silence. When he reentered his square he dropped to the ground, and, sprawled on his back, waited for the fire in his lungs to die down.

"Things never turn out the way you want them with the Turks," his father had told him. Vlad had inwardly derided the remark as banal. As if one couldn't say the same thing about any other people: Hungarians, Germans, even Wallachians. But now, recalling all the ways he'd been thwarted since crossing the Danube at Nicopolis, he had to admit Father was right. Nothing turned out Vlad's way in this heathen empire.

An hour passed in silence. Then a shout came from upfield, and soon there was hollering and cheering. *They found the fucking stone.* Vlad rose and headed for the shoreline, not even glancing at the place where everyone must've been gathering. As he thought about what was going to happen to him tomorrow, despair welled inside him. Dull pressure behind his eyes blurred his vision and shot a throbbing pain into his left temple with every step.

He came to a small cove he'd noticed from the camp the day before, and knelt on its muddy shore. Then he dipped his face into the frigid water and remained still until his skin began to sting. When he straightened up he licked his lips, imagining he tasted among the salty drops the sweet ones that had flowed from the Danube into the Black Sea, and down to this spot with the Bosphorus current.

"Stop looking for the stone, Vlad," he heard Mehmed shout. "We've found it."

Stung back to reality, Vlad jumped to his feet. With a start, he noticed a fisherman's boat moored to a nearby tree. For an instant every cell in his body came alive, and the thought of having just been saved flashed through his mind. But when he approached the boat he saw it had been abandoned there long ago, the flaked and discolored paint leaving the hull mottled like an old cheese. Without oars and nearly rotten, the craft couldn't be of use to anybody, least of all to someone trying to depart in a hurry. A series of notches carved onto the starboard gunwale seemed to mark some past significant events. Big fish caught? Harsh storms survived? Absentmindedly, he counted the notches, and his skin turned to goose flesh. There were nine of them.

This boat is meant for me, after all. He felt as if old man Theodore was somewhere nearby, looking on him with his sightless eyes.

By the time Vlad reached the search party, Tirendaz and Zaganos were descending the slope from the plateau, followed by most of the people in the camp.

"Guess where the stone was," Mehmed said.

"Are you sure it's the right one?" Vlad asked, just to say something. He didn't care if Mehmed found the philosophers' stone.

"Come see for yourself," Mehmed said. His face was flushed, and it seemed to Vlad the boy couldn't stop grinning. "It was in my own square."

The two-foot-long marble tile lay about three inches below the surface where Mehmed discovered it. It was brown with age and dirt, except for a fresh light-colored chip where his spear must've made impact.

Mehmed dropped to his knees, and tugged at Vlad's sleeve to do the same. "Read what it says, and tell me if it isn't the right stone."

With his mind still reeling from the discovery of the boat, Vlad obeyed.

On the thirteenth day of Dhu al-Hijjah, during the feast of Eid al-Adha, the year 795 of Hegira, Iskender Bursalı, humble slave of the Great Khan Beyazid Yıldırım, with the blessings of Allah, whose 99 names he recited before the event, shot an arrow from this spot across the water to mark the site of Anadolu Hisari.

When Tirendaz reached the site of the footstone, everyone fell silent. One of his pages set a fresh marble tile for him, three feet behind Bursali's. Tirendaz took up his shooting position by setting his left foot on his stone, bow in hand and an ivory-tipped arrow in his sash. When every inch counted, Vlad marveled at Tirendaz's willingness to relinquish an entire yard, in what had to be a form of homage to his predecessor.

"*Allāhu Akbar,*" Tirendaz intoned, and all present echoed the chant. He held the bow by the limbs and touched it to his forehead. Then he kissed a white bone chip embedded in the bow's grip, and nocked his arrow against the string.

The sun had already risen above the hills on the Anatolian side. Tirendaz squinted, and aimed his arrow at some point only he saw above the Bosphorus. Then he prayed, "*Ne hava vü ne keman-ü kemankeş Ancak erdiren menziline nidayı,* Not the wind, not the bow, not the archer cast the arrow to its target. Only you—" He pulled the string in one smooth motion past his right ear and, without a pause, loosed his arrow into the sky. Then he let out a prolonged shout, to complete his prayer, "*Ya Haaaakk,* Oh, Loooord."

Vlad heard a whoosh, and saw the arrow as a white flash before it disappeared in the sun's glare. When Tirendaz's shout died down, Vlad found himself holding his breath. Moments passed in silence, then a green flag unfurled on top of the Anadolu Hisari ramparts. The shout of "*Allāh*" exploded from the crowd around Tirendaz.

Mehmed gave a yell and rushed over to Zaganos, who stood at the edge of the crowd with a grin on his face. The two of them had an animated exchange, then hugged each other. Zaganos headed for the camp, and Mehmed returned to congratulate Tirendaz.

Vlad followed Mehmed, and whispered, "It's a good omen that *you* found Bursali's stone, not someone else."

Mehmed turned to Vlad with a giddy expression. "Now Lala Zaganos and I are convinced Tirendaz is the one who'll mark the spot for Rumeli Hisari, when the time comes."

"Your fortress on the European shore and your gate to history," Vlad said.

"Let's go celebrate," Mehmed said, visibly pleased with Vlad's remark.

Back in the camp, fire pits blazed and the kitchen hands were busy skinning just-slaughtered sheep. A crowd had formed in front of Tirendaz's tent, and everyone spoke cheerfully at once. Vlad observed with satisfaction that even the camp guards had joined the merriment. From inside the tent came a continuous stream of joyful shouts and boisterous laughter.

"Come, let's get inside," Mehmed said, and began to elbow his way through the throng.

Vlad waited until the tent flap closed behind Mehmed before he walked to the edge of the plateau. When a look back assured him no one was watching, he took a few steps down the slope, then stopped. *This is the point of no return. The next step will mean either freedom, or…* A muscle twitched in his thigh, and a vein in his neck began to throb. Would he get an asthma attack right now? He breathed deeply, and listened to his breath, but heard no sound of wheezing. Then he crossed himself three times and began to lope toward the shoreline.

34

An Unplanned Adventure

When Vlad reached the boat he pounced upon the line that moored it to the tree. The line was made fast to an iron ringbolt on the bow, the rope expertly knotted. When he tried to undo the knot he found it stiff and unyielding. He looked around with mounting concern for a sharp object he could use to tease the knot loose. Nothing that could serve the purpose lay in sight. As precious seconds rushed by, he tried to untie the knot with his teeth. But the sunbaked cord resisted his attempts, as if made of rigid strips of cowhide. The knot at the tree end of the line was equally hardened.

Vlad thought he could break the ringbolt with a rock, and began to search for one. That moment he heard his name shouted in different voices from the camp, and his heart cramped with a sharp pain, like an overstretched muscle. Three figures stood on the edge of the plateau, gesticulating. He was discovered. Away from the camp on his own, and trying to free up a boat from its mooring … clear evidence he was trying to get away. Then there was the money hidden in the tail of his shirt, if more proof were needed. The only thing worse than failing to escape was being caught trying.

There was one subterfuge he could use to justify his presence by the water. He turned his back to the camp, then slowly unlaced and removed his boots. Next he stripped down to his drawers, and folded his clothes methodically. Whoever was coming after him could see he was in no hurry. The voices drew closer, but he resisted the temptation to look behind him. Instead he walked into the water until it reached over his head, then swam under the surface for about twenty yards.

"What are you doing here?" Mehmed shouted when Vlad resurfaced. He was standing on the shore, flanked by Hamza and Yunus, all three breathing hard from their run. "You're missing the feast."

Vlad looked past the three men, and saw no one else. People in the camp hadn't figured out what he was up to. Though once again his plan was being thwarted, at least his true intentions might not be exposed.

"You Turks have your heated *hamams,*" Vlad shouted back, "we Wallachians prefer cold baths."

"You aren't supposed to be here without permission," Hamza said.

"Zaganos Pasha ordered us to bring you to him immediately," Yunus said.

That was a lie. If Zaganos knew what Vlad had done he would've sent the soldiers after him, not a ten-year-old and his two pathetic minions. All Vlad had to do now was keep the conversation light, and he'd stay out of trouble. "Will your *lala* let you swim in cold water, Mehmed? Or hot water only is acceptable for the next sultan of the House Osman?"

"None of us are getting wet," Hamza said.

Yunus stepped in front of Mehmed, as if to protect him, and repeated, "None of us."

"This cove doesn't have a women's section," Vlad said, "so you two can be excused for staying dry. But don't speak for Mehmed."

"If the water isn't too cold for you," Mehmed said, "it isn't for me either." He disrobed quickly, and dove in before Hamza and Yunus could stop him.

Vlad had been treading water until now, and his flesh began to get numb. He swam to the boat, and climbed in. "Come to my *hot room*," he said, then pulled Mehmed after him. The boy's teeth were chattering and his lips were bluish, but he kept a brave face.

"I love adventures," Mehmed said. "But Lala Zaganos won't let me have any. At ten my brother could do anything he pleased, and his *lala* wouldn't say a word. You should hear the troubles Aladdin used to get himself into."

Mehmed's mention of adventures sparked in Vlad an idea for reviving his escape plan. But Hamza and Yunus had to be sent away first. "You two, don't stand there like turds in the grass," he called out to them. "Go get us some towels."

The youths gaped at Vlad's insolence.

"Vlad's right," Mehmed said. "Make yourselves useful."

When Yunus and Hamza began to trudge back to the camp, Vlad jumped onto the shore. He felt through Mehmed's pile of clothes, and found the boy's dagger. He discarded the scabbard and concealed the blade in his left hand, then tossed Mehmed's clothes into the boat. "Put these on, and I'll tell you of an adventure your brother wouldn't even dream of."

Vlad waited until Mehmed was dressed, then he said, "How would you like to do something your father tried to do, but failed?" Then he threw his own clothes into the boat and, while Mehmed was distracted catching them, cut the line with a swipe of the dagger.

"That's a trick question, isn't it?" Mehmed said, unaware the boat was now adrift. "Father never fails at anything."

Vlad glanced up at the camp, and concluded things were still quiet. He leaped onto the boat, put on his clothes swiftly, then sat on a bench with his back to the bow. The dagger he slipped into his left boot. "Ah, but your father *did* fail at one thing he wanted badly to accomplish in his youth."

"I don't know what you mean," Mehmed said, with the smile of someone anticipating an amusing trick. "I still think you're trying to play me."

"Think hard," Vlad said. "What city did every Muslim ruler since the time of the Prophet dream of getting into, but couldn't?"

Mehmed's lips puckered into a tiny circle, and his eyebrows arched almost up to his shaved scalp. "Constantinople?" he said in a pitched tone. "Lala Zaganos would never hear of me doing such a thing."

Vlad couldn't help chuckling at the boy's astonishment. "With Zaganos it's hard to tell who's the prince of the blood, and who's the slave," he said. Mehmed frowned, and Vlad pressed his point. "Till what age is an heir to Empire of the Crescent Moon supposed to take orders from a mere slave?"

He tore a board off his bench, and began to paddle on one side. The boat turned away from the shore, and now he could survey the plateau with ease. The alarm still hadn't been sounded.

"Even if I acted against my *lala*'s wishes, how am I supposed to get away unnoticed, and travel five miles to the city, without him sending his men after me?"

Vlad began to alternate his paddling from side to side, and the boat glided toward the opening of the cove. His confidence grew with every stroke.

"It's simply impossible," Mehmed said, dejected. Then he sat on the bench facing Vlad.

Angry shouts erupted from the camp, but Mehmed, his back to the shore and eyes on Vlad, didn't react to them. The entire edge of the plateau was now crowded with people. Vlad's heartbeat quickened. For an archer like Tirendaz the distance to the boat was trivial. But would he take a shot at Vlad, and risk killing Mehmed? Vlad maneuvered the boat so Mehmed's body would hide him to the view from above.

"Impossible, you say?" Vlad winked at Mehmed. "Not at all. We're already on our way to Constantinople. Not unnoticed, but decidedly unstoppable."

Mehmed jumped to his feet and looked around, startled. Vlad struggled with the idea of pushing him overboard, to spare the boy from Murad's recriminations for this misadventure. But in that brief interval of indecision, the boat cleared the cove's mouth and was captured by the current. Now the light craft heaved, pitched, and yawed violently. In the cold, rushing waters Mehmed was certain to drown, and Vlad was unwilling to see that happen.

"Sit down and hold on tight," Vlad shouted, as he himself was almost thrown overboard by an unexpected roll of the boat.

When they reached the middle of the stream the water became calmer, but moved faster. Behind them the cove and the plateau had already vanished from sight, hidden by the hill south of the camp.

"Let Zaganos try to tell us now what we can and can't do," Vlad said.

Mehmed laughed with a joy that proved he had no misgivings left. He stood on his bench, face flushed with excitement and arms raised like a prophet addressing his followers. "Woe onto you, Constantinople, city of the Seven Hills," he shouted into the wind, "when a young man will lay siege to you, and your mighty walls will come down."

And that young man will be you, of course.

Vlad stopped paddling, and turned to the bow. In the distance to the right, the Golden Horn yawned wide, just as he remembered it from Mehmed's model. Hundreds of anchored ships with their barren masts gave the inlet the appearance of a defoliated forest strewn with huge boulders. To the right of the opening, Galata's walls crept up the hillside in a staircase fashion, dominated from the summit by the imposing Christea Turris, Christ's Tower, with its conical roof. To the left of the opening rose Constantinople's outline, compelling in its richness of forms, colors, and textures. Emperor John's red and gold banners fluttered from the tops of wall towers, and hundreds of gold crosses glittered above church cupolas.

"My promised land," Vlad wanted to shout, taken by a heady feeling.

"There's Cape Saint Demetrius," Mehmed said, breathless, "and the Hill of the Acropolis, and beyond it Hagia Sophia, and—"

"Can you point out the Third Hill?" The Pantelimon Monastery would be there on its north slope.

Mehmed didn't seem to hear him. "When Beyazid laid siege to Constantinople, he marked on his war map all the places he wanted to visit when he took the city. There were many of them, but Hagia Sophia was going to be his first stop."

"Your great-grandfather was a dreamer, like you," Vlad said, and turned his back to the city. "In eight years of siege, he got no closer to the city than the Walls of Theodosius." *And you wouldn't be doing it either, were it not for me.*

"When my brother hears I set foot in Constantinople he'll croak with envy. The Prophet, may Allah's peace be upon him, said that he who—"

"I heard your father has spies all over Constantinople," Vlad said. "Might one of them recognize you?"

"Yes, if they saw me with Father in Edirne. But they won't if I undo my turban." Mehmed unwrapped the white cloth wound around his fez, and said, "I'll use this as a sash and keep the fez as my cap." When he girded himself he realized he'd lost his dagger, and the corners of his mouth drooped. "It was a present from Lala Zaganos on the occasion of my circumcision—"

"We've got something more urgent to worry about than your dagger," Vlad shouted. He'd just noticed the boat had sprung a leak, and had already taken in a couple inches of water.

"Are we sinking?" Mehmed shrieked, and clutched Vlad's arm. "I can't swim more than a few yards."

Vlad guessed the shore was at least five hundred yards away. He removed his right boot and handed it to Mehmed. "Start bailing the water, while I try to steer us into the Horn." He spoke as calmly as if he were asking Mehmed to pass the salt. No need to let him know that Vlad too was afraid they might not make it. "We need to escape the current, or we'll overshoot the inlet, and end up in the Sea of Marmara."

"I can promise you I won't be attacking Constantinople by water," Mehmed said. "We Turks are better fighters on land."

"A reassuring thought to the defenders of Constantinople," Vlad said. He asked again about the location of the Third Hill.

"It's that second hump to the right of Hagia Sophia," Mehmed said. Then, scooping water with Vlad's boot, he resumed talking about his designs on Constantinople.

But Vlad stopped listening. He followed the line from the Third Hill to the seawall where Ca' Loredano appeared on Mehmed's model of the city, and that reignited his memories of Donatella. Only a few hours, and he'd see her again. Perhaps this very moment she was looking down over the water from the height of her palace, wondering if he was going to come. What perfume would she have chosen for this special day? Myrrh, perhaps, or damask rose. No, it would be lavender, he decided. Recalling the scent of her skin gave him such a surge of vigor that his paddling became wild and unbalanced.

"What's gotten into you, Vlad?" Mehmed said, amused. "It looks as if you're ready to conquer Constantinople all by yourself."

Vlad laughed, embarrassed at his own display, yet pleased he was able to share his secret excitement without having to explain the reasons. "This city's got something for everyone. I'll leave the conquering to you, and chase after my own dreams."

When they passed in front of the Tower of Eugenius, Mehmed pointed to a large cluster of floating platforms under the walls. "Those must the buoys used to float the big chain that closes the Horn in times of war. They say not even the largest carracks can break through it."

"That shouldn't be of concern to you, since you'll be attacking from the landside," Vlad said. "For now, keep on bailing."

"No amount of mocking will discourage me, Vlad," Mehmed said, self-assured. "Did you know Emperor Constantine predicted a thousand years ago the city would fall to someone coming from Asia? His statue on top of the column in the Forum Tauri used to point across the water to the east, before an earthquake toppled it."

"He couldn't have meant you, born in Edirne as you were. Perhaps he had your brother in mind."

Mehmed's head snapped in Vlad's direction, as if the remark had touched a sore spot. "Aladdin is under the influence of Khalil Pasha's peace-loving ways. I can promise you my brother will never conquer anything."

The city harbor was choked with small vessels offloading the large ships of merchandise that had traveled across many seas to reach Constantinople. Vlad and Mehmed wended their way through the floating maze, and reached the wharf just as their boat filled with water, and sank. In the morning hubbub, nobody paid attention to the two youngsters climbing onto the dock, drenched and laughing.

35

Captain Throatcut

"I want to see everything my great-grandfather wanted to see," Mehmed said. He and Vlad were sitting on the edge of the wharf outside the Gate of Eugenius, wringing their clothes dry. "It would be like paying my respects to the great man. The Forum of Constantine, the Hippodrome, the Emperor's Palace—"

"We don't have time for Beyazid's grand tour," Vlad said. "A short visit, then you must find your way back to Galata and your company."

"What about you?" Mehmed asked, alarmed. "Aren't you coming back with me?"

Vlad had decided not to let Mehmed on to his plans until they were inside the city, away from the custom officers. "We both need to get out of Constantinople as soon as possible," he said. "Now, choose one place you want to visit, and let's get moving."

"If I must, I'll choose," Mehmed said, disappointed. "But I've got to eat first."

Impatient and annoyed with Mehmed's whining, Vlad cut the bottom of his shirt above the knot containing his money, and tossed this improvised purse to Mehmed. "Here, buy yourself something."

Mehmed took the money as if it were his due, and scampered over to a nearby food vendors' stall. Vlad took advantage of his departure to approach a Greek-looking monk loitering on the wharf.

"Pantelimon Monastery?" the monk repeated after Vlad. He tugged at his beard, then removed his *skufia* cap, and scratched his head with a show of concentration. "Past this gate turn right, then cross the Genovese, Pisan, and Amalfitan Quarters. Just before the Venetian Quarter turn left, up the hill. Once you pass the Tower of Eirene, you're almost at the monastery. Can't miss it. It's the only gate on a dead-end lane."

Vlad turned to check on Mehmed, and noticed three rough-looking youths hovering around the boy. "*Ce dracul?* What the Devil?" Vlad said under his breath. "Trouble so soon?" He closed the distance to the food stall in a few quick steps. Mehmed had spilled Vlad's aspers on the counter, and appeared to be searching among them, looking perhaps for copper coins. If the three ruffians were local Greeks, they'd probably understand some Turkish, so Vlad called out to Mehmed in Persian, "Gather your coins and let's go."

Mehmed glanced over his shoulder, and understood the threat at once. He swept the coins back into the cloth purse and rejoined Vlad. The three youngsters melted into the crowd.

When Vlad and Mehmed tried to enter the city gate, an officer barred their path. "Stand in line there and show your papers," he said, indicating a kiosk nearby with his baton.

Vlad experienced a moment of panic and almost dashed past the officer, thinking to get lost among the people on the other side of the gate. But then he noted a stream of porters laden with sacks and bundles, walking past the kiosk unchallenged.

"Come," he said to Mehmed, "get into that line and pick up a parcel."

They eased their way into a throng of porters queued up to offload cargo from a barge. Vlad placed a cotton bale on his head, and Mehmed took hold of a small sack of rice. Once inside the walls they dumped their loads onto the first cart they came to, then took off in the direction of the Acropolis. When a hundred feet farther Vlad glanced behind, he noticed the three Greeks from the food stall were tailing them. He lengthened his stride, but thought it unnecessary to alert Mehmed.

The neighborhood behind the Gate of Eugenius stretched up the north slope of the Acropolis Hill in a labyrinth of twisted lanes. Rows of wooden houses were cantilevered over these passages, making it difficult for daylight to reach the ground. Clothes hung to dry between the buildings further diminished whatever light did filter down. Even with the sun high, shops kept their oil lamps lit. Crowds of shoppers choked the lanes and filled the murky space with their chatter while they moved about their business in a molasses-slow shuffle.

Vlad and Mehmed weaved their way through this multitude as fast as they could. But when Vlad looked back again, the three men were still only a few dozen steps behind them. Murad's spies? Bounty hunters? Whatever these folks were, they seemed more determined than ordinary pickpockets looking for an easy mark. Now he had to tell Mehmed. "We've got to shake off our friends. Whatever they want with us can't be good."

When they arrived at the next crossing, Vlad doubled over to escape detection and turned the corner, Mehmed close behind. They stepped into a coppersmith's shop just in time to see the three strangers charging up the hill in their pursuit. A few minutes later, Vlad and Mehmed retraced their steps downhill for the space of several alleys, then resumed climbing through a new set of passageways.

"Have you decided on the one site to visit?" Vlad asked when they were out of the warren of houses, and could see the crest of the hill in the near distance.

"Hagia Sophia, of course," Mehmed said, and pointed to a cupola rising above a row of giant trees. "Beyazid said he would—"

"I've had enough of Beyazid," Vlad snapped. "Let's just keep the pace and be done with this." He decided that sightseeing was a poor idea.

But when they cleared the trees, and saw the church in its full, awe-inspiring dimension, Vlad changed his mind. Despite the structure's enormous size, the graceful combination of domes, half domes, arches, and buttresses induced a feeling of harmony and peace upon Vlad. To have come into the city, and not seen this ancient masterpiece, would've been a mistake.

"I think my father's entire castle would fit inside," he said, mostly to himself.

"My father's too," Mehmed said.

They came to an open portico supported by a row of immense brick pillars, and Mehmed said, "You go in by yourself."

"What? I brought you all the way here so you'd stand outside and—"

Mehmed assumed a grave mien that, as at the *hamam,* made him look like a grown man in the boy's body. "You need to know that the day I set foot inside, this church will become a mosque."

"Oh, I forgot," Vlad said, thoroughly annoyed. "You want to fulfill Beyazid's ambition." He lost interest in entering the church himself, and turned to leave. "I guess I too can put off seeing the inside until that day."

"Wait," Mehmed said. "There is one thing I want to do before we go away." He picked up a rock, and walked over to the portico. Before Vlad understood what was happening, Mehmed smashed the rock against the corner of one of the pillars, and broke off a brick chip the size of his fist. "I swear by Allah, the most glorified," he said with full solemnity when he returned to Vlad's side, "I'll restore this chip to its rightful place next time I return here. Until then, this will be my amulet."

They walked back toward the harbor in silence. At the first food stall they encountered, Mehmed bought two pieces of pita bread stuffed with grilled onions and eggplant. Vlad's hunger was sharp by now, and the aromas rising all around made him feel a weakness in his stomach. But, still upset at Mehmed's capricious behavior, he declined his share. Mehmed shrugged, and ate Vlad's portion without visible concern.

They were about midpoint on their way back to the Gate of Eugenius when a man of about forty, whom Vlad had just noticed leaning against the wall, stepped abruptly onto their path.

"I am Captain Throatcut, of His Majesty's Purse Relief Regiment," he said in Greek, with the deep, gravelly voice of a drunkard. "And who might you two lovebirds be?" The so-called captain had a shaggy mane that fell onto his shoulders, and a sparse beard that didn't cover suppurating purple sores on his cheeks. His clothes were mere rags, and he reeked appallingly of sweat and feces.

It's a trap, flashed through Vlad's mind, and blood rushed to his face. A man with a name like that didn't operate alone. When Throatcut's lips twitched Vlad knew it was a signal and he swiveled around quickly, raising an arm for protection. A heavy club landed upon his elbow, and the painful blow enraged him. As he snatched the club from his attacker, Vlad recognized him as one of the three youths from down by the wharf. The man's two cohorts stood by his side, grinning.

"Drop it, or your lover here gets a new breathing hole," Vlad heard. He turned to see Mehmed trapped under the captain's left arm, a knife at his throat. From the corner of his eye Vlad observed people passing by with no concern to what was happening in the middle of the lane. No help was going to come from them.

With the club in hand—a sturdy hickory ax handle—it would be child's play for Vlad to fight his way out of this mess. These young bullies weren't likely to have the training in close-quarter combat he did. But the older man looked the type who'd enjoy carrying out his threat against Mehmed. Vlad's mind raced. Fight, and see Mehmed killed? Or drop the club and hope they'd be just robbed, then let go? Robbed, no doubt. But let go? Quite improbable. Both he and Mehmed might still be stabbed to death after Vlad surrendered. His mouth went dry.

"So you're a feisty one," Throatcut said with a grin that showed a mouthful of decayed teeth. "Well, then take this." He gave his knife a quick jerk, and Mehmed screamed.

The man had only nicked Mehmed's skin but the sight of blood helped Vlad make up his mind. He let the club fall and dropped to his knees, joining his hands in prayer. "Have mercy on us, my good lord," he said in the most supplicating tone he could muster.

Guffaws erupted behind him, and the captain said, "That's better. Now which one of you has the money?"

"He does, my lord," Vlad said. "And it's all yours."

"You take the purse from the little boy, and toss it to my friends over there." From Throatcut's relaxed manner it was evident he had practice with this type of transaction, and relished the process perhaps as much as the proceeds. "Then tell us whom the precious one belongs to. I've got the feeling this pretty birdie's worth a lot more than the money he's got on him."

"Yes, for sure, my captain," Vlad said. He looked Mehmed in the eye, trying to convey the need to remain calm. "You guessed right. The boy can bring you a fortune in ransom, just don't hurt him anymore."

Vlad's thought flew back to Michael, who years ago insisted on teaching him to fight with either hand. "A knife in the right hand lacks the element of surprise," Michael warned Vlad. "But, in the left hand ..."

When trying to save a friend with a blade at his throat, nothing but a big surprise would do.

Vlad reached slowly with his right hand toward Mehmed's sash. While doing this he raised his right knee off the ground, and lowered his left arm to the knife in his boot, all in one smooth, dance-like motion. Next instant his left hand shot upward and planted the knife into the man's right armpit. The force of the thrust was such that the blade's tip emerged through the hollow of the man's neck, and lodged in his jawbone. Vlad took but a second to see that Mehmed had sprung loose, unharmed. Then he swept the club off the ground and pivoted around to confront a would-be attacker. None of the three youths had the chance to react. Behind him Vlad heard a thud as the captain's body hit the ground.

He shouted in Persian, "Run, Mehmed, while I hold back these scoundrels."

"Here's your money, sons of leprous whores," Mehmed screamed in Greek, his tone frightened and overwrought. Then came the sound of a coin shower. Instantly the scene was transformed into a seething mass of crawling bodies, as practically all men in the vicinity dove to the ground hoping to partake of this unexpected manna. Vlad took advantage of the confusion to get away. He skipped nimbly from one bent back to another, then dove downhill, club in one hand, Mehmed's arm in the other.

"Great idea, the coins," Vlad said between gulps of air. "But the brigands will still be coming after us, and they won't be kind next time."

"I saved some of the coins for just such an eventuality," Mehmed said.

"Good thinking," Vlad said, and laughed despite the strain of the chase. "Just remember, easy money breeds bad habits."

They ran blindly, bumping into people, upsetting hawkers' carts, and raising a chorus of curses in their wake. Vlad had to temper his speed so as not to lose Mehmed, knowing their new enemies would find and slaughter the boy. When they reached the main road, Vlad saw the Gate of Eugenius half a mile in the distance. He looked behind and was shaken to discover a mob of about twenty stampeding down the alley, less than thirty yards away. "We won't make it at this pace," he shouted. "Have to split up. Take this road straight to the gate, and use the coins to pay for the ferry to Galata."

"Don't … leave … me," Mehmed cried, nearly out of breath. He was flushed, and spittle ran down his chin.

"You're short enough to hide in the crowds," Vlad said. "I'll distract them from following you, then lose them and join you in Galata."

He let go of Mehmed's hand, resumed running at full speed, and took the first alley on his left without looking back at the boy. The rolling uproar behind him indicated his pursuers were determined to settle their account wherever he'd lead them.

After zigzagging through a dozen narrow streets, Vlad found himself on a wider road running parallel to the seawall. He guessed he was in the Pisan Quarter. Crowds were sparser here, allowing him to run faster. But a glance back revealed that his chasers also picked up the pace, and some began to gain on him. The first to close the gap was one of the original three youths who started this entire affair. He pulled even with Vlad, but kept himself at an arm's length distance. Below the man's huge beaked nose was the grin of a runner confident in his speed. His intention to outrun Vlad and trap him against the rest of the mob was obvious. *You're fast, but dumb.* Vlad slammed his club across the man's face without breaking stride and without looking. A crackling resembling that of kindling crushed in the fist told Vlad the beaked nose had taken the hit. The mob responded with a howl, and the sound of footsteps fell back, perhaps as the men attended to their injured comrade.

Vlad had no way of telling where the Pisan Quarter ended and the Amalfitan one started. Or where the Amalfitan Quarter gave way to the Venetian one. If he overshot his turning point for the Tower of Eirene, he'd find himself without a place to take shelter. But asking for directions wasn't something he could do while people with knives and clubs were chasing him at close range. The uncertainty gave him a painful stitch in the kidneys.

Unexpectedly a man with a basket of bread on his head blocked Vlad's path. *Great timing.* Vlad sidestepped the man, and crashed into a monk who just then emerged from a side street on the left. Both Vlad and the monk tumbled to the ground. Vlad's club flew out of his hand and rolled away.

"*Luate-ar dracul, vagabondule,* the Devil take you, tramp," the monk cursed Vlad in Romanian.

Never did words spoken in anger sound sweeter. "*Mulțumesc părinte,* thank you, Father." Vlad sprang back to his feet and threw himself headlong in the direction from which the monk had come, certain it led to the Pantelimon Monastery.

After about fifty yards the street's grade steepened, and broad wooden steps replaced the cobblestone pavement. Vlad's heart felt close to giving out, and his breath became a scorching flame. He felt a burst of joy when, two crossroads later, he came upon a tower he believed to be that of Eirene. Beyond this point there were no more houses, only ten-foot brick walls on both sides. The street narrowed into a lane that dead-ended in a stone archway fitted around a massive gate. Just like the monk on the wharf said.

Vlad stopped and looked behind him. The crowd of his enemies had thinned out a bit and fallen hundreds of feet behind. *I'm saved.* He wouldn't be butchered by the mob to become a nameless corpse no one would be able to identify. Anonymity in death troubled him, not death itself.

Slightly refreshed, he resumed his uphill run. The gate, two enormous oak panels reinforced with iron studs, was locked. Vlad looked for a bell rope, but there wasn't one. No Judas gate either. He pounded with his fists on the heavy planks, but they yielded only a dull sound. Behind him, an explosive clamor bounced off the walls. The pursuers had just entered the cul-de-sac to find Vlad trapped in there.

The mob stopped, and seemed to deliberate. Vlad thought they might be asking themselves whether finding their quarry in a blind alley wasn't a ruse meant to entrap them. Seemingly satisfied that it had to be pure luck, they set in motion again. As they advanced with slow, pompous steps, some twirled their clubs and knives to show off their dexterity. Vlad continued to pound vainly on the gate, while he watched with growing terror the approach of his enemies. With about thirty yards left to cover, one of the rogues lost his patience and broke ranks with the rest. He charged toward Vlad, hollering and brandishing a knife. Not to be deprived of the chance to carve a piece of their victim, the others followed. Vlad pressed his back against the gate and faced them with fists raised, as the jaws of an implacable vise seemed to squeeze his chest. He closed his eyes and felt the ground run from under his feet, while his body began to float weightlessly.

So, this is what it's like to die?

36

Pantelimon Monastery

An old monk was dragging Vlad by the shoulders, screaming, "Shut it, Patrocles, shut the goddamn gate, in the Virgin's name, or they'll kill us all." Vlad realized that instead of being dead he was now lying on the stove pavement behind the gate. A stinging pain on the back of his head served as explanation of how he ended there. Patrocles, a much younger monk, was straining to close the gate, but something was impeding his efforts. Vlad jumped to his feet and noticed the fingers of two hands were stuck in the center jamb between the door panels, keeping them ajar. He kicked the gate hard with the sole of his boot. Three of the fingers popped off and hit him in the chest; the others remained in place, dangling from bits of skin. The panels closed, and Patrocles secured them with a crosspiece he dropped onto iron brackets.

The mob's response was a collective bestial howl.

"Take me to the abbot, Fathers," Vlad said.

Patrocles seemed delighted by the unexpected disturbance at his monastery. When Vlad glanced at the door with concern over the hammering of clubs occurring on the outside, Patrocles said, "Don't you worry about this gate. It was built to withstand an attack by the Huns."

"Don't say such stupid things, Patrocles." The elder monk crossed himself. "Hurry up and lead our visitor to the office. The Reverend Father will be wondering what this clamor is all about."

"You should address me as Brother, not Father," Patrocles said when he and Vlad were on their way to the abbot's quarters. "I haven't been tonsured yet. I'm only a novice."

The abbot professed to be overjoyed when he learned who Vlad was. "King Dracul has always been generous to our monastery with his gold in the past," he said. Then he shook his finger like a scolding teacher. "But not lately. Our winepress broke down two years ago, and we haven't been able to replace it. And our fishing boat is in need of repair. But if he sent his son to us, the king must've finally heard our grievances."

"Gold, Reverend Father," Vlad said, "is something that my father—"

"Yes, gold is what this monastery needs, Son. Not beeswax, or hides, or furs ... all useless things that the God-fearing boyars of Wallachia keep sending us. Only gold will buy winepresses and repair boats." He leaned forward in his chair, and assumed a conspiratorial air. "I had a dream last night that a yellow bird shit on my head. Then today, my left palm itched all day. And now, praise be to the Mother of God, here you are with the good news." The corners of his eyes crinkled, and a dry laughter that sounded like wood rubbing on wood escaped his throat.

"My father is short of gold at the moment, Reverend Father. But he has an ingenious plan to—"

"What?" the abbot cried, and rose halfway in his chair. "If not to deliver your father's gift of coin, then what are you here for?" He turned an angry face to Patrocles, as if the novice were responsible for this sad misunderstanding.

Vlad gave an account of his father's visit to Edirne, and his own transformation into a hostage. At the word, "escape," the abbot gulped several times before he could speak. His oversized Adam's apple jerked up and down, desperate to escape from under his leathery dewlap. "Does anyone know you are in the city?"

"My Turkish guards on the other side of the Horn will have learned of it by now," Vlad said. "And I ran into a spot of trouble with some local folks, but they don't know who I am."

"Some street robbers chased the prince to our gate, but we managed to keep them out." Patrocles gave Vlad a wink and a proud smile.

The abbot's face acquired the yellowish tint of rancid fatback. "Harboring an escapee from the Turks is a violation of the peace treaty that could lead to war." He blessed himself three times. "All Murad needs is a pretext."

Vlad didn't believe a peace that had lasted twenty years could end on account of an insignificant person like himself. "I request nothing else from you, Reverend Father, but a place to rest until dark. Then I'll head to the Venetian Quarter, where friends await me. I'll be out of the city tonight, and no one will ever know I've been at your monastery."

"Yes, yes," the abbot said, absentminded. "You must rest, of course. Nothing else. Go rest, my son." He dismissed Vlad with a flick of his hand. "I must pray for heavenly guidance."

The room where Patrocles led Vlad was barely large enough to hold a narrow cot. "You may wait here in my cell, Prince Vlad," the novice said, "and I'll go steal some food from the kitchen. The monks won't feed you until after the Vespers service, and you look in need of something now."

The youth's un-monastic attitude amused Vlad. "What are you doing in this place? You don't appear to have the calling."

Patrocles chuckled. "I left Wallachia to see the world, and got as far as Constantinople before I ran out of money. That landed me in the debtors' prison. Fortunately, the Pantelimon monks took pity on me, so now here I am, ready to serve the Lord."

The fish stew Patrocles produced five minutes later tasted watery, but served to quiet Vlad's hunger. When the novice returned to his duties in the garden, Vlad tumbled onto the cot. He tried to review the events of the day, but fell asleep before reaching the breakfast in Mehmed's tent.

"Wake up, Prince Vlad, wake up." Two arms shook Vlad much harder than needed to awaken him. He recognized neither his surroundings nor the person leaning over him who shouted, "You've been sold out."

That jarred Vlad into full wakefulness. "What are you saying, Patrocles?"

"I just overheard the Reverend Father tell the deacon to go fetch the emperor's guards."

The bite of a viper couldn't hurt more. Vlad's fist closed over the hilt of an imaginary sword so tight that his arm quivered. But when he addressed Patrocles, he feigned indifference. "So, the good abbot did receive his heavenly guidance?"

Patrocles smiled. "Hurry, My Prince. The guards have barracks nearby, and they'll be here any moment."

Vlad leaped to the door, and saw there was about an hour left before sunset. He had no choice but to show up early at Donatella's palace. "You're taking a great risk helping me, Patrocles. Why not join the abbot in betrayal?"

"The wall at the rear of the orchard is only six feet high," Patrocles said. "It gives onto a dry creek bed that runs down to the Venetian Quarter."

Vlad took off at a run across the orchard. He was astride the wall when he remembered he hadn't thanked Patrocles. He turned to look for him, but the novice had vanished from sight. From the direction of the gate came the sound of shouted orders and people running on the stone pavement with heavy boots.

37

Bounty Hunters

Vlad recognized Donatella's Venetian palace from far away. It stood at the highest point on the street running along the Golden Horn seawall, surrounded by lesser buildings, as he remembered from Mehmed's model of the city. The building's facade reminded him of similar structures he saw in engravings owned by Father Lorenzo in Târgovişte. Soaring three stories high, the structure was pierced by tall windows graced with pointed arches and traceries in white marble.

When Vlad approached the palace he saw two men seated on the ground by the gatehouse, playing dice. He recognized them as members of Donatella's Edirne staff. The men gave Vlad indifferent looks and returned to their game. He knocked on the gate, and had a warm feeling when it was Spencer who opened it.

"You've made it, little brother," Spencer said, and gave Vlad a happy grin. "We were expecting you to show up tonight. But what's the idea of coming here in daylight when everyone can see you?" He pulled Vlad by the sleeve through the gate.

"Are those the Grimaldi's spies?" Vlad said, and pointed his thumb at the gatehouse.

"Ignore them. All they care about is that Bianca doesn't leave the palace without them." Spencer gave Vlad a hug, then shot up his arms in surprise. "You're drenched in sweat. Trouble?" Without waiting for an answer he stepped onto the street, and glanced left and right.

"Where's Lady Donatella?"

"Follow the *portego*, the hallway, and you'll find a staircase mid-point on your right. The mistress is above on the *piano nobile* with Lady Bianca."

"Emperor John's guards are looking for me," Vlad said over his shoulder, and dashed toward the stairs. "I've been betrayed by my own people."

"What?" Spencer shouted, but Vlad didn't stop to explain. As he raced up the shallow marble stairs, taking them two at a time, all he could think of was he'd see Donatella in a few seconds.

The staircase was ablaze with candles, and decorated with tapestries depicting naval battle scenes. On the second floor, the stairs gave onto another *portego* supported by two rows of red porphyry columns. This hallway connected the facade of the palace with the rear wall, whose windows opened over the Golden Horn. The light of the setting sun shimmering on the water far below entranced Vlad. *That's where I'll be tonight.*

"There is a better view of the Horn from my salon." Donatella's voice came from behind him.

In the two and a half months since he'd last heard her speak, Vlad forgot just how much that voice evoked in him the touch of velvet, or that of young moss. Not a sharp tone in it, not an unexpected inflection. Now, when it rang at such a close distance, it enveloped him in a warm glow that seemed to erase the gloomy weeks leading to this moment. He turned to her, and saw she had her arms extended, ready to embrace him. When he took an impulsive step forward, she dropped her arms and looked bashful. Her hair was pulled back and held in a filet of pearls, allowing her tall forehead to glow in the slanted sunrays. She had on a silk-and-gold-brocade overgown, sleeveless and split on the sides. Underneath, she wore the same blue velvet gown he knew from his sickroom in Edirne. Vlad wondered if she'd chosen it on purpose for this day. The summer heat, even in this airy palace, had to be oppressive to a person dressed in so many layers. Yet Donatella managed to appear as cool and comfortable as if she wore only a gauze chemise.

"I know I was supposed to come after dark, but—"

"I was afraid you wouldn't come at all," she said, and smiled with a joy she hadn't displayed in front of him before.

"Who's there, Mamma?" With a shriek, Bianca emerged from a nearby room and ran to Vlad with open arms. She almost knocked him off his feet as she slammed into him.

"Bianca Pia!" Donatella exclaimed. She frowned at her daughter, but didn't lose her smile. That gave her face a funny look Vlad found adorable.

"Let Vlad catch his breath. Can't you see he's been running?" With a discreet tug, Donatella extracted a purple handkerchief from between her breasts. "Here, Bianca, wipe Vlad's brow, then let's take him to a place he can rest for a bit."

Bianca complied with evident pleasure.

"I'm not tired," Vlad said. With a casual gesture he took the handkerchief from Bianca, and dabbed his cheeks. *I was right*, he thought, giddy from inhaling Donatella's lavender perfume. He felt that having guessed her choice of fragrance placed him into a more intimate contact with her. He tucked the precious piece of fabric into his pocket, and saw Donatella acknowledge his innocent larceny with a near suppressed smile.

"Tired or not, you'll sit down and tell us everything about finding your way here," Donatella said. She took him by one hand, Bianca by the other, and together they led him to the salon.

The sparsely decorated room owed its warmth and intimacy to dark wood paneling and soft Persian rugs. The furniture was light, reduced to a couple of slender cupboards and a writing desk decorated with inlaid gold. In the room's center stood a pair of wooden chests overflowing with articles of feminine clothing. Next to them were two low stools upholstered in needlepoint. Vlad guessed Donatella and Bianca had been sitting on them when he arrived.

"There," Donatella said. She tugged at a swath of damask fabric that lay in a pile on the floor to make room for him. "Sit down and let's have your story."

"These *cassoni* hold my trousseau," Bianca said indicating the chests. "And this mountain of *damaschino* will one day be the cover for my matrimonial bed. Mother's been embroidering it forever, but it's still far from being done." She giggled, then blushed.

"Bianca accuses me of acting like Ulysses's Penelope," Donatella said. "According to her, I unravel at night the work that I do in the daytime."

"Mother thinks procrastinating with her embroidery will delay the day of my departure."

"I don't wish to alarm you, Lady Donatella, but I've been betrayed by the abbot of the monastery where I was hiding. The emperor's men are looking for me, and might pick up my trail soon."

Donatella blanched. "Then you must get away without delay," she said, her voice crimped by fear.

She picked up a lantern from the windowsill. "I hope Captain Andrea will see my signal, with the daylight still so strong." She opened the window and swung the lantern outside a few times. "He might be wondering why I'm calling him so early. But he's a clever man, and he'll guess there is a reason to hurry."

"Captain Andrea's galley is the one next to that Portuguese carrack," Bianca said. "Can you imagine, Vlad, being only a few feet away from freedom?"

Vlad estimated the "few feet" to be more than a hundred, if one measured the elevation of the *piano nobile* above the waterline. But, indeed, he *was* only feet away from freedom. Yet, the feeling of exhilaration he'd anticipated at the arrival of this moment wasn't there. Instead, he felt torn between the desire to climb down the seawall, and the longing to remain in this very room forever. Remain to do what? He couldn't say. His soul felt like a hawk flapping its wings, while a cruel master held onto its claws.

"The galley's moving," Donatella and Bianca shouted in unison.

The hawk's wings flapped harder, but the grip on its claws remained firm.

"I've just decided I'm going with Vlad, Mother," Bianca said, then bit her lip, perhaps anticipating her mother's shock.

Donatella gasped, and her eyes widened. She struggled to say something, but produced only a tremulous whimper. Vlad guessed she had gotten used to the chronic pain of losing Bianca in the future, and had difficulty accepting the acute pain of losing her now, without preparation, and not knowing when they'd be reunited.

"But your dizziness, your fear of heights?" Donatella said finally. "You'll panic again, and give both of you away."

"With Vlad I'm not afraid," Bianca said. "I'd go with him anywhere."

Donatella kneaded her hands with a look of despair.

"She'll be safe with me," Vlad said. If he took Bianca away from her uncle's nefarious designs, he'd be repaying in part Donatella's kindness to him.

His reassurance had a more powerful effect upon Donatella than he anticipated. Her face relaxed, and something close to excitement came into her eyes.

"How do we keep Grimaldi's maids from sounding the alarm?" she said. "If they find out what we're up to—"

"I'll get them to try on some of your clothes, Mother," Bianca said. "They'll be thrilled, and while they're busy doing that I'll sneak away."

"Excellent idea," Donatella said. "Fetch Paola and have her lock the maids in my dressing room. Once you're free of them, put on the sailor's clothes I prepared for you last time, and return here quickly."

Bianca dashed out of the room, and Donatella let herself fall onto one of the stools. Vlad noticed she covered her mouth to stifle her sobs, and would've loved to comfort her, but didn't know how. He turned his face away, embarrassed. As he did so, a loud commotion erupted somewhere on the ground floor.

Donatella jumped to her feet with a sharp cry. "My God! They're here. They've tracked you down."

Vlad didn't need to be told this. He heard the harsh soldiers' voices, the rattling of their weapons, and felt as if he'd just fallen into a sinkhole. The first thought that came to mind was to forget about Bianca and bolt, to save himself. He met Donatella's eyes, and a flame of shame flared up inside him.

Donatella rushed to the writing desk, and returned with a key. "Here. It opens the door to the stairs that lead up to the wall-walk at the rear of the garden." She spoke very fast but in the cool tone a parent would use to quell a child's panic. Yet Vlad knew she had to be on the verge of hysteria.

"I'm not leaving without Bianca," he said.

"The rope ladder hangs between those two merlons marked with crosses," she said, pointing to the seawall through the open window. "Jump into the garden, and I'll stall the guards until you vanish from sight."

"Not without Bianca," Vlad repeated. He regretted his self-destructive stubbornness but could see no way around it. "I promised to take her with me and she's counting on that. There's got to be a place in this palace I could hide."

A babble of protests resounded from the *portego* below. Spencer's voice rose above the din, then came a yelp of pain. *They've killed my friend.* Vlad's feet became heavy, as if shod in iron boots.

Footsteps boomed now on the stairs, and hobnailed boots ground against the marble treads. Vlad cast about the room for a place to hide, but there was none. Now he wished he'd fled, but it was too late.

Grim-faced with determination, Donatella took his elbow and pulled him toward the stool. There she forced him to his knees, then sat down in front of him. A moment before the door flew open she pushed his head onto her lap, and covered him with the matrimonial spread.

"Where is he?" a coarse voice hollered from the doorway.

Vlad felt Donatella's thighs tremble like a rabbit caught in a net. He squeezed them hard to still them, while his own fear thumped in his temples. He remembered that feeling from his encounter with Omar and his brothers. But this time something new lurked on the fringes of fear. It was pleasure, he realized, and felt guilty.

"Who are you, and how dare you invade my home?" Donatella shouted with sincere outrage. "Don't you know who I am?"

"We know very well who you are, Lady Loredano," the man who'd spoken before said in an insolent tone. "We also know you're harboring a fugitive who's Sultan Murad's subject."

"Do you see anyone being harbored around here, Captain?"

The man didn't reply. Instead he stomped across the room, and Vlad assumed he looked out the window at the garden below. "He escaped through here, but can't have gotten too far. Quick, men, to the garden. Check the ground behind the palace, and that of the neighboring residences." The heavy steps returned from the window, then the door slammed shut.

38

The Flight of the Hawk

In the silence that descended in the room, Vlad could hear the blood pulsing in his ears. He wanted to let go of Donatella's thighs, but his hands wouldn't budge. She too remained still, seemingly waiting for the soldiers' sounds to die down. Finally she threw the spread aside, and crouched next to him with a wild look of concern. He was shocked at her pallor, and reached out a hand to reassure her. Perhaps not understanding his gesture she flinched, and tumbled backward. At the last moment she grabbed his shirt for anchor, and dragged him with her to the floor.

Vlad landed on her, cheek-to-cheek, and the touch of her skin brought white heat to his face. Then the raw scent of her sweat, with its forbidden promises, robbed him of all reason. He clamped his mouth over hers with the fierceness of a starving man pouncing on the last morsel of food. She struggled to free herself, and that sent an icy shock through him. *What have I done?* Mortified, he raised his face from hers.

She stared at him with wide, reproachful eyes ready to incinerate him with their ire. He was about to apologize, when she sank her nails into his cheeks and drew him to her for a clumsy kiss. Then she pushed him away, but without conviction. Her tepid resistance unleashed in him a fathomless desire he was unable to trammel. His mouth sought hers again, and this time she reciprocated. The two abandoned themselves to a frenzy of bites, moans, and growls that betrayed their long-concealed hunger for each other. Somehow, their game reminded him of two wolves he saw once playfully devour a lamb, jowl to jowl, and that distant image aroused him further.

Carried by passion, Donatella's bites became increasingly harder until they drew blood. She must have tasted it, because she pushed his face from hers to examine his lips. Her look tensed, and he feared she regretted her display of ardor. Then he realized she was straining to lift her gown, pinned under his weight. He helped her, only to discover that under the blue velvet folds there were more fabric layers. These unexpected and treacherous obstacles frustrated his search for a passage to his intended destination.

There has to be a way. He saw Donatella smile teasingly, and that emboldened him. He maneuvered through the bewildering array of ribbons and laces, and tore at the last barrier with his nails. The flimsy fabric yielded, and granted his hand access to that proof of feminine desire familiar to him by now.

When it was over, they stood, and looked away from each other. Vlad's mind, freed of lust, drifted quickly to the impeding descent of the wall, and a new surge of energy filled his breast. He'd headed for the window, to check on the galley's progress, when he heard movement by the door. He turned swiftly, and his hand flew to the place where he'd normally find his sword. Bianca stood in the doorway dressed as a boy, hair concealed under a sailor's cap.

"I know what you did with Vlad, Mother," she said, reproachful as only a child can be. Vlad felt the words whip him. How long had she been there?

Donatella said, self-assured, "Whatever nonsense are you talking, Bianca? Did you hear the soldiers were here, looking for Vlad?"

Donatella's attempt at changing the subject didn't work. The girl pointed an accusing finger at her, and said, "You told me you didn't love him, and now—"

"You must hurry, child," Donatella said, and walked with firm steps to the window. "I don't see the galley anymore, which means Captain Andrea has reached the base of the wall. Let's not make him wait there too long and draw unwanted attention to his ship."

"I'm not leaving anymore." Faced buried in her hands, Bianca burst into tears. "You both have betrayed me."

Vlad wasn't prepared for this new set of difficulties, and was unsure how to act. Women … they moved the world one moment, and brought it to a halt the next. He walked over to Bianca, and took her into his arms.

"Of course your mother loves me," he said, his eyes on Donatella. "And I love her. But I also love you, and it's *you* I've waited for. And *you* will be leaving with me, not your mother. So let me take you away from this dangerous place."

Bianca raised her face to his, with the look of someone who wanted to believe. He wiped her tears with his thumbs.

"I'll lead the way," Donatella said, garden key in hand.

"How soon will I see you again, Mother?"

Donatella faltered, and reached out a hand to Vlad. Would she break down at this crucial moment? He gave her hand a squeeze, and she regained her composure. "With Grimaldi no longer threatening to take you away from me, I can sell my estate here and join you in Venice. It won't take more than a year."

"*Nooo*," Bianca wailed. "That's too long, Mamma."

"My aunt Lucretia will be like a mother to you, until I come." Donatella put her arm around Bianca's shoulder and led her out of the salon.

On the ground floor, the servants surrounded them with agitated chattering. Donatella silenced them with an imperious gesture.

"Has anyone been hurt?" she said.

"Spencer took a knock on the head but he'll be fine," the steward replied.

"Give your belt and sword to Prince Vlad," Donatella ordered him. "Then make sure the front gate is bolted and that Grimaldi's men remain on the street."

Vlad could tell from the sword's heft that it was a weapon of inferior quality. But he cinched the belt to his waist anyway, then followed Donatella and Bianca into the garden. Donatella opened the rear gate, and the three of them climbed a rusty spiral staircase. It led to a sentry box that opened onto the wall-walk. They waited there, listening for sounds that might betray the presence of soldiers nearby.

"I kept the rope ladder rolled up since the last time we tried to use it," Donatella whispered, "so it wouldn't be noticed from the boats passing below. But when I heard you arrived outside Galata, I had Spencer release it."

"It's quite slippery," Bianca said. "That's why I got so scared last time."

"You've got nothing to fear with me," Vlad said, unconvinced. "I'll check to see that everything's in order."

He crouched and scooted across the walkway in five steps, then ducked into the embrasure between the two marked merlons. The Golden Horn was speckled with dozens of ships of every size. He recognized the Venetian, Genovese, and Catalan standards from his manuscripts. There were also many standards he couldn't identify. Small boats crowded the space around the larger vessels, probably delivering supplies. An isolated Venetian galley floated fifty yards off the base of the wall, below the place where he stood. The crew was lined up along the deck, its members appearing to stare in his direction. "Can you imagine being only a few feet away from freedom?" Bianca had asked. *Yes, that's freedom down there.* His mind said those words calmly, as detached as if they were the most banal words in the world. But his heart thrashed in his breast, drunk with a mixture of love, gratitude, and longing it had never tasted before.

When he looked straight down the wall, he felt a shooting pain in his groin. The vertical drop of more than ninety feet ended on a rocky outcrop covered in sea foam. *I wouldn't want to be carried down there on anybody's back.*

The top of the ladder was anchored just below the lip of the crenel from two large ringbolts set in lead-filled sockets. The first ten feet of lashing were iron chain, while the rest was hemp rope. He leaned over and felt the wooden rungs, found them solid and dry.

"Come, Bianca," he called, and the girl shot across the wall-walk without hesitation. Behind her, Donatella stood inside the sentry box, hand covering her mouth. Her eyes drilled into his, and he read in them the unquenched desire he'd felt himself only minutes before. But now the sap of freedom overflowed inside him, leaving no room there for other want but that of returning home.

The hawk's claws had finally been released, and it was now soaring into the violet sky.

He took hold of the ringbolts and lowered himself onto the ladder. "Close your eyes, and climb onto my back," he ordered Bianca, in a firm tone meant to bolster her confidence. She complied, gripping his neck so tight he could barely breathe. He said nothing for fear she'd loosen her hold and fall. The girl's weight on his back felt lighter than the armor he wore in swordplay with Gruya and Marcus. *It's going to be easy.*

The chain portion of the ladder was stable and he had no difficulty descending the first ten feet. But when he reached the rope lashing, his footing became uncertain. The rungs had been made of perfectly round dowels that would rotate inside their rope sockets, causing his foot to slip. The first time it happened he found himself dangling over the abyss, hanging on with one hand. Bianca shrieked, and tightened further her hold on his neck. He turned his head to the side to reduce the pressure on his windpipe. Then, she began to tremble and whimper. He worried that, in her panic, she would impede his moves, the way a drowning man hinders his rescuer. "How well do you know the geography of the seas?" he asked, to take her mind off the unstable ladder.

She didn't answer but stopped whimpering, showing she heard him.

"I've got a game for you. Every three rungs I'll call out the name of a place and you—"

"I know all about my *nonno*'s, grandfather's, sea battles." Her trembling ceased. "I could draw you a map of the Mediterranean with my eyes closed."

"So you'd know if a place was too far out of the way for our galley to make a stop there?"

"Try me."

"One … two … three," Vlad counted, placing his feet on rung after rung with utmost care. "Gallipoli?"

"Yes," Bianca shouted, gleeful. "*Nonno* Pietro defeated the Ottoman fleet there in the year fourteen-sixteen."

Vlad counted three more steps. "Smyrna?"

"No." Bianca giggled. "Too far east."

"Thessalonica?"

"Too far west."

Negroponte drew a yes. Athens a maybe. Crete, a yes. Rhodes, a firm no.

Vlad glanced downward, trying to guess how many more places he'd have to name before they reached the water. They were about sixty feet above the rocky ledge. Even though the going was slower than he'd anticipated, things would turn out well.

Then a high-pitched shout of, "Vlad," came from above. Donatella was leaning through the crenel, her hair disheveled now and hanging over her face. "Hurry, Vlad, they've spotted you."

The bells of a nearby church began to toll that instant, with the rumbling energy of a thunderclap and a regret-laden timbre. Those of another church farther away echoed them in a golden voice full of pleading and contrition. Soon hundreds of bells throughout the city rang in a myriad of tones and rhythms. A deafening, maddening, exhilarating call to Vespers. Constantinople was speaking to God, and He, no doubt, was ready to receive its prayers.

Donatella disappeared, and several heads popped up above the parapet. In her place now stood a burly soldier wielding an ax. He swung it at the chain lashing, but the sound of the blow was washed over by the bells' din. Vlad felt the ladder shake, and saw sparks fly from the iron links.

Bianca screamed, "Mamma."

Vlad crossed himself and said a hurried Paternoster. "There is nothing to fear, Bianca Pia." He imitated Donatella's calm tone from earlier that afternoon, though his own knees had begun to quiver. "It will take that ax an hour to cut through the chain, and by then we'll be in the Sea of Marmara. Just close your eyes and hold on tight."

He resumed the descent, counting. "One … two … three. Corfu?"

Bianca didn't reply.

A shower of stone fragments rained down on them. The man was now attacking the stone around the lead sockets. That would go much faster. In a few minutes, one of the sockets would spring loose and the ladder would collapse on one side, becoming unusable. Then the other socket would give in under the unbalanced weight; he and Bianca would be done for.

"One … two … three. Durazzo?"

Still nothing from Bianca.

Vlad took another look at the water through more stone shards flying by. They were now about forty feet above rocks. Alone, he could jump clear of them from this height. But he couldn't do it safely with Bianca on his back. And continuing to descend at this slow pace would sentence them both to death.

"Can you swim?" Vlad said, and felt her nod. "Great. Then grab onto a rung and continue down by yourself." She started to wail but he didn't relent. "Count ten rungs, then think of Syracuse. Ten more, and you're in Ragusa. Ten more yet, and you've reached Venice. Then jump into the water and swim to the galley." When she didn't move he took one of her hands, and forced it onto the rung above his head. His skin prickled at thought the ladder might break at any moment. "It's me those men want, not you." He slipped away from under her, and slithered into the space between the ladder and the wall, holding all along onto the belt of her breeches. Face-to-face with her, only inches apart, he noticed that her blue eyes had flecks of gold in them.

The rock splinters kept falling; time was running out. "I'll go pretend I'm ready to surrender, and that'll make them stop what they're doing. It will give you time to reach safety. Then I'll join you."

He gave her a peck on the nose, then regained the outside of the ladder and began to climb. As he had anticipated, the soldier stopped swinging the ax. After a few feet Vlad stopped. The ax struck again. *They've guessed my game, and won't be fooled.* Bianca had only descended two or three feet. He'd have to continue climbing, to give her more time.

But when Vlad resumed his ascent, the soldier didn't stop the ax work. His cohorts, peeking over the merlons, sounded amused by the spectacle and kept goading the axman.

"Murad pays for captured runaways dead or alive," Spencer had said. *So, these good Christians decided on murder.* Fury overtook Vlad as he thought of Bianca lonely and scared down below. He closed the remaining distance to the top in a frenzied scramble, and drew his sword just as the socket gave in, and the right side of the ladder collapsed.

"The other boy's fallen," a man shouted, and the rest of the soldiers cheered.

Holding on to the chain with one hand, feet entangled in the lashing, Vlad tried to look down but couldn't manage.

"He's swimming to the galley," the same man said. The soldiers' cheers turned to curses.

Against the odds, Bianca was safe. But the price for her safety was Vlad's doom. A sharp claw of anger and hatred clutched at his insides. He stabbed with his sword at the axman's foot but missed. The soldiers laughed, and someone shouted, "Let him have it, Gregorius."

When Vlad stabbed at him again, the man struck Vlad's sword with his ax. The blow caught the blade against the stone wall and shattered it. But Gregorius had leaned over the crenel too far, and began to teeter. He let go of the ax and flailed his arms, trying to grab onto something. For a moment it looked as though he'd manage to regain his footing. But then he tumbled over, and plunged headlong past Vlad, letting out a perplexed groan and a lungful of garlicky breath.

A storm of curses erupted on the battlement, and two halberds were lowered in Vlad's direction. Their hooks tore into his tunic and gouged his flesh. The halberds lifted Vlad over the parapet, then dropped him onto the wall-walk. There, hobnailed boots began to kick him.

39

The Price of Sin

When Bianca crossed the wall-walk to join Vlad, and disappeared with him over the parapet, Donatella felt something inside her tear like an overstretched piece of fabric. The pain left her disoriented, and reminded her of the feeling she had when her daughter was born and Donatella lost a part of herself.

She'd known for more than two years her baby would be torn away, a weaned lamb from the ewe. But now when the separation came, albeit with Donatella's consent, it found her as ill prepared as the day Grimaldi announced his ghastly news of Bianca's "betrothal."

At least this separation was temporary, Donatella reminded herself. Bianca had escaped Murad's gilded cage, and was headed for a better place where mother and daughter would be reunited one day. Yet that reasoning didn't mend the tear in her breast, nor did it assuage her fears for Bianca. A sea voyage was fraught with perils. Storms sank dozens of ships every year, and pirates captured many more. Her mind thrashed with thoughts of dangers present and future.

Without thinking of peril to herself, she rushed over to the parapet and peeked down the wall through the crenel's opening. She saw Vlad and Bianca swaying with the movement of the ladder, and had to choke back a cry of terror. Vlad said something to Bianca, and the sound of his voice had a searing effect on Donatella. It reminded her the pain she felt was not only from seeing her child go, but also from losing … what was she losing by Vlad's departure? She'd never asked herself what he meant to her. But now that he was about to vanish forever, that question forced itself upon her. Besides her love for Bianca, he was everything that meant life to her.

Her reason rebelled. How could a youngster nearly half her age be anything but a ward to her?

Age had nothing to do with it, her heart retorted. He'd proven that only minutes ago through that act that forever pierced the wall separating them. But the recollection came wrapped in shame and guilt. Her hand dropped to her groin like the protective fig leaf in a fresco of naked Eve she'd seen once in Verona.

That moment, heavy steps resounded behind her, and she yelled out Vlad's name without thinking, or looking back to see who it was.

When the soldiers tried to remove her from the battlement, she clawed at them and screamed. On the captain's orders, two of them dragged her back to the garden and locked the staircase gate with her own key. She ran upstairs to her salon, waving the servants out of her way. There she rushed to the window and leaned out so far she nearly toppled over the sill.

She saw a soldier hacking with his ax at something on the wall's outer face, and knew it had to be the ladder. The horror she felt was blacker than any she'd ever experienced. Another soldier pointed at something below, and all the others leaned over the parapet to look, then made gestures of disappointment. Did that mean Bianca and Vlad had reached the bottom? Donatella dared to hope again.

"You were a mother too, Holy Virgin," she whispered. "You understand my pain. Save my child and I'll build you a most beautiful chapel." She knew such a bargain wouldn't satisfy the Almighty;

He would want more. She thought about her consummated lust for Vlad and said, "I'll pay any price you want for my transgression, God, just please save Bianca." She joined her hands, beseeching, barely able to breathe.

Then she saw Vlad being hoisted over the battlement on the hooks of two halberds, and bit her hand, expecting they would bring up Bianca next. When the soldiers turned their backs to the water, she understood Bianca had eluded them. But was she safe, picked up by Andrea? Or had she fallen and … anguish and uncertainty crushed what remained of her spirit. A venomous curse escaped her lips, against this miserable city, its emperor, and his vile servants.

On the wall-walk the soldiers were elbowing each other to kick Vlad, whom she couldn't see, but whose pain she felt in her flesh. She realized his capture was the price set on her sin. Drained of all strength but brimming with resentment against a God who couldn't put off His revenge, she crumpled to the floor, both heart and eyes dry.

She had no sense of the passing of time as her mind closed in on itself, trying to keep the pain at bay. When a voice called her name, she didn't recognize it as Paola's.

"Tella, Tella," Paola wailed, "what have they done to you?" She caressed the top of Donatella's head, then helped her rise. "Look, my child. There is a signal down there on the water. It must be Captain Andrea's."

Those words tore through Donatella's stupor and brought her back to the moment. In the darkness that had descended, she saw the flames of two torches describing circles as they twirled back and forth. It was indeed the signal she and Andrea had agreed upon. "The passenger's on board, and we're on our way."

"The Virgin has answered my prayer," she cried, the pendulum of her emotion swinging back to the bright side.

The signal would be repeated until acknowledged from above, or until the galley was out of sight. "Hurry, Paola, light up the lantern for me."

When Captain Andrea's torches went dark, Donatella's mind snapped back to the scene she'd witnessed before her collapse.

"What did they do to him?" she said, and she couldn't recognize her own voice. "Did they—?" She was unable to utter the word "kill."

"Calm down, Tella," Paola said. "You've had enough trauma for one day."

"But—"

"The steward found out they took Prince Vlad across the water to Galata."

He's not free but lives. Her earlier resentment against God forgotten, Donatella raised her eyes to the sky. "Now, please help him find his way home."

Donatella stood, absentminded, while two maids began to undress her, but had removed only her *giornea* and her *gamurra* when Paola dismissed them. With the maids gone, she lifted off Donatella's chemise and took it over to a candelabra to inspect. She grunted in surprise, then returned and knelt in front of Donatella to untie and roll down her chausses. This time, she gasped. "I was wondering how you managed get your chemise wet, but now I see how that might've happened."

Donatella didn't reply. She wasn't embarrassed about anything in front of her old nurse, and kept no secrets from her. But now she had no desire to speak.

Paola removed Donatella's pantaloons and touched the fabric's torn edges with a squeamish expression. "I see you must've been in a hurry," she continued, relentless and acid. "Or, should I say, 'Someone was in a hurry'?" She rose with a sigh, and turned to leave. "I'll throw these away, and have the seamstress make you a new pair."

"Don't bother, Paola." Donatella snatched the garment from her nurse. "I'm done with wearing pantaloons. They do nothing but get in the way."

Later in bed, her mind was on Bianca as her arms held the guilty pantaloons close to her bosom. Bianca would be crying now. She'd be feeling lonely and fearful for what was going to come. *We've never been apart, even for one day. But, unlike me, you're getting your life back, while I ...*

When her tears began to flow, Donatella told herself they were for Bianca. With that lie on her lips, and the only trace she had left of Vlad clutched in her fists, she finally fell asleep.

40

Zaganos's Judgment

To Vlad's relief, the soldiers' fury was short-lived. They soon began to talk about women and wine, and their kicks devolved into perfunctory thrusts. From their banter Vlad gathered Gregorius hadn't been quite right in the head, and had always served as the regiment's laughingstock. The soldiers didn't seem to regret his demise, and Vlad pitied the unfortunate fool.

"Enough play," the captain barked after a while. "You two," he said to men Vlad couldn't see, "tie him up, and take him to Galata. Don't forget to get a receipt from the watch officer, so I can collect the reward tomorrow. The rest of you, forget drinking and whoring and return to the barracks."

The two soldiers charged with escorting Vlad bound his hands behind his back. Then they lit a torch and walked him to the Gate of Saint John nearby. On the way, Vlad had to bite his lip to hold back groans of pain. *They must've cracked my ribs.* He knew it would take him months to heal. Then he remembered that what awaited him in Galata made this injury inconsequential. The Brankovich boys had been blinded on mere suspicion they planned to escape. Vlad had actually *tried to escape,* so for him there could be no other punishment than death.

The soldiers borrowed a boat from the gatekeepers and shoved him facedown into the hold. Even with two strapping slaves rowing in earnest, the crossing of the Horn took nearly half an hour. To Vlad it felt like five minutes. Too short an interval for the tumult of thoughts that crowded pell-mell his mind.

Some thoughts were mere flashes: a name here, an image there. Others lingered, pitiless in their ability to inflict longing and remorse. Oma came to him repeatedly, both tender and chiding. "There is no such thing as 'glory'," she kept repeating. But when Vlad tried to explain that glory wasn't his quest she'd just shake her head, skeptical.

Wolves, manuscripts, bells tolling for no reason … Father, Michael, Marcus, Gruya, Gunther …

Was his life meant to be so short? So meaningless? His father had been right regarding the prophecy. It hadn't meant anything.

Would Father be saying, "I told Vlad he'll end up badly"? That would be unfair, since Vlad knew what he was doing; he did nearly escape, after all. And, as Bianca put it, he made it to within a few feet of freedom. That should count for something, as far as his abilities went.

Ah, Bianca. There was something that went right tonight. She was leagues away by now from that unscrupulous Grimaldi. And something else went right, as well. He touched with his tongue the place Donatella had bitten his lip. More than right. He hoped she wouldn't find out how he died. But of course she would, like everyone else. He was ashamed at the thought he'd be pitied by all, like some clumsy rider who broke his neck in a fall. Being executed by the Turks wasn't like dying in battle, an arrow in your chest or steel in your guts.

He wondered who would inherit Timur. Lash would care for the horse as lovingly as Vlad had done it, until a new owner claimed him. Remembering the horse's habit of rubbing its head against his shoulder whenever they were reunited gave him a feeling akin to jealousy. Would Timur do that to his new master? The possibility saddened him. *How can I think about a horse at a time like this? Damn it all. Damn Hunyadi and his letter that caused this entire disaster.*

When the boat bumped into the Galata pier, Vlad reflected he still had a few hours before facing Zaganos's "justice." They'd have to wait for the predawn *adhān*, when the vizier would rise to do his prayers. Tirendaz and Mehmed would also get up then. The boy had to be in trouble as well. Nothing like Vlad, of course, but trouble nonetheless. And not so much for sneaking into Constantinople without his *lala*'s consent, but for losing Murad's precious prisoner. Knowing how Mehmed "lost" him made Vlad feel sorry for the boy. He might be the sultan's son, and thus every Christian's enemy, but Mehmed was still only a ten-year-old kid, unfairly accused of something grievous. Vlad resolved to take full blame for the Constantinople adventure when he saw Zaganos.

Upon being dragged out of the boat Vlad discovered, to his dismay, that facing Zaganos would happen earlier than anticipated. From the chatter around him, Vlad gathered his and Mehmed's flight to Constantinople had sent the Third Vizier into a state of blind rage. He beat Hamza senseless as the messenger of bad news. Then he asked Podestà Grimaldi to keep Galata's port gate open all night, in case Vlad was captured and returned by the Byzantines. And now, here Zaganos stood at the top of the wharf, tapping the blade of his *kılıç* against the palm of his left hand. Flanked by a dozen slaves bearing torches, the vizier looked like a victorious general soaking in the humiliation of a defeated foe.

Hamza, face covered in bruises, and Yunus, grinning self-importantly, stood beside him. There was no sign of Mehmed.

"'Endure you patiently, for your patience is from Allah'," Zaganos recited grandly, "'and your enemy shall be returned to you'."

"You aren't planning anything hasty, Zaganos Pasha, are you?" Vlad heard Tirendaz say behind him, and had a flash of hope. Next, Vlad felt his wrist bindings snap loose, releasing the pressure on his injured ribs and allowing him to breathe more comfortably. "Let the hostage get some rest, and we can question him in the morning."

"There is nothing 'hasty' about carrying out the punishment of a runaway," Zaganos said. "The sooner the sultan receives this boy's head, the sooner he'll realize King Dracul and his son played a nasty trick on His Majesty."

Tirendaz planted himself between Vlad and Zaganos. "Even though you have the authority to sentence Vlad to death, you may not carry out such a sentence without a *kadı*'s approval."

Zaganos knitted his brow and shook his head, clearly vexed with Tirendaz's interference. "Remove the prisoner's shirt," he ordered no one in particular. Hamza rushed to Vlad and stripped him to the waist. "You know well, Tirendaz, the nearest *kadı* is in Izmir, four days' travel from here. You can't expect me to let this traitor live that long." He stepped around Tirendaz, and removed Vlad's medallion. "You won't be needing this charm anymore."

"I most certainly expect you to let the Izmir *kadı* review Prince Vlad's case," Tirendaz said, determined.

Zaganos placed Vlad's medallion around his own neck, and appeared to reconsider the matter.

He might give in. Vlad clutched to that thought, as a sinner to prayer beads on his deathbed. He knew that any *kadı* was apt to give in to Zaganos's authority and irrefutable arguments. But a four-day reprieve was a lifetime.

"Check his pockets," Zaganos ordered, and Hamza turned Vlad's pockets inside out. Donatella's handkerchief fell to the ground.

Zaganos appeared disappointed. "What? No money? Where's the silver you took from Mehmed before you left him among the infidels?"

What story did Mehmed spin his *lala* to get himself out of trouble? "Mehmed himself tossed the coins to the people who attacked us." Vlad wanted to add the silver had been his to start with, but knew that wouldn't change anything.

"The word of a liar and a coward," Hamza said.

Vlad wouldn't have thought anything could aggravate him further. But Hamza's words inflicted a fresh wound to his pride. "What cowardliness are you speaking of?"

"You abandoned Mehmed in the hands of some ruffians, to save your skin," Yunus said. "He had to fight his way free at knifepoint."

"He said *that*?" Vlad looked at Tirendaz, and was disheartened to see him confirm Yunus's claim with a nod.

"And what's this?" Zaganos said. He speared the handkerchief with his saber, and raised it to Vlad's face. "Whom did you steal this from?"

"Now you're just looking for a pretext to take your vengeance on Prince Vlad," Tirendaz said.

Vlad snatched the kerchief. The soft tissue with its delicate scent took him back to Donatella's salon, and the remaining strength in his legs seeped away. "It belongs to Lady Loredano, in the city," he whispered. When Zaganos began to laugh, Vlad realized the answer he gave confirmed the vizier's theft accusation.

"Yunus, you're a diligent student of the Qur'an," Zaganos said in a sugary tone. "Tell us what it says about the punishment Allah ordains for thieves."

Yunus stepped forward, and shut his eyes in a show of concentration. His face shone with pride as he recited the Qur'anic verse that required no scholarly knowledge, and was probably known even to illiterate peasants. "'As for the male thief and the female thief, cut off from the wrist joint their right hands as a recompense for that which they committed, a punishment by way of example. Allah is All-Powerful, All-Wise'."

"Get him ready for Allah's justice," Zaganos ordered, no longer sweet. Several people jostled to get hold of Vlad. Yunus looped a cord around Vlad's right wrist, and began to drag him toward a mooring bollard.

Vlad tried to break his movement by digging his heels into the boards of the wharf. He craned his neck to see Tirendaz, but the *musahib* had vanished, probably tired of defending Vlad against Zaganos's wrath. Eager hands pinched and pushed Vlad, and excited murmurings spread through the crowd on the wharf.

Irreversible ... irretrievable ... irremediable ... incalculable. The words lashed Vlad with rabid fury. He knew of no warrior who'd ever made a name for himself while missing his sword-hand. Hannibal lost an eye, and still reached greatness; Caesar suffered seizures, yet he was a peerless general. But losing the sword-hand? Powerless and confronted with the inevitable, he fell to a grim despair that made him quiver violently.

"I beg you—" Vlad couldn't finish. Hamza had grabbed him in a tight headlock and forced him to his knees.

"You've got a front-row seat, Vlad, so watch the show," Hamza hissed.

Yunus pulled hard on the cord, cutting the blood circulation in Vlad's wrist. Donatella's handkerchief protruded from Vlad's whitened fist, a purple flower incongruously blossoming on top of the mooring bollard.

"Let the prince speak," Zaganos said. "There is no sweeter music than an infidel's call for mercy."

Hamza relaxed his hold, but kept Vlad on his knees.

"I beg you to cut off my head, instead of my hand. I don't want to live without—"

"Oh, no, My Prince," Zaganos said with sham regret. He tested the sharpness of his sword by shaving a patch of hair on his arm. "You heard Tirendaz Agha: only a *kadı* can decide on a death sentence. But this little operation is something I can do on my own authority."

Before Vlad could understand what was happening, Zaganos flourished his sword above the chopping block, as a calligrapher might flourish a quill above his parchment. Vlad felt a sting in his wrist and noticed, with consternation, a red line appear across it, like a bracelet. A skilled swordsman, Zaganos had marked his target.

Instinctively, Vlad turned his head sideways, wishing to avoid the sight of his own mutilation. But his eyes remained fastened on his hand that, numb from the tightness of the rope, he could no longer feel.

Zaganos raised his arm for the second time, now in a deliberate movement. As his *kılıç* floated ever so slowly upward, the flames of a dozen torches danced on its curved blade and turned it into a brilliant crescent moon.

The End of Book Two

The author wishes to thank you for your interest in his book. Please visit Amazon.com and write a review reflecting your impression of this read.

THE JOURNEY CONTINUES

For someone uprooted forcefully from his native soil there is no stronger desire than to return home.

It's such a desire that burns in Vlad's chest as he finds himself sinking deeper and deeper into the turbid waters of the Ottoman Empire.

As he plots his way back to freedom Vlad learns, like countless heroes before him, that the obstacles on his way won't always take the shape of physical dangers.

Temptations of the flesh and soul can thwart the wayfarer in his aims as much as poison and steel.

Join the adventure.

www.draculachronicles.com

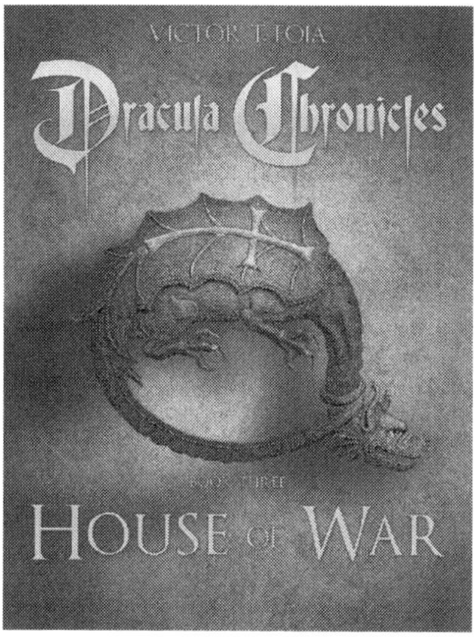

Glossary

Note on spelling of the word "Allah": When the word is used in an English-language sentence, no diacritic is employed over the letter "a"; when the word is used in a quotation from the Arabic, it is italicized and presented in two spelling variations using a diacritic over the letter "a": *Allāhu* and *Allāh.*

Note on Ottoman Turkish: To get a sense of the difference between Turkish and Ottoman Turkish, please refer to *Story World of Dracula Chronicles.*

Note on pronunciation: A pronunciation key in square brackets [...] is provided for selected words; the syllable stress is indicated by a diacritic or underlining.

Adhān: Word of Arabic origin representing the Islamic call to prayer recited by the muezzin at prescribed times of the day

Agha: Turkish for a title used to designate a high-level civil or military officer

Akinci: Ottoman Turkish word designating a member of the Ottoman light, irregular cavalry, specializing in raiding enemy territories

Al-Fātiḥah: Arabic for the first chapter of the Qur'an

Alea jacta est: Latin for "The die has been cast"; phrase attributed to Julius Caesar as he led his army across the Rubicon River in Northern Italy in 49 BC

Allāhu Akbar: Arabic for "God is the greatest"
Arte biondeggiante: Italian for the art of turning the hair color to blonde
Asper: Ottoman silver coin
Asr: Arabic for "afternoon"; one of the five obligatory daily prayers for Muslims
Ayah: Arabic for the smallest unit of the Qur'an, usually called a verse
Ayat: Arabic for the plural of "*ayah*"
Ayran: Frothy Turkish beverage made of yogurt mixed with cold water and salt
Bade [ba̲h-déh]: Romanian title of respect used in addressing men from the countryside in Wallachia, Moldova, and Transylvania
Baksheesh: Word of Persian origin meaning tip, charitable giving, or bribe
Bastonata: Italian for "bastinado", a punishment consisting of beating the soles of the feet with a stick in a systematic manner
Bedestan: Turkish for the central building of the commercial part of a town; a covered market
Beg: Same as bey; perhaps a Persian variant of bey
Bey: Turkish word signifying, among other things, lord, chieftain, emir, governor of a fortress or of a small province
Boyar: Romanian for a person of noble rank in Wallachia and Moldova; Romanian spelling: "*boier*"
Ca': Venetian abbreviation for "casa (house)"; customarily applied to a palace
Caftan: Also known as "kaftan"; a front-buttoned coat or overdress with long sleeves, usually reaching to the ankles
Camicia: Italian for "chemise"
Caravanserai: Fortified roadside inn encountered throughout the Ottoman Empire and other Muslim territories in Asia Minor
Cassone: Italian for a type of wooden chest usually associated with the storage of a bride's trousseau
Cassoni: Plural of "*cassone*"
Çavuş: Ottoman Turkish for messenger, or emissary; also title of an officer at the Ottoman court carrying out the duty of usher, sergeant, or ambassador to foreign princes and states

Ceruse: Also known as "Spirits of Saturn"; Venetian Renaissance cosmetic made with lead, and used as a skin whitener
Chausses: Renaissance woolen leggings; stockings
Chopine: Italian for Renaissance platform shoes
Coazzone: Italian for a broad plait or roll of hair hanging down the back
Coglione: Italian for "testicles" (vulgar)
Colletto: Italian for "*partlet*", a chemisette intended to fill the open front of a dress
Damaschino: Italian for an ornate silk fabric originating from Damascus (damask)
Dar al-Harb: Arabic for "House of War"; the name for the regions where Islam does not dominate, and where submission to Allah is not observed
Dar-al-Islam: Arabic for "House of Islam"; the name for the region where Islam dominates, and where submission to Allah is observed
Dar al-Sulh: Arabic for "House of Treaty"; name for a region benefitting from a truce or a peace treaty with the Ottoman Empire
Dervish: Word of Persian origin designating a Muslim believer belonging to a mystic brotherhood and usually following an ascetic path
Dhuhr: Arabic for "noon"; one of the five obligatory daily prayers for Muslims
Dio: Italian for "God"
Djellaba: Word of Arabic origin for long, loose-fitting, unisex outer robe with full sleeves
Doamne ajută, bade: Romanian for "May God help you, *bade*"; see entry above for *bade*
Dracul [dr**á**h-kool]: In the Romanian of 15th century Wallachia, the word meant both "dragon" and "devil"; not capitalized when used as a common noun
Dracula [drah-kool-ah]: In the Romanian of 15th century Wallachia, the word meant "Son of Dracul," hence "Son of the Dragon," or "Son of the Devil"
Efendi: Also spelled as "effendi"; Turkish honorific word used in the Ottoman Empire as a title of respect or courtesy, equivalent to the English "Sir"

Fajr: Arabic for "dawn"; one of the five obligatory daily prayers for Muslims

Falaka: Arabic for "bastinado"; foot whipping, variously known as "*falanga* (*phalanga*)", and "*falaka* (*falaqa*)"; a form of corporal punishment in which the soles of the feet are beaten with an object such as a cane, rod, or a stout leather bullwhip

Fātiḥah: Arabic word **("Al-** Fātiḥah**")** designating the first chapter of the Qur'an

Figa: Italian for "female genitalia" (vulgar)

Flight shooting: Ottoman archery exercise where the objective is distance, not accuracy; both the bow and the arrow used in flight shooting are different from other forms of archery (target shooting and war)

γαμώ [gah-mo]: Greek for "fuck"

Gamurra: Italian for a basic version of a woman's gown at the time of the Renaissance

Gazi: Also spelled "*ghazi*"; word of Arabic origin referring to a frontier warrior in Islam

Ghazwa: Word of Arabic origin for a battle or military expedition associated with the expansion of Muslim territory

Giaour [gya-oohr]: Offensive Turkish term used to describe non-Muslims, particularly Christians

Giornea: Italian for a long, sleeveless overgown at the time of the Renaissance

Grand Vizier: Second-highest official in the Ottoman Empire, outranked only by the sultan; see entry for *Vizier*

Hamam: Turkish word designating a bath involving dry heat treatment followed by scraping of the skin and deep massage

Hadith: A report of the deeds and sayings of Prophet Mohammed

Hekim: Turkish for "doctor"

Hoja: Also spelled "Hoca"; Ottoman Turkish for a title given to a teacher or a sultan's advisor

Insha'Allah: Arabic for "If it is God's will"

Janissary: Ottoman Turkish word designating an infantry soldier belonging to the Ottoman sultan's household troops and bodyguards

Jinn: Word of Arabic origin designating magic spirits believed to take human form and serve the person who calls them; spiritual creatures who inhabit an unseen world; mentioned in the Qur'an
Jo no parlo grec: Catalan for, "I don't speak Greek"
Jo sóc català: Catalan for, "I'm Catalan"
Jubbah: Word of Arabic origin designating a long outer garment resembling an open coat with long sleeves; worn formerly in Muslim countries, especially by public officials and professional people
Kadı: Ottoman Turkish for "judge"
Kadıasker: Ottoman Turkish for "supreme judge"; one of the highest officials in the empire
Kash-kash: Poppy seeds
Kiliç: Ottoman Turkish for a type of one-handed saber with a slight curvature and a sharpened back edge at the final section of the blade
Kilim: Turkish for a flat tapestry-woven carpet or rug
Kumis: A fermented dairy product traditionally made from mare's milk
Kurva bitang: Hungarian for "You, whore's bastard"
Lala [láh-lah]: Ottoman Turkish designating an experienced man assigned as tutor, mentor, and advisor to a young prince
Lenza: Italian for a fine, adorned string crossing the forehead
Luate-ar dracul, vagabondule: Romanian for "The Devil take you, tramp"
Maghrib: Arabic for "sunset"; one of the five obligatory daily prayers for Muslims
Mamluk: Ruling military caste in medieval Egypt that rose from the ranks of slave soldiers who were mainly of Kipchak Turk, Circassian, and Georgian origin
Manger: Ottoman copper coin worth approximately 1/8 of an asper at the time of the story
Mantello: Italian for "over-cloak"; long, and most often of wool
Mehterân: Ottoman military band
Mein Gott, nimm mich!: German for, "My God, take me!"

Menzil zor ile atılmaz, sanat ile atılır: Turkish proverb meaning, "A flight-arrow record comes from the skill of the bowman, not from his strength"

Minaret: Word of Arabic origin designating a tower structure associated with a mosque and used for issuing the call to prayer

Mosque: Word of Arabic origin designating a place of worship for followers of Islam

Muezzin: Word of Arabic origin designating the person at a mosque who leads and recites the call to prayer (See entry for *Adhān*)

Mujahideen: Islamic guerrilla fighters especially in the Middle East

Mullah: Word of Arabic origin designating a Muslim man educated in Islamic theology and sacred law

Mulţumesc părinte: Romanian for "Thank you, Father"

Mumia: "Miracle" drug made from ground mummies; widely used in the time of the Renaissance in Italy, the Byzantine Empire, and the Ottoman Empire

Musahib: Word of Arabic origin meaning companion, advisor, friend; in some cases it came to signify the favorite of a prince or sultan

Nana [náh-nah]: Romanian title of respect used in addressing women from the countryside in Wallachia, Moldova, and Transylvania

Ne hava vü ne keman-ü kemankeş Ancak erdiren menziline nidayı ya Hak!: The prayer an Ottoman flight archer would utter at the moment of loosing his arrow for an attempt to establish a new distance record; Turkish for, "Not the wind, not the bow, not the archer cast the arrow to its target. Only you, Oh Lord"

Ney-flute: End-blown flute that figures prominently in Middle Eastern music

Nonno: Italian for "grandfather"

No pot parlar: Catalan for, "He can't speak"

Nullus melior amicus, nullus peior inimicus: Latin for, "No better friend, no worse enemy"; epitaph the Roman dictator Lucius Cornelius Sulla wrote for his own tomb in 78 BC

Oh, dolç Jesús: Catalan for, "Oh, sweet Jesus"

Oma: German for "grandmother"

Opincă [oh-peen-kah]: Romanian for the traditional moccasin-style footwear used by peasants in Wallachia, Moldova, and Transylvania

Opinci [oh-peench]: Plural of "*opincă*"

Orthodox: Major branch of the Christian Church; not under the jurisdiction of the Vatican and the Pope

Ottoman: A Muslim inhabitant of the Ottoman Empire and subject to the sultan. Can be a person of any ethnicity, and may be a free person or a slave

Palazzo Podestàle: Italian for, Podestà's palace (See entry for *Podestà*)

Pasha: A high title in the Ottoman Empire political system, typically granted to governors, generals, and dignitaries

Persian language: An Iranian language within the Indo-Iranian branch of Indo-European languages; Farsi

Peşkeş [pesh-kesh]: Ottoman Turkish word designating diplomatic gifts given by an inferior authority to a superior one

Pianelle: Italian for "slippers"

Piano nobile: Italian for second floor in Italian villas and palaces; used primarily by the owners of the dwelling and their guests

Podestà: Italian for Chief City Magistrate; governor of a Genovese colony

Portego: Italian for a hall that went the length of a Venetian palace, from the front to the rear of the building; usually supported by columns

Provveditori alla Sanita: Italian name of the Venetian Public Health Board

Rakija: An alcoholic beverage common in Southeast Europe produced by the distillation of fermented fruit; alternate spellings: "*raki*", "*pálinka*", "*palincă*"

Qur'an: Arabic for "the recitation"; it represents the central religious text of Islam, which Muslims believe to be the verbatim word of Allah; also known as, "Koran", "Al-Coran", "Coran", "Kuran", and, "Al-Qur'an"

Salah: Arabic for "prayer"; alternate spelling: "*salat*"

Saltarello: Italian for a type of lively, merry dance practiced in Italy in the 14th and 15th centuries

Sanjak: Ottoman Turkish for an administrative district of the empire, under the command of a bey

Schmetterling: German for "butterfly"

Sema: Word of Persian origin for the ritual dance practiced by dervishes

Ser: Tuscan honorific term roughly equivalent to "Sir"

Shalwar: Loose pajama-like trousers; alternate spellings: "*salwar*", "*shalwar*"

Sharia: Word of Arabic origin for the moral code and religious law of Islam

Shaytan: Arabic for "Devil"

Sheikh: An elderly Sufi authorized to teach, initiate, and guide aspiring dervishes; the head of a dervish lodge

Sikke: Word of Persian origin for the truncated conical hat worn by Mevlevi Dervishes

Sipahi: Ottoman Turkish word designating a member of the Ottoman heavy cavalry

Skufia: Greek for the black cylindrical cap worn by Orthodox monks

Solak: Ottoman Turkish word designating left-handed archers, famous for being the most skilled archers in the empire, employed as bodyguards to the sultan; even though the bodyguard corps consisted of both right-handed and left-handed archers, it bore the moniker of "Solak Archers, Left-Handed Archers"

Solakbaşı: Ottoman Turkish for "Commanding Officer of the Solak Archers imperial bodyguard" (See entry for *Solak*)

Sufism: A mystic movement defined by some scholars as the inner, mystical dimension of Islam

Tavla: Game played in Turkey; similar to backgammon

Terra incognita: Latin for "land unknown"; meaning land not mapped or documented

Theriac: Medical concoction of more than sixty ingredients, reputed to be a "wonder drug" from the antiquity, through the Middle Ages and the Renaissance, and on to the 19th century

Tirendaz [teah-ren-dahz]: Word of Persian origin meaning master archer, accomplished bowman, skillful individual

Trinzale: Italian for a sort of fine fabric or metallic cap covering the back of a woman's head; decorative headdress item in late Middle Ages and the Renaissance

Tuğ: Ottoman Turkish for "horsetail banner"; there could be one, two, three, or four horsetails, depending on the dignitary's rank; the sultan's *tuğ* was the only one to have four horsetails

Ṭuğrā: Ottoman Turkish for a calligraphic monogram, seal, or signature of an Ottoman sultan that was affixed to all official documents and correspondence

Ulema: Word of Arabic origin representing the educated class of Muslim legal scholars engaged in the several fields of Islamic studies; alternate spelling: "Ulama"

Vèneto: Romance language spoken in the Veneto region of Italy before the adoption of Italian; continues to be spoken in Venice by certain groups to this day

Vergiß nicht deine Zukunft, Sohn des Drachen: German for "Don't forget your destiny, Son of the Dragon"

Vino puro, cazzo duro: Italian for "pure wine, hard cock"

Vizier: Turkish for minister in the Ottoman government; there were up to four viziers, with the Grand Vizier being the most senior

Ya Hakk: Ottoman Turkish for the traditional shout of flight archers at the moment they loosed their arrows, meaning "Oh Lord", or "Oh Truth"

Zoroastrianism: A religion and philosophy based on the teachings of the prophet Zoroaster, also known as "Zarathustra"

Zweifle nie an deinen Samen, König Drache: German for "Never doubt your seed, Dragon King"

WHO IS WHO AND WHAT IS WHAT

A difficulty arising for readers of historical fiction is remembering the names of characters and places. This stems from unfamiliarity with foreign names, and from the reoccurrence of names with variations in spelling. Dracula Chronicles has sought to alleviate this burden for its readers by making appropriate name substitutions.

In cases where the name of a historical character has been altered or replaced, the original name is provided for reference.

Names and places in **bold** font have a particular significance in the current story.

Birth dates provided only for characters that play a more-than-casual role.

Death dates withheld and marked with *** in cases that could constitute plot spoilers.

A pronunciation key in [...] is provided for selected characters and places; the syllable stress is indicated by a diacritic or underlining.

Adrianople: A town founded by the Romans in Eastern Thrace, the northwestern part of Turkey, close to the borders of Greece and Bulgaria; became a Byzantine city, then the second capital of the Ottoman Empire, under the name of Edirne

Aladdin (b. 1425 – ***): Sultan Murad's oldest living son; Mehmed's older brother; governor of Eastern Anatolia with the seat of government in Amasya (see *Houses of Dracula Chronicles*)

Alba Clan: Wealthy family of Wallachian boyars (see *Houses of Dracula Chronicles*)

Alba, Dan (b. 1401 – *)**: Head of the Alba Clan in the time of Dracula; treasurer at the court of King Dracul (see *Houses of Dracula Chronicles*)

Alba, Esmeralda (b. 1427 – ***): Dan and Helena Alba's daughter (see *Houses of Dracula Chronicles*)

Alba, Helena (b. 1403 – *)**: Dan Alba's wife; Esmeralda Alba's mother (see *Houses of Dracula Chronicles*)

Alba, Julius (b. 1420 – ***): Peter Alba's son (see *Houses of Dracula Chronicles*)

Alba, Peter (b. 1403 – ***): Dan Alba's brother; Julius Alba's father (see *Houses of Dracula Chronicles*)

Alexan: Armenian masseur at the *hamam* in Edirne

Alexander (b. 356 BC – d. 323 BC): Alexander of Macedon; also known as "Alexander the Great"; King of Macedonia

Alexander Basarab: King of Wallachia; founder of the House of Basarab (see *Houses of Dracula Chronicles*)

Amalfitan Quarter: Constantinople district; Amalfi's business outpost in the Byzantine Empire (see *Maps of Dracula Chronicles*)

Amasya: Ottoman town in northeastern Anatolia

Anadolu Hisari: Turkish for "Anatolian Fortress"; fortress erected in 1394 on the eastern shore of the Bosphorus by Beyazid I (see *Maps of Dracula Chronicles*)

Anatolia: The Asia Minor zone of the Ottoman Empire; region corresponding roughly to the Asia Minor part of modern Turkey (see *Maps of Dracula Chronicles*)

Andrea: Venetian galley captain in Donatella's employ

Arif: Omar's spiritual guide at the Mevlevi convent

Aśka [osh-kah]: Aśka of Rzeszów, Princess Lubomirska; Polish princess taken into slavery by the Turks

Athos: also known as "Holy Mount Athos"; peninsula in northern Greece; host to a large number of Orthodox monasteries (see *Maps of Dracula Chronicles*)

Azarian: Armenian slave auctioneer in Edirne
Aziz: Janissary guard at the Macedon Tower
Baba [báh-bah]: see *Novak, Baba*
Baragan [burr-a-góhn] Plain: Vast field stretching east and west in the space between the Devil's Belt Forest and the Danube River (see *Maps of Dracula Chronicles*)
Basarab: Royal Wallachian Dynasty (see *Houses of Dracula Chronicles*)
Bedreddın: Shaik of the Mevlevi lodge frequented by Omar
Bey of Nicopolis: Ottoman Governor of Nicopolis (see *Glossary* for *bey*)
Beyazid (1354 – 1403): Ottoman sultan; nicknamed "Yıldırım", meaning, "the Thunderbolt"
Bianca Pia, Loredano (1430 – *)**: Donatella Loredano's daughter
Black Sea: Body of water situated southeast of Wallachia (see *Maps of Dracula Chronicles*)
Boruele Grimaldi (b. 1380 – *)**: Podestà of Galata; Bianca Loredano's uncle, Donatella Loredano's brother-in-law (see *Glossary* for *podestà*)
Bosphorus: Alternate spelling "Bosporus"; narrow waterway draining the Black Sea into the Sea of Marmara; separates Europe from Asia Minor (see *Maps of Dracula Chronicles*)
Brankovich, George (b. 1377 – ***): Original name "**Đurađ Branković**"; King of Serbia (see *Houses of Dracula Chronicles*)
Buda: Fortress town situated on the Danube River; capital of the Kingdom of Hungary
Byzantine: Greek inhabitant of the Byzantine Empire
Byzantine Empire: Empire established on the foundation of the Eastern Roman Empire with the capital at Constantinople
Ca' Loredano: Donatella Loredano's Venetian-style palace in Constantinople (see *Glossary* for *Ca'*)
Caesar (b. 100 BC – d. 44 BC): Julius Caesar; Roman statesman, general, dictator
Cape Saint Demetrius: The most northeastern point of the peninsula on which
Constantinople is situated (see *Maps of Dracula Chronicles*)
Cardinal Cesarini (b. 1398 – ***): Full name "Julian Cesarini the Elder"; papal legate to the Kingdom of Hungary

Captain Andrea: See *Andrea*

Carpathian Mountains: A range of mountains forming an arc across Central and Eastern Europe; the second-longest mountain range in Europe

Christ's Tower: Largest of the Galata defensive towers; known today as "Galata Tower"

Christea Turris: Latin for Christ's Tower, the ancient name of the Galata Tower

Çiftkule Kapısı: Turkish for "Two Tower Gate"

Constantine: Constantine the Great, Roman Emperor from 306 AD to 337 AD

Constantinople: Capital of Byzantium; capital of the Eastern Roman Empire; capital of the Latin Empire; seat of the Orthodox Ecumenical Patriarch

Cozia [k**ó**h-z-ya]: Monastery and nunnery on the Olt River; King Justus's burial place

Crimea: See *Crimean Peninsula*

Crimean Peninsula: Peninsula on the north shore of the Black Sea (see *Maps of Dracula Chronicles*)

Dalmatia: Croatian historical region; situated on the eastern shore of the Adriatic Sea

Dan: See *Alba, Dan*

Danakil (b. 1422 – *)**: African eunuch slave in Zaganos's service

Danube: Europe's second-longest river; it originates in the Black Forest, Germany, and drains into the Black Sea through a delta (see *Maps of Dracula Chronicles*)

Dar al-Harb: See *Glossary*

Dar al-Islam: See *Glossary*

Dar al-Sulh: See *Glossary*

Dardanelles: Narrow waterway draining the Sea of Marmara into the Aegean Sea; it separates Europe from Asia Minor (see *Maps of Dracula Chronicles*)

De' Medici: Florentine political, banking, and ecclesiastical dynasty

Devil's Belt Forest: Vast forest in Wallachia, extending east and west in the space between the Baragan Plain and the southern Carpathian Mountains (see *Maps of Dracula Chronicles*)

Don Enrique: Don Enrique of Aragon and Pimentel, son of the Duke of Segorbe; Ferran's assumed identity

Donatella Loredano (1416 - *)**: Venetian lady residing in Constantinople; Bianca Donatella's mother; Giovanni Grimaldi's widow
Dracul [dráh-kool] **(b. 1398 – ***)**: Original name "Vlad"; King of Wallachia as Vlad II; Dracula's father (see *Glossary* for the meaning of the name)
Dracula [drah-koo-ah] **(b. 1428 – ***)**: Son of Dracul (see *Glossary* for the derivation of the name)
Draculoğul: Turkish for "Son of Dracul"
Duke of Segorbe: See *Don Enrique*
Edirne: Formerly "Adrianople"; capital of the Ottoman Empire in the time of Dracula (see *Maps of Dracula Chronicles*)
Eisenmarkt: "Hunedoara" in Romanian; fortress town in Transylvania; seat of the Hunyadi Clan (see *Maps of Dracula Chronicles*)
Elizabeth (b. 1403 – d. 1442): Emperor Sigismund's only child; widow of Albert II, King of Hungary; regent of Hungary on behalf of her infant son Roland (see *Houses of Dracula Chronicles*)
Emirzade al-Tabrizı: Emirzade of Tabriz; name assumed by Vlad with Kasim ibn Jihangir, the Karaman prisoner in the Macedon Tower
Emperor Frederick: See *Frederick*
Emperor John: See *John*
Enea Silvio Piccolomini (b. 1405 – ***): Poet Laureate at the Vienna court of Emperor Frederick III
Esmeralda: See *Alba, Esmeralda*
Fabrizio Garzoni: Majordomo of the Venetian Consul in Edirne
Ferran: Catalan pirate; prisoner in the Edirne underground dungeons
Filibe: Today "Plovdiv"; town in Bulgaria
Fioravanti: Venetian apothecary in Edirne
Forum Tauri: Latin for "Market of the Bull"; Constantinople's largest public square
Frederick: King of the Germans; Holy Roman Emperor as Frederick III
Galata: Also known as "Pera"; Genovese colony on the north shore of the Golden Horn (see *Maps of Dracula Chronicles*)
Gate of Eugenius: Gate in Constantinople seawalls; located near the Tower of Eugenius (see *Maps of Dracula Chronicles*)

Gate of Saint John: Saint John de Cornibus; gate in Constantinople seawalls; located near the Venetian Quarter (see *Maps of Dracula Chronicles*)

Genova: English Genoa; city-state in Liguria (Italy), on the Tyrrhenian Sea; one of the so-called "Maritime Republics" (Repubbliche Marinare), along with Venice, Pisa, and Amalfi at the time of the story

Genovese: Citizens of Genova

Genovese Quarter: Constantinople district; Genova's business outpost in the Byzantine Empire (see *Maps of Dracula Chronicles*)

George: See *Brankovich, George*

Giovanni Grimaldi (b. 1400 – d. 1429): Donatella Loredano's late husband; Boruele Grimaldi's younger brother; Bianca's father

Golden Horn: Inlet of the Bosphorus; separates Constantinople from Galata (see *Maps of Dracula Chronicles*)

Gregorius: Member of the Byzantine imperial guard

Gregory Brankovich (b. 1415 – ***): King Brankovich's oldest son; Mara Brankovich's brother; Ottoman hostage blinded by Murad's order (see *Houses of Dracula Chronicles*)

Grimaldi: See *Giovanni* and *Boruele Grimaldi*

Gruya [gr<u>ew</u>-ya]: See *Novak, Gruya*

Gunther (b. 1380 – d. 1442): Christian slave escaped from the Ottoman Empire; Vlad's tutor in things Ottoman; Vlad's teacher of Turkish, Persian, and Arabic

Hagia Sophia: Church of Holy Wisdom in Constantinople; Greek Orthodox patriarchal basilica; largest Christian church in the world at the time of the story

Hajji Mustafa: Edirne merchant who lent Omar money for his raid into Wallachia

Hamza (b. 1422 – *)**: Mehmed's slave, bodyguard, friend

Hannibal (b. 247 BC – d. 181 BC): Carthaginian general

Hassan Bey: See *Hassan*

Hassan Pasha: See *Hassan*

Hassan: Governor of Nicopolis; also addressed as "Hassan Bey" and "Hassan Pasha" (see *Glossary* for *Bey* and *Pasha*)

Helena: See *Alba, Helena*

Hermannstadt: "Sibiu" in Romanian; fortress town in Transylvania (see *Maps of Dracula Chronicles*)

Hill of the Acropolis: Hill in the northeast district of Constantinople; in the vicinity of Hagia Sophia (see *Maps of Dracula Chronicles*)

House of Basarab: Dynasty of Wallachian kings or *voievodes* (see *Houses of Dracula Chronicles*)

Hungary: Danubian kingdom located on the Pannonian Plain; capital at Buda

Hunyadi [hoon-ya-deeh] Clan: Hungarian lower nobility family (see *Houses of Dracula Chronicles*)

Hunyadi [hoon-ya-deeh], **Janko** [y**á**hn- koh] **(b. 1405 – ***)**: Governor of Transylvania; Captain General of the Kingdom of Hungary (see *Houses of Dracula Chronicles*)

Hussein: Edirne innkeeper

Ibrahim Bey: Sultan of Karaman

Ignatius: Wallachian boyar; member of King Dracul's Royal Council; master of the horse

Iskender Bursalı: Iskender of Bursa; legendary archer from the court of Beyazid I

Ismail (b. 1422 – ***): Tirendaz's slave; personal secretary

Janko [y**á**hn- koh]: See *Hunyadi, Janko*

John (b. 1392 – d. 1448): Emperor John VIII Palaiologos; penultimate reigning Byzantine Emperor, ruling from 1425 – 1448

Julius: See *Alba, Julius*

Justus (b. 1353 – d. 1418): King of Wallachia; original name "Mircea" [meer-cha]; also known as, "Mircea the Elder"; King Dracul's father; Dracula's grandfather (see *Houses of Dracula Chronicles*)

Karaman: An Islamic province neighboring the Ottoman Empire on its southern Anatolian border (see *Maps of Dracula Chronicles*)

Kasim ibn Jihangir (b. 1425 – *****)**: Karaman prisoner in the Macedon Tower; grandson of the Karaman Sultan

Katharina: Saxon girl from Kronstadt; Thomas and Elsa Siegel's daughter

Khalil Pasha (1404 – *****)**: Family name "Çandarlı"; Grand Vizier at the court of Murad II; member of the Imperial Council

Kilia [key-lee-yah]: Wallachian outpost near the Black Sea in the Danube Delta

King Justus: See *Justus*

Kosovo: Town in the Balkan Peninsula; site of a great Ottoman victory in 1389 against the Kingdom of Serbia

Kronstadt: Brasov in Romanian; fortress town in Transylvania (see *Maps of Dracula Chronicles*)

Lala Tabrizı: Lala of Tabriz; spectator addressed by Sultan Murad on his way to the Friday Mosque; here *lala* is used as an honorific

Lash (b. 1424 – *)**: Dracula's Gypsy manservant

Loredano: See *Pietro, Donatella,* and *Bianca Loredano*

Lorenzo: Abbot of the Târgoviște Catholic monastery

Lubomirska: See *Aśka*

Lucius Cornelius Sulla (b. 138 BC – d. 78 BC): Roman statesman, general, dictator

Macedon Tower: Tower in Edirne used as temporary prison

Mahmud Pasha: Governor of Iznik; tried in the Imperial Council for abuse of power

Mamluk: Alternate spelling: "Mameluke"; ruling military caste in Egypt between 1250 AD and 1517 AD; risen from the ranks of slave soldiers, mainly of Kipchak Turk, Circassian, and Georgian origin; ruled Egypt and much of the Middle East at the time of the story (see *Maps of Dracula Chronicles*)

Mara Brankovich (b. 1416 – *)**: One of Murad's four wives; King George Brankovich's daughter; Gregory and Stefan Brankovich's sister (see *Houses of Dracula Chronicles*)

Marcus (b. 1426 – *)**: Original name "Mircea" [meer-cha]; King Dracul's oldest son; Dracula's older stepbrother (see *Houses of Dracula Chronicles*)

Marmara: See *Sea of Marmara*

Mathilda: See *Novak, Mathilda*

Mecca: Holiest city in Islam; located on the Arabian Peninsula

Mehmed (b. 1432 – *)**: Sultan Murad's youngest living son; governor of Western Anatolia with the seat of government in Manisa (see *Houses of Dracula Chronicles*); Aladdin's younger brother

Mevlana: Also known as "Mevlâna"; popular Turkish sobriquet for Muhammad Rūmī, Persian poet and mystic; known widely in the West as "Rumi"

Mevlevi Dervish: Dervish belonging to the Mewlewī Sufi order, founded in 1273 by the Persian poet Rumi's followers after his death; known in the west as "whirling dervish" (see *Glossary* for *Dervish*)

Michael: See *Novak, Michael*

Moldova: See *World of Dracula* Chronicles; see *Maps of Dracula Chronicles*

Mühlbach: "Sebeş" in Romanian; fortress town in Transylvania (see *Maps of Dracula Chronicles*)

Murad (b. 1404 – *)**: Ottoman Sultan during Dracula's youth; known as "Murad II"; Aladdin and Mehmed's father (see *Houses of Dracula Chronicles*)

Nestor (b. 1420 – *)**: Original name "Vladislav" [Vl**á**hd-y-slahv]; nicknamed "the Usurper"; Wallachian prince from the House of Basarab; Dracula's second cousin (see *Houses of Dracula Chronicles*)

Nicopolis: Fortress town on the right bank of the Danube River; site of the last Crusade before Dracula's time (see *Maps of Dracula Chronicles*)

Novak Clan: Wallachian boyar house

Novak, Baba [b**á**h-bah] **(b. 1402 – ***)**: Wallachian boyar; King Dracul's sword-bearer; member of King Dracul's Royal and Small Councils; Michael Novak's son; Gruya Novak's father (see *Houses of Dracula Chronicles*)

Novak, Gruya [gr<u>ew</u>-ya] **(b. 1426 – ***)**: Dracula's squire; Baba Novak's son; Michael Novak's grandson (see *Houses of Dracula Chronicles*)

Novak, Mathilda (b. 1382 – ***): Michael Novak's wife; Baba Novak's mother; Gruya Novak's grandmother; Dracula's governess (see *Houses of Dracula Chronicles*)

Novak, Michael (b. 1380 – *)**: Wallachian boyar; chancellor at the court of King Dracul; member of King Dracul's Royal and Small Councils; Baba Novak's father; Gruya Novak's grandfather; Dracula's mentor (see *Houses of Dracula Chronicles*)

Olt River: River in Wallachia; it originates in Transylvania; tributary of the Danube River (see *Maps of Dracula Chronicles*)

Oma: German for "grandmother"; Dracula picked up the habit of using this term as a child in the Saxon town of his birth, Schassburg

Omar Amasyalı (b. 1407 – *)**: Omar of Amasya; Akinci raider; Redjaï, Sezaï, and Zekaï's oldest brother

Ottoman Empire: Turkish empire founded by Osman in early 14th century; began in Anatolia and spread to Europe, Middle East, and northern Africa; lasted until early 20th century (see *Houses of Dracula Chronicles*)

Pantelimon Monastery: Wallachian monastery in Constantinople; located on the Third Hill (see *Maps of Dracula Chronicles*)

Paola: Donatella Loredano's nurse, governess, head chambermaid

Patriarch Metrophanes: Patriarch of Constantinople at the time of the story

Patrocles (b. 1426 – *)**: Wallachian monk at the Pantelimon Monastery

Persia: Territory covering parts of today's Iran, Afghanistan, and Iraq

Peter: See *Alba, Peter*

Philotheou Monastery: Wallachian monastery on Mount Athos

Pietro Loredano: Venetian admiral; Donatella Loredano's father; Bianca Loredano's grandfather

Pisan Quarter: Constantinople district; Pisa's business outpost in the Byzantine Empire (see *Maps of Dracula Chronicles*)

Plutarch: Greek historian

Pope Eugene (b. 1383 – d. 1447): Eugene IV, pope during Dracula's youth

Ragusa: Maritime republic located on the Dalmatian coast; Dubrovnik

Redjaï (b. 1413 – d. 1442): Akinci raider; Omar's brother

Rumeli Hisari: Rumelian Fortress; fortress Mehmed envisions building if he becomes Ottoman Sultan; to be erected on the European shore of the Bosphorus, as companion to Anadolu Hisari

Rumelia: The European zone of the Ottoman Empire; region corresponding to parts of current Bulgaria, Serbia, and Northern Greece (see *Maps of Dracula Chronicles*)

Sea of Marmara: Body of water between Anatolia and the southeastern shores of Europe (see *Maps of Dracula Chronicles*)

Rzeszów: City in southeastern Poland

Sadeddin Hoja: Kadıasker, or Chief Judge, of the Ottoman Empire; member of the Imperial Council (see *Glossary* for *Kadıasker*)

Schassburg: "Sighişoara" in Romanian; fortress town in Transylvania; Dracula's birthplace (see *Maps of Dracula Chronicles*)
Selim bin Sedad: See *Tirendaz*
Sezaï (b. 1415 – d. 1442): Akinci raider; Omar's brother
Sheikh Bedreddın: Head of the Mevlevi Dervish lodge visited by Omar (see *Glossary* for *Dervish* and *Sheikh*)
Silk Road: Ancient commercial road with numerous branches; stretches from China to Asia Minor
Skanderbeg (b. 1405 – *)**: Ottoman general; former Albanian hostage converted to Islam
Solomon: Hekim Solomon; physician at Sultan Murad's court in Edirne (see *Glossary* for *hekim*)
Spencer (b. 1415 – *)**: Englishman captured and raised by Calabrian corsairs; Ottoman slave in Edirne
Stefan Brankovich (b. 1417 – ***): King Brankovich's second-oldest son; Mara Brankovich's brother; Ottoman hostage blinded by Murad's order (see *Houses of Dracula Chronicles*)
Sulla: See *Lucius Cornelius Sulla*
Tabriz: Town in Persia
Târgovişte [tahr-**gó** -veesh-teh]: The capital of Wallachia at the time of Dracula (see *Maps of Dracula Chronicles*)
Tella: Donatella Loredano's nickname used by Paola, her nurse
Theodore (b. 1341 – d. 1441): Blind seer; recipient of the prophecy foretelling the advent of the Son of the Dragon; nicknamed "the Old Man of the Forest"
Third Hill: One of the seven hills on which Constantinople was built
Thomas Siegel: Saxon from Kronstadt, Transylvania; alderman of the Weavers Guild; Katharina Siegel's father; Ottoman slave
Timur: Dracula's horse
Tirendaz [tea-ren-dahz] **(b. 1408 – ***)**: Nickname of Selim bin Sedad; Sultan Murad's *musahib; agha* of the sultan's bodyguard (see *Glossary* for *Musahib* and *Agha*)
Tower of Eugenius: Defensive tower on Constantinople seawalls; located at the mouth of the Golden Horn (see *Maps of Dracula Chronicles*)
Tower of Eirene: Bell tower of Hagia Eirene in Constantinople; situated on the Third Hill

Transylvania: Region of the Kingdom of Hungary (see *World of Dracula Chronicles*; see *Maps of Dracula Chronicles*)
Trabizond: Also known as "Trabizond Empire"; small Christian Orthodox remnant of the Byzantine Empire; situated on the southeastern shore of the Black Sea (see *Maps of Dracula Chronicles*)
Üç Şerefeli Mosque: Edirne mosque built by order of Murad II; the name derives from the unusual fact that its minarets had three balconies, a first in the world of Islam
Ulfer: King Dracul's teenage German nickname; means "warrior fierce as a wolf"
Varlaam: Orthodox Archbishop of Wallachia; member of King Dracul's Royal Council
Vienna: Capital of the Duchy of Austria; seat of Holy Roman Emperor Frederick III
Venetian Quarter: Constantinople district; Venice's business outpost in the Byzantine Empire (see *Maps of Dracula Chronicles*)
Vlad [vlohd; rhymes with "pod"] **(b. 1428 – ***)**: Prince of the House of Basarab; King Dracul's second son; nicknamed "Dracula"; also known as, "the Impaler" (see *Houses of Dracula Chronicles*)
Wallachia [vah-lóck-y-ah]: Kingdom situated between the southern Carpathian Mountains and the Danube River (see *World of Dracula Chronicles;* see *Maps of Dracula Chronicles*)
Walls of Theodosius: Constantinople defensive walls protecting the city on the (western) landside (see *Maps of Dracula Chronicles*)
Ialomiţa: River flowing in the vicinity of Târgovişte
Yunus (b. 1424 – *)**: Mehmed's slave, personal secretary, friend
Zaganos (b. 1402 – *)**: Ottoman officer; third vizier at the court of Sultan Murad II; member of the Imperial Council
Zekaï (b. 1427 – d. 1442): Akinci raider; Omar's youngest brother

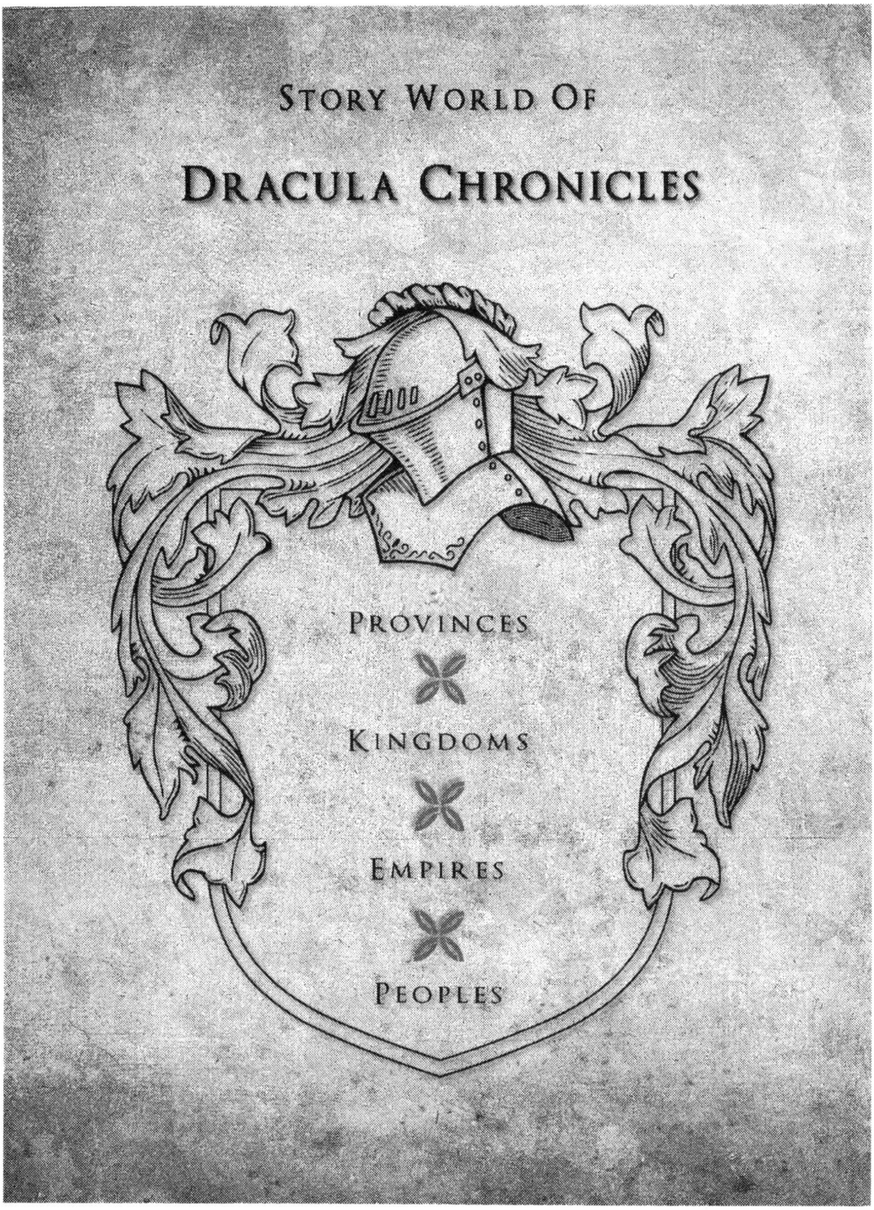
Story World Of
Dracula Chronicles
Provinces
Kingdoms
Empires
Peoples

ROMANIA: Its regions and peoples

General

Romania is a relatively new country, formed and recognized as a kingdom by the European powers only in the second half of the 19th century. It consists presently of three major provinces: Wallachia, Moldova, and Transylvania.

Prior to the emergence of Romania, these three provinces led a separate political existence and were ruled by voivodes (alternate spelling: "voievod"). Although the title of voivode had different connotations throughout Eastern Europe, in Wallachia and Moldova it was equivalent to that of king. Therefore, in the ***Dracula Chronicles*** the title of "king" is used for the rulers of Wallachia and Moldova. In Transylvania, the voivode, or *vajda*, was an appointee of the Hungarian king, and as such was equivalent to a governor.

Wallachia and Moldova were inhabited preponderantly by Romanians. Transylvania had a mixed population, consisting mainly of Hungarians, Saxons, and Romanians.

The Hungarians conquered Transylvania sometime in the 10th century and maintained control over it until the 20th century, when it was incorporated into the Kingdom of Romania.

The Saxons (people of German ethnicity) were invited by the Hungarian kings to colonize parts of Transylvania in the 12th and 13th centuries. The Saxons were instrumental in the building of numerous fortress towns and the development of the various crafts and industries essential for life in the Middle Ages.

Origin of Romanians

The Romanians living in Wallachia, Moldova, and Transylvania of the 15th century were a relatively homogeneous group, sharing a common ancestry, a common language, and a common religion.

The Romanians consider themselves descendants of the Roman colonists brought to parts of present-day Romania, following the conquest of the region by the Roman Emperor Trajan at the beginning of the 2nd century AD.

The Roman conquest targeted mostly Western Wallachia and Transylvania, inhabited at the time by Dacians. The occupation of the region, which the Romans called Dacia Felix, or "Happy Dacia", lasted until the second half of the 3rd century AD. At that time the Roman military forces and imperial administration withdrew south of the Danube, leaving stranded behind them tens of thousands of Roman colonists. Romanian scholars believe these abandoned colonists formed the stock from which the Romanians of Wallachia, Moldova, and Transylvania emerged.

Some of the minorities living in Wallachia, Moldova, and Transylvania were the Gypsies, Jews, Szeklers, Armenians, Tartars, Bulgarians, Serbs, and Poles.

Language of Romanians

While there has been controversy over the origin of the Romanians for centuries, it is a universally accepted fact that the language spoken by Romanians is closely related to the Vulgar Latin. Romanian is recognized without debate as belonging to the surviving group of approximately forty-seven Romance languages and dialects, alongside French, Italian, Spanish, Portuguese, Occitan, and Catalan. None of Romania's minorities or neighbors speaks languages of a Latin origin.

Religion in 15th Century Wallachia and Moldova

Christian (Greek Orthodox dominant, Catholic insignificant). In Wallachia and Moldova Judaism was tolerated, but Islam was not.

Religion in 15th Century Transylvania

Christian (Catholic dominant, Greek Orthodox practiced only by the Romanians of Transylvania). In Transylvania Judaism was tolerated, but Islam was not.

HUNGARY: Its regions and people

General

Hungary is situated on the Danube River, in the northwest of the Balkan Peninsula. In the 15th century, Hungary was an independent kingdom that included Transylvania among its regions. Even when, for a few decades, the King of Hungary was Sigismund of Luxembourg, also Emperor of the Holy Roman Empire (HRE), Hungary was not part of the HRE.

Origin of Hungarians

Hungarians, also known as "Magyars", are a people originating in Central Asia. They settled in the current territory of Hungary in the 9th and 10th centuries AD. Soon thereafter they conquered Transylvania, which remained a province of Hungary, with some interruptions, until the 20th century.

Language of Hungarians

Hungarians speak a Uralic language that does not belong to the Indo-European group of languages spoken by all their neighbors. Instead, Hungarian belongs to the Ugric group of languages spoken by certain peoples of Western Siberia.

Religion in 15th Century Hungary

Christian (Catholic in the Kingdom of Hungary proper; Catholic and Greek Orthodox in Transylvania). In Hungary and Transylvania Judaism was tolerated, but Islam was not.

BALKAN SPACE: Its states and peoples

General

The turbulent history of the Balkan region renders it difficult to make firm observations regarding state lines, since these lines moved continually throughout the Middle Ages. Moreover, with the expansion of the Ottoman Empire starting in the second half of the 14th century, most of these states ultimately ceased to exist, only to reemerge in the second half of the 19th century, and after WWI.

The political formations extant in the region in the 14th and 15th century can be most easily identified by their current names, since the actual names used at the time are too challenging to follow in a work of historical fiction. Thus, we can mention Bulgaria, Serbia, Bosnia, Croatia, Slovenia, Montenegro, Macedonia, and Albania.

Origin of Balkan Space Peoples

Bulgarians, Serbs, Croats, Slovenes, Bosnians, Montenegrins, and Macedonians (those not of Greek ethnicity) are designated as "South Slavs" and constitute the southern ethnographical branch of the Slavic peoples. It is hazardous to posit hypotheses on the ethnic composition and origins of these peoples, since modern DNA science has revised many of the traditional views on this subject and will continue to do so.

Most historians consider Albanians as descendants of the populations of the prehistoric Balkans, such as the Dacians, Thracians, and Illyrians.

Languages of Balkan Space Peoples

The South Slavs speak variations of Old Church Slavonic, a language belonging to the Indo-European group.

Albanians speak a distinct Indo-European language that does not belong to any other existing branch of that group.

Religion in 15th Century Balkan Space

Christian. Both Catholic and Greek Orthodox religions were practiced by the peoples of the Balkans. In the Christian zone of the Balkan space, prior to the Ottoman conquest, Judaism was tolerated, but Islam was not. Following the Ottoman conquest, some Christian groups converted to Islam, presumably by choice.

BYZANTINE EMPIRE: Its regions and peoples

General

At its height in the 6th century AD, the Byzantine Empire, or Byzantium, encompassed all territory known today as Greece, as well as many regions bordering the Mediterranean and Black Seas. By the time of Dracula, the empire had lost most of its territory, reduced to a small area consisting of the capital city of Constantinople, its immediate surrounding region, a few islands in the Aegean Sea, and the Despotate of Morea (Peloponnesus). Of the territory that had been Greece in antiquity, most fell under Ottoman, Venetian, and Genovese occupation.

In the Western Mediterranean, former Byzantine holdings became kingdoms and city-states in the Italian and Iberian Peninsulas. In the Eastern Mediterranean and the Black Sea, the Byzantine Empire lost ground to the Ottoman, Trebizond, and Mameluke Empires.

Origin of Byzantine Empire Peoples

The majority of the inhabitants of what remained of the Byzantine Empire by the 15th century were Greeks. A large variety of minorities was also present, consistent with the multicultural tradition of the empire.

Languages of Byzantine Empire Peoples

The official language of imperial administration and of most Byzantines was Greek. However, having encompassed many ethnically diverse territories over the centuries, Byzantium inherited other languages, such as Latin, Arabic, Georgian, Armenian, Aramaic, Slavonic, and Turkish Roma (the language of the Gypsies).

Religion in 15th Century Byzantine Empire

Christian (Greek Orthodox dominant, Catholic minority). In the Byzantine Empire Judaism was tolerated, but Islam was not.

TREBIZOND EMPIRE: Its region and peoples

General

Trebizond broke away from Byzantium in the 13th century. It occupied a small portion of the southern coast of the Black Sea. In resisting occupation by the Ottoman Empire until the second half of the 15th century, Trebizond became the longest surviving of the Byzantine Empire successor states.

Origin of Trebizond Empire Peoples

The majority of the Trebizond inhabitants were Greeks.

Languages of Trebizond Empire Peoples

The official language of imperial administration and of most inhabitants of Trebizond was Greek. However, having once been part of the Byzantine Empire, Trebizond inherited other languages, such as Latin, Arabic, Georgian, Armenian, Aramaic, Slavonic, and Turkish.

Religion in 15th Century Trebizond Empire

Christian (Greek Orthodox dominant, Catholic minority). In the Trebizond Empire Judaism was tolerated, but Islam was not.

VENETIANS AND GENOVESE: Their activities in Eastern Mediterranean and Black Sea

General

In the 15th century, both Venice and Genoa were maritime merchant republics with a particular interest in the Eastern Mediterranean and the Black Sea. Thousands of their ships plied these waters, dominating the shipping trade that brought goods from the Silk Road to Western Europe, and manufactured goods from Western Europe to the countries of the Middle East. As was the case with other republics throughout history (e.g., the Athenian Republic in the 5th century BC, and the Roman Republic in the 1st century BC), their republican status at home did not prevent Venice and Genoa from establishing empires abroad. In the case of these two Italian city-states, the empires they spawned were of primarily a commercial nature, though military power was never kept too far out of sight.

Venice's primary theater of operation was the Adriatic, Ionic, and Aegean Seas. In the Aegean Sea Venice exercised control, or strong influence, over most of the islands, including Cyprus, Crete, and Euboea. Venetians also held intermittent control over portions of the mainland around Thessaloniki and on the north coast of the Peloponnesus.

Genoa dominated the maritime trade through the straits of Bosphorus and the Black Sea, which the republic considered practically a Genovese lake. The intense commercial activities of the Genovese, at such a long distance from their home base on the northwest coast of Italy, were supported by two colonies established by the Genovese Republic: Galata, also known as "Pera", on the Golden Horn, across the water from the City of Constantinople; and Caffa, in Crimea on the Black Sea.

As Christian powers, both the Venetians and the Genovese professed to be allies of Byzantium. This religious affiliation did not prevent them, however, from trading with the Ottoman Empire in times of peace. During times of war between the Ottomans and their Christian or Muslim foes, Genovese and Venetian ships would occasionally help the Ottomans with ferrying their troops to and from Anatolia, across the straits of the Dardanelles and the Bosphorus, also known as "Bosporus".

Origin of Venetians and Genovese

The Venetians were at their origin refugees from Roman towns of the mainland region bordering the lagoons. The Genovese were descendants of the ancient Ligures, who were conquered by the Romans in the 2nd century BC.

Languages of Venetians and Genovese

In the 15th century the Genovese spoke Ligurian, while the Venetians spoke Veneto. Both of these languages belong to the group of Romance languages, derived from the Vulgar Latin and modified by other linguistic elements specific to each geographical region. While Ligurian and Veneto continue to be spoken by some groups, the standard Italian language dominates at the present in Genoa and Venice.

Religion in 15th Century Venice and Genoa

Christian (Catholic). In the Venetian and Genovese Republics, Judaism was tolerated, but Islam was not.

OTTOMAN EMPIRE: Its regions and peoples

General

The Ottoman Empire had its roots in the remnants of the Sultanate of Seljuk, which controlled roughly three quarters of Anatolia from the 10th through the 13th century AD. The Seljuks were leaders of nomadic Turkish warrior tribes who arrived in Anatolia from Central Asia. In mid-13th century, the Seljuks became vassals of the advancing Mongols. In the first decade of the 14th century the Sultanate of Seljuk finally disintegrated, leaving behind a number of small emirates, or beyliks, led by Turkish warlords.

One of these beyliks, that of Osman Bey, neighbored the shrinking Byzantine Empire on the western tip of the Anatolian Peninsula. It was Osman who, through the strength of arms and diplomacy, managed to rally many of the other beyliks around him and form a strong army. Motivated by both religious fervor and thirst for conquest, Osman's army launched relentless attacks on the Byzantine Asiatic holdings. From this struggle there emerged, at the beginning of the 14th century, a growing power that was destined to become the longest-lasting empire of the Christian era, the Ottoman Empire. By the mid-15th century, when Dracula's story begins, six sultans of the House of Osman had already been in power, and the Ottomans had conquered all of the Byzantine Anatolian lands and most of its European holdings. The great city of Constantinople, believed impregnable and under the protection of God, remained standing, as a tantalizing prize for the sultan strong enough to smash through its gigantic walls.

Origin of the Ottoman Empire Peoples

The Turks belong to the group of Turkic peoples whose branches also include the Kipchak, Karluk, Siberian, Chuvash, and Sakha/Yakut. They began to migrate westward in the 7th century AD, from the Central Asian region of the Altai Mountains. Ultimately they settled in Anatolia, from where their empire grew to engulf in time much of Europe, the Middle East, and North Africa.

Naturally, not all inhabitants of the Ottoman Empires were ethnic Turks. There were also Arabs, Jews, Armenians, Georgians, Kurds, Persians, Afghanis, Greeks, Gypsies, Wallachians, Moldovans, Bulgarians, Albanians, Serbs, Slovenians, Hungarians, and Croats. To a small degree, representatives of virtually all other nations in Europe, Asia, and Africa were present in the empire. Some of these minorities were free people, while others were slaves. People in some of the conquered territories were already Muslims; and some Christians from conquered lands chose to convert to Islam, adopting the clothing style and the language of the Turkish conquerors. All of these non-Turkish Muslims were lumped together by the Europeans outside the empire under the designation of Turks. However, since many of them were not ethnic Turks, a more appropriate designation would have been that of Ottomans.

Languages of Ottoman Empire Peoples

The ordinary Turks of the 15th century spoke Turkic, a language belonging to the Altaic language family, together with the Mongolic, Tungustic, Japonic, and Korean languages. The languages of the Altaic family are spoken in a wide area, from

Northeast Asia, through Central Asia, Anatolia, and Eastern Europe. Other languages spoken in the empire were: Greek, Latin, Arabic, Persian, Georgian, Armenian, Aramaic, Slavonic, Romanian, and Roma (the language of the Gypsies).

The educated classes, which included slaves in the military and the administration of the empire, spoke Ottoman Turkish, a variant of Turkish rich in words borrowed from Arabic and Persian. Ottoman Turkish was largely unintelligible to the less-educated classes and is practically unintelligible to the Turks of today.

Religious terminology related to Islam was either Arabic or of Arabic derivation. The Qur'an and other Islamic literature were available only in Arabic. Scientific literature was typically in Arabic, and often represented translation into Arabic of ancient Greek and Roman materials. General literature, including poetry, was primarily written in Persian.

In the 15th century manuscripts written in Ottoman Turkish began to appear. Among these were original writings pertaining to some of the Sufi mystic orders. However, most were translations from Arabic or Persian.

Religion in 15th Century Ottoman Empire

Islam (Sunni dominant, Shi'a minority). In the Ottoman Empire, Christianity, Judaism, Zoroastrianism were tolerated religions, with no forcible conversion to Islam evident as a widespread phenomenon. However, boys recruited at an early age for the Janissary Corps from among the Christians (by either force or acquiescence) were forcibly converted to Islam.

Houses Of

Dracula Chronicles

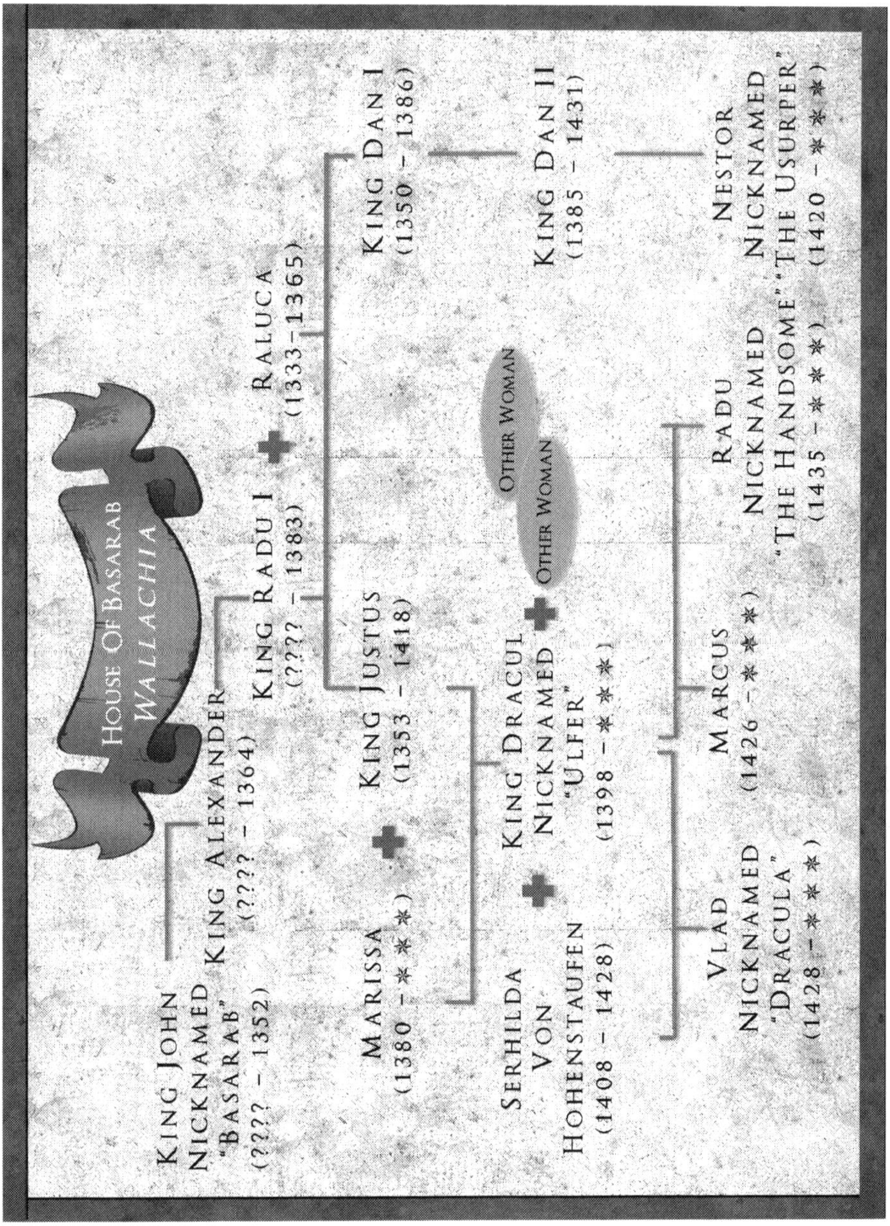

House of Basarab

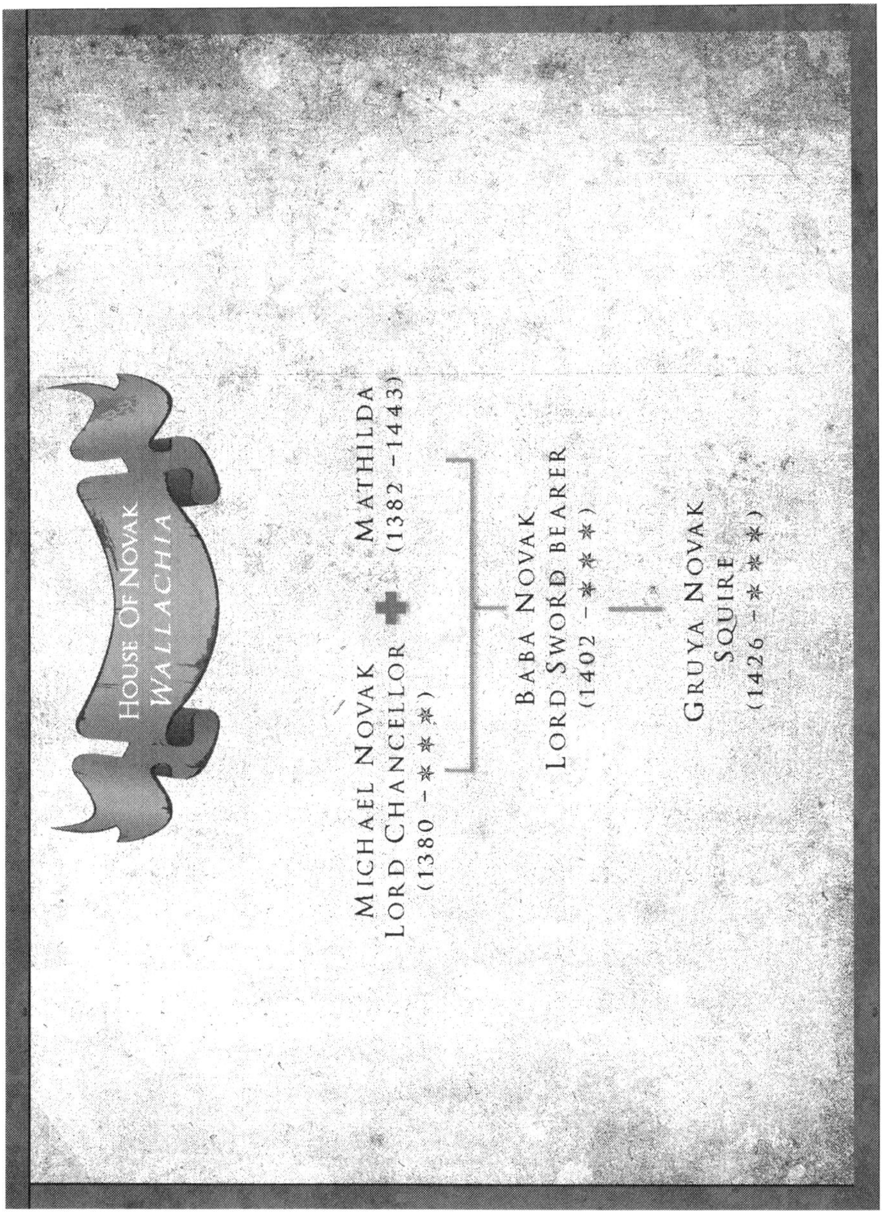

House of Novak

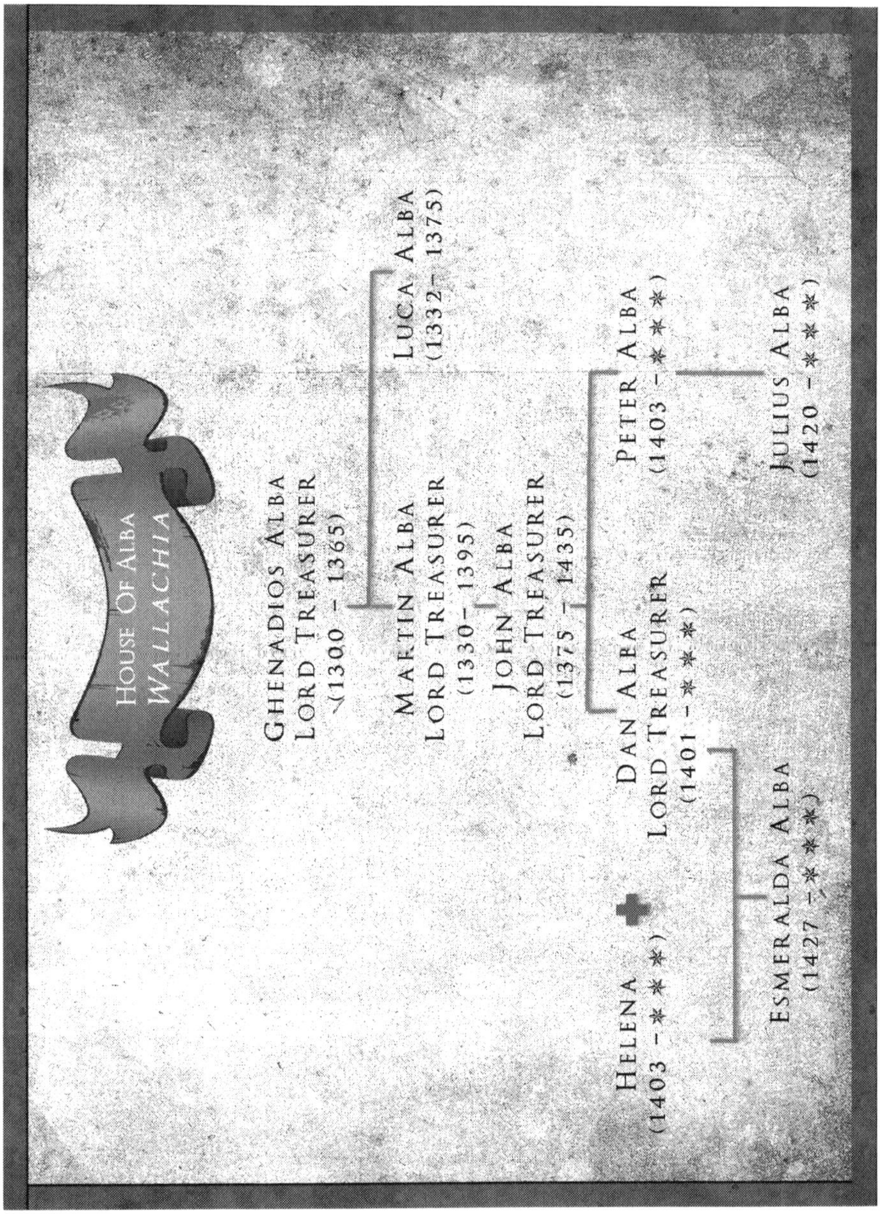

House of Alba

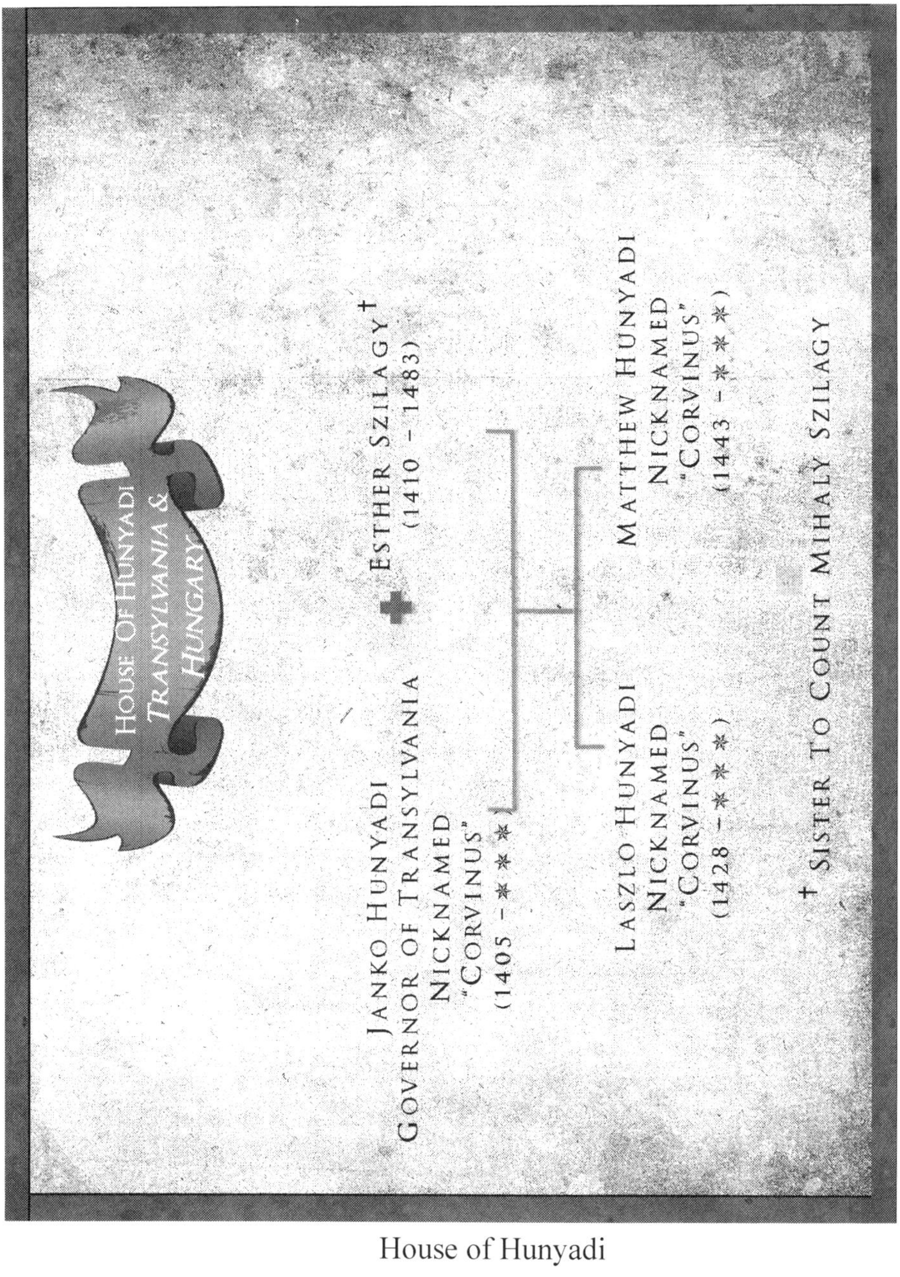

House of Hunyadi

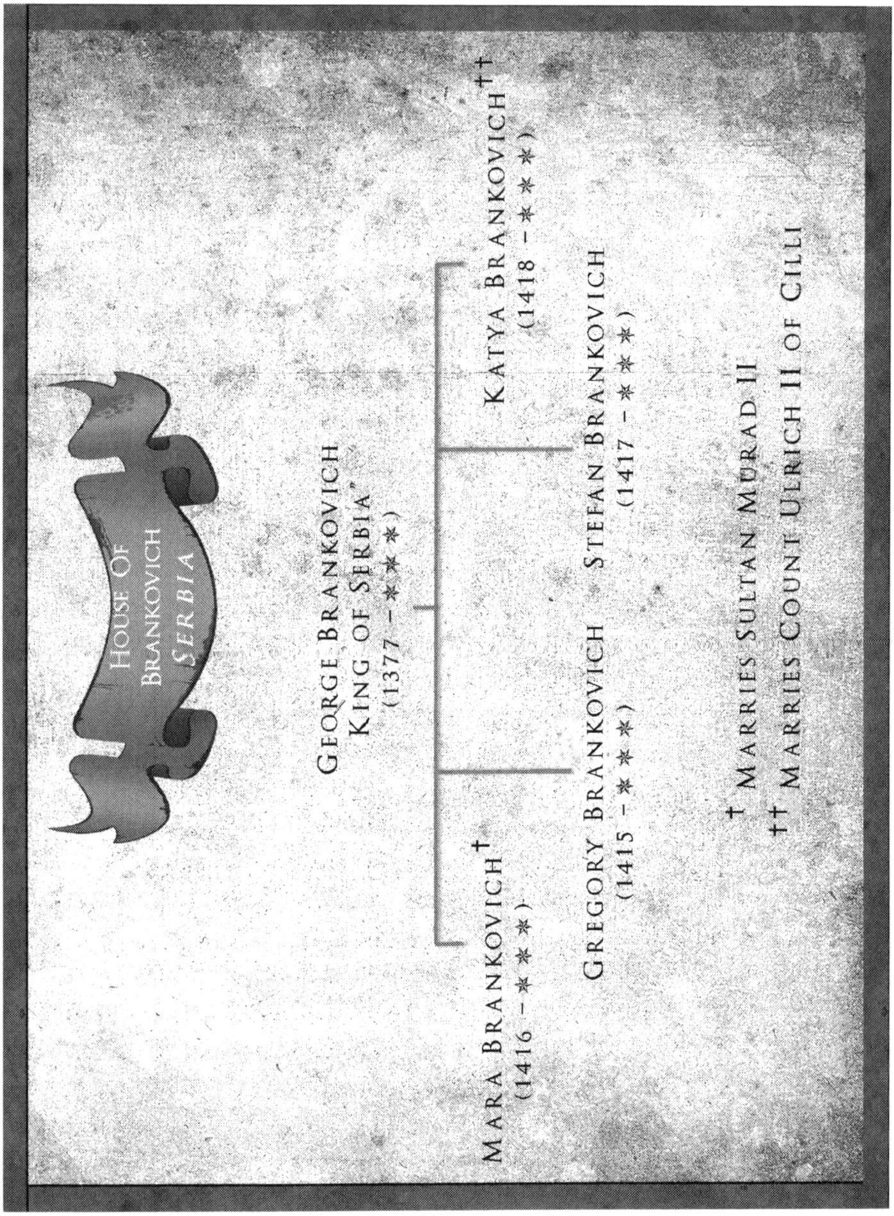

House of Brankovich

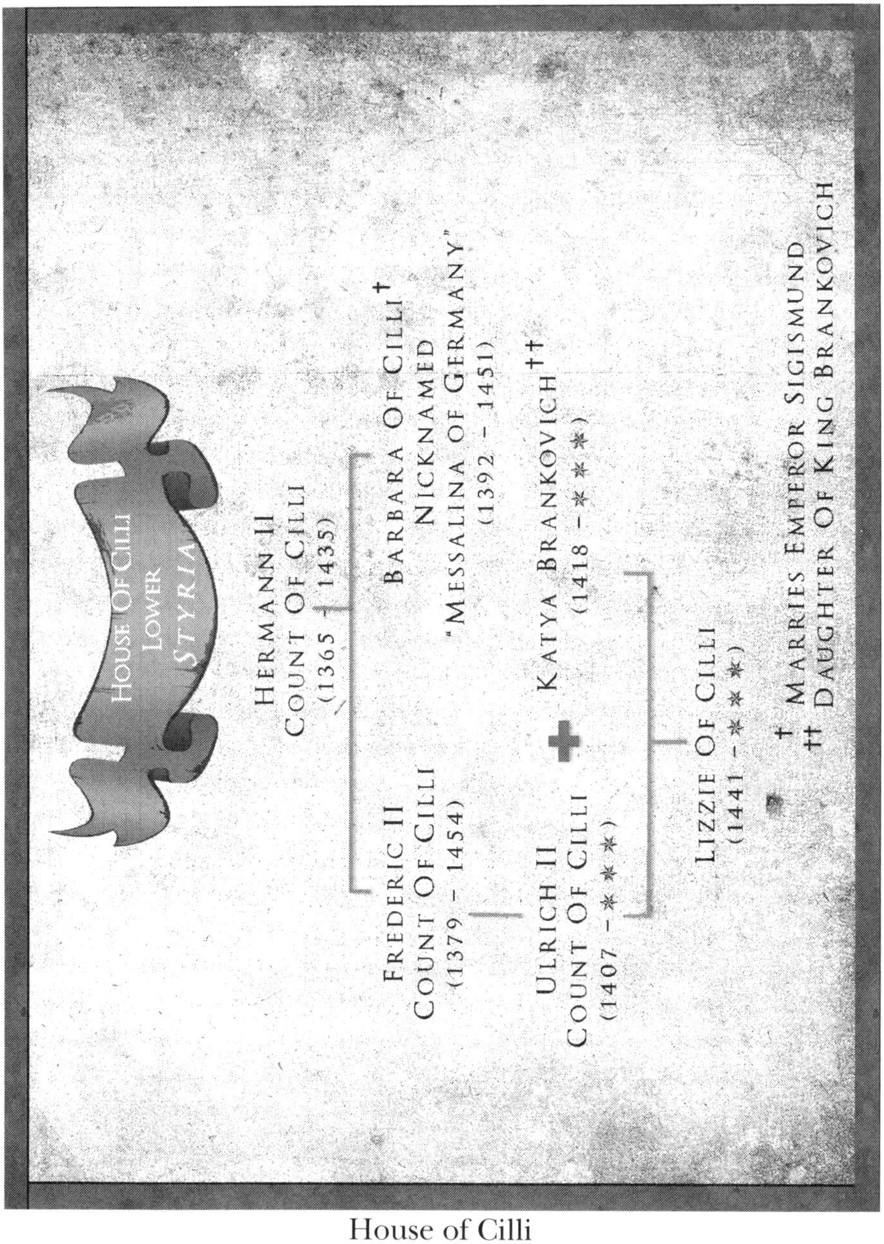

House of Cilli

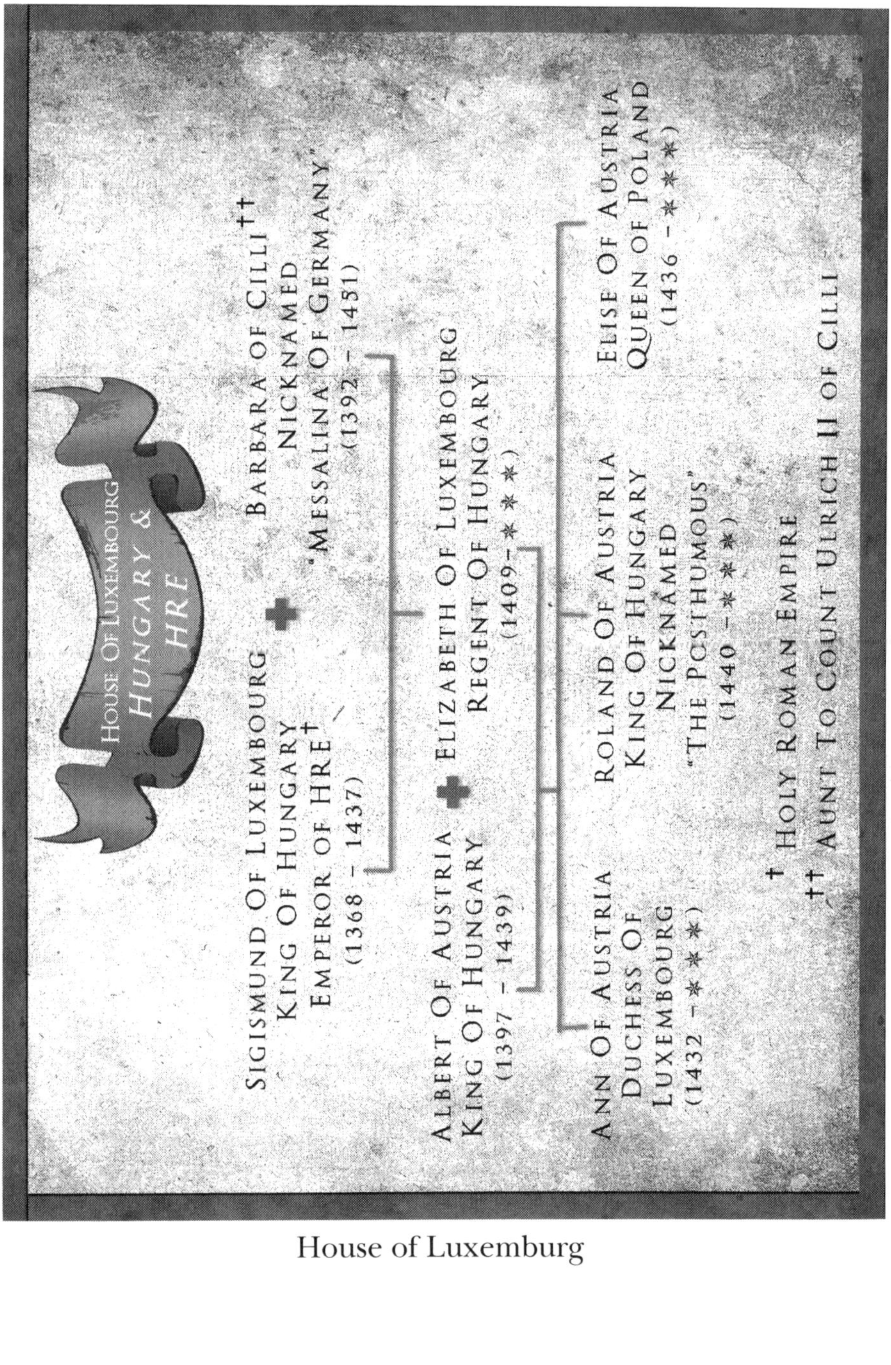

House of Luxemburg

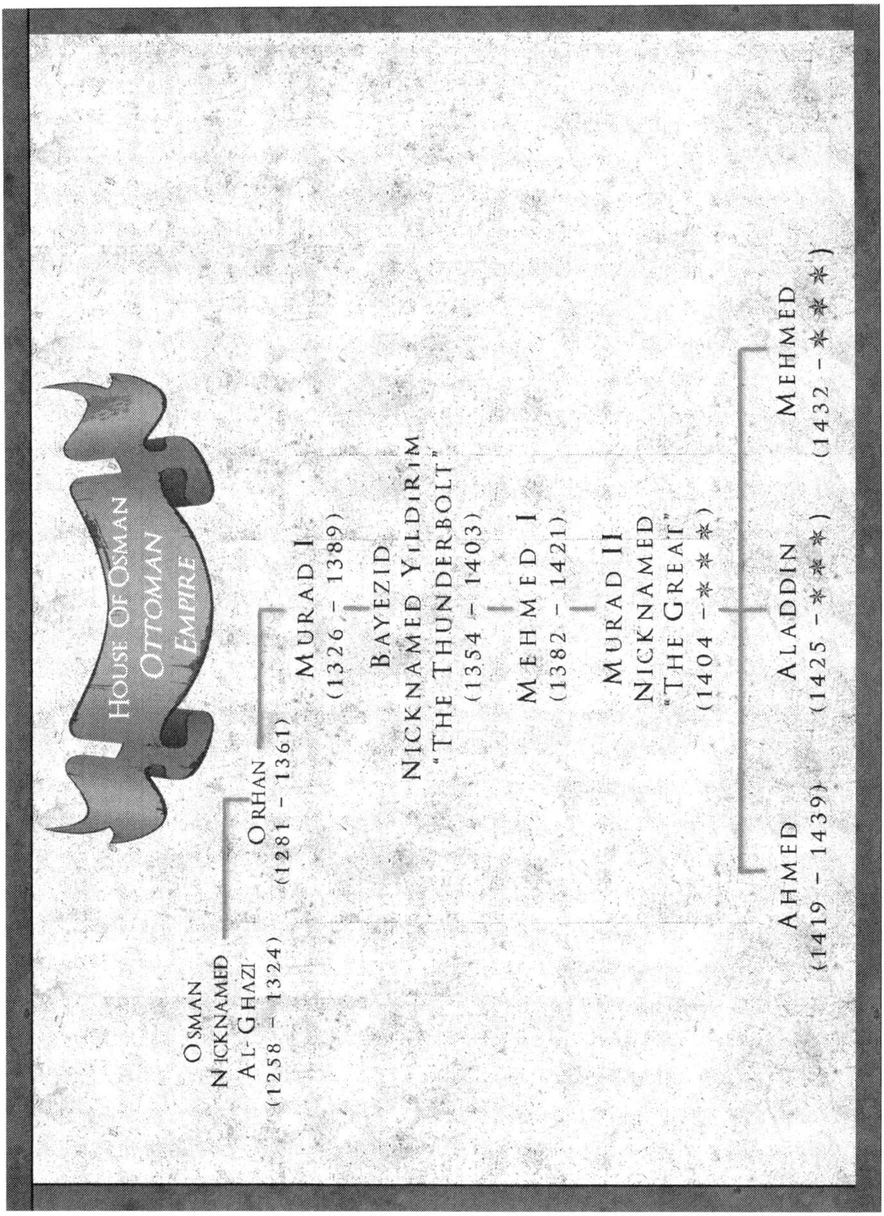

House of Osman

ACKNOWLEDGMENTS

I am grateful to numerous persons who've encouraged and assisted me along the path leading to the creation of this book.

In alphabetical order:

Julian Balog, Georgia Beutler, Ken Beutler, Tim Christofferson, David Detert, Suzette Donisan, Robert Donisan, Sarah Jenny Engering, Samantha Hernandez, Helen Jarvis, Radu Ion, Gloria Klopf, Gregory Klopf, Stephen Klopf, Margaret Larkin, Judy LaVine, Jeanne Majeski, Steve Malzberg, Aurelia-Mihaela Manache, Mary Casey Martin, Samuel McClary, Bill Moller, Cecilia Monacelli, Jim Morgan, Joanna Morgan, Gemma Norman, Carlette Norwood, Michelle Palmer, Patrick Palmer, Maureen Gaynor Ross, Jeffery Pritchett, Christopher Ruddy, Janet Sakal, David Sackeroff, Sally Slattery, Milena Soree, Ann Strainchamps, Marika Suval, Julie Berns Tadych, Krystyna Walc, Jenna Waters, Judith Wills, Kenneth Wills, Spencer Wills, Tom Wills, and Steve Winkle.

Special thanks to my editors, Arlene W. Robinson and Terry Lee Robinson. As most writers know, a manuscript is not fit for public consumption until it has been hammered into shape by professional editors. Their contribution to literature must not go unacknowledged.

Above all I am grateful to my wife Diane for her encouragement, advice, and formidable sense of humor, an attribute indispensable when witnessing the creative process up-close.

ABOUT THE AUTHOR

Victor T. Foia was born in Transylvania where he studied theoretical physics at the Babes-Bolyai University. At the age of twenty-two Victor escaped from behind the Iron Curtain and defected to Italy. After a waiting period of months spent in UN refugee camps, he emigrated to the United States. There Victor graduated from the Universities of Illinois and Dallas. He then embarked upon a career as an international corporate executive, culminating in the position of CEO of an international corporation. Presently he is engaged full time in writing historical fiction.

Victor's interest in Dracula dates from the age of six, when he first visited his compatriot's birthplace, only a hundred miles from his own. Soon this interest became a lasting passion for research into Dracula's life. Over a period of four decades Victor visited castles, fortresses, and monasteries throughout Eastern Europe and the Middle East. In doing this, he aimed to gaze beyond Dracula's iconic image and try to ferret out the essence of the man behind the legend. Victor's journey has taken him to virtually all the places where Dracula lived, loved, fought, and was imprisoned. In the end, by the empty tomb from where the prince disappeared without a trace 535 years ago, Victor felt his journey of discovery was complete, and now the story of the ***real*** Dracula could be told.

Visit our Home Page:
www.draculachronicles.com

Like us on Face Book:
www.facebook.com/draculachronicles

Follow us on Twitter:
twitter.com/VictorFoia

Contact us:
info@draculachronicles.com

47780968R00237

Made in the USA
Charleston, SC
17 October 2015